For testimonials from law enforcement,
visit Carolyn Arnold's website.

An absolutely unputdownable crime thriller

CAROLYN ARNOLD

She's been living with a secret far too long…

PAST DEEDS

A Brandon Fisher FBI Thriller

HIBBERT & STILES
PUBLISHING INC.

Hibbert & Stiles Publishing Inc.
hspubinc.com

This is a work of fiction. Names, characters, places, and incidents are the products of the author's imagination or are used fictitiously. Any resemblance to actual events, locales, or persons, living or dead, is entirely coincidental.

Names: Arnold, Carolyn, 1976
Title: Past Deeds / Carolyn Arnold.
Description: 2021 Hibbert & Stiles Publishing Inc. edition. | Series: Brandon Fisher FBI Series ; book 8

Identifiers: ISBN (e-book): 978-1-988353-96-8 | ISBN (4.25 x 7 paperback): 978-1-988353-97-5 | ISBN (5 x 8 paperback): 978-1-988353-98-2 | ISBN (6.14 x 9.21 hardcover): 978-1-989706-13-8

Additional formats:
ISBN (5 x 8 paperback): 978-1-989706-69-5
ISBN (large print editon): 978-1-989706-14-5
ISBN (audiobook): 978-1-989706-18-3

PAST
DEEDS

CHAPTER ONE

The sun was just coming up, and the sniper's hands were sweaty as she looked through the rifle's scope to the streets eight stories below and point eight miles away. In mere minutes, the target would be dead, and she would walk away. Scot-free. But a lot of variables needed to be accounted for to pull off the shot, including the vehicle and pedestrian traffic that was picking up and the wind coming out of the west at two miles an hour. None of this was a challenge to her, given that she was a skilled sniper, but her nerves threatened to upset the entire operation. She wasn't a killer by nature, but she was good at it—and maybe that meant she was supposed to do it.

She'd do as she was taught and remove emotion from the equation, focus on her purpose, and the end result. Her target certainly deserved to die—and he was one of many.

She checked the time on her watch. *5:56 AM.*

"*Fortuna favet fortibus,*" she chanted. Fortune favors the strong.

She readjusted the rifle's stock, letting it sink comfortably into the meat of her shoulder, pocketed there. The rifle was like an extension of her body, another appendage. Peering through the scope again, she took a few grounding breaths.

The terrain was different from her past. In place of desert was concrete jungle. Instead of emptiness, people scurried along sidewalks, rushing to get to wherever they needed to go. They had no idea what was about to take place just outside Wilson Place, a few blocks to the south.

Her mark was currently inside the building, but he'd be emerging in mere minutes. His routine was boring and predictable, which made it easy for her. She knew that every Tuesday, Thursday, and Saturday morning, he'd leave the condo structure at six o'clock in the morning and head to his office.

She was homed in on the front door and watched as the doorman, who had been standing sentinel to the right of it, sprang into action. She held a breath, prepared to take the shot when a thirtysomething woman stepped outside and headed east.

The doorman closed the door after her and returned to his post, but quickly hurried back to open the door again.

This is it!

The sniper took another calming breath, intensifying focus through the scope.

The door was opened, and the target emerged.

Right on time.

The sniper slowly squeezed the trigger and watched the bullet find its mark.

CHAPTER TWO

A sniping took place in Arlington, Virginia, in the Clarendon District about an hour ago, at oh-six-hundred hours, outside of a condo building called Wilson Place."

FBI Supervisory Special Agent in Charge Jack Harper started his briefing with one heck of a punch. Jack was my boss and the leader of a team with the Behavioral Analysis Unit, which consisted of myself Brandon Fisher, Paige Dawson, and a new member, Kelly Marsh. Kelly was a former homicide detective with the Miami Police Department and had recently replaced Zach Miles, who took a desk job as an FBI analyst because he was starting a family and wanted to increase his chances of returning home at night. Risk was minimal behind a monitor versus staring down the barrel of a gun held by a psychopath—which we did far more often then I'd like.

The team was in a conference room at the FBI office in Quantico, Virginia, and I was seated directly across the table from Jack. Arlington was essentially our neighbor, but I wasn't overly familiar with the city's segments. "Clarendon? What kind of neighborhood is that?"

"Clarendon is in the downtown area, near the Courthouse District. Lots of condo buildings, upper-class." Jack responded without enthusiasm, proof he wasn't too thrilled that I'd cut in with questions before he'd finished laying out the situation. He continued. "Several civilians have been taken to the hospital for stress-induced illnesses. Panic attacks and the like, but there is only one reported casualty. A prosecuting attorney by the name of Darrell Reid."

I'd keep my thoughts to myself for now, but prosecutors, by the very nature of their jobs, attracted enemies—though revenge usually took the form of a bullet from a handgun or a stabbing, maybe strangulation. So why had he been taken out so dramatically?

"We've been asked to look at the evidence, establish a profile on the sniper, and conduct a threat analysis," Jack said. "We need to know what we're dealing with here. Was this an isolated incident, or are more attacks planned?"

I looked at Kelly, her shoulder-length brown hair, brown eyes, and…neon-green nail polish? *To each her own*, but I also couldn't help but think that for her first case with the BAU, she'd netted an anomaly. Our team was normally assigned to profile and track down serial killers, but a shooting like the one in Arlington, given its vicinity to Washington, DC, needed to be handled swiftly.

"My guess is the area's busy this time of day," Paige started. "The fact there was only one death makes it seem like Reid was targeted."

"I thought the same," I admitted, "but why such a drastic means for taking him out? Regardless, we're looking for a skilled sniper. Someone who is former military or law enforcement? Someone who still is?"

Jack looked at me with a serious expression.

"The sniper might be skilled, but not necessarily intelligent." Kelly tossed out, and we all looked at her.

"We're listening," I said, challenging her to continue. When Kelly and I had first met during an investigation this past spring, we hadn't exactly hit it off: we butted heads repeatedly. It had taken facing down a serial killer together to morph the dynamics of our relationship into something congenial.

"Let's say Reid was the target." She gestured, her arm shooting out emphatically, her green polish grabbing my attention again. "Why not shoot several people to throw off the investigation? We wouldn't know who the intended victim was, and it would take longer to hunt down motive."

"We're just getting started. Motive is likely still a long way off," I peacocked. "Besides, it's also possible the sniper could have missed the intended target and hit Reid by mistake."

"Not based on what's come in to us," Jack stated sourly. "Reid was hit directly in the chest. Now each of you has a folder." He laid a hand on his and gestured to the ones in front of each of us on the table. "Nadia prepared them, but there's very little there."

Nadia Webber was our assigned analyst who worked out of Quantico along with us. But while our work mostly took us into the field, she remained holed up in a windowless office.

The three of us opened our folders. As Jack had said, there wasn't much. Only Reid's driver's license photo blown up to letter size, his basic background, and contact information for the building's management.

"Nadia's in communication with officers on the ground and is gathering as much intel as she can," Jack added.

Kelly held Reid's background in one hand and pressed a fingertip to the full-page photo of Reid. "What do we know about him besides he was a prosecutor?"

"Nothing much. Everything we know is in there." Jack nudged his head toward the file. "Keep in mind that the first rule of profiling is never jump to a motive. We do that, and we might as well hand in our badges. Our priority right now is whether or not we can rule out terrorism."

Kelly slid her bottom lip through her teeth, clearly uncomfortable by Jack's mini lecture. But she'd appeared frazzled from the moment she came in the door this morning, as if she were running behind and trying to catch up. She'd come to realize soon enough that this job usually felt like that. After all, we were usually steps behind the unsubs, the unidentified subjects.

Kelly scanned the file. "You mentioned terrorism, Jack, but on the surface, Reid doesn't seem your typical terrorist's target. And don't terrorists like to make a bigger splash? The more blood spilled, the better?"

"It's far too early to rule out Reid's attractiveness to a terrorist. We don't know enough about him," Jack replied and studied his new agent as if he were just getting to know her. But part of why I hadn't liked Kelly at first was because she and Jack seemed to know each other too well. As it turned out, Jack had served in the military with her grandfather and had known Kelly from her days at the FBI Academy.

Kelly's eyes pinched with concentration. "As a prosecutor, sure, he'd make enemies, but given how he was killed, maybe we're looking at a hired gun."

"Which would also imply he was targeted, but it's too soon." Jack's tone was cool, correcting, and one I recognized well from my days as a rookie agent—days that were only two years behind me. Any concern I had that Kelly would receive special treatment due to her past connection with Jack was eroding with his rebukes.

"Let's move." Jack stood, and the rest of us followed and headed toward the door. "Brandon, you'll be with Paige, and Kelly, you'll come with me. We'll meet at ground zero. When you get there, ask for Captain Anthony Herrera from the Homeland Security Division of the Arlington Police Department."

My heart paused in dread: *I am paired with Paige.* Guess I should have seen it coming. Jack had mentored me as a new agent, and now it was Kelly's turn. I put on a smile for Paige's benefit, and she returned it, but her expression faded as quickly as mine. Let's just say we had a past, which held no place in the present.

I'd been a student at the FBI Academy, and she, a teacher. In a moment of weakness, I'd ignored the fact I was married, and we fell into bed together—more than once. Big mistake, and nothing to be proud of. That might have happened four years ago, but our efforts to bury the past were thwarted when we'd both ended up on Jack's team. And it didn't help that a lingering attraction and unexplored feelings were still there.

"That's not a problem, is it?" Jack had his gaze set on me. He had found out about Paige and me, but he let us sort things out, making it clear it wasn't an option for us to fraternize romantically and remain on his team.

"No, not at all. It's fine." That's what I said, even as sirens were sounding in my head.

I was divorced now, not because of my affair with Paige, but rather just irreconcilable differences. My ex couldn't stand my job with the FBI. Again, nothing to do with Paige being my colleague. Anyway, Paige and I were making the best of it, and I was currently in a relationship with Becky, an officer from a neighboring county.

"Just keep your mind about you out there," Jack cautioned all of us. "The sniper's probably long gone, but there's the chance they've stuck around to peck off some law enforcement. Vests are mandatory."

Before the four of us made it to the door, Nadia entered the room.

"I haven't been able to uncover any other shootings in the DC/Virginia area that are similar to this one," she informed us.

"Expand the geography and keep looking." Jack brushed past her.

The one thing that Kelly would quickly learn about Jack was that he liked answers, not updates for the sake of updates. Sometimes even those of us who had worked with him for years failed to remember that if we weren't providing new information, we were a hindrance.

CHAPTER THREE

Kelly felt like she was starting her life from scratch with a knot in her gut reminiscent of the first day of school after summer break. Jack had meant so much to her grandfather—and her grandfather to her—that she just wanted to impress him. It had taken her six wardrobe changes until she settled on a cream blouse and a black pantsuit devoid of all personality, but it was clean, crisp, professional, and it communicated confidence. She might not be feeling it, but that didn't mean her outfit couldn't say it.

She split her attention between looking at the road and glancing over at Jack in the driver's seat. Sometimes it was hard to believe she was actually here—her dream of becoming an FBI agent finally realized. She'd wanted this since she'd graduated the academy eleven years ago, in her early twenties, but life had other plans for her, and the bumps in the road all started with her mother.

She wasn't exactly the saint of motherhood—who was, really? But Kelly's mom had served time for murder. Self-defense, really, even if the victim had been Kelly's father. Kelly had been six at the time, but in her twenties when her mother was released from prison and ran off. After Kelly's granddad had a heart attack, Kelly left Virginia to live and care for him in Florida. The dream of being FBI had become nothing more than a flickering memory. It wasn't until this past spring, when she'd called Jack to Miami to help with a case, that she realized she still hungered to be FBI. And now that she had the job, she was determined to keep it, and that would mean impressing Jack.

She opened the folder in her lap and eyed…*bright green nails!* She'd meant to go with something more neutral before today and resisted the urge to sit on her hands.

Come on, Marsh, pull yourself together. Get your mind back on the case!

The information packet didn't offer much. On paper, Darrell Reid looked like a regular guy: father, husband, prosecutor. What had he done to get himself killed? Was he even the true target?

Jack's caution that it was too soon to conclude anything, including motive, wasn't far from her mind, but she felt she had to say something useful. She scanned Reid's background, groping.

"Reid's married and has a seventeen-year-old son." The instant the words were out, she felt like a rambling fact giver. Jack could have read that much from the file himself; he probably had. She needed to offer something fresh and intelligent, or Jack might start to rethink bringing her on board. "He's worked for the commonwealth's attorney's office for ten years," she added. "That's certainly enough time to build up enemies…assuming he was the true target." She was starting to feel she couldn't say anything right.

Jack remained silent, lowered his window, and lit up a cigarette. Technically, he shouldn't be smoking in a government vehicle, but who would be brave enough to give Jack grief about it—or anything for that matter?

"You know, smoking isn't good for you." She'd heard the words in her head as carefree banter, but they landed with more weight.

Jack angled his head toward her, and her stomach flopped. She should have kept her mouth shut.

"I shouldn't have—" She scrambled to backpedal.

Jack smiled at her. "You sound like Brandon."

"Ouch. Of all the things for you to say." She returned his smile. It hadn't been much of a secret that she and Brandon hadn't gelled immediately. Sadly, she'd come to realize part of the reason was they were too much alike. "I take it he doesn't care for your habit, either."

"Nope." Jack sucked back on the cigarette and blew the smoke out the window.

The cigarette cartons she'd seen in an airport duty-free shop flashed to mind. The warning was clear, printed in an open-face font about an inch high on a white band: SMOKING KILLS. She spoke the words out loud.

"So does our sniper," Jack countered drily.

She could have smacked herself for letting her guard down. They were headed to the scene of a fatal shooting; it wasn't the time for mindless chitchat. She would also do well to remember that Jack had the reputation of being one of the best FBI agents the Bureau had ever seen, and it would take more than a personal connection to remain part of his team.

She went back to burying her head in the file, wishing for a miraculous epiphany, but none came. Maybe she was stressing too much about impressing Jack and should let things flow naturally. It wasn't like she was a floundering rookie new to law enforcement. She'd solved countless murders during her six years as a homicide detective with the Miami PD.

Jack entered Arlington, and she marveled at the buildings and architecture. *The city is beautiful*, was her thought, just as Jack pulled up to the outskirts of the crime scene.

He parked the SUV and got out, and she wasn't far behind him. He held up his credentials to one of the officers securing the perimeter, and she followed his lead, feeling pride in displaying hers.

"I'm Supervisory Special Agent in Charge Jack Harper with the Behavioral Analysis Unit, and this is Probationary Agent Kelly Marsh. She's with me. We need to speak with Captain Herrera."

Kelly couldn't wait for the "probationary agent" to drop, but she had twenty-four months left before it technically wouldn't apply. She tried to tell herself that the time would go fast—it always did.

The officer studied her while she studied him. The name tag on his uniform read PEREZ.

"Sure, just give me a sec." Perez spoke into his radio, and voices came back telling him where to find Herrera. He went to repeat what was said to Jack, but he was already on the move.

"Thanks," Kelly called over a shoulder to Perez as she hurried to catch up with her boss.

Past the tape, Kelly took in three ambulances and ten police cruisers parked haphazardly, at different angles, lights flashing. Responders were moving about the area at a hustle, stark looks on their faces, each person driven by his or her mission.

She went past one ambulance that had its back doors open; a man in his forties was sitting on the back step, breathing from an oxygen mask. A female paramedic was by his side, and a police officer was standing nearby.

The voices of panicked civilians carried past the barricade—some in hushed tones, others shrill with excitement and fueled by adrenaline. But it was impossible not to feel the tendrils of death clawing in the air, clinging to the skin as gauze.

This "energy" was a reliable companion where there had been a fatality, and it was something Kelly was certain everyone felt—law enforcement and civilians alike. The only exemption would be the inanimate. The buildings that towered overhead, unable to feel anything. If she thought about it for too long, she'd become envious of the edifices, who stood as silent witnesses with no way of telling their stories.

A trim man of just over six feet, with a head of silver hair, was rushing toward them. His face was chiseled with resolve, but years of experience had left weariness lingering in his pale blue eyes and lines etched in his brow. He held out his hand toward Jack. "I'm Captain Anthony Herrera."

"Supervisory Special Agent in Charge Jack Harper and Agent Kelly Marsh."

Agent Marsh. Kelly liked the sound of that much better than *probationary* agent.

Herrera directed Kelly and Jack to follow him to a command trailer that had its front driver's wheel up on the curb. Someone didn't know how to park, but the vehicle was nestled in a pocket of calm surrounded by chaos.

"As you can see, it's still a bit of a gong show," Herrera said, pointing around. "By now, you know the victim was Darrell Reid, a prosecuting attorney. He had his wallet on him and his identification, so that preliminary step was easy. Of course, his wife will need to provide the formal ID. She has yet to be notified, and we're doing our best to keep his identity out of the media until that happens. Sometimes that's easier said than done." Herrera flailed a hand toward the growing crowd of pedestrians. Back to Kelly and Jack, he said, "The other injured are being treated, and the DB is still on the ground."

Dead body.

"Other injured?" Kelly prompted. She recalled Jack mentioning panic attacks and wanted to confirm that's all they were looking at.

"Collateral injures. Just minor stuff…well, mostly." Captain Herrera squinted into the rising sun. "One woman has since been taken to the hospital, complaining of chest pain." Herrera pointed past a crowd of responders to a tall building across the street. "Shall we head that way?"

Jack started in the direction of Wilson Place, Kelly and the police captain in tow.

"The medical examiner on the way?" Jack asked over his shoulder.

The captain and Kelly scurried to catch up with Jack.

"Should be here any minute," Herrera said. "I put the call in just after arriving on scene at six fifteen."

That was only fifteen minutes from the time of the shooting. "Fast response time," she commented.

"We try."

An officer who had been standing in front of the victim stepped to the side as the three of them approached.

The body was supine on the sidewalk. His gray hair was groomed short, and his skin was pale. His brown eyes were large and open, unseeing marbles. His lips were curled in a mask of horror. Blood had poured from the chest wound and pooled to the left of the torso. Kelly kept her eyes on the corpse; she had never been fazed by the sight of death. Maybe it was because she had been exposed to it at such a young age, watching her father shot before her eyes. To her, death was nothing more than the logical progression of life—even when it was aided along.

Kelly hadn't thought of it earlier, but being there and seeing the body, it sank in that only a highly skilled sniper could have pulled off a shot like this one—through a crowd, vehicle traffic, and net no other casualties. A head shot would have been far easier to execute.

Reid was dressed in a black suit, tailored to his fit frame, and a white-collared dress shirt with a tie. He wore a platinum wedding band on his left hand and a gold pinkie ring on his right. Peeking out from beneath his left sleeve was a Bulgari watch. Not that they were within Kelly's price range, but her best friend Brianna back in Miami had one, and it had cost five figures. Everything about the man's wardrobe was high-end, down to his Salvatore Ferragamo shoes, the toes of which pointed upward.

Kelly lifted her gaze, her eye on buildings farther away and her mind on where the sniper may have built a nest.

Another take at the body, she started to make deeper observations. Who had this man been in life, besides a prosecutor? The shoes, watch, and cut of suit didn't testify to someone working on the right side of the law. If Reid had been a defense attorney, the expensive wardrobe would be much easier to reconcile, as criminals paid much better than the government.

"Prosecutors make, what, fifty thousand a year?" she asked.

"Somewhere around there, depending on the office where they work," Herrera said.

Jack faced her, one eyebrow raised in curiosity. Maybe she should take that as a cue to keep quiet, but she felt doing so would be more of a crime than speaking up. Besides, she finally had a contribution worth making.

"The file we have on Reid said he worked out of the commonwealth's attorney's office. He was fifty-five, had seniority, but still, his clothes don't match up with his earnings." Kelly watched Jack as she spoke for any tells that she was displeasing him somehow, but she couldn't see any.

"What do you think that means?" Herrera was studying her, his eyes squinting in the rising sun.

She glanced at Jack, briefly tempted to elaborate on her leanings toward Reid possibly being involved in criminal activity or on the take, but without anything to back up her suspicions, she thought it best to keep quiet. "Too soon to say," she said, pegging that as the safe road and determined to remain there. She recalled Jack telling them this neighborhood was near the Courthouse District. "Do we know why Reid was here this morning?"

"Wish I could tell you," Herrera replied.

"Could be for his job," she tossed out.

"Sure, but we don't know for sure. It's still something we need to figure out. That guy—" he gestured with his head toward the man sucking back on an oxygen mask "—is the building's doorman. He might talk to you, but my men haven't been able to get much out of him."

Kelly was eager to head right over, but Jack remained grounded, his gaze on Reid. As she looked back at the gaping wound in the man's chest, she was pretty sure the bullet had struck his heart. If it had, was that where the sniper had aimed and, if so, was it of any significance?

CHAPTER FOUR

It wasn't often that we were called to investigate a case this close to home. It certainly made it easier than needing to set off across the country on a government jet. But it was still sobering that someone had been killed and we needed to catch the bad guy—and preferably come out the other end alive. That's where the bulletproof vest came in, but it wouldn't do much against a knife or a shot to the head. I tried not to dwell on that, but the severity of the situation was never far from mind as the vest added a good thirty pounds to my lean frame.

Paige and I got snagged in traffic on Interstate 95 all because a car broke down on the side of the road and everyone slowed to gawk, making the drive about forty minutes longer than it should have been.

As we approached the scene of the shooting, people were huddled in masses, crying and hugging, pointing, and trying to make sense of what had taken place.

Being here emphasized our shooter had no qualms about making his or her kill in a very public place. Seeking to "make a splash?" With the numerous buildings facing Wilson Place, it would make it rather easy for the sniper to do the deed and get away.

After Paige parked and we cleared the barricade, we found Jack and Kelly standing with a man at the front door of Wilson Place, a corpse at their feet.

The man with them held out his hand to Paige and me and introduced himself as Captain Herrera.

Paige looked up at the building, and I followed the direction of her gaze. Residential, at least fifteen stories tall. People pressed their faces against windowpanes or stood gawking from their balconies.

What is it with people and gawking?

"Do we know what brought the prosecutor down here?" Paige asked.

"We," Herrera referred to Jack and Kelly, "were just talking about that, matter of fact, but we don't know yet."

"I'd say something likely brought Reid here regularly," I concluded. "Either that or he had this visit planned in advance. The sniper would have needed time to select a perch and plan this out."

"Running with the assumption that Reid was the mark," Kelly interjected. "But even if he was, it could just be that the right person—or wrong person, really—knew where he'd be and when to strike."

"The doorman might be able to help us fill in some blanks." Jack nudged his head toward a man at the back of an ambulance.

I thought the place looked nice enough to warrant a doorman, but that would mean… I looked down at Reid's body and its positioning. It wasn't that far from the entrance, and the way he was lying would suggest he'd just come out of the building. "He was shot upon exiting?"

"That's right," Herrera confirmed.

That meant our sniper had the timing fine-tuned. "Was the doorman injured?" He was being tended to by a female paramedic, but I was more interested in the extent of his injuries.

"He's just shaken up," Herrera said. "He got some blood on him."

I let the picture play out in my mind—the doorman holding the door for Reid, Reid walking through, getting shot in the chest. "Our shooter knows what they're doing," I drove home again.

"I'd say so. Kill shot through a crowd, and only one person taken down." Herrera crossed his arms and puffed out a breath of air. "So, what do you think we're looking at here? Is the threat still active, the first in a series of planned shootings, or a one-off?" Herrera was looking at Jack for answers.

"It's too soon to know for sure," Jack said, tapping a hand over his shirt pocket where he kept his pack of cigarettes. I wasn't a certified shrink, but it was easy to conclude they were his coping mechanism.

I scanned the area, taking in the surrounding buildings, curious where our sniper had built a nest. "Have you been able to figure out where the shot originated?"

Herrera shook his head. "We figure the sniper set up a nest thataway." He pointed north. "But that's about it. We'll need to determine the angle of the shot to figure out any more, and for that, we first need the body examined by the ME."

And any answers on that front probably wouldn't come until after the autopsy. From there, it would take a lot of calculations to triangulate the direction of the sniper's nest—and given the number of buildings in the area, we'd likely have to eliminate a few before we found what we were looking for.

"Anyone recall seeing anything?" Jack asked. "A flicker of metal in the sunlight?"

Jack was reaching, especially if we were dealing with a professional sniper. The gun—lock, stock, and barrel—would be black or covered in flat, black tape for the purpose of concealment.

"Nothing that's surfaced yet," Herrera confirmed.

Jack gestured up the side of the building. "We need to get officers knocking on doors, talking to these lookie-loos. Someone might have seen something from their apartments."

"I was going to get that started when you showed up." Herrera waved over an officer, instructing him to gather other officers and knock on every door in the building.

The officer scurried off to carry out his captain's orders.

"It's time to start getting some answers." Jack put his attention on Herrera. "You said Reid's family hasn't been notified."

"That's right."

"Kelly and I will take care of that."

Herrera nodded. "Have at it. Not my favorite part of the job, anyway."

None of us touched that because notification was the dark cloud of law enforcement.

Jack looked at Paige. "You and Brandon go talk to the doorman." Then he turned to Herrera. "Do we know his name?"

The captain nodded. "Ronald McBride."

Jack said to Paige, "See if you can get any answers as to why Reid was here. When you're finished there, I want you to stay on the ground, talk to as many eyewitnesses as you can, and join the officers knocking on doors."

Somehow I managed to bite my tongue, but canvassing was the job of uniforms, not FBI profilers.

"You got it, Jack," Paige said.

"We'll meet back at the Arlington PD at—" Jack consulted his watch "—let's say two o'clock this afternoon. We'll have a better idea where we stand by then."

"I'll have a conference room ready for you," Herrera promised.

Paige and I set off in the direction of the doorman, and I saw two men cutting through the street toward the victim. The younger of the two was pushing a gurney and trailing a gray-haired man with a determined stride and carrying a medical bag.

"Looks like the ME and his assistant are here," I said, and Paige simply nodded.

As we got closer to McBride, I'd put him in his fifties, though he looked older at the moment. His eyes were bloodshot, and his face pale except for the splotches of blood on his cheeks and forehead. He was breathing with an oxygen mask, and a paramedic had a hand on his shoulder. She was advising him to take slow, deep breaths. She scowled at our approach.

"Are you Ronald McBride?" I asked, ignoring the woman's apparent attitude.

The man nodded, the apparatus bobbing with the movement.

"We have some questions for you," Paige said with kindness and respect, but it did nothing to soften the paramedic's grimace.

"Mr. McBride has been through an awful lot. Maybe a little later would be better." She packaged her request like a suggestion, but I wasn't fooled for what it really was. But there was no way I'd be going back to Jack and telling him we'd been stonewalled by a paramedic.

I squared my shoulders. "Unfortunately, we don't have the time to wait around. There was a murder, and it's imperative that we get the bottom of exactly what transpired here."

The paramedic met my gaze, and her body stiffened, but she eventually stepped aside. "Keep it brief."

"Mr. McBride," I said, "we have just a few questions for you."

McBride went to pull off the oxygen mask, and the paramedic made a motion to keep it in place, but he shooed her away and removed it.

The paramedic shook her head and wandered off.

"I'll help in whatever way I can," McBride said.

"We appreciate that," I said. "Can you tell us what happened…from your perspective?"

"I…I was just holding the door—" he took a hit of oxygen, lowered the mask again "—the door open for him. It all happened so fast."

Paige sat on the ambulance's back step next to McBride. "It must have been terrifying."

He looked over at her. "Never seen anything like it. Hope to never again."

"Did you see or hear anything before the man went down?" I asked.

"No, like I said, it all happened so fast."

"Fair enough." It was probably too much to hope that he'd been looking in the direction of the sniper and caught a glimpse of something that would expose the nest.

"There was..." McBride licked his lips, "a woman who came out just ahead of him. She's fine, as far as I know, but don't quote me. I kind of lost track of everything after..."

"Do you know who she was?" Paige asked.

"Even if I did, I'm not at liberty to say, Miss."

"Did the man who was shot and the woman know each other?" I was trying to feel out if there was any sort of relationship between the victim and this woman.

McBride clamped his mouth shut, and that told me there was a connection between Reid and the woman, but he wasn't about to confirm it.

"Did you know the victim well?" I kept leaving Reid nameless to aid in objectivity.

"Can't say as I did. But today was only my fourth day on the job."

If McBride was being honest, which I had no reason to suspect he wasn't—his employment record could be easily verified—then maybe his predecessor would be able to provide us with some insight. "Did you know the doorman you replaced?"

"Just his first name. Gerald. He retired. Age sixty-eight. All the standing was getting to his knees."

I nodded. We could get Gerald's information through Nadia and building management.

"Is there anything you can tell us about the victim?" Paige asked.

"I know he was some bigwig. Had money."

"And how do you know that?" The money part was rather easy, given Reid's wardrobe, which I'd noted upon arriving on scene.

McBride seemed to hesitate, but Paige and I waited him out.

"Roy told me after the man got on the elevator," he eventually said.

Paige leaned in toward McBride. "And who's Roy?"

"He mans the front desk, calls up to tenants to clear their visitors."

I looked around. "Where could we find Roy?"

"Knowing him, he's probably still at his post. He's one of those guys who takes his job almost too seriously."

"When did the man show up?" I inquired.

"Last night about eleven."

Two things occurred to me. One, if Reid had an interview related to his job as a prosecutor, eleven at night was rather late—and it didn't explain why he'd be there all night. Two was, "You have a long shift," I said to McBride.

"Everyone at Wilson Place does, the doormen and the people at the front desk. You're either on from ten at night to ten in the morning or the opposite. The long hours are probably another reason why all this is affecting me so much."

"You saw a person shot right in front of you. No matter how tired or alert you are, it makes sense it would affect you." Paige, ever the empathizer.

McBride took another hit of oxygen. "I suppose you're right."

"Do you know why he was here?" If we could get an answer to that, we might have motive, and it could also give us some suspects.

McBride shook his head. "Again, try Roy. Not sure he'll be able to tell you, though, due to confidentiality issues."

"We appreciate your help." Paige took her card out of a pocket and handed it to McBride.

"Not sure how much help I've been, but Roy has a sign-in book for visitors. That might get you somewhere."

Paige pointed to her card in McBride's hand and stood. "If you think of anything else, call me. Anytime. Day or night. Okay?"

"I will, but I don't think there will be anything."

"Thank you for your help," I reiterated, and once Paige and I were out of earshot, I said to her, "We'll need a background pulled on McBride, even if it's just to rule him out."

"Makes sense to me," she said. "In the least, I believe McBride knows a lot more than he's telling us. Not sure how we're supposed to get it out of him, though. He seems pretty comfortable hiding behind his employment's confidentiality clause."

"Me neither. Not sure he's involved, but we need to consider everyone a suspect until they're ruled out." Not that I needed to say as much to Paige. She'd also know that those who appeared innocent were often the guilty ones. What's to say McBride didn't have some beef with Reid and fed information to the sniper? He was, according to his own words, a new employ, so that made me wonder what had led him to Wilson Place.

"For sure," Paige agreed, "and we'll need a report on the former doorman as well and to have a chat with him."

"Yep." I pulled out my phone, called Nadia, and made the requests. As I did, I scanned the area. The initial buzz was dying down, and I could see the medical examiner and his assistant working on Reid. Herrera was towering over the two of them, arms crossed. I thanked Nadia and hung up. "She's getting us the backgrounds on McBride and Gerald Whoever-he-is."

"Knowing Nadia, that won't take too long. Why don't we go have a word with the ME?" She nudged her head toward him.

If talking to him would delay canvassing, then I was all for it. "Sounds like a plan."

CHAPTER FIVE

Kelly was riding shotgun again as Jack drove them to the Reids' house. It was located in an area of Arlington known as Woodmont. Jack was smoking away, a cigarette perched between two fingers that dangled out the open window.

Nadia's voice was coming over the speakers. She'd already told them that Darrell's wife was Arlene, and she was eight years her husband's junior at forty-seven. She'd never worked outside the home.

"Arlene Reid was born Arlene Pryce to a wealthy British family in Wales," Nadia elaborated. "Arlene's parents followed her to the States when she came here for schooling, and none of them returned home. She met and fell in love with Darrell, and she married him soon after she graduated law school."

"Yet she never practiced law?" Kelly asked, thinking that was such a waste of money and education.

"Not that I see."

The whims of the rich, she supposed. They had to spend their time somehow, and much better it be in the pursuit of knowledge than frivolous endeavors.

"Any luck on finding similar shootings in any of the US that fit today's?" Jack asked.

Luck? As if he wanted other shootings to be discovered. Tragic—but it would give them something else to analyze and compare, and clues may surface. She concluded Jack must suspect Reid's shooting hadn't been an isolated incident.

"None yet."

"Well, keep looking."

"Will do, Jack."

With that, Jack ended the call and pitched the SUV back into an awkward silence that begged to be filled, but Kelly was at a loss for what to say.

He turned down a street of large homes, mature trees, and beautifully manicured lawns. It was autumn, but in such a neighborhood, the grass dared not turn brown just yet.

If it hadn't been for Arlene's family's money, Reid probably wouldn't be able to afford living here.

Jack pulled into the driveway of a redbrick, two-story home, though it had three levels of living space; they could see the basement windows just above ground level. Two sets of staircases joined at a landing and led to double front doors that were hugged by sidelights and a transom window and set back under two columns and an overhang. The word *regal* came to mind.

Jack got out of the vehicle, and she hurried to catch up to him. He poked the doorbell, and a rendition of some classical song chimed throughout the home and spilled through to the front step. Kelly wouldn't have expected anything less from a place like this.

The door was opened by a pleasant-looking brunette who looked years younger than forty-seven. She was wearing a light-pink, silk blouse paired with pressed pants and teardrop earrings. Her eyelids were painted in shades of purple, and her lips were glossy pink. Her perfume smelled heavenly— and expensive—and was probably sold by the ounce.

"Mrs. Arlene Reid?" Jack asked while holding up his credentials. Kelly hurried to follow his lead and had hers displayed by the time Arlene's eyes went to her.

"Yes." Her one word held both caution and curiosity.

"I'm FBI Supervisory Special Agent in Charge Jack Harper, and this is Agent Marsh. Can we come in for a moment?" Based on Jack's body language, the way his leg rested, how his foot was positioned, his question wasn't so much a question as a request.

"Sure." Arlene stepped back and let them inside. She closed the door behind them and watched them, expectant.

"Do you have somewhere we could sit down?" Jack asked.

Arlene seemed to pry her eyes from Jack before turning and taking them to a sitting room that was to the right of the entry. Sunlight drenched a space that was stuffed with furniture along with antique trinkets and collectibles. She sat in a beige chair, and Jack and Kelly sat in matching ones across from her.

"We're here about your husband," Jack started. "He was killed this morning in a shoot—"

Arlene's mouth fell open, and tears immediately pooled in her eyes.

"We're sorry for your loss, Mrs. Reid," Kelly offered, trying to soften the blow, though realizing the futility.

Arlene met Kelly's eyes and sniffled. "What am I supposed to tell Riley? Thank God he's at school right now."

Riley was the Reids' teenage son.

Arlene blew out a deep breath. "How?… Where?… Why?"

Jack gestured for Kelly to answer. She'd been given a little rope; now she just had to be careful not to hang herself.

Kelly cleared her throat and pressed her hands down on her slacks. "Your husband was shot in Clarendon."

"The sniper…" Arlene looked across the room as if she was seeing something, but there was nothing there to see.

"I'm sorry," Kelly said, "but I'm not sure—"

Arlene met her gaze. "I saw it on the news…the shooting." *The media never missed a beat.*

"They said that a man was killed and—" She stopped, her chin quivering. "Others were injured."

"We're trying to figure a few things out. Do you know why your husband would have been in that area this morning?" Kelly asked.

Arlene slowly shook her head. "No idea, but I didn't keep tabs on his calendar. He was a respected prosecutor. Good at his job." Her brown eyes turned to burnt charcoal. "Was it what got him killed?"

"It's too soon to say," Jack jumped in. "We're trying to figure out exactly what happened ourselves."

"My husband was shot." Venom licked her words. "What else is there to figure out?"

"In order to find who did this, it helps us to know what might have made him a target," Jack responded coolly, not giving any indication that her outburst had affected him.

"Ohmigod." Arlene slapped a hand over her mouth, and tears spilled down her cheeks. "He was targeted? Why? Why would anyone do this?"

Arlene's emotions were all over the place, and Kelly struggled to remain objective and discern whether it was due to grief or an act that the wife was performing. "We intend to find out," Kelly said. "That's why it would help us to know a little bit more about your husband, starting with why he might have been in that neighborhood. Given the circumstances, it would seem that the shooter was aware he'd be there when he was."

Jack looked over at Kelly, his mouth in a straight line. She must have been talking in absolutes more than Jack cared for. "Again, this is just one angle we're working on," Kelly said, trying to backpedal.

"One angle?" Arlene cocked her head.

"Yes, ma'am. It's also possible that your husband was an unintended victim of the shooting." This pained Kelly to say because she could easily conjure up the picture of that perfectly placed hole in Reid's chest.

"I don't understand." Arlene snatched a tissue from a nearby box, dabbed her nose, then scrunched it in her hand, her fingers tugging on the corners.

"All Agent Marsh means is that it's too early to conclude exactly what took place."

"There's that word *exactly* again." Arlene's eyes scolded Jack.

"What more can you tell us about your husband? Do you know of anyone who didn't like him?" Jack asked, shifting the spotlight from why her husband was in Clarendon.

"I'm sure my husband had his enemies." Arlene straightened her back, jutted out her chin just slightly. "No one gets to his position without them."

"Anyone specific come to mind?" Kelly said gently, aware she was braving it by speaking in definitives—both with Mrs. Reid and Jack.

Arlene made a long, raspy sigh. "My husband was responsible for putting away a lot of very bad men. It could be any of them. I wouldn't even know where to start with names. You'd best be going down to the commonwealth's attorney's office for those answers."

"We will be, but just curious if Darrell happened to mention any recent cases he was working on?" It was possible that a conviction had led to revenge, but Kelly couldn't close her mind to the possibility it could have been an active case.

"Darrell kept his work to himself. He kept a lot to himself." Arlene's gaze fell to her lap. For a few seconds, the confident debutante slipped away. Then she squared her shoulders and lifted her head high. "I respect...*respected*...that about him."

Even if Darrell had skeletons in the closet to find, they weren't getting to them with Mrs. Arlene Reid guarding the door.

Silence stretched out for a couple of minutes before Arlene spoke.

"You said he was shot in Clarendon, and I caught as much on the news, but missed where exactly." Arlene watched Jack, seeking an answer.

"In front of Wilson Place." Jack paused, blatantly observing Arlene. Her brow wrinkled, and she sniffled. "Does that ring any bells for you?"

"No." Arlene was quick to answer. "Why would it?"

"Your husband was coming out of the building when he was shot," Jack disclosed.

"Oh." She rubbed at her neck, where the skin had become blotchy.

"Do you know something you're not wanting to tell us?" Kelly did her best to present the inquiry as coming from an equal, a friend, not law enforcement digging for a lead.

Arlene met her gaze and shook her head.

Kelly could tell right away she was lying. Mrs. Reid was holding back—but what was it and did it have anything to do with her husband's murder?

CHAPTER SIX

Paige wasn't surprised when Jack paired her with Brandon. Jack liked to work alongside his new agents, but understanding his reasoning didn't make working so closely with Brandon any less uncomfortable. He might have moved on with that officer named Becky, but Paige was single, and her feelings for Brandon were still very much alive—no matter how much she wished they'd die.

She led the way across the street to Wilson Place. Reid's body was still on display, and he had an audience of three surrounding him: the medical examiner, his assistant, and Captain Herrera.

The ME looked up, squinting in the sun, from where he was crouched next to Reid when she cast a shadow over the body. It appeared he was about to say something when his eyes went to the acronym in large, yellow letters on the front of her vest. He grimaced and returned his attention to the body.

"I'm FBI Special Agent Paige Dawson, and this is Brandon Fisher." She gestured to Brandon, but it was lost to the back of the ME's head.

"I'm Clayton Shaw." The ME's assistant smiled weakly.

"Nice to meet you, Clayton." Paige shook his hand.

"You'll have to excuse Simon," Herrera said. "He's much better with the dead than the living."

Simon paused his work and glanced up at the captain. "As if you're one to talk."

Paige wasn't going to touch on the tension between the two men. "Simon…?" She was looking for a last name, and just when she thought he'd leave her hanging, he replied, keeping his focus on the body.

"Fleming."

"What are we looking at?" she asked.

"Gunshot to the chest. Instant death." Simon's gloved fingers prodded Reid's body here and there as if he were on an Easter egg hunt.

"That I could have concluded myself," she said with a little heat. "I was hoping for more specifics."

Seconds ticked off, and eventually, Simon looked at her. "I don't like to speculate or hypothesize. And I especially don't like to do so before the body's on a slab."

What a piece of work!

She puffed out her chest, took a deep breath, and tried to pull on patience from deep inside. "Do you have any idea what type of bullet we're looking at here?"

"A round from a sniper rifle."

Trying to get answers from this man is excruciating!

Paige turned to Brandon, and she noted the subtle smirk on his lips. She narrowed her eyes at him and went back to the ME. "When do you think you'll have him 'on your slab'?" So uncouth, but she matched the ME's attitude.

The ME's assistant backed up a few feet. So did Herrera.

Simon got to his feet, his blue eyes like ice. "As soon as I'm finished here, we'll be loading him up and taking him back to the morgue. The less chitchat, the faster we finish up here and get Mr. Reid on a table for autopsy."

Paige's jaw dropped open, then she snapped it shut.

"Are we done?" Simon huffed out.

She'd never met anyone so rude in her life—and she was used to dealing with serial killers, for goodness sake! "For now."

"Best I can hope for, I suppose." Simon returned to the body.

Paige glanced at the other men. Herrera blew out a breath, Clayton winced, and Brandon's mouth was twitching like he was fighting off laughter.

She walked off a few feet away, and Herrera kept close. She turned to him. "You'll keep us posted on the autopsy?"

"I will."

"I'm right here," Simon barked, "and I'm more than capable of—"

Paige took the few paces back to the ME and stuck her business card in his face. He snatched it and tucked it into a back pocket.

"We need to talk to the front-desk clerk," she said to Herrera and nudged her head toward Wilson Place. "He still in there?"

"Yep, I'll come with you."

Herrera probably wanted away from the miserable ME just as much as she did—not that she could blame him.

"He always like that?" she asked once they were inside.

"Simon? Oh, yeah, and to think you caught him on one of his good days."

"I'd hate to see one of his bad ones," she mumbled and bumped Brandon's arm when she caught him grinning like a fool.

Wilson Place's lobby smelled like money with its plush carpeting, stiff-looking furniture, and marble waterfall counter. A man in his fifties was standing behind the latter, ignoring the chair that sat off to the side. At the end of the lobby was an elevator with a uniformed officer stationed next to it.

The man at the desk took in Paige and Brandon, his gaze briefly dipping to the FBI acronym on their vests before seeking out Herrera for an explanation.

"Roy Hall, these are FBI agents, Dawson and Fisher."

Roy's eyes returned to Brandon's vest, and he paled.

"Mr. Hall," Paige started, "we have some questions we're quite certain you could help us with."

Roy's body stiffened, and he put his hands on the counter for support. "I'll do my best."

"The man who was shot…" Paige paused, watching for Roy's reaction, but he was as impassive as stone. "Did you know him?"

"Uh-hum, yeah."

Paige didn't say anything for a few seconds.

Roy went on. "He was a prosecuting attorney, right? His name was Darrell Reid?"

"That's right." Paige had the feeling Roy was more familiar with Reid than he was letting on.

Roy was looking in her direction, but more or less through her. "I've seen him around," he volunteered.

"Here? In this building, before today?" she tiptoed but applied some pressure.

"I'm not really at liberty to say." Roy's gaze drifted to Brandon again.

"I'm guessing you've worked here a long time," Brandon said, and Paige could appreciate he was trying to establish a comradery with Roy.

"Yeah." Roy stood a little taller. "I've been here twenty years."

"That's impressive."

"My guess is you haven't been an agent near as long."

"Just over three years." Brandon smiled, and Roy returned the expression.

"Aw, you're just getting started."

"That I am, but I can appreciate that you would do anything to protect a job you love." Brandon's gaze flicked to her just briefly. "But I think sometimes we need to make judgment calls in life. Do what might not necessarily be *right*—" he added finger quotes "—but that actually is."

"I don't know where you're going with this, Agent Fisher."

"I think you do." After a few seconds, Brandon asked, "You ever see Reid here before?"

Roy's shoulders sagged as if all his breath had left him, and he slinked across the counter to the chair, where he lowered himself. "I may have." Roy kept his gaze on the floor.

"Did he come here regularly?" Paige asked in a gentle tone.

He raised his eyes to meet hers. "I'm not going to say."

Apparently, Brandon's attempts to loosen Roy's tongue hadn't worked. Paige stepped toward Roy with care, so as not to intimidate or startle him. "We understand that Mr. Reid came here last night and left this morning. Do you know what business he had here?"

"I couldn't tell you even if I knew, but apparently, someone has a big mouth." Roy's gaze shot past them to outside.

"We understand that you have a sign-in book for visitors," Paige said. "Is there any way we could see that?"

"Sure, with a warrant. Doing so without one would get me fired." He glanced at Brandon, seeking understanding.

"We understand," Brandon assured him.

"Not counting last night and this morning, when was Mr. Reid last here?" Paige wasn't about to give up trying to get more out of Roy, but he clenched his jaw. Maybe another approach would work. "Did he always come to visit the same person or people?"

Still, Roy said nothing.

"We'd appreciate it if you would answer our questions," Paige said.

"I'm sorry, but I can't."

"Can't or won't?" she countered.

Herrera tugged down on his suit jacket. "Mr. Hall, a man was just killed outside of this building. The more information we get, and the sooner we get it, the better chance that we'll catch his killer. Do you understand that?"

As each word left the captain's mouth, Roy's body language become more and more closed off—arms crossed, jaw tight, eyes resolved. "Do you understand that I'm not going to get fired over this?" Roy slapped back. "I am sorry that man was killed. I truly am, but it's not my fault, and I'm not going to lose my job over this."

"You respect your job, the people in this building. You have the chance to help someone." Brandon was back to playing diplomat, Mr. Relatable.

"Too late for him, from what I understand." Tears glistened in his eyes.

"You don't have to tell us anything," Paige started.

"Well, thank you very much."

"We'll contact Property Holdings Group."

"You do that. Now, is that all?"

Paige had thought maybe she could call the clerk's bluff, but it turned out he really didn't want to be involved.

"Can I go back to work now?"

Paige wasn't sure what Roy had in mind, given that the building was on shutdown. Anyone who arrived here would be turned away, including the clerk showing up for the next shift. But the thought of busying himself probably calmed Roy's nerves. "You can go back to work," she said, feeling for him.

CHAPTER SEVEN

I left Wilson Place with Paige and Herrera and glanced back through the glass doors at Hall. He had returned to his post, standing there expectant for the next person to walk through the door—as if it were any ordinary day. Sometimes clinging to the normal and familiar was how people coped with tragedy.

"Poor guy's so shaken up." Herrera jacked a thumb over a shoulder to indicate Roy Hall. "Do you think he's holding something useful back from us? Maybe he's behind the shooting in some way? Connected with the sniper?"

I shook my head. "I'm not getting that from him."

"Me neither," Paige said and looked at me, "but we still should pull his background."

"I can do that for you," Herrera offered.

"We can get our analyst back at Quantico to take care of it." The words came out in a rush. "No offense."

"None taken," was what Herrera said, but I think I caught a spark of offense flash across his eyes.

Herrera went on. "I'll get on the warrant for the sign-in book?" He posed it like a question, but neither Paige nor I touched it. He added, "I have a good relationship with Judge Whittaker, a local. He'll give authorization over the phone, and I'll follow up with a signed version later, but that will get the book in our hands fairly quickly."

Paige was nodding. "While you're at it, if you could get a subpoena for the tenant list from Property Holdings Group for Wilson Place, that would be useful as well."

"I'll see what I can do."

"Brandon and I will be staying on the ground a bit longer. Jack's wanting us to do some door knocking, see if we can dig up anything pertinent to the case. Who should we see about that?"

"You saw the officer standing next to the elevators in there? Name's Officer Byrd…Stewart. He's young but a great cop, and I put him in charge of the inside. He's to make sure people go back to their apartments if they come down, and he's overseeing the progress of the canvassing officers."

"Thank you," Paige said.

Herrera dipped his head. "Once I get the warrant and collect the book, I'll be going back to the station to get the conference room set up. Hopefully by then, we'll have a better idea what we're looking at. And if luck's in our favor, some solid leads." With that, Herrera walked off toward the command center.

"Before we start knocking on doors, I say we get Nadia started on the background for Roy Hall," Paige said.

"She probably already has the info on McBride and the former doorman by now." I pulled out my phone and dialed Nadia on speaker.

She answered on the third ring. "Ah…hey, hi."

I raised my eyebrows. "It's me and Paige. Is everything all right there?"

"I…don't know. I'm following a hunch, and it's not a good one."

I glanced at Paige. "What is it?"

"I don't want to say just yet. I want to do some more digging first, but I feel horrible for lying to Jack."

"You lied to Jack?" *Brave woman.*

"Not one hundred percent, but he asked if I found any other shootings similar to today, and I told him no."

"So, you have?" Paige exclaimed.

"Safe to say I'm working on a hunch. But you know how Jack is. He wants facts, not theories. What can I do for you, Brandon?"

"We need another background," I said and requested one on Roy Hall. "Also, if you could update me on—"

"I was about to send you the reports on McBride and the information for Gerald Stevens—that's his last name, by the way. Neither man looks suspicious on paper. But I got a little distracted."

I squinted, not recognizing this Nadia. "Something to do with that hunch of yours?"

"Probably more fact than hunch," she mumbled, then clicked off.

"Okay," Paige dragged out.

"Someone's not herself," I said needlessly.

"I'd say."

"I guess we'll have to wait it out to hear about this 'hunch' of hers."

"Guess so." Paige smiled subtly.

"Want to go talk to Stevens now? He doesn't have to worry about confidentiality issues anymore. He might be more open to talking." I was hopeful my argument would get me out of knocking on doors.

"Nope. Jack told us to stay on the ground and do some canvassing—and that's exactly what we're going to do."

"Yippie," I griped.

Paige angled her head. "You make it sound so horrible."

"Well, it's not my favorite assignment."

"Sometimes we have to do things we don't like."

"Someone's sounding quite mature."

She moved toward the door, but I didn't.

"The most important thing is finding the sniper, right?"

She stopped walking but didn't turn around.

"Well, to do that, it would be helpful to find out more about Reid," I said quickly, while I had her attention. "The former doorman might be able to—"

She faced me but didn't say anything.

I had her hooked and felt a twinge of triumph. "Nothing about this so far strikes me as an act of terrorism. One man was taken out, and I believe that man was targeted by a skilled sniper."

"So you say...And I tend to agree. It just would have taken one small miscalculation and we'd be looking at more fatalities. I already have my theories."

"Well..." I prompted, hoping she'd be more willing to share than Nadia had been.

She took a deep breath and shrugged her shoulders. "Just like you hypothesized in our briefing. Our sniper is highly trained and someone with a military or law enforcement background."

"Yep, or self-taught is also possible," I said, downplaying my own idea. "Could even be someone who didn't quite make the grade to become a cop or who wasn't approved for military service."

"A person like that would be mad at the world. That wouldn't explain one casualty."

"One victim in this shooting." The skin on the back of my neck tightened. "Nadia has a hunch, so I'd say she's uncovered something. Maybe other shootings? Other victims?"

"Sure, but we'll have to wait on Nadia." Paige worried her bottom lip. "Sniping off a person is just such a drastic measure to take. There has to be a specific reason this is the method our killer prefers—again assuming this wasn't a one-off. If we can answer why our sniper chose this method of operation, it might get us closer to understanding motive."

Both of our phones pinged. I looked at mine and saw that it was a message from Nadia with the backgrounds for McBride, Stevens, and Hall. I scanned through them quickly and came to the same conclusion Nadia had: nothing seemed suspicious about the doormen. A quick look at Hall's gave me the same impression.

"If either doorman was involved with orchestrating the shooting," I said, "we'll need Nadia to dig much deeper than this. Financials, associations."

"I'm not seeing enough to justify doing that just yet." Paige pocketed her phone. "Let's get on with doing what Jack wants us to." She sounded about as thrilled as I was about the prospect, but she pointed a finger toward the building—the message being *move it*.

I got the door for her.

Hall's shoulders squared up to his ears. "What—"

Paige stayed him with a raised hand. "We need to speak with the tenants."

"There's already cops spread all throughout the building."

"And now there will be two Feds." I smiled pleasantly at him.

"Hold up. The tenants of this building expect a certain amount of privacy."

"I can respect that," Paige said, "but I bet they didn't expect a shooting outside their front door. I'm sure some of them would be happy to speak with us. Even if it's for reassurance there's nothing to fear."

"Is that true?"

"We believe so," Paige said, pulling off the misdirection like a pro. Hall's softening posture told me he took her words to mean we'd be comforting people, but Paige never actually said as much. There'd be no way either of us would be making any promises or guarantees of safety—not when we weren't even sure what we were looking at.

Paige and I went over to Officer Byrd. He was standing with his shoulders squared, chin lifted high, and hands clasped.

"Captain Herrera said you could help us out," Paige said. "He left you in charge of the canvassing officers."

"That he did, ma'am."

Paige stiffened at the address. "Can you tell us the attack plan?"

Byrd's mouth twitched at her words. "Sure. There's six officers other than myself. They're assigned in pairs, a floor per team, starting at the top—the fifteenth floor."

"So, that puts them currently…where?" I asked.

"Well, each team is to check in with me when they finish a floor before heading to the next. Only one team's checked in so far."

I tried to do the math in my head, but that subject had never been my strong suit. "That makes the next available floor to work…"

"The eleventh. I'll let the officers know you'll be there."

"Thanks." Paige reached for the Up arrow, but Byrd beat her to it. "Thanks," she said again.

"No problem, ma'am." Byrd smiled at her, and a pang of jealousy fired in my chest. He might have been addressing her as *ma'am*—and she was probably twenty years older than him—but the officer was attracted to her. And that was enough to have me disliking him, even if a little bit.

CHAPTER EIGHT

The sniper didn't need to close her eyes to see death. It was there in front of her eyes most of the time. The memories never far away. She should be on the open road with Arlington in the rearview mirror, but she had never been good at leaving things behind. Whether wanted or not, the past was haunting, always present, and ready to consume. She felt like a zombie—eyes wide and blank, roving about on autopilot. It was the same way after every kill, though she stupidly expected a different outcome. The anticipated high was never quite achieved. There was no fulfillment of desire, no culmination, no feeling of reward—just a mission set and mission accomplished. Taking life was like attaining a long-desired goal, only to realize reality stripped it of its charm.

She was settled in a corner table at a coffee shop about eight blocks from Wilson Place. There was a TV mounted on a facing wall where the events from that morning were being broadcasted as "Just in."

She stirred her coffee, watched as the liquid swirled like a mini whirlpool, the cream creating little bubbles. Just like agitated water, around and around, furiously pounding, and currents meeting and reacting. She removed the spoon from the coffee but dropped the piece of cutlery on the table, causing a clatter.

Three groups of people looked over with sharp expressions on their faces. She stared back at them blankly, and they returned to their idle conversations.

Their reactions to a dropped spoon were about the same as the people at the site of the shooting—brief and fleeting. Sure, a crowd liked to hype up disaster, but eventually, folks returned to their own lives, moved on, with little regard for what had taken place. That is unless they were personally touched by the tragedy—and sometimes even so, humans were much like wild animals, feeding off the carcass of misfortune, sucking it bone dry for their own advantages, whatever those may be. This had been quite evident when she had stood at the edge of the police tape with a gathered crowd and had asked one officer what had taken place. In response, like a zombie, his eyes blank, the officer had said, "For your safety, I ask that you stay back."

The people weren't saying much, either—at first. Just whispers carried on a breeze, marked with curiosity and suspicion. *"I think someone was shot." "I think there was a sniper."* As time passed, the speakers became self-assured, talking in the definitives, establishing themselves an authority, trying to magnify their own importance. As if they had something meaningful to offer the world with their juicy tidbits of knowledge.

The sniper picked up the spoon again and stirred the coffee. The stainless steel struck against the ceramic mug—*clink, clink, clink*—and some coffee sloshed over the rim.

The female television newscaster went on about the shooting, but the people in the coffee shop paid her no attention. They were too absorbed in their own trivialities and selfish ambitions.

While the sniper couldn't hear what was being said on TV, the ticker tape at the bottom read AN ACT OF TERRORISM?

Of course they'd leap there!

That's how the media always liked to portray unexplained acts of violence. Blame it on a foreign enemy or one who infiltrated themselves onto native soil. Don't understand something, and it must be an evil entity at work. It was sickening, as was the human condition.

So many of them paranoid, scampering, trying to carve out a life of meaning but failing desperately to reach the mark. The solution was to stop searching for purpose when none existed. The sniper was all too familiar with the unfairness of the world. Enough to know that no matter who was to blame, it didn't erase the consequences. They rippled out, like water from a stone tossed into water. Spreading... *spreading.* Some waves caused destruction; others were hardly felt.

The sniper had turned her life around by harnessing the darkness, befriending it, welcoming the churning waves and riding them. She took charge of her own existence, paved her own way. Any lesser person would have been destroyed, *broken,* a word she couldn't stand. It was a sweeping label that excused responsibility, though in that context it held some appeal.

She stirred her coffee a few more times, then let the spoon clang to the tabletop again. This time, only one woman looked at her, bearing a scowl and arched brows. Unmoved, she took a slow draw on the coffee, and when she lowered the cup, her eyes landed on the TV screen and the ticker tape.

THE *FBI* TO INVESTIGATE THE SHOOTING IN ARLINGTON, VIRGINIA

The sniper let go of her cup. It hit the edge of the table and smashed to the floor.

Everyone was staring—the sniper could feel it—but her eyes were on the television. Sweat was gathering at the base of her back and neck. If she had any hope of finishing her mission, it was time to move.

CHAPTER NINE

Kelly debated sharing her thoughts about Arlene Reid with Jack. Speaking her mind so far in this case hadn't netted her any favors. She snuck in glances at his profile while he drove them to the Arlington commonwealth's attorney's office.

"Do I have something on my face?" Jack took a quick drag on a cigarette and turned slowly to face her.

She shook her head. "Sorry if I've been staring."

"A penny for your thoughts?"

He'd asked for them, but was she ready to part with them? She feared being shut down, accused of jumping to conclusions. How was she supposed to work like that? She cleared her throat. "Gramps used to smoke...until I made him quit."

"You made that old goat quit?" Jack took another inhale. "That's impressive."

"I can be persuasive."

"Good skill for an agent to have." He flicked some ash out the window.

"I like to think so." She briefly looked out her window, catching her reflection. "Actually, Jack, I was thinking something else."

"Figured you probably were."

"Mrs. Reid's hiding something. I think she knows what her husband's connection was to Wilson Place."

"I do, too."

She was ready to defend herself and snapped her mouth shut.

"We'll find out—if not from her, then someone else," Jack said. "Unfortunately, we can't force people to talk. Good news is things have a way of coming out." He pulled into the lot for the commonwealth attorney's office, and both of them got out. He extinguished his cigarette on the pavement with a twist of his shoe.

"You can let me handle this in there," Jack told her. "Sometimes these types aren't too open to talking."

"'These types' being lawyers?"

"You got it." He smiled, and she nodded. Jack wouldn't be the first person who wasn't a fan of lawyers. Considering an incompetent one had played a role in her mother's murder conviction when it should have been self-defense, as a whole, lawyers weren't Kelly's favorite people, either. Her friend Brianna, who was a defense attorney, was the exception.

At the front desk, Jack announced them as FBI with urgent business for the commonwealth attorney. The young woman told them Margaret Holmes would be with them shortly. It was less than five minutes later that another woman, introduced as Danielle by the receptionist, asked that they follow her. She led them down various hallways to an office with its door open and rapped her knuckles on the doorframe.

"Yes?" A woman's voice—presumably Margaret Holmes—responded. Just the articulation of that one word attested to her authority.

Danielle stepped into the opening. "FBI Agents Harper and Marsh to speak with you, ma'am."

"Send them in."

Danielle moved to the side to allow Jack and Kelly room to enter the office. A woman in her fifties with short, dark hair was perched behind an oak desk, her eyes intelligent and curious, small wrinkles outlining them and marking her brow. Margaret was a handsome woman, and probably not much got past her attention. She stood and extended a hand toward Jack.

"I'm FBI Supervisory Special Agent in Charge Jack Harper, and this is Agent Kelly Marsh."

"Margaret Holmes." She gave a perfunctory glance at Jack, but there was a spark in her eyes when she met Kelly's gaze. Kelly picked up on the unspoken message that the attorney liked seeing another woman in a position of power.

"You both may take a seat." She gestured toward two chairs that faced her desk before sitting in her own again.

"We appreciate you seeing us on such short notice, but as you are likely aware, there's been an incident in Clarendon," Jack said.

"Yes, I'm aware, and I'm not surprised to see you here. I thoroughly expected to be seeing someone from the FBI's office. The mayor's looking at me for answers. Do you have any that I can pass along? Are we looking at an act of terrorism?"

"There's nothing yet to indicate that." Jack took a pause, and Kelly wondered if he'd picked up on the same thing she had: Margaret didn't know that Reid had been killed. "Are you aware, ma'am, that the victim was Darrell Reid?"

"Dar... Reid?" the attorney stammered. Her previous composure was gone, and she sank back in her chair, folding in on herself.

"We're sorry to be the ones breaking this to you," Kelly said kindly. "It must come as quite a shock."

Margaret ran a hand over her mouth. "Yes, you could say that." She cleared her throat, blinked her eyes, and leaned forward, a show of resuming a stance of control and confidence—except that her energy betrayed her vulnerability. "What happened?"

"Mr. Reid was leaving Wilson Place this morning at six AM when he was shot," Jack laid out candidly. "We'd like to get some information from you about Reid—"

"You believe his murder might somehow be connected to one of his cases."

"We do," Jack admitted.

"Anything's possible, I suppose."

"Would you know why Reid may have been at Wilson Place this morning and last night?"

"Last night? The way you say it makes it sound like he stayed over."

"He may have."

"Well, if he did, I can't imagine him being there for official business."

"Is there someone who could provide more insight into Mr. Reid's schedule?" Jack asked.

"Reid's aide, Brad McCarthy, manages his calendar. If anyone could shed some light here, it would be him." Margaret picked up her phone and requested that Reid's aide be sent to her office forthwith.

"While we're waiting, tell us what you do know," Jack encouraged.

"I know that this is hitting me right out of left field. I'm well aware this job pits us against some pretty violent criminals. You just expect there to be a barrier between us and the madness." She glanced at Jack. "As crazy as that might sound."

Jack didn't say anything, and Kelly thought the attorney's ideal sounded naive. But she gave her a pass, given the circumstances.

Margaret continued. "I know Darrell was currently working on a few large cases—one quite high profile compared to the rest."

"Tell us about that one," Jack said.

Margaret clasped her hands over her lap. "The son of a local businessman drove drunk and killed a family of three."

Tragic to be sure, but Kelly wasn't sure if such a case on its own would be considered "high profile," so it would have to be the players involved. "What is the man's company?"

"The man is William Pratchett, and he founded and runs Pratchett Group." She paused as if expecting Kelly or Jack to reply. She clarified, "Pratchett Group owns hundreds of newspapers and numerous television networks. The man is like a god in some circles. Most people have heard of him."

"It seems you found two who haven't," Jack said drily. "Tell us more about the case as it involves Reid."

"Well, Darrell was gunning for the heaviest sentence available by law. If he got his way, Darrell would rewrite the law on the sentencing for drinking and driving causing death."

Kelly glanced at Jack but kept her mouth shut. Maybe Pratchett didn't take too kindly to his son being used as an example and had decided to shut Reid down.

Margaret went on. "There's a real hype in the media about the case. Of course, any papers owned by Pratchett Group approach the story from taking mercy on William's son. The ones outside of his control are making it their full-time endeavor to do what they can to taint the public against William and his son. I'm sure Pratchett Group stock has been affected."

Another motive for William Pratchett.

"And what's the son's name?" Kelly figured it was always best to work with names.

"Adrian." Margaret's eyes went contemplative. "Do you think Darrell's death had something to do with that case?"

"Nothing's off the table yet," Jack said. "We'll need all the pertinents on that case."

There was a knock on the door, and Kelly and Jack turned. A man in his early twenties stood there. Dark hair, fair complexion, and lean frame.

"Brad, these two are from the FBI." She looked at Jack, then Kelly. "This is Brad McCarthy, Mr. Reid's aide."

Brad's gaze went over them, and he awkwardly tucked his hands into his pockets.

"Here, you can have my seat." Kelly stood and gestured for Brad to take her chair.

"I'm good to stand," Brad said, "but thank you."

"When you find out why they're here, you might change your mind," Margaret cautioned.

Brad looked leerily at Kelly and dropped into the chair she'd vacated. "Thanks."

"No problem."

Margaret made the formal introductions, then said, "Mr. Reid was shot and killed this morning outside of Wilson Place in Clarendon."

Brad's mouth gaped open, and his eyes glazed over, his mind processing what he'd just been told. "He was…" That was all he got out.

"Mr. Reid was murdered." Kelly put it as delicately as she could. The attorney hadn't exactly delivered the news with much tact. "We're trying to figure out why he was at Wilson Place, and Ms. Holmes told us you might be able to help us since you kept Mr. Reid's calendar."

"I can certainly look…" Brad pulled a tablet out of an inside jacket pocket. "What time…did it…" He pulled nervously at his collar.

"Six o'clock this morning, but it's believed he might have spent the night there."

Something flicked across Brad's eyes before he put his gaze on the tablet. "One moment, if I may?" His fingers moved across the screen as fast as a skilled pianist's played over keys.

"You certainly know how to get around that thing." Kelly had said it to offer a moment of levity, but Jack gave her a cold look.

Brad's movements slowed a bit. "Ah, he was supposed to have a meeting this morning, but there's nothing in the calendar about an overnight." Brad paled and glanced at Margaret.

"What is it, Brad? It might help us find our killer." Kelly hoped to appeal to his humanity and that it would surpass any concerns he might have about damaging Reid's character.

Brad waved a hand in the air. "Oh, it's probably nothing. He was to meet with a defendant and his attorney."

"At Wilson Place? Overnight?" Jack blurted out the questions with skepticism in every word. "Did Mr. Reid make a habit of sleeping over with defense attorneys and their clients?"

"Heavens, no!" Brad exclaimed.

Jack angled his head just slightly, and Brad's shoulders sagged.

"And the meeting wasn't to take place at Wilson Place. It was set for eight o'clock at the defense attorney's office across town. That's the opposite end of the city from where he was…shot." Brad frowned. "I don't have any idea why Mr. Reid would have been at Wilson Place." He glanced again at Margaret.

If Kelly's gut was telling her something was off with Reid's character before, sirens were now sounding with flashing red lights. "Brad," she started and waited for him to look at her, "did you manage any personal affairs of Mr. Reid's? I ask because sometimes assistants are asked to cross a professional line. For example, pick up their boss's dry cleaning or things like that." If she wanted Brad to voice his suspicions about Reid, she needed to play it diplomatically—especially with Margaret listening intently, leaning forward, elbows perched on her desk.

Brad chewed on his bottom lip. "No dry cleaning."

Kelly decided to tug a little harder on the string, curious what it might unravel. "But he did have you handle some personal errands?"

"Not really. Well, I guess he had me buy gifts for Mrs. Reid on his behalf. But in his defense, he had a full calendar." He blushed.

It was time to pry open this can. "Is there something you think we should know?"

Brad swallowed roughly; his Adam's apple bobbed, and his eyes darted about the room. "I'd say I don't want to get Mr. Reid into any trouble, but I guess that doesn't matter now." He held eye contact with Margaret while he continued. "Mr. Reid would sometimes miss appointments, interviews with defendants, and so on."

Margaret sat upright suddenly, posturing full authority. "Why is this the first time I'm hearing of this?"

Brad's cheeks fired to crimson.

"Why was he missing appointments? Mr. McCarthy, I demand that you tell me right now."

"I wish I could say with certainty."

"Out with your suspicions. Now's not the time to keep quiet." Margaret's tone had teeth.

Brad nodded. "Whenever I'd question him, he'd get defensive, tell me he didn't answer to me. He'd even accuse me of not keeping his calendar properly. But I assure you, Ms. Holmes, that I took the utmost care with his schedule. Any appointments that I made for him or he told me about, I placed into his calendar immediately—day or night. Mr. Reid had access to his calendar on his phone, but sometimes I wondered if he even looked at it. He'd double-book himself, and I'd have to move previously existing appointments around to accommodate the new ones he made."

Margaret was scowling. "The calendar was your responsibility, Mr. McCarthy, not Mr. Reid's. But with that said, Mr. Reid had a responsibility toward this office and his commission to place importance on his schedule. Yet, I'm having a hard time accepting in all the time you worked together, you never found out where he'd been or why he'd miss appointments."

"With respect, ma'am, as I said, Mr. Reid would tell me that it wasn't my place to question him, and I didn't want to pry into his life."

"By not prying, you've placed the reputation of this office at risk. Did that ever occur to you?"

Brad's shoulders lowered, along with his gaze that fell to the floor. "No...I..."

"You and I will discuss that matter later."

"Yes, ma'am." Brad waited it out for a few seconds, then added, "I would like to be excused."

Margaret's face etched into stone. "You are *not* excused. You gave us the impression you had suspicions about where Mr. Reid went or what he was up to. I'd like you to share those with us." She splayed her hand across the room to indicate Jack and Kelly, then crossed her arms.

Brad seemed to shrink in his chair. "Oh…I'm not sure I should…if the reputation of this office is at stake."

Margaret leveled a stare on the aide that could have frozen lava.

Brad drew a deep breath. "I'd like to start by saying I have no concrete proof, but—"

"Mr. Reid was cheating on his wife," Margaret stamped out, seemingly with a lick of distaste for all men.

Brad's eyes met hers. "I wondered that sometimes. Yes."

"Just because of the missed meetings?" Kelly squeezed in before Margaret could sink her talons more deeply into the aide's flesh.

Brad looked at her. "Sometimes women would call for Mr. Reid, but they wouldn't leave their names or numbers. And before you ask, they always blocked their numbers."

"This happen often?" Jack asked.

"Probably once a month or so."

Kelly studied the aide, and based on his slightly more relaxed body language, he was telling the truth as far as he knew it.

Had Arlene Reid known about her husband's affairs? The way she'd talked about Darrell, it would seem she idolized him, but maybe that had been an act. Kelly had learned a long time ago that the images people project rarely reflect reality. But if Mr. Reid had numerous lovers, it really opened up the suspect pool. Did one of those women decide to take him out? Or was Mr. Reid's murder not related to matters of the heart, but rather professionally motivated—or something else entirely different, such as the case against Pratchett?

"Were you aware of anyone who disliked Mr. Reid and made their hatred evident?" Kelly asked.

"I'm not sure where to start with answering that question, Agent. He made a lot of enemies with his job."

"Maybe he received hate mail or threats?" Jack suggested.

"Nothing in writing, but he had his share of people who were unhappy with the outcome of their cases."

"The convicted are never happy—innocent or guilty," Margaret chimed in.

"As we mentioned to Attorney Holmes before your arrival," Jack started, "we'd like to get some information on the cases Mr. Reid was working recently, including ones that closed. Any you recall that stirred a lot of animosity toward Mr. Reid could prove especially useful."

Brad looked at Margaret, who nodded. "Sure, I can compile that for you." He put his hands to the arms of the chair as if about to propel himself up and out of the room. He seemed eager to leave, probably to deal with the news of his boss's death in private. "Oh, am I excused, ma'am?"

Margaret gestured for him to leave. With the aide gone, she said, "He's really a good kid, but he doesn't always consider the big picture. And that's what we need in our employees around here."

Jack and Kelly saw themselves out. While they were leaving with a fresh perspective on their victim, which expanded a field of possible motives, Kelly still couldn't help but feel for Brad McCarthy. He'd just done his job as best as he knew how. He'd been loyal to his boss—to a fault, it would seem. She glanced over at Jack, and she certainly didn't want to end up in the same spot. She had to remember the job came first, approval second.

CHAPTER TEN

Being confined with Brandon in an SUV was one thing; an elevator car was another. All Paige could smell the entire way up to the eleventh floor was Brandon's aftershave. It was the same one he'd used when they'd been together, and it was causing the past to resurface with sensory force—and she hated it. She happily stepped off the elevator the second the doors opened.

"Did you want to pair up or split?" Brandon asked.

She looked over at him, his question catching her off guard, and she realized it was all business. "Let's stick together." Splitting up might result in faster coverage, but if they worked together, they could pick up on things the other missed when questioning a tenant.

"Sure. We've always made a great couple—I mean, team," he said. "We make a great *team*."

"Right. You be sure to correct that. I don't think Becky would like it." She attempted a smile but failed, and when they met each other's eyes, she saw he was feeling just as uncomfortable. "Okay, you ready to get started?" She gestured to the end of the hall, which faced the back of the building and not the front where Reid had been shot. The people in those apartments were less likely to have seen anything with regard to the shooting, but they could have something to say about Reid and whether he had been here before or why he had been leaving this morning.

The eleventh floor, like the lobby, was well maintained. The plush carpet was a neutral pattern, and the air smelled pleasantly of lavender-scented cleaner. The walls were wainscoted with a creamy-white bottom and warm gray on top. Decorative fixtures were mounted to the walls and provided enough light to eliminate shadows, but not so much she wanted to squint.

They set out and worked their way through most of the floor. They found one person at home—an older lady by the name of Ruby MacIntosh. She'd enticed them inside by saying she could tell them something about Reid. She just hadn't clarified it would be her stand on Reid's professional life.

"He's far too lenient on these criminals. He should push for harsher sentences." Ruby slurped tea from a floral china teacup.

Paige and Brandon were seated on a floral couch with doilies on the arms covered in plastic sleeves. The place was starting to feel like the Mafia—once you were in, you didn't get out.

"Did you know Mr. Reid?" Paige did her best to be kind to the woman, but she had to consider that the clock was ticking while they were wasting time in here.

"No. I've never met him. But you can tell a lot from a man just from seeing him on camera," Ruby punched out and added an energetic head bob for emphasis.

"Did you ever see him in this building?" Paige was pulling from somewhere deep inside herself for patience.

"No, can't say as I have."

Paige glanced at Brandon and stood. "Well, thank you for the tea, Mrs. MacIntosh, but Agent Fisher and I need to get on and speak with your neighbors."

Ruby frowned.

"Yes, I suppose you don't have time to just shoot the shit with an old lady." She slurped back the rest of her tea and placed the teacup down rather heavily on the table next to her chair.

Paige beelined for the door, a tad hesitant to put her back to the old woman, but was highly motivated to escape.

"Perhaps another time," Brandon said cordially.

Out in the hall, Paige nudged his elbow. "Why did you say that?"

"I was just trying to be nice."

"Try less. She's the type to hold you to your word."

"Good luck pinning me down." Brandon was laughing, but Paige wasn't.

Not being able to "pin" Brandon down had been a source of regret and pain for years. Not that she thought about it constantly, by any means, but their time together had a way of filtering back into her thoughts.

They hit the next—and last—door on this floor, apartment 1135. It was at the end of the hall and faced the front of the building where Reid had been shot.

A twentysomething woman answered after the first knock. Her hair was tied back into a ponytail, and her silver eyes were locked on Brandon. She seemed to hang off the door as she smiled and said, "Yes?"

"Do you know him?" Paige put a copy of Reid's license photo in her face, blocking her view of Brandon.

"Sure, but who are you?"

Paige exchanged the photo for her badge. "FBI Agents Dawson and Fisher." She nudged her head toward Brandon.

The woman squinted. "Why is the FBI interested in Mr. Reid? I agree it's a crime he isn't sitting in Margaret Holmes's chair. She's far too lenient on sentencing recommendations, if you ask me."

The exact opposite of how Ruby McIntosh felt about Reid.

"You seem to know a lot about the attorney's office," Brandon said. "Hobby?"

There was a subtle curve to her lips, but it carried flirtatious overtones. "Let's just say it's out of professional interest."

"You're a lawyer?" Brandon smiled.

She shrugged off his question with a grin. "You could say that. I've got a law degree and passed the bar."

"But you don't practice," Paige concluded.

Her face soured. "No, I don't, and I don't have any real interest. The schooling and passing the bar, I did for Daddy. But I must admit, it provides me with a unique perspective on things." She paused as if expecting Paige or Brandon to say something. When they didn't, she added, "You don't know who I am, do you?"

"Can't say that I do." Paige gestured to Brandon. "You?"

"No."

The woman pouted. "I'm Cindy Beat. And, wow, you really don't know me. Okay—" she planted a hand on a hip "—I'll try not to be offended."

"There's no need to be offended," Brandon said, and Paige fought off rolling her eyes. "Neither of us live in Arlington."

"But you do live on planet Earth?" Cindy shot back, and Paige was tempted to give her a dose of a reality check. Cindy continued. "I host *Keeping a Pulse on Law & Politics*. It's a podcast—one of the most listened-to podcasts in the entire US. Not just in its genre, but overall."

"Our jobs don't leave us much social time," Paige said.

"That's too bad." Cindy eyed Brandon like a hungry tigress.

"Could we come in and talk?" Paige cut in. "You can tell us more about your podcast." It wasn't really at the top of Paige's list for topics of conversation, but talking about the show might relax Cindy and get her opening up about Reid.

"I'd love to." Cindy opened her door wider, and Paige and Brandon went inside.

Unlike Ruby MacIntosh's apartment, there were no doilies in sight. The space adhered to the minimalist look, and what existed of furnishings were modern and high-end. Gleaming hardwood floors were accented by faux-fur area rugs.

Cindy guided them to a living room that was framed by two walls of windows, including a glass patio door that led to an outdoor living space. From what Paige could see, it had been decorated with a minimalist brush like the apartment.

"Your place is beautiful," Paige complimented.

"It should be for what I pay for it." She gestured for Paige to sit in a chair made of oak and laminate with metal legs and a thin cushion.

Paige complied and found it as uncomfortable as it looked. She wiggled, trying to find an agreeable position.

Cindy sat in a round accent chair with deep, navy cushions and a back pillow, and Brandon dropped himself into its twin.

"As I was saying, *KPL&P* is— That's just what I call the podcast for short."

"Makes perfect sense," Paige said, even if the acronym was a mouthful.

"On the podcast, I speak my mind on everything law and politics. Don't even get me started on Trump."

"No worries there," Paige said quickly. "I'm guessing you spoke a lot about Mr. Reid."

"When he was newsworthy, yes."

"You ever meet him or interview him?" Brandon asked.

"Absolutely. I don't just like to give my opinion—though my listeners tune in for that—but like an investigative journalist, I really dig into my subjects. It makes for much more interesting and reliable content."

"What was your take on Mr. Reid," Paige started, "besides he should have been in the commonwealth attorney's chair?"

"You mean personally?" With the question, Cindy's voice cracked ever so slightly.

"Sure."

"He seemed like a nice man, but very driven. Ambitious. He had a bit of a suffocating quality to him, but he was also…" Cindy worried her bottom lip and kept eye contact with Paige. "Woman to woman? He was magnetic, charismatic, but also somewhat chauvinistic. Somehow he knew how to work the three together and—"

"He was hard to resist," Paige finished. She'd known her fair share of men who could be summed up the same way. "Did you and Mr. Reid ever—"

"Hook up? No, but that's only because I don't do married guys."

Paige suddenly felt sick and full of remorse. She wished she'd adhered to that code of ethics. Then she wouldn't have gotten together with Brandon in the first place, and there wouldn't be any awkwardness in her life now. But in her defense, she hadn't known right away, and by the time she had, she hadn't cared—as awful as that sounded. Even now, with Brandon currently in a relationship, it was a fine tether that held her to a higher course of morality.

"That's a good philosophy to live by," Brandon offered, his voice a little strained.

Cindy puffed out a deep breath. "I think so. Sleeping with married guys only complicates life—and life's complicated enough. Why compound things?"

Yeah, why compound things? Paige cleared her throat. "Did Mr. Reid ever make a move on you?"

"Oh, yeah, on several occasions."

"Did you interview him more than once?" Brandon asked.

"Absolutely. Like I said, whenever he was newsworthy, which was often. But we'd also run into each other at different events. He definitely knows what he wants." Cindy crossed her legs, and a serious expression blanketed her face. "You never did answer my question. Why is the FBI interested in Mr. Reid?"

"You are probably aware that something transpired outside this building this morning," Paige said, doing her best to remain still, though her butt was going numb on the hard chair.

Cindy nodded. "I know there's been a lot of police activity. From what I gather, someone got shot. I've called my contacts and haven't gotten far, which is very unusual for me. Oh"—her mouth gaped open—"Mr. Reid was the one who was shot."

"That's right," Paige confirmed.

Cindy sank into her chair, putting her elbow on the arm, a hand to her forehead. "I think a part of me knew that was why you were here...and asking about Reid. I just didn't want to believe it."

"We're trying to figure out what brought Reid to the building this morning. Would you know?" There was no advantage to feeding a rumor mill that it seemed the attorney had spent the night somewhere in the building, presumably with *someone*.

"Wow. I'm going to have to start recording our conversation."

"We need to ask that you don't," Paige rushed out.

"Why wouldn't I? This is news."

"Yes, it's news," Paige said tersely, "but there are people behind the story. His family is in the process of being notified." It was likely Jack and Kelly had already finished with the notification, but that was neither here nor there.

"I guarantee you, someone out there already has broken the story. It's probably already trending online. God, I hate being behind, especially as I was right here." Cindy pulled out her cell phone and ran her finger over the screen—then stopped. "'*Did Reid's ambitions catch up to him?*'" She held the screen toward Paige and Brandon, not that either of them could read it from where they were seated, and then stuck her nose in her phone for the next few seconds. "The article suggests a hit was taken out on him." She continued to scroll. "Other articles note a shooting—leaving Reid nameless—and mention the possibility of terrorism."

Paige's life experience had taught her that people liked to sensationalize things any chance they got to make a name for themselves. More interesting to Paige was that a hit was being speculated.

"Do they say why they think Mr. Reid was targeted?" Brandon asked, beating Paige to the question.

"I would know the answer to that one, even without reading the entire piece." Cindy lowered her phone. "Mr. Reid was currently working a case against a drunk driver who took out a family of three. It was the driver's first offense, but Reid was pushing to get him a harsher sentence than mandated by law. Reid was hoping to rewrite the penalties for drinking and driving causing death."

"What is the textbook sentence in Virginia?" Brandon asked.

"First of all, it's considered DUI manslaughter when a person kills someone while driving under the influence in Virginia. Some states, it's DUI homicide."

Paige lifted her left butt cheek and stretched out her leg; tingles spread down to her toes. "Like Florida."

"Could be."

Is. Earlier this year, the case where they'd met Kelly involved hunting down a serial killer targeting drivers who had drove drunk and killed from behind the wheel, so she knew the law in Florida.

Cindy went on. "With it being the driver's first offense, the prison sentence could be as little as a year with a cap at ten years, unless it can be proved the offender had a very high blood alcohol count. Then it could be as much as twenty years. Keep in mind, these numbers are based on one death. The driver in this case killed *three* people—a mother, a father, and a ten-year-old boy. There's also a maximum fine of twenty-five hundred," Cindy tagged on as an afterthought.

"Despicable," Brandon muttered, and Paige glanced over at him.

As FBI agents, they were to keep their personal feelings out of it—especially in front of civilians. The fact that she and Brandon held differing views on the topic probably didn't help her aggravation.

"Well, that's how Mr. Reid felt, and he was determined to rewrite the law book. Reid wanted to push for a sentence of fifty years to life. He stressed that three lives had been lost, and his reasoning was: why should DUI manslaughter come with a lighter sentence than outright murder when the result was the same?"

Brandon was nodding, while Paige remained motionless. She needed to ignore the urge to open a debate. Driving under the influence could be prevented, yes, but drinking to the point of drunkenness was also a disease. Sure, it was regrettable when a person under the influence got behind the wheel and killed someone—more than regrettable—but she couldn't sweep such accidents in with murder. She could understand why Reid's stand on the matter could have made enemies. "Who was the driver?"

Cindy gave a brief, sly smile. "That's where it gets really interesting. He's the son of some bigwig who owns and runs several publishing companies and networks."

Paige glanced at Brandon. A man like that would have the power—and the means—to make his enemies disappear.

Cindy tucked her phone back into a pocket. "Do you think someone killed him for that?" she asked casually, as if she weren't inquiring about the fate of a man's life.

"It's too early to say, but it's certainly an avenue worth exploring." Paige realized that Cindy never said or even speculated why Reid had been in the building, and it was time to revisit that. "Do you know why Mr. Reid would have been here?"

"Your guess would be as good as mine, but I have interviewed him here—in my apartment—in the past."

"Where he made the moves on you?" Paige asked.

That question elicited a relaxed smile. "Yeah, he made moves."

So Reid wasn't opposed to spending time alone with women—not his wife—in those women's homes no less. Was Cindy Beat an exception or the norm for Reid? Paige would guess more likely the latter. And if he was a philanderer and Mrs. Reid found out…well, that could spell trouble—and more to the point, motive for murder. "When was your last interview?"

"Say six months ago, give or take a few days."

Paige shot to her feet, and both Brandon and Cindy looked at her. She held up a hand. "Just needed to stretch." *And get feeling back in my ass!*

Brandon slowly took his gaze from her and put it on Cindy. "What was the interview about?"

"Oh, Mr. Reid was representing a college student who had been raped by the school's dean. I thought the story was worth covering. It was a *male* student," she said, emphasizing the last part with a slight raise of her brows.

Sadly, sexual assaults and rape were perpetrated far too often by people in a position of power or someone the victim had trusted. "Definitely a story worth telling—whether the student was male or female," Paige said.

"True, but less common for a guy to come forward."

Paige and Brandon excused themselves and thanked her for her time and insights. While they waited for the elevator, Paige said, "Well, wasn't she Miss Informative?"

Brandon looked over at her and smirked. "She really was. Gave us an insight into Reid and at least a couple possible motives for his murder."

"Personal, if he was a cheater and his wife found out, and professional, if his stand got him targeted. The guy had it coming from all directions."

"What now? The next floor or…"

Paige consulted her watch, and it was close to two in the afternoon. "It's time to meet with Jack and Kelly at the Arlington PD."

"So happy to hear you say that."

Paige nudged him in the arm. "Canvassing really that bad for you?"

He lolled his head side to side. "I'd rather have a root canal."

Paige laughed. "Nuff said."

CHAPTER ELEVEN

Kelly couldn't get poor Brad McCarthy out of her mind. He'd just done his job, as far as he was concerned, by covering for his boss—but he was facing a reprimand. Maybe loyalty was overrated. Or at least in certain cases. She and Jack beat Paige and Brandon to the police station. They'd just asked the clerk at the front desk for Captain Herrera when the two of them walked in, and Herrera entered the lobby from a back hall.

Herrera's gaze swept over all of them. "Perfect timing. Everyone, follow me."

He led them through a small maze of corridors and showed them to a conference room. Two officers were putting up some photos on a whiteboard that spanned the length of the room.

"These are Officers Green and Chase. They're here to help with whatever is needed. Their next task will be to pull backgrounds on all Wilson Place employees to see if anything stands out."

Chase was in her late twenties, given the maturity in her eyes and the confidence with which she carried herself. She kept what was probably shoulder-length hair in a bun. Green resembled his name: he looked like a newer recruit. Crew-cut blond hair and blue eyes. He smiled at Kelly at his introduction, and she dipped her head in acknowledgment. *Why is it always the younger ones?*

Kelly took a seat at the table, as did Jack and the rest of the team.

Herrera took position at the head of the table. "I was able to get the sign-in book from Wilson Place, and I took the initiative to start looking at it. I have yet to find a time and date where Mr. Reid had signed in."

"Really?" Paige said, her voice a little tight. "That doesn't make sense, in light of what Brandon and I have learned. The doorman on duty this morning said that Mr. Reid entered the building at eleven last night."

"I don't know what else to say, but he's not in the book."

"Huh," Paige huffed out.

Herrera held up his hands. "Can't give you what I don't have."

"What makes Reid an exception to the building's protocol?" Kelly asked, the possibilities swimming in her mind with the foremost being that Reid held sway over the clerk and used his influence because he didn't want anyone to know he was there—but why? What was he hiding? There was another likelihood, though. "If Reid had an apartment there, he wouldn't need to sign in," she said, answering her own question.

"That occurred to me," Herrera said. "I've already requested the tenant list from the building management company, and I suspect it should be here any minute."

Paige nodded. "You were there when we tried to get some answers from the front desk clerk, Captain." She turned her attention to Kelly and Jack. "The clerk was afraid to speak to us and betray the privacy of the tenants and their visitors."

"He feared for his job," Jack concluded.

"That's right. Now, the doorman we spoke to only started three days ago, but he recommended that we speak to the former doorman."

"He's no longer in the employ of Wilson Place, so he could be more open to talking," Jack surmised.

Paige gestured to Brandon. "That's what we thought. Then again, there might be a confidentiality agreement that surpasses term of employment."

"Only one way to find out," Jack said. "Let's talk to him."

"Can do, Jack. Brandon and I did some canvassing, the entire eleventh floor to be precise, and we spoke with a podcaster who said she interviewed Mr. Reid in her apartment about six months ago." Paige shot a look a Herrera. "Nothing in the book for Reid then, either?"

Herrera sat back, appearing flustered and sighed deeply. "We can certainly dig into the book more, but I'm telling you, I never saw one instance of Reid signing in." The room fell silent, and Herrera tapped his chin. "You said she was a podcaster?"

"Yeah. Name's Cindy Beat. Runs something about…" Brandon seemed to be searching his memory.

"*Keeping a Pulse on Law & Politics*," Paige chirped in.

"It's a huge podcast." Officer Green lowered a photo he'd been about to stick to the whiteboard as everyone looked at him.

"Go on," Herrera prompted.

"I listen to it sometimes. She's sure a loudmouth, but it's what makes her podcast lively. She says what other people wouldn't dare to say. Gotta respect that."

Kelly puffed out her chest and smirked. Herrera frowned, and his reaction probably reflected how most people in positions of authority felt about that statement. They'd rather their underlings not question their directives. Jack, whose opinion mattered to her, looked indifferent to Green's comment.

"Anyone who can make politics lively…Now there's a gift," Brandon muttered.

Paige faced him. "Have you been living under a rock? Something 'lively' hits Twitter every day."

Kelly smiled to herself. If only her grandfather had lived to see Trump in office and how politics had taken the stage of social media; he'd die all over again. She put her focus

Jack was scowling, and Kelly could tell he really didn't want to press Pratchett and stir up that hornet's nest.

"Okay, devil's advocate," Brandon started, "if we're thinking a hired gun, maybe Reid's wife hired them—or a jilted lover."

Herrera blew out an exasperated sigh. "The elusive motive."

"Uh-huh." Jack pulled out his cigarette pack and knocked it against the table.

Herrera's phone buzzed, and he looked at the screen. "Just got word from the ME. Autopsy's in an hour. You and your team joining me, Agent Harper?"

"Ah." Green lifted his head from the laptop, face pale, and held up a finger as if asking to be called on in class. "William Pratchett did serve time in the military."

"We can't ignore that connection," Paige said, and Kelly looked forward to the time when she could speak her mind as freely with Jack.

"Fine. But tread carefully. Don't ruffle the man's feathers."

"Understood."

"Kelly and I are going to speak with the former doorman, e if he has anything to offer where Reid is concerned. tain Herrera, if you would keep us posted on the ME's ings and anything else your team uncovers," Jack said.

f course. I'll have them see if any Wilson Place yees have any sort of military background, too."

yone got up at once and rushed for the door.

back on the case and what Paige had said. "Don't you find it strange this podcaster interviewed Reid in her home?"

"Not really. She works out of her apartment."

"Oh." Kelly was having a hard time releasing the aide's expressed suspicions about Reid's infidelities. "Do you think there was more going on between them?"

Paige shook her head. "Definitely not. She made it very clear to Brandon and me that she doesn't get involved with married men."

Kelly caught Brandon glimpse briefly at Paige before he put his gaze on the whiteboard, and she was curious if there was an underlying narrative there.

"Okay, so Reid wasn't with this podcaster for romantic interests," Kelly began, "but we still need to know why Reid didn't sign in."

"That will be something we need to find out," Jack stated.

"Now, just because Cindy doesn't get involved with married men doesn't mean that Reid wasn't interested." Paige looked around the table. "Apparently, Reid did make moves on her."

Kelly found herself breathing easier. "It's interesting that you say that." She glanced at Jack, whose face was unreadable and all hard lines. "We just came from the attorney's office, and Reid's aide had reason to suspect Reid might have been cheating on his wife."

"Might have been," Jack emphasized.

Kelly wasn't sure why Jack hesitated to consider the aide's statements as relevant to the case. It felt like he would be more than happy to shuffle them aside as inconsequential. But jealousy was the number one motive for murder. There was one textbook problem with the theory of a woman scorned, however. Murders of passion were usually executed in the moment, up close and personal. But "textbook" would become skewed if someone was paid to kill. "Our sniper very well could be a hired gun."

Everyone in the room looked at her. Paige and Brandon paled a little.

"It's possible, Jack." Brandon was the first to agree with Kelly, and she almost fell off her chair. "When we were with the podcaster, she did an internet search and found an article on Reid's murder that suggested he was taken out."

"Wow." Jack shook his head. "We take our cue from the media now."

Brandon grimaced.

"Do you think we should get out in front of this? Do a press conference?" Paige asked and received a glare.

"I'd suggest we say nothing until we have something more concrete to say," Herrera suggested.

Jack looked thoughtfully at the captain. "I'd normally say that something needs to be said—an acknowledgment of what happened at least. Even if it's just to show that we're taking this incident very seriously, but until we know more about what we're dealing with here, we can't risk saying the wrong thing and enticing the sniper to possibly act again."

"Do you think there's a risk of that?" Herrera sought out Kelly's gaze, and she grasped that he was on board with her theory about a hired hit, and she found some more courage.

"When Jack and I were at the attorney's office, we found out about a recent case Reid was working on."

"The one with the drunk driver who killed a family of three?" Brandon asked.

Kelly's heart raced. "Yes, that's the one. Reid was planning to use the case to change laws on sentencing for drinking and driving causing death. Maybe William Pratchett took justice into his own hands."

"Now that's an assumption," Jack reprimanded.

"He'd have the money. I'm sure he'd have the contacts to make something like that happen." The words were out in a torrent, and internally, she winced, though it felt good to stand her ground.

"Hmm," was all she got out of Jack. Whether that was a good thing or a chord of displeasure, she wasn't sure.

"I don't think we should rule Pratchett out." Paige cut Kelly a look of reassurance that she had her back.

Jack leveled a glare on her. "Then you suggest that we go to the owner of a media conglomerate and start interrogating him?"

Kelly shrank—for herself and Paige. She hadn't thought that part through.

"I suggest that we do, yes." Paige stiffened her shoulders. "We can't just turn our backs on him because of who he is and what he does."

Jack and Paige locked eyes. Kelly could understand both sides. Jack was concerned about Pratchett making the FBI look like a clown-run circus, and Paige didn't want to leave the avenue of Pratchett unexplored. No one spoke for about a minute until Herrera broke the silence.

Herrera started with looking at Jack and swept his gaze over the team, one by one. "It seems like you're somewhat divided, but is it safe to say that we can rule out an act of terrorism? No one's come forward, and there was only casualty. But where does that leave us? The hired gun? sniper is one, have they killed before, will they again? any established pattern we can follow?" Herrera r back of his neck.

"Only time will answer those questions, b has mentioned before, our sniper is likely so with the military or law enforcement," Ja active duty or formerly."

"Now, Jack and I got a call on the aide," Kelly said. "None of Reid's ope involved former military, but wha have any association with the m She was feeling more embold

"I can pull a quick backgr laptop that was on the ta clicking away.

"All it takes is one finger on the table. mean he doesn't k man like him would ne

CHAPTER TWELVE

I stuck my nose in my phone while Paige drove us to Pratchett Group headquarters. I whistled at the sight of the company's net worth. "The guy's worth a mint. There's no doubt if this guy wanted to hire a hit, he could afford it. Maybe even get one of his former military buddies to carry it out."

"A man like that would also be able to afford an army of lawyers."

"So you don't think he's behind Reid's murder now? You sounded like you thought he was back at the police station."

"Because I felt for Kelly. Jack's being tough on her. Have you noticed?" She stopped hard for a yellow light and looked over at me. "Is it just me, or is he more brash than usual? He really seems to be putting Kelly through the wringer."

I laughed.

"What am I missing?"

"He was the same way with me when I came on board. You just didn't notice."

Paige put her attention back on the road, but we weren't moving anywhere anytime soon. "No, if he had been, I would have noticed."

"Maybe you've just forgotten."

Nothing was said for a few beats. The light turned, and we started on our way again.

"Okay, maybe Jack applies a lot of pressure to his new agents." Her admission came a few blocks later.

"You think?" I laughed again. "There were days I wanted to curl up into the fetal position."

"Come on, really?"

"Not quite, but close." I held my fingers to within half an inch of each other. "I thought for sure he was going to break me some days. He's certainly the strong and silent type."

"So what? He's not a conversationalist. He only says what he feels is important."

"No wasted words; I get it." I paused and took in the city streets. All the people going about their lives with no thought about murders and killers. I continued. "It must be a shock for Kelly, though. Jack was much nicer to her in Florida when she was just helping us out."

"Ah, maybe that's why I'm noticing that he's different." Paige signaled to turn left into the underground garage of a towering high-rise. "You came on board as an agent from the get-go. I had no previous interactions to base his treatment of you on."

"Could be, but..."

"What?" She eyed me skeptically.

"It's going to sound sexist, but maybe you just notice because Kelly's a woman."

"Oh, please."

I hitched a shoulder. "Just saying."

"Well, unsay it. Besides, it's not like Jack would ever treat any of us differently for that reason."

"I never said that. I said that's why you're noticing how he's treating her and never noticed how he treated me."

"Oh, so I'm the one who's biased?"

I chuckled at her serious tone, probably shouldn't have. Her eyes fired lasers. I tried to salvage myself. "I'm just saying that you're a woman, so is Kelly, so you probably empathize with her more."

"Uh-huh." She turned into the lot.

The attendant directed us to a temporary parking section on P1. Paige pulled into a spot near the elevator and we took it up to the building's lobby. We unloaded into an immaculate space, just as one would expect from a Fortune 500 company with no expense spared. There were a fountain and a pond, and I surmised there'd be koi in there. As we walked past it to the front desk, I looked in, and sure enough...

I whistled again, and Paige chuckled.

"Good day. Welcome to Pratchett Group. How can I assist you?" The receptionist's proportions resembled a troll doll with a head that was comically large atop her narrow shoulders, and her wide pressed-lip grin also didn't help her image.

Paige and I held up our badges.

"We'd like to speak with William Pratchett," Paige told her.

"Sure. Do you have an appointment?"

"We do not."

Troll winced. "That's going to be a problem. Mr. Pratchett's calendar is quite packed." She looked at the monitor. "He's in a meeting now, matter of fact."

"I'm sure he could squeeze us in for a couple of minutes." Paige flashed a smile. "We can wait until he's finished. When do you expect that will be?"

"Give or take another fifteen minutes."

"Great. We'll wait. If you'll just be so kind as to notify him the minute you can that we're here."

"I can do that." Troll flashed a toothy smile. "In the meantime, you can help yourself to a latte or cappuccino if you'd like." She pulled out two red pieces of paper the size of standard business cards and pointed to a café nestled inside the lobby. "These will get you complimentary ones."

"Oh, wow. Thank you." Paige took them.

"You're very welcome."

Paige and I headed to the café. Caffeine was always a good idea—*free* caffeine even better, aside from the fact we shouldn't be accepting anything free in case it was construed as a bribe.

A few minutes later, we were armed with our drinks and headed back to the reception area, where we took a seat.

"Guess we should be happy the guy's even here," I said, getting comfortable on a couch. I took a sip of my black coffee. "He could have been anywhere in the States covering a story or dealing with business."

"That's very true. I thought it was a long shot when Jack told us to head over right away, but I'd much rather be here than attending the autopsy."

I grinned. "And miss out on seeing Mr. Congeniality?"

"Wasn't that ME a piece of—"

"Excuse me." A slender woman in her thirties approached us. "You're here to see Mr. Pratchett, correct?"

"We are," Paige replied.

"Please, then, follow me." She smiled politely, but the expression faded quickly. She took us up the elevator to the twenty-first floor and down a series of hallways. She stopped outside a door, rapped her knuckles on it, and waited for an acknowledgment before opening it.

Inside, four men sat around a table. William Pratchett was easy to pick out, and not just because I saw his driver's license photo, but he had an energy exuding from him that clearly communicated he was the man in charge.

"Mr. Pratchett, these are FBI Agents Dawson and Fisher," the twentysomething woman said, gesturing to the two of us.

"Come in, have a seat," Pratchett said cordially. "Thank you, Connie."

With that, the woman left, closing the door behind her.

Pratchett kept his eyes on Paige and me as we took a seat. My gaze briefly went over the three other suits, all aged somewhere between fifty and ninety, given the deep lines in the eldest's face and his stock of white hair.

"These are my lawyers." Pratchett tugged down on his suit jacket and tilted out his chin. "I'm sure their presence isn't going to be a problem."

My guess was the man lived for confrontation and wanted us to challenge him.

"No, not at all," Paige said.

"Good. Now, what brings you here?"

"There's been an unfortunate turn of events," Paige began. "Prosecuting attorney Darrell Reid was shot and killed this morning."

Pratchett's body tensed—just slightly—enough to tell me he already knew about Reid's death. "Tragic, to be sure, but I'm not sure what this has to do with me."

"We understand that he was going to be trying a case against your son, Mr. Pratchett." Paige set that out there far more delicately than I could have managed. Guys like Pratchett were bullies, and I had no tolerance for bullies.

"He was, but I'm not sure where you're going with this."

Paige continued. "I guess to start, we wanted to know if you knew Reid's plans for his case against your son?"

"That he was going to blow the entire event out of proportion?"

Out of proportion? *Three people are dead! His son should pay for that!* I clamped my mouth shut for fear I'd say something I might regret.

The youngest lawyer held out a hand to stay Pratchett, and the man snuffed out derision at the gesture.

"Ah, I see…" Pratchett leaned back in his chair, a sadistic-looking grin on his face, and rubbed his chin. "You think I had something to do with Reid's death."

"We never said that," Paige was quick to say.

"Good, because you'd be greatly mistaken. Besides, I'd have no reason to kill him." Pratchett gestured to the lawyers. "These three men are but a small sampling of the legal team I have at my fingertips, agents. Reid wouldn't have gotten anywhere with his grandiose plans to make a mockery of my son. He made one teeny mistake, and the boy's to sit behind bars for life? Not as long as I'm drawing breath."

I balled my hands into fists under the table. This guy was reprehensible! Easy for him to sit in his ivory tower and downplay the severity of three lives lost when they weren't people close to him. Though I suspected Pratchett didn't hold many—if any—intimate relationships or let himself care too greatly about other people. He was probably even more concerned about his image than his son's fate.

"Things don't always go as planned," I said at a low volume. "There was the possibility that Mr. Reid would have met with success."

"What are you implying?" Pratchett hissed.

"We're simply here to get a read on things," Paige mediated.

Pratchett's face shot a bright red. "To see if I—"

The middle-aged lawyer seated next to Pratchett put a hand on his forearm. He took me in for less than a millisecond but leveled his gaze on Paige. "Unless you have evidence of Mr. Pratchett's involvement in the death of Mr. Reid, this meeting is over."

"You mean in Mr. Reid's *murder*?" I slung back, not able to restrain myself any longer.

The lawyer clenched his jaw but said nothing.

"We're sorry that we've upset you, Mr. Pratchett," Paige said, shooting me a molten-lava glare. "That was not our intention. I hope you can appreciate that, as a matter of procedure, we had to speak with you, though."

"A matter of procedure," Pratchett mumbled. "As I said, I'd have no reason to kill him. I have enough money to fight for my son for a lifetime. Besides, my defense team had every confidence that they could get the charges against him tossed out. He was never going to see a day behind bars—Reid or no Reid."

The last claim stung like alcohol poured on an open, fresh wound. Anger swept around the back of my neck and heated up my core. The audacity that he would think his son could kill three people and get away with it was preposterous. I had to get out of this room, away from this piece of shit. I stood and headed for the door.

"That's right. We're done here," one of the lawyers said to my back.

"Thank you for your time, Mr. Pratchett," Paige said and joined me in the hall. "You better hope none of what happened in there gets back to Jack."

"You heard that douche—"

"Ahem." The low volume of someone clearing their throat. It was Connie, the woman who took us to see Pratchett. She rose from a bench and didn't say a word as she took us back to the lobby.

"Unbelievable," Paige exclaimed as she slammed her door shut on the SUV.

"Yeah, that piece of work is!"

"I meant you," she fired back.

"Me?" I snapped. "You've got to be kidding me. He thinks the murder of three people shouldn't come with a sentence. He thinks his little boy should just walk." I mimicked the action with my fingers.

Paige shook her head. "Jack told us to tread carefully. Do you really think—"

"I'm not sure I care."

She smacked the steering wheel.

"I wish that Reid had the chance to stick it to Pratchett Junior," I seethed.

"I'm sure you do."

"You don't?"

"Argh. We've been through this before. My feelings about drinking and driving aren't as strong as yours. But it doesn't mean I think he should walk."

I flailed my arms in the air as if to say *there you go.*

Quiet passed between us, and warm air started blowing from the vents.

"I tried to swallow my temper. I really did."

Paige glanced over at me. "I saw you clench your fists in there."

"Yeah, and aren't you happy one didn't come up and punch Pratchett in the nose."

"Ah, very." Paige's mouth twitched like she was refusing to laugh but losing—and she did. "Can you imagine…the guy's face if…"

I grinned. "Priceless."

"Oh, but can you imagine Jack's?"

Her question had us both sobering.

"Yeah, that wouldn't be a good face," I admitted.

"No. Do you think Pratchett's behind the shooting?"

I shook my head. "I think he's actually egotistical enough to think his son would have walked. Like he said, 'I have enough money to fight for my son for a lifetime.'" I pushed out my chest and held my arms like an ape, best as I could in the confines of the SUV.

"God, you look just like him."

"I really did want to knock the smug look off the cocky son of a bitch's face."

"I know you did."

"Props for self-control?"

"Well, he was infuriating."

"There. You finally admit it."

"Here's something that just occurred to me." Paige's face fell serious. "Father might be cocky, but what's Junior like? Maybe he didn't have as much faith in his father's ability to make the charges go away, and he took action on his own."

"Could be. I mean, it's possible. He likely has access to his own spending money."

"I think we should speak with Adrian Pratchett."

I already had my phone out, looking for his home address.

CHAPTER THIRTEEN

Kelly shadowed Jack up the steps to Gerald Stevens's townhouse. She was thinking how she'd really gone from being the big fish in the small pond of the Miami PD to the small fish in the big pond of the FBI. There were moments she felt in over her head, but she recalled how her grandfather had told her about Jack's obsession with perfection. Until now, she thought he'd exaggerated on that point.

Jack knocked on the door, and footsteps padded toward them from inside.

The door swung open, and an imposing sixty-something man of six-four stood there.

"Can I help you?" He eyed them with curiosity.

Jack held up his badge and identified himself and Kelly. "Are you Gerald Stevens?"

"I am." Gerald crossed his arms in front of his expansive chest.

"We'd like to talk to you about your time as a doorman at Wilson Place. Could we come in?"

Gerald stepped back and gestured for them to enter, but he didn't invite them to a sitting room. He closed the door and tilted his head in inquiry.

"You might have heard there was a shooting at Wilson Place this morning," Jack began.

"A shooting? At Wilson Place? Really?" Gerald's hands moved about, not sure whether to settle on his hips or in his pockets. "No, I hadn't heard, but then again, I don't watch or listen to the news. Don't read a paper, either." He tucked his hands in his pockets. "Anyone hurt?"

Or go online, because the news is all over the internet, Kelly thought.

"There was one fatality." Jack pulled up Reid's license photo on his phone and angled the screen toward Stevens. "Do you know him?"

"Yeah, um…yeah." Gerald rubbed the back of his neck.

"Name?"

"Darrell Reid. He's a prosecutor for the commonwealth attorney's office."

"That's right." Jack backed out of the picture and tucked his phone away. "How do you know him?"

Gerald chewed his bottom lip as if hesitating to answer that question. Was it because he still held on to a sense of loyalty to his former employer, have a confidentiality contract still in place, or was there some sort of connection between him and Reid's shooter? A look at his background didn't show a military record—but there was always that blasted one degree of separation Herrera had brought up.

"I didn't really *know* him."

"All right," Jack said leisurely. "How did you recognize him just now?" His eyes studied the man.

"He came to Wilson Place from time to time."

"Often?" Kelly asked.

Gerald licked his lips and looked at her. "I don't know if I should be talking with you two about him."

"We're FBI, Mr. Stevens. It's usually a good thing to talk to us." Jack's face was expressionless, but there was no missing his tone that made it obvious cooperation was the right route.

"Very well." Gerald tucked his hands back into his pants pockets. "Mr. Reid came to the building often."

"How often?" Kelly rushed out and was sorry she had when Jack glanced over at her. She understood the reprimand in his gaze to rein in her excitement at this possible lead. But this was the closest they'd gotten to finding out Reid's purpose there.

"Usually a few times a week."

Kelly bit back the urge to immediately counter with *what days* and *what times?* She let a few seconds of silence wade between them. "With any sort of regularity? Specific days? Times?"

"Now, I'll have to think on that." Gerald tugged at the stubble on his chin. "I know he came in on Wednesdays and Fridays…" More whisker tugging, then, "And Monday nights, come to think of it."

"Do you know who he was visiting or why he wouldn't have signed in at the front desk?" she asked.

Gerald shook his head. "Not my place. You speak to the front desk clerk?"

"Yes, we have." Kelly spoke slowly, locking eyes with the former doorman and getting the feeling he knew the reason Reid didn't sign in. Maybe he didn't want to soil the reputation of a dead man, but the thing with death was it was better than truth serum: with it, everything had a way of coming out. "Did he usually show up at night?" She didn't think she should ask Gerald outright if he thought the attorney was having an affair with someone in the building. If Reid had been, it was definitely something he wouldn't want found out.

Gerald planted a hand on his hip. "Nah, not always. He'd come on Fridays in the afternoon."

"But at night on Mondays and Wednesdays?" Kelly asked.

"That's right."

"Did he ever stay overnight on Mondays and Wednesdays?" Kelly toed carefully.

Gerald put up his hands in surrender. "I'm not answering that one."

"Okay," Kelly said. "When he did show up, was it like clockwork, same times, reliable?"

"I don't know if I'd set my watch by it." He paused and smiled, light twinkling in his eyes. "But, yes, I'd say it was with some regularity."

It would make sense how the sniper knew when and where to strike. Had Gerald fed that information to the sniper? If he had, he could win an Academy Award for acting. "Do you know what brought Mr. Reid to the building? Maybe he was visiting someone?" She did her best to keep suspicion of a mistress out of her voice.

Gerald shook his head. "I know I don't work there anymore, but I pride myself on my discretion, and I always have."

"So, you know but are choosing not to talk to the FBI?" Jack raised his brows.

"I never said that."

Kelly softened her stance, pushed her hip a little to the left. "Was he alone when he'd show up?"

Gerald pointed a finger at her. "I see that you're still trying to get me to tell you something that could hurt a dead man's character, but I'm not going to fall for it. Actually, I've said all I'm going to. If you'd kindly leave." He maneuvered around Jack and Kelly for the door.

"Just a couple more things." Kelly's adrenaline was pumping. The former doorman's reaction told her Reid had a mistress at Wilson Place; she just wished he'd put it into words.

Gerald turned the handle and swung the door open.

"Please," she rushed out. "We understand that your last day working at Wilson Place was this past Sunday."

"Is there a question in there?"

"Here's the question. Did Mr. Reid keep the schedule you mentioned of Monday, Wednesday, and Friday up until last Friday?"

"He did." Gerald looked out the door to his front steps, a not-too-subtle hint for them to leave.

"And for how long before that? As in, how long had he been showing up on Mondays, Wednesdays, and Fridays?"

"That I can't tell you for certain."

"Weeks, months, years?"

"Oh, you said a couple of things." Gerald tapped his wrist. "Off you go."

"Please, Mr. Stevens," she pleaded.

"Fine, I'd say the better part of a few years." He swept a hand in front of him, motioning for them to get going.

Jack pulled out a business card and extended it to Gerald. "Call if you feel like talking some more."

Gerald tucked Jack's card into a back pocket of his pants. "I wouldn't be waiting by the phone, Agent. Good day."

Kelly and Jack stepped outside, and behind them, the door was shut with force.

They got into the SUV, and Kelly did up her seat belt.

"Sorry if I came across too strong in there," she said.

Jack turned the vehicle on and looked over at her. "You need to get a better handle on your emotions. They don't have any place in an investigation."

His words came as a blow. She'd half-expected her apology to be met with a rebuff, some off-cuff remark about it being unnecessary.

"I'm not saying that we don't feel emotions," Jack added. "We can't help that. They will come up, but we need to rise above them."

"So approach life like a Vulcan?" The words rushed out, and she balled her hands into fists so tightly her nails dug into her palms, a habit of hers. The pain would cause her to slow down and consider her next steps. As her grandfather always stressed to her, "pick your battles wisely."

"Like a what?"

"You know *Star Trek*?"

Jack's face pinched.

"Never mind. And yes, I understand." *That you want me to be Vulcan, suppressing my emotions in favor of logic.* As far as she was concerned, there was a place for both emotions and logic in proper balance, but she'd suck it up. "At least now we know that Reid went to Wilson Place on a regular basis."

"And he kept that schedule up until last week."

"Predictable. That would have made it easier for the shooter. They'd know when to strike."

"How they knew is still a question we need to answer. Did they track Reid, or were they fed the information?"

"If it is a hired gun, it's quite likely the latter. Maybe a little reconnaissance of their own, but we still don't know why the sniper chose Wilson Place. Was it to call attention to Reid being there and to expose his purpose?" Jack didn't say anything, and she considered holding back her suspicions—for a second. "The way Stevens clammed up, I bet he knows Reid was there to see a woman. Just speaking out loud, but what if Wilson Place was chosen for the hit because the motive was driven by revenge for adultery?"

Jack tore the cellophane from a new package of cigarettes and tapped one out.

Kelly would try another tack. "We both felt that Arlene knows far more than she's telling us about her husband and Wilson Place."

Jack waved his unlit cigarette. "Go on."

The gaping hole in Reid's chest—had he been shot in the heart? A literal translation of how Arlene had been wounded by Reid's affairs? Running with the assumption he was sleeping around and Arlene was aware.

"Talk, Marsh," Jack prompted.

She flinched, much the same way a pooch shook under harsh rebukes from their owner. She hated that she felt that way with Jack, but she was uncomfortable with his condemning attitude and all the corrections—especially in front of other people. But she was powerless to do anything about his treatment of her. She didn't need to go mouthing off or losing her cool and her job along with it. But she couldn't keep biting her tongue, afraid to talk, either. And he was asking for her opinion...

She met his gaze, hoping she wasn't stepping into a trap. "You've made a point of telling me that we can't rush to any assumptions, so for now, I want to keep some of my theories to myself. Respectfully." She held her breath.

"I can respect that." Jack put down his window and lit up a cigarette.

"Actually," she blurted out, "can I speak freely?"

Jack waved his hand that held his cigarette in a casual manner that said, *Go ahead.*

"If Stevens saw Reid go in that building, you can bet there are other doormen from different shifts who might have—and who might be more talkative. Maybe Reid was there on other days of the week, different times."

"They'll clam up, hide behind fear of job security and confidentiality clauses."

Shot down in less than a second...

"Possibly, but we don't know unless we try. And maybe there are other retired doormen from the building out there we can speak with."

Jack didn't say anything, just took a few puffs of his cigarette.

"Or retired front-desk clerks?" she grasped.

"I'd be more interested in them if they had a record of military service or law enforcement with training in sniping."

"Herrera's officers are looking into that. Want me to follow up on—"

Jack's phone rang over the SUV's speakers.

Kelly read the caller ID on the front display: N WEBBER.

Jack answered.

Nadia started talking right away. "Jack, I have a theory, and I'm still doing some digging, but I need to tell you what I know so far." The sentence came out on one breath. She continued, talking a tad slower. "I believe our sniper has struck before. More precisely, three different times. And in all three cases, there was a sole victim, a man."

"All shot in the chest?" Kelly asked, but purposefully didn't look at Jack.

"Direct hit to the heart," Nadia punched out. "What about with Reid? Do we know yet?"

"The autopsy's underway as we speak," Jack said. "We'll know soon enough."

"Nadia, were all the men married?" Kelly queried.

"They were."

Tingles ran down Kelly's back, and her heart picked up speed. She tried to get control of her pesky emotions before speaking again. "Were those men cheating on their wives?"

"I don't know, but I can find out." Nadia's voice held uncertainty as to why that mattered.

Kelly filled Nadia in on what they'd been finding out about Reid's character.

"Nothing's proven on that front yet," Jack inserted.

"Well, if it is, maybe we're looking at someone targeting cheating spouses?"

Kelly felt reassured hearing her unspoken suspicion coming from Nadia's lips.

"Too soon to know," Jack stated firmly. "Where were the shootings?"

"Albuquerque, New Mexico; Little Rock, Arkansas; and Knoxville, Tennessee."

"Hmm."

Kelly glanced at Jack, not sure what to make of his *hmm*. "What did these men do for a living? What were their ages?" she asked.

"Varied backgrounds. Guy in New Mexico was—"

"Nadia, gather all this information together and send it over to me. I'll call you back in about an hour or less, once the team's back together at the Arlington police station."

"You got it." With that, Nadia hung up, and Jack made another call.

"Paige, I need you and Brandon to head back to the station— No, put off seeing Pratchett Junior for now." Jack ended the call, flicked his cigarette out the window, and took off in the direction of the station.

"You don't think we're looking at a hit man?" Kelly ventured, based on the sharp look in Jack's eyes. Nadia's news pushed her thoughts about Wilson Place employees to the side for now.

"Not sure whether our sniper gets paid, but I think Nadia's just found us proof that we're after a serial killer."

And the real hunt begins…

CHAPTER FOURTEEN

Paige had just gotten herself fired up to talk to Pratchett Junior when Jack called them back to the police station.

"He didn't say what he wanted?" Brandon asked.

"Nope."

"Do you think Pratchett complained about us?"

That's exactly what she was thinking, but then that didn't align with Jack's tone of voice on the phone. He wouldn't wait to confront them in person—or would he? "If Jack asks how things went with William Pratchett, leave it to me."

"No argument here."

"Huh-uh." Just like Brandon to happily take the easy road.

They entered the room where things were set up and found Kelly and Jack already there.

"Hey, Jack." *Approach things calm, relaxed, casual.* "What's going on?"

"Nadia has a theory."

Paige's lungs expanded a little further. This wasn't about Pratchett. She glanced at Brandon, wondering if it was Nadia's hunch realized. "Great. What is it?" she asked with true enthusiasm.

"She's found three other shooting incidents, three other victims—all male."

Previous murders connected with their open case? No wonder Jack wanted her and Brandon back at the station immediately.

"All married," Kelly added.

"We still don't know if it's the same sniper, but if it is, he or she is mobile." Jack went on to tell her and Brandon the shootings had taken place in different states.

Mobile was one thing, but New Mexico, Arkansas, Tennessee, now Virginia? That was a long journey, and she wasn't sure how it meshed with their earlier thoughts. "How does that fit with a hired gun?"

"Doesn't mean the sniper comes cheap," Kelly put simply.

"When were the shootings?" Brandon asked.

"We'll get all our questions answered soon enough. Just waiting on Officer Chase to return with the printouts of the briefing packet Nadia sent—"

There was a rap on the doorframe, and Officer Chase entered, holding a stack of paper in her hands. "I have what you asked for, Agent Harper."

Jack took the pile from her. "Thanks." With one word, Jack managed to be polite and also dismissive. Officer Chase left the room.

Jack distributed the binder-clipped reports. Paige took the one Jack gave her, examined the thickness, which was at least a quarter-inch. "Wow. Nadia's outdone herself."

"We'll see about that, but what she started telling Kelly and I was promising. Now that everyone's here and we have the report…" Jack's voice disappeared, and he called Nadia on speaker. When she answered, he said, "The team's here, Nadia, go ahead."

"You received my information packet?"

"We've all got it in front of us in print."

Nadia was quiet for half a beat. "I'm assuming none of you have had a chance to read it as of yet."

"You assume correctly," Jack said. "Give us the highlights to start."

"Paige and Brandon, I'm not sure how much Jack and Kelly have shared with you, but there were three previous shootings where there was only one causality, and in each case, that was a man. The shootings took place in—" and she went off to list the states again.

"When," Brandon cut in, "did they happen?"

"New Mexico six months ago, Arkansas three months ago, and Tennessee one month ago."

"Huh. Three months between the first two, and only one month between Tennessee and here," Paige voiced. "Why? Did our killer have a schedule to keep? Or were they rushed for some reason? A last-minute job?"

"All good questions, Paige, but I have much more information for you."

By the look of the report, Nadia wasn't lying.

Nadia went on. "All three victims were in their mid-fifties and married. This matches up with Darrell Reid's profile. Now, the three men were shot in the heart. Direct hit. Do you know—"

"Not yet," Jack interrupted. "Hopefully soon."

Whatever they were discussing wasn't going to be resolved soon enough for Jack, but the subject wasn't entirely clear. "Do you mean where Reid was shot?" Paige asked.

"Yeah," Nadia said. "Now, there are differences between the previous cases and our current one. None of the victims were in the same line of work. One was a plumber, one a public-school teacher, and one was an unemployed electrician. If Reid was a victim of this same killer, you know he was a prosecutor."

Paige studied her colleagues. "It just means the victims weren't targeted based on their profession. Are we sure that the murders are linked?" She hated calling Nadia out, but it was a necessary question.

"No doubt. All three men were shot with a 7.62×51mm NATO bullet, believed to be fired from an M40."

"That's standard Marine issue," Jack said.

"That's right," Nadia replied.

Brandon shifted in his seat. "There's a confirmed military connection."

"Nadia, do the victims share a military background?" Jack asked.

"Not that I could find. None have a record of service, in fact. They were all born in different states, too, and lived in different cities, so no way to connect their pasts that way, either."

Jack nodded, not that Nadia would have seen. "Herrera's officers haven't found any military or law enforcement connections in Wilson Place employees, either."

"Were the bullets fired from the same weapon?" Paige asked. When a bullet was fired from a gun, it left behind grooves and impressions that could then be compared to databases and net a manufacturer—sometimes even gun type. But there were characteristics intrinsic with the gun itself.

"Unfortunately, of the three bullets fired, only one remained intact enough inside the body to get some grooves and striations. That didn't leave much for ballistics testing to definitively conclude the bullets were fired from the same weapon. I'm guessing you don't know what bullet was used on Reid yet?"

"We don't," Jack told her.

Paige was trying to understand how Nadia connected the shootings without the identical weapon coming up in the system, so she asked.

"I started first looking at sniping incidents where there was only one victim, who was male, and branched out from there," Nadia replied.

"We might not know for sure if the bullets were fired from the same gun, but it would seem the same person's pulling the trigger," Kelly concluded, but withered under Jack's eye.

What's up with the hostility toward the new girl? Paige could understand the importance of not jumping to conclusions—or becoming laser-focused—but Kelly was just basing her comment on what was before them. In that, Paige saw no harm. It's nothing she and Brandon wouldn't do. Heck, if Kelly hadn't said it, Paige might have.

"Kelly," Nadia interjected, "you'd asked if the men were cheating on their wives when I called before. I can tell you all their marriages were in shambles. One couple was in counseling, another argued a lot, according to their neighbors, and the other one… This is horrible to say, and I'm just quoting, but one of the widows said, 'Thank God for small miracles; burying him will be cheaper than getting a divorce.'"

"Brr. That's cold." Brandon mocked shivers.

Jack leaned back in his chair and tapped an unlit cigarette against the table. "Did investigators have any suspects?"

"No one solid," Nadia replied. "But the men's wives were looked at closely. A hit man was considered, but investigators hit a wall when none the widows' finances supported one."

Jack's mouth set into a straight line. "I can't believe no one linked these shootings before now."

"As I said, Jack, I was looking at very tight parameters. Sniper shot with one male causality."

"Yeah, and I can't imagine shootings involving a sniper are too common," Paige reasoned.

"More common than you'd like to think, sadly," Nadia responded.

"Where's Zach to give us the statistics on that one?" Brandon bumped Paige's elbow, and she shook her head, trying to stay focused on the seriousness of the topic. But if Zach were here, he'd know the stats. He was a genius and a walking encyclopedia.

"I should add," Nadia said, "that in the shooting from a month ago—the one in Tennessee—the widow received compromising photos of her husband in the mail. Him with another woman having—"

"We get the picture," Jack interrupted.

"Anyway, local law enforcement really looked at the wife."

"That the one who celebrated her husband's death?" Brandon asked.

"That would be her."

"No wonder," Paige said, completely understanding where LEOs would have been coming from.

"Were any photos sent to the previous two widows?" Brandon asked. "The ones in Albuquerque and Arkansas?"

"Not that's on record," Nadia replied. "What about with your vic?"

"None yet, that we know of." Jack slid a glance at Kelly, and Paige took it to mean they weren't confident Mrs. Reid had been forthcoming.

"This is in your packets, but all the murders took place along the I-40/I-81/I-66 corridor."

While Kelly might like the hired-gun theory, Paige wasn't so sure. There was the geographic distance between murders to consider, and there wasn't any proof of a contract killer being hired. Paige felt their sniper was acting on a personal agenda. Now, what that was, she didn't know yet. "What else can you tell us about the places where the victims were shot? Did they have any meaning to the men?"

"Here's the thing…" Nadia seemed to leave those three words out there as a dangling teaser. "Two of the three men were sniped outside their regular haunts. They were as predictable as the rising sun."

"And the third?"

"Sherman, in Tennessee, had never been to the restaurant he was shot at before."

"If we're looking at a hired gun, they could have been provided information on where and when to find their targets," Brandon said.

Kelly pounced on that. "And that seems feasible. Three months between the first and second victim, two between the second, and now only one between number three and Reid."

"Still doesn't explain Sherman being pecked off somewhere he didn't frequent." Paige took a deep breath. "I don't think we're looking at a hired gun."

Kelly's shoulders sagged.

"I do think all four victims had something in common," Paige said. "We need to figure out what."

"Better yet, *whom*," Jack said. "Thanks, Nadia. We'll take it from here." With that, he ended the call. "Paige, I want you and Brandon to stay here and go through the packet with an eye for detail. If the three previous shootings relate to our case, I want to know without a doubt. How did you make out with William Pratchett?"

Paige resisted the urge to glance over at Brandon. Jack didn't need to know what Jack didn't need to know. She said, "As I've made clear, I don't think we're looking at a hired gun, but does Pratchett have the means to hire someone for his dirty business? Sure, but I don't think he did. And now that we're talking about three previous victims spread out across the country, I think it's safe to rule out the Pratchett family."

"I agree about the Pratchetts, but I'm not ruling out a contract killer just yet." Jack gripped the edge of the table as he stood. "Kelly and I are going to talk to Mrs. Reid again, see if we can shake any more out of her, like possible knowledge of her husband's affairs or his connection with Wilson Place. If we're lucky, she might give us a lead."

Paige wasn't going to continue to argue about a hit man. She'd let things sit and see what she and Brandon discovered in Nadia's information packet.

CHAPTER FIFTEEN

There were three cars in the Reids' driveway, and Kelly's heart sank. Family and friends would be inside—all there to support each other through this rough time. It would be ideal if she and Jack could turn away, but it was crucial they speak to Arlene. Kelly couldn't let herself be influenced by emotion, as Jack had more recently reminded her.

Jack had his hand out to press the doorbell when the door was opened by a silver-haired man. Kelly would peg him in his seventies, but he was in terrific physical shape and had piercing gray eyes.

"Can I help you?"

Jack lifted his badge, and so did Kelly. "We need to speak with Arlene."

The skin at the corners of the man's eyes pinched, and he let his gaze take in first Jack, then Kelly. "She's not doing so good." The man stepped back, letting them inside the home. "Please don't upset her any further."

"We shouldn't be too long," Kelly said softly.

The man dipped his head.

"Are you a relation to Arlene or Darrell?" Kelly asked.

"I'm Arlene's father. My name's Bert Pryce."

Solemn voices filtered down the hall toward the entry.

Bert looked over a shoulder in the direction of the conversation, then back to her and Jack. "Beverly's by Arlene's side—that's my wife and Arlene's mother."

"From the looks of outside, there are a few friends and

family here," Kelly said.

Bert nodded slowly. "Arlene's brother and his wife. And my wife and me."

"Grandpa?" A teenage boy, who could have been a young Darrell Reid, stepped up next to Bert, and his gaze danced over Kelly and Jack. "Who are they?"

"Riley, these are FBI agents investigating your father's death." Bert sought out Kelly's gaze for reassurance. They hadn't gotten out yet that they were investigating the case in so many words, but Kelly nodded her head in confirmation.

"His *murder*, gramps. You can say it." Anger flashed through the young man's eyes as he locked them with Kelly's. "You find out who did this to my dad?" Riley's shoulders were rigid, his body wired tight like a wild cat about to spring on its prey, but there was so much unspoken vulnerability to him. Grief had chipped into his soul and was washing away his innocence.

"We're sorry for your loss, Riley," Kelly offered and gazed over at Bert to carry the condolence to him as well.

Riley's shoulders relaxed, just a bit, but he recovered his tough-guy act by thrusting out his jaw. "Mom needs to know who did this."

"We're still working to find out that answer," Jack said.

Bert put an arm around his grandson. "Why don't you go see if your mother needs anything?"

Riley gave one more withering look at Kelly before leaving in the direction from which he had come.

Bert glimpsed after his grandson, and when he disappeared up a back staircase, Bert turned around to them. "He'll be fine. He'll recover, bounce back. It's just been quite a shock."

"Understandably." At face value, Bert's words could sound callous, but Kelly could also see the sad truth in them. Life would go on. A new normal would be found.

"If you could take us to Arlene…" Jack gestured down the hall.

"Yes, of course. This way." Bert led them to a different sitting room than where they'd been earlier that day. When they stepped inside, all conversation stopped, and four sets of eyes were on her and Jack.

Arlene was sitting in a loveseat with an older woman beside her. A man and woman Kelly pegged in their forties sat on a couch, nestled close to each other. This was probably Arlene's brother and his wife.

"Arlene," Bert started, "the FBI wants to speak with you."

Arlene's eyes sagged like a hound's and were puffy. She had been twisting a frilly handkerchief in her hands to within inches of its life, but she stopped and sat up straighter. "Agents, did you find his killer?"

"Not yet, but we have some questions for you." Jack put his gaze on everyone else in the room in turn. "Alone, if that's possible."

The Pryces looked at each other, not quite seeming to understand why they had to leave, but the brother and sister-in-law were the first to comply.

The mother took Arlene's hand. "I would prefer to stay."

"Mom, I'll be fine."

"You sure?"

"I'm sure." Arlene squeezed her mother's hand and let it go, and the mother got up.

Bert held out his hand for his wife to take, and the couple left the room.

"We appreciate you talking with us alone." Jack took one of the recently vacated spots on the couch. "We have some questions we need to ask you about your husband, and they might make you uncomfortable, especially with your family around."

"Whatever it is, I'm sure it would have been fine, but I appreciate you considering my feelings." She started working over the handkerchief in her hands again.

Kelly sat next to Jack, and he gestured for her to talk. She wanted to jump right to asking if she was aware her husband may have been cheating on her, but that would have been too direct a place to start. "Mrs. Reid, did your husband have any friends or enemies who might have had a connection with the military?"

"Um, not that I know of. Maybe?" Arlene was peering into her eyes, trying to read them. "My husband knew a lot of people. There's no way I'd know of all of them. Do you think that someone in the military killed him?"

"All that seems likely is whoever killed your husband had experience with firing a rifle at long range," Jack told her.

"I don't know why anyone in the military would want to kill him. Maybe if it's related to a case?" Her eyes sparkled briefly with hope at her epiphany but dulled just as quickly. "I don't know why anyone would have wanted to kill him." Her voice cracked, laden with grief. "I wish I could help you."

Kelly sat back and relaxed, hoping her body language would make Arlene more comfortable, like she was in the company of friends, not FBI agents. "Mrs. Reid, this is a delicate question, but do you know if your husband was having an affair?"

"Dad would never do that," Riley snarled, storming into the room with the force of a gale wind. He was holding a glass of water.

"Riley, please," Arlene petitioned her son. "Go be with your grandparents."

"No, Mom, no way." Riley dropped next to his mother and handed her the glass, and she let the handkerchief drop into her lap.

Kelly leaned forward. "We're not saying that your father—"

"Yes, you are. You think he cheated on Mom," Riley interrupted.

Kelly couldn't deny that one and remained quiet.

Arlene sniffled and blinked away tears. There was an electricity of anticipation in the air like secrets were about to come out.

"We just need to ask these kinds of questions," Kelly explained. "It's part of the process." She gave Riley a reassuring smile, but the teen was unmoved.

He shook his head and looked at his mother, who now had tears streaming down her face. "It's a stupid process, then. You're upsetting my mother."

"Unfortunately, murder investigations usually cause discomfort. But trust me when I say that we wouldn't ask the questions we do unless it was absolutely necessary," Kelly said.

"Trust you?" Riley scoffed.

Arlene put a hand on her son's shoulder. "They're just doing their jobs."

"Well, I don't like it." He stormed from the room.

"I'm sorry. He's…"

"There's no need to apologize." Kelly thought Riley was doing quite well, considering his world had just been shattered. A grown woman of thirty-three, she didn't think she'd handle news of her estranged mother's death as well— or her brother's, for that matter.

"He wasn't close with his father," Arlene volunteered, then took a sip of the water, setting the glass down on a side table. "Darrell was always so busy with his work, and it came first. I just hope Riley realizes that Darrell loved him as much as his own heart." She picked up the handkerchief and started kneading it in her hands. "The timing of Darrell's death is probably what's making this all the worst for Riley." Her chin quivered, and more tears fell. These she dabbed with the handkerchief. "He and Darrell had an argument yesterday afternoon. Their last words to each other were angry ones." Arlene licked her lips, and the admission seemed to suck the air from her. Her body sagged.

Sadly, there often wasn't any closure, no pretty bow tying everything up nice and neat.

"You said 'yesterday afternoon.' Was Darrell not around last night?" Kelly figured Arlene had opened things for her to work her way back to the topic of affairs.

"No, he worked late. Sometimes he slept in his office."

Kelly peered into Arlene's eyes, trying to figure out if she was afraid to voice her suspicions about a cheating husband for fear of making them real or if she intentionally was withholding the fact that she knew about it. "Mrs. Reid, do you think your husband was having an affair?" There were times the direct approach was called for, but Kelly put it out there as tactfully as she could.

"Darrell and I had our problems. We often didn't see eye to eye, but that was what I loved about the man. He challenged me to think differently. There's no growth when everyone around you is just like you. Sometimes the people who rub us the wrong way make us flourish the most."

Arlene's phrasing *rub us the wrong way* could imply their problems were quite significant.

"Did your husband feel the same way?" Jack asked.

"I'd like to think so."

Jack crossed his feet at the ankles. "You don't think he ever sought out companionship with someone more like-minded with himself?"

Kelly admired the way Jack used Arlene's own reasoning as a springboard to press such a delicate topic as infidelity.

"If he did, I didn't know about it." Arlene glanced from Jack to Kelly. "We still made love regularly. He always had time for me."

But not for his son? Kelly was skeptical about Arlene's claims, but she couldn't exactly come out and call the woman a liar.

"If anyone's told you that Darrell cheated on me, they are either lying or wanting something," Arlene said adamantly. "Our family does have money, and that can bring out the haters, people who are jealous we have it all. Or at least did." She had gone from hapless widow to a woman of independent means and influence. Someone who was proud and had an image to protect. Someone, who if cheated on, would be humiliated and might even take things into her own hands—or hire someone else to get dirty. And Arlene would have enough money to afford a high-end killer.

"Thank you for your time, Mrs. Reid." Jack nudged Kelly's arm, and they saw themselves out.

"Shouldn't we be talking to the rest of the family? Even to get their take on the Reids' marriage?" she asked.

"No one in that household is going to talk to us." Jack lit up a cigarette outside the driver's-side door of the SUV. "I'm going to have Nadia subpoena her financial records."

"In case she hired someone?" Hope lit in her soul—he hadn't abandoned the hired-gun theory as she was certain Paige had.

Jack took a drag on his smoke. "Exactly."

CHAPTER SIXTEEN

The sniper cut in front of a minivan full of kids, and the suburban mom behind the wheel honked and gave her the finger. That was the problem with the world today. *Some example, Mom.* But everyone was out for themselves, and that meant no one was reliable. Those who tried to convince others that human beings were mostly good were lullabying themselves into a coma, shutting out reality. Even well-meaning "friends" offered advice or sentiments tainted with their own personal ambitions. Like when her mother had died, and the nurses told her that Mother was in a better place. She found that hard to believe. It was easier to accept that the nurses just wanted to project self-importance—as if anyone was an authority on what happened to the dead.

In her last few years of Mother's life, doctors claimed that a disease was eating her mind, but the sniper wondered if maybe her mother had been the most lucid of her life, attaining some elevated state of awakening. After all, the moments of clarity seemed to hit so intensely, the erratic swings from bitter heartbreak and devastation to acceptance and forgiveness so fierce, the sniper felt as if she'd experienced them firsthand.

Mother had gone on about the vileness of people in a hot rage some days, and on other days excused them. As if her suffering had been of no consequence—or even her own fault. And while her mother may have been willing to forgive and sweep over transgressions, the sniper wasn't. And it didn't matter how many days passed or how far she traveled.

The past was strapped to the bumper, clanging like a bunch of tin cans against the road in her wake. But every once in a while, a small voice would slither from the darkness and whisper that what she was doing was wrong. Like an interlude of conscience that would roll in with the fierceness of a tidal wave. Destructive yet restorative. At these times, she reminded herself she was simply defending herself against a world that had gotten her in its jowls, bit down, and shook her like she was in the throes of a rabid dog. So what if her actions were technically wrong—at least when measured against society's standards? She couldn't stop herself. Even with the FBI looking for her, she was determined to keep going until she finished her mission. And to complete said mission, she had to continue moving forward. To turn around now, to go into hiding would only be weakness.

"Fortuna favet fortibus!"

Fortune favors the strong.

She merged onto Interstate 395 East, headed toward her final stop, prepared to put an end to this mission once and for all. But her mind kept going back and forth, balancing the scales of good and bad and which way her actions would weigh heavier. Maybe she should heed the soft voice trying to be heard.

She reached into the console, pulled out an orange prescription bottle, and shook it. Empty. Just like she was— empty and adrift, with nothing to lose. She tossed the container into the back seat and pressed harder on the gas pedal, focused ahead.

CHAPTER SEVENTEEN

Cheating husbands get taken out. I could imagine the headline, and I hated it—not that we knew they were all cheaters yet. I'd like to think there was a deeper motive to the killings than a wayward spouse. *You cheat on me, so I kill you. Ouch!*

I glanced over at Paige, who was set up on the other side of the conference table. She had one foot up on her chair, her bent knee to her chin, and she read the reports from the folder in front of her, her lips moving slightly at she did so. I couldn't miss the irony that I was holed up with Paige—whom I'd had an affair with—digging into men's lives who seemed to have been a little less chivalrous than morals demanded. I also had a hard time ignoring the fact every time I looked at Paige, my heart picked up its pace. But I would ignore it as long as we worked together, and I had Becky in my life. Cheating once was enough, and I thought I'd buried all the guilt that came with it, but apparently, it had just been lying dormant beneath the surface, ready to bubble up and overwhelm me. For a brief moment, I wondered if it was this guilt that kept holding me back from finding any sort of comfort in a committed relationship. Maybe on some level, I didn't think I was worthy of one.

But these men, even if they were unfaithful… It would hardly seem possible that one person had been wronged by all four men and decided to take them out. That reasoning lent itself to a hired gun, even if there wasn't a money trail to support it.

I peeked up at Paige again, taking in how her red hair hooked over a shoulder, how her lipstick had faded more from her top lip than her bottom one.

I put my folder down and made it obvious I was watching her.

She slowly pried her eyes from what she was reading and looked at me. "Yes?"

"Do you think we're looking at the same killer in all these murders?"

"Seems likely. Same MO—as far as we can see. Straight to the heart. The ME hasn't confirmed it yet, but I wouldn't be surprised to hear that Darrell's heart was hit, given the location he was struck."

"I know you were leaning away from a hired gun, but what if someone out there makes it their business to rid loyal spouses of their problems?" Something cinched in my chest as the last segment of my sentence came out. It was a severe judgment passed upon myself. If the criteria for becoming a target was adultery, I could be a victim, too. But it wasn't like I'd set out to be a bastard. I'd certainly been raised better and was even given the example of a long-lasting and faithful marriage in my parents.

"Assuming all four victims were even cheating. Nadia only confirmed one widow got pictures. So far, Reid's a rumor. With the others, all we know is they had marriage problems."

"Cheating being a significant marriage problem," I tossed back, and her eyes flicked to mine. Guilt tightened its grip. While my brief affair with Paige hadn't been the culprit behind the dissolution of my marriage, it was an obvious symptom that something was wrong to start with. *It wasn't the disease; it was a symptom...* Maybe if I told myself that enough times, I would be able to tamp down my remorse. They say it takes two for a marriage to work. Then, by deduction, it would take two to fall apart. Sometimes I wasn't as generous at forgiving myself.

Paige held my gaze for seconds but didn't say anything. I sensed she could tell what I was thinking, how I was feeling. She put her leg down and glanced away at the whiteboards, and when she turned back to me, her expression hardened. "The locations of the hits cover a lot of territory with—what?—hundreds or thousands of miles between them."

"Just means our unsub is mobile. But if Zach was here, he could tell you the distance off the top of his head."

"Man, I miss that guy, *Pending*." Paige winked at me. "Pending" was Zach's nickname for me. He easily dispensed with it during my two-year probationary period, but even when I became a full-fledged agent, he still found occasion to pull it out—just because he knew it bothered me.

Good ol' Zach.

"Let's not start with that again—unless it's directed at Kelly."

Paige laughed.

"But in all seriousness," I started, "I still think we might be looking at a hit man."

"You're forgetting there's nothing to prove the transfer of money."

I held Paige's eye. "So what? Our sniper is acting on their own prompting—why? And why these men?" I gestured to pictures of all the victims I'd set on the table in front of me.

"Don't know, but there's something personal there—between the sniper and those men." Paige's gaze went to the photos. "I mean, they were shot in the heart."

It was the second time that Paige had pointed that out in less than so many minutes. Was Paige feeling the connection to her own life? She hadn't been the one to cheat on a spouse, but she'd been a mistress. I met Paige's eyes and considered saying something about our past, but her phone rang.

"Special Agent Dawson," she answered. "Uh-huh. Okay. Great." She put her phone on the table. "That was Captain Herrera. The ME confirmed the shot was a direct hit to the heart. Death would have been instant for Reid. And the bullet fragments have been removed and are being sent to the lab for analysis, but it's believed to have been a 7.62×51mm NATO bullet."

"Same as in these three cases." I pointed to the report from Nadia.

"Uh-huh."

"We need to call Jack."

"Herrera's on that." Paige spun her phone on the table. "But there's more. Since Crime Scene Investigators now have the angle at which the round entered Reid's body, they're on the street figuring out the triangulation and where the shot may have been fired from. With any luck, within an hour or two, Herrera figures we'll have a good idea of where the sniper set up."

"That's a start." I should be more excited about her news, but I couldn't bring myself to feel it.

"*A start*? Don't get all excited on me," she teased.

"It's just there's not likely to be any evidence to find—at least nothing that's going to get us to our shooter."

"Someone's gone dark."

She has no idea! There were times it was difficult working with Paige; being paired with her, on this case no less, was a cruel trick of fate.

"This is a tough case." She spoke so softly I wondered if I'd imagined hearing her voice.

I nodded. It was all I felt like doing. To say anything would just complicate things more than they already were.

There was a knock on the door, and Officer Green entered the room.

"I found something you might like to know. It's from the tenant list. One of the condos is registered to a corporation, and it's owned by Bert Pryce."

I could tell Green thought this finding was a gem, but— "Who's Bert Pryce?"

"Reid's father-in-law."

"Oh." I glanced at Paige, back at Green. "He lives there?"

Green shook his head. "The Pryces live out in Washington."

"What does the company do?" Paige asked.

"Source high-end artwork for corporate offices and hotels," Green replied. "It's likely the condo's used for schmoozing out-of-town clients."

"The question now is whether Reid was going to Pryce's place or visiting someone else," I laid out.

"And if Reid was going to his father-in-law's condo, was he using it as his personal bachelor pad?"

"Ballsy…if so." I looked at Green. "Thanks for the update."

"Uh-huh." Green left the room.

"We've got to call Jack right away," Paige started. "Maybe we'll catch him and Kelly while they're still at the Reids' house, and they can press Arlene about this."

CHAPTER EIGHTEEN

Kelly swallowed the feeling of validation at finding out that Reid had been shot in the heart. It seemed her suspicion about him—and the other victims—being targeted for their cheating ways was spot-on. Still, she told herself not to get attached and lose all objectivity. The investigation was still young.

Jack's phone rang, and he answered without putting the call on speaker. His face turned to granite, and his gaze hardened as he listened to his caller. Whatever he was hearing obviously wasn't pleasing him.

"We're still here." With that, he pocketed his phone and looked over at Kelly. "That was Paige. Apparently, Bert Pryce owns a condo at Wilson Place."

Another rush of vindication tore through her. She'd been right: Arlene was hiding something.

Jack knocked on the door with the subtlety of someone notifying homeowners their house was on fire.

Riley got the door. "Too soon to ask again if you caught my dad's killer?"

Sarcasm, Kelly noted. One surefire way of hedging grief.

"We need to speak with your grandfather," Jack told him.

"Grandpa," Riley shouted over a shoulder and took off down the hall, leaving the door open.

Kelly and Jack stepped inside but didn't leave the front entry.

Bert came toward them, scowling. His energy had hardened with a protective demeanor that would require a chisel to penetrate.

"We need to speak to you," Jack said, "somewhere private."

Kelly never took her eyes off Bert. She was curious why he'd never mentioned owning a condo in the building where his son-in-law was shot. Were both father and daughter hiding their knowledge of Wilson Place for a reason?

"This is not a good time," Bert stonewalled.

"Mr. Pryce, it's either we speak here or down at the Arlington police station. Your choice."

Bert's gaze traced over Jack as if assessing whether his threat held merit. Kelly, on the other hand, didn't even need to glance at Jack to know that it did.

Bert waved for her and Jack to follow him.

"We'd also like for Mrs. Reid to join us," Jack requested.

Bert stuck his head into the sitting room and motioned for his daughter to get up and come with them. Arlene cocked her head, pressed her eyebrows down, but relented.

This time, Bert took them to a study lined with bookshelves full of law tomes. A mahogany desk took up residence in the room, along with a deep-green leather couch and two matching pub chairs. Bert sat in one of those; Arlene on one end of the couch. Kelly parked next to her, and Jack took the other chair.

"Why didn't you tell us that you own one of the condos at Wilson Place?" Jack said, his gaze on Bert.

Way to just come out with it, Jack!

Bert clenched his jaw and crossed his legs, running a hand down his slacks as he did so. Arlene was watching her father. Neither of them said a word.

"It's come to our attention that you own unit 1035 under your company's name," Jack laid out.

Bert's face flushed.

Jack turned his attention to Arlene. "Did you know about that?"

"I…" Arlene faced her father. Her hands were trembling in her lap.

"Just leave my daughter out of this." Bert's tone had heat. "I don't know where you think you're going with this, but whether or not I own a condo in that building has nothing to do with Darrell's death."

That was the second time he'd referred to Darrell's murder as a death. The first time was to his grandson. Was it an intentional downplay or an indication there was no love lost between father- and son-in-law?

"Are you sure about that?" Jack countered.

Bert's nostrils flared. "You come in here and accuse me of—"

"No one's accusing anybody, but we do need some answers. Some straightforward ones."

Neither father nor daughter made a move to speak.

"It might help us to know why Darrell was there this morning," Kelly put out there, aligning herself as an ally, "and why he frequently went to the building."

Arlene turned to face Kelly. "He—" She stopped there and rubbed her throat.

Kelly put her focus on Bert. "Did Darrell have a reason to go to your condo?"

"I bought that condo mainly for business purposes."

"That still doesn't answer Agent Marsh's question," Jack said.

Bert glanced at his daughter, then back to Jack. "If Darrell was there, I have no idea why. And you said 'frequently'? I am at a loss." Bert was breathing heavier than before and kneading the back of his neck.

Jack leaned back in his chair. "We've found out that Darrell had been going to Wilson Place on a regular basis for years. Unless he visited someone else in the building…"

Arlene flushed.

"He had to have been going to my condo," Bert jumped in. "Not sure why he'd be going there. Not even sure how he'd have gotten in. It's not like I gave him a key. The only people who have one are Arlene and my wife. Oh, and Jeff… That's Arlene's brother, whom you've met already."

Arlene was picking at her pants.

"Did you ever go there with Darrell?" Kelly asked her. "Or give him your key, perhaps?"

Arlene slowly looked up and shook her head. "I never gave him the key. I promise Daddy."

Bert clenched his jaw.

"I'd go sometimes—but by myself—to check on things if Dad asked me to," Arlene continued. "I might have taken Darrell there once. If I did, it was a long time ago."

"So, you still have your key?" Jack asked Arlene.

"Yes, of course."

"Can you check that for us? We'll wait."

Fire glinted across Bert's eyes in response to Jack's request. Arlene wetted her lips and headed for the door.

"I'll be right back," she said.

The door shut behind her, and Bert leaned forward.

"Do you think that son of a bitch got into my condo and—" His voice quivered with rage, and his face was bright red. He wasn't that stupid, after all.

"We're here trying to get some answers," Jack said.

"It seems to me you're looking at me to provide 'em, and I can't."

"Did you and your son-in-law get along?" Kelly tried to present the question in an upbeat manner to slice through the tension.

"He made my daughter happy; that's what mattered to me."

Classic diversion…

"Did he make *you* happy?" Kelly asked more pointedly.

Bert met her eyes. "Suppose he really didn't have to, did he? But if you wonder if I'm happy he's dead or think Arlene's better without him, you'll never hear me say that. And a boy needs his father. Riley will recover, but it will take time."

He'd made a similar comment when they'd arrived before. "You lose your father as a young boy?"

"I did, and I ended up just fine."

Arlene came back into the room and extended a key ring toward Kelly, with one key pinched between her fingers. "That's the one for Dad's condo," she declared proudly, her chin tilted up and out.

Kelly nodded, but the fact she still had her key didn't prove that Reid had never used it. And it was possible Reid had a copy made. Kelly would point that out to Jack when they left. There was one thing Kelly needed a little clarification on. "You said you have the condo for business?"

"I do."

So, if Darrell went regularly, he had to have known when the place would be available unless— "Did you make often use of the condo? For you and clients?"

"A few times a year, if that. But it's a legitimate business write-off."

If Darrell had availed himself of his father-in-law's condo, he would likely have known that it was rarely used. But they still didn't know for sure that Darrell had been going to Bert's condo. "Would we have your permission to look around your condo, Mr. Pryce?"

"I don't know what you expect to find, but I don't see why not. As long as I can come with you."

Kelly looked at Jack, who nodded.

"Do you think you're going to find proof Darrell was there?" Bert asked.

Arlene's hands were shaking, and she dropped the key ring to the floor. Kelly picked it up for her.

"I think we should take a look. Even if it's to rule out that Darrell hadn't gone there," Kelly said.

"Very well. Let's head over there right now and get this over with." Bert stood, and Arlene followed.

"It might be best if you stayed here, Mrs. Reid," Kelly suggested.

"Actually, she's welcome to come if she wants to," Jack said, overriding Kelly. She felt her cheeks flush at her stupidity. Of course they'd want Arlene present when they searched the condo.

A few minutes later, in the warming SUV, Jack turned to Kelly in the passenger seat.

"Do you know why we want Mrs. Reid to come with us?"

"I do. I slipped up in there. If we find proof of Reid's infidelity in that condo, we want to see her reaction."

Jack smiled at her. "You got it."

"There's something else. I mean, you probably thought of it, but Reid could have made a copy of his wife's key to the condo."

"Yes, I thought of that."

He had a way of lifting her up one second and deflating her the next. She was going to stay humble on Jack's team.

CHAPTER NINETEEN

Page grabbed two coffees from the bakery in the same plaza as the Arlington PD. One for her, one for Brandon. It didn't matter that it was going on nine o'clock at night. She was starting to drag, and she needed to get out and clear her head—and put space between her and Brandon. And to think she'd only been penned up in the conference room for over an hour; it felt so much longer than that. Brandon was obviously sorting something out, given his shortness and awkwardness. She'd guess he was visiting their past, and it made her more than a little uncomfortable. She didn't want to talk about it, and she got the inkling he might want to. Hence, the need to leave for a bit.

Kelly had called to confirm she and Jack were headed over to Pryce's condo to take a look around to see if there was any evidence that Reid had been there and, if so, his purpose there. It would seem the answer to that question was obvious, but Paige learned a long time ago that reality didn't always turn out to be what was assumed.

She entered the conference room, holding out a cardboard cup toward Brandon, sort of like a shield.

"Thanks." Brandon took the coffee from her. "How is it?"

"How is..."

He bobbed his head toward the coffee in her hands.

"Oh...pretty good." She took a sip as if on cue. "I got a call from Kelly." Paige filled Brandon in.

"I'm interested to know what they find."

"Me too. How's the research going?"

"A lot slower than if Zach was here to read it."

"True that." Zach was a speed reader. She slid into the chair she had been in before she left. "Find out anything while I was gone?"

"Well," Brandon started, a seriousness reflecting in his eyes, "all the victims—the ones that Nadia found—and Reid are the same age range. Fifty-five to fifty-six."

"Huh. Is the sniper picking a type based on someone else?" She'd seen it before, where a killer targeted people who simply reminded them of the actual person they were angry with.

"Obviously, we don't know yet, but I got looking more into the victims' lives. Their occupations and where they were killed. As Nadia mentioned, two of the three were in a regular routine of going where they were shot. Three of four, including Reid." Brandon lifted a photograph from the spread of papers in front of him. "This is Robert Wise. He was the victim from six months ago in New Mexico. He frequented the pub he was shot in front of. Ironically called the Lucky Pub."

"Frequented? How often?"

"Monday through Friday after work. He was a plumber for a mom-and-pop company. A note on witness statements said he had a standing reservation for five thirty on the patio, weather permitting. Same table."

"Making it easy for the sniper to plan their attack. What about the others?"

"Well, we know from what Jack and Kelly found out that Reid showed up at Wilson Place on a regular schedule. Miller from Arkansas was a public-school teacher—"

"Don't tell me he was taken out at the school." Paige's heart sank at the thought of all the school shootings that were plaguing the country. But maybe that's what happened when kids were raised on first-person shooter video games and subjected to violent TV shows and movies. It also didn't help that the internet made committing a crime easy if you knew how to navigate it.

"Thankfully not." Brandon moved his cup around but didn't take a drink. "Miller was shot outside of a bookstore where he'd go every Saturday to grade papers and have a coffee. He was hit on the way out."

"And the one from a month ago?" Paige prompted.

"Sherman from Tennessee was the unpredictable one, and the interesting one, if you ask me."

Paige cocked her head. "Why's that?"

"He was unemployed at the time of his death, and he was taken out on a restaurant patio. Staff said they'd never seen him there before, but Sherman had told them he was waiting on someone."

"Now, that's interesting. If we're after a hired gun, it would be easy for the wives—assuming they ordered the hits—to let the shooter know their husbands' routines." She still couldn't get past the lack of a money trail, but she'd play hypotheticals. "Did Sherman tell anyone who he was waiting for?"

Brandon shook his head. "Nope. All we know for sure is it wasn't Sherman's wife. She confirmed as much."

Paige sat up straighter, remembering what she'd said about her husband's death being a cheaper alternative to divorce. "Can't say that's a surprise."

"Yeah, cold as ice to say her husband's death saved her money on a divorce."

A theory was starting to shift into focus. "And she was the one who received damning photos of her husband with another woman…"

"Yes." A few seconds passed, and he asked, "What are you thinking?"

"That you should have led with Sherman. There's no way that our sniper would know he would have been at the restaurant at that time, on that patio, unless—"

"The sniper arranged to meet him there."

"Uh-huh. And what could get a man with a wandering eye to someplace new?"

"Our sniper's a woman," they said in unison.

"Whoa." Brandon flopped back in his chair.

Adrenaline was fusing through her system, but she worked to rein it in. "Do we know if Sherman was waiting on a man or a woman?"

"Sadly, no, not from the records, anyhow. I'm sure that question would have been asked of the restaurant staff."

Paige shook her head. "It's easy enough to accept that Sherman wouldn't even have said."

"Agreed."

"But if our sniper did arrange a meetup, what's to say the shooter wasn't someone they knew and trusted? Sherman might not have had any clue he was in trouble," Brandon suggested.

"Knew and trusted could apply to a man, as well." Her stomach sank. "It could have been a business meeting? Maybe a job interview?"

"Okay, fine, we still don't have gender nailed down," Brandon said, "but if it is a woman, did she have a personal connection with all the men?"

"Your guess would be as good as mine, but one thing in our favor is our sniper seems to have sped up their timeline. And killers in a hurry make mistakes."

"Sure, but do you really want a sniper making any?"

Paige gulped at Brandon's grim volley. "We've got to find this person—and quick."

"Well, no shit."

She narrowed her eyes at him, and he laughed, then took his first sip of coffee. He licked his lips and nodded.

Apparently, the brew passed the test...

"There are more victims here than just the men," she concluded; the theory starting to crystalize. "Maybe we've been too focused on the murder victims. At least one widow was slapped in the face with her husband's adultery via photographs. It didn't mean the others weren't, just that it wasn't part of the record. The sniper could be trying to hurt the widows. First by killing their husbands, then by exposing their infidelity. In a way, the wives are also victims."

"You think the men were murdered to get revenge on the women?"

"Just thinking out loud."

Brandon drank more coffee, and he looked weary.

She pointed to the papers in front of Brandon. "Did Nadia include information on the wives?"

"Nothing beyond their names and that they were cleared of their husbands' murders."

Paige lifted a pen off the table and scribbled on the corner of a report: *have Nadia probe wives' backgrounds.*

"What are you looking for?" Brandon asked.

"A connection, a motive. Something that ties the women together somehow."

"Well, there is something else you should know," Brandon said, baiting the hook.

She raised her eyebrows.

"In all three cases, no forensic evidence was left in the sniper's nests, but they held two things in common. A circular hole was cut out of the windows, and they were all located in hotels, on the same floor."

She'd seen the crime scene photos, but— "You said the same floor?"

"Yes, the eighth."

"Huh. I wonder if that holds any significance."

"I'd guess it does."

"Me too. Curious how the forensic guys are making out with their trajectory calculations. Let's head down there and find out." On the way, she texted Nadia about the widows.

CHAPTER TWENTY

Kelly had called Herrera on the way to Wilson Place to have him bring the keys taken from Reid's body. They were curious to know if one of them would fit the lock to Bert Pryce's condo.

"Good day, sir." The desk clerk at the building smiled at the sight of Bert, but gave a brief look of derision to Jack and Kelly. His gaze drifted through the front windows to the sidewalk where CSIs were fervently working on figuring out where the shot might have been fired from.

Bert met the clerk's greeting with an attack. "You let anyone into my condo without my knowledge?"

"I…" The clerk straightened his tie. "I…not that I—"

"It's a yes or no," Bert barked.

"He told me that you told him it was all right. And he had a key." The last word came out in a high octave.

Kelly's heart sped up. They had their confirmation that a man had been in Bert's condo, but not that it had been Darrell Reid specifically. "He, who?" she asked.

The clerk's eyes went to her. "Mr. Darrell Reid."

Arlene squeezed her purse, a deep-purple number the size of a paperback novel that hung from a long strap slung over a shoulder, and averted eye contact.

"You never cleared it with me or my daughter." Bert gestured to Arlene.

The clerk's gaze darted back to Bert. "I…I'm sorry, Mr. Pryce."

"I don't need your apologies. I need your ass out the door. You can bet I'm going to be talking to management about this." A thick vein popped in Bert's forehead as he stared down the clerk.

"Would Mr. Reid come by himself?" Kelly ventured.

The clerk's gaze cut to her. "I'm not at liberty to—"

"You're going to answer her question right now," Bert scolded.

"Yes, of course, Mr. Pryce." His eyes fluttered to Arlene, and he pulled on the collar of his shirt. "He sometimes had company."

"*Female* company?" Jack pressed.

"Yes," the clerk confirmed.

Arlene gasped and turned to Kelly for emotional support. Kelly put her hand on the woman's shoulder, but there was something about Arlene's reaction that seemed staged— either her demeanor or the subtle way in which she shifted under Kelly's touch.

"When was he here last?" Jack asked.

"Last night, this morning…obviously." The clerk swallowed roughly after his tart response.

"Was he with a woman last night?" Arlene inquired in a low voice.

"Yes, ma'am."

She didn't respond but walked over to the elevator bank. The rest of the group followed her. Nothing was said on the way to the tenth floor where Bert's condo was located.

When the doors opened, Arlene lamented, "I can't believe that Darrell came here. I don't understand."

"He was a selfish man," Bert slapped out.

"Dad, please don't say that, especially now that he's—" Arlene's words stopped there, her face knotted with what Kelly would peg as disappointment. Arlene was probably tired of defending her husband.

"I apologize if what I said hurt you, darling, but he had his secrets. Obviously." Bert gestured toward the door marked 1035 and took out his key ring.

Jack snapped on gloves and held out a hand for the keys. "It would be best if you waited in the hall."

"Wha— Why let us come down here?"

Jack held up the key ring. "Which one?"

Bert pointed to a silver one with a rounded top.

"Why did you let us come?" Arlene repeated her father's question.

"You both wanted to come down here with us, and that's fine, if you stay in the hall. I can't have you coming in and possibly contaminating evidence."

They had wanted to see their reactions if it was proven that Darrell Reid had been bedding other women—and they had that.

"What sort of evidence? He was killed outside," Arlene said.

"We still don't know why your husband came here, Mrs. Reid," Jack said. "Or anything about the company he kept."

"Oh, please. That bastard was sleeping around on my girl, and he had quite the balls to do it in my place. If he wasn't dead, I might kill him myself!"

"Father!" Arlene cried out.

"I'm not apologizing anymore. I refuse." The older man clamped his jaw tight.

Tears beaded in Arlene's eyes, but none fell. "Do you think his lover took him out?"

Jack slipped the key into the lock. "We need to consider every—"

The elevators dinged, and everyone looked down the hall to see Captain Herrera unloading with two uniformed officers. Herrera led the way, holding up a key ring.

"What's this? What's going on?" Arlene split her gaze between Jack, Kelly, her father, and Herrera. "What's he got there?"

Herrera came to a stop in front of Arlene and looked at Jack for an introduction.

"Captain Herrera, meet Mrs. Arlene Reid," Jack said. "And that's Bert Pryce, her father—"

"And the man who owns this condo." Bert pointed to the key ring Herrera held. "You didn't answer my daughter's question."

"This? It's the key ring that was taken from your husband's pocket, Mrs. Reid." Herrera spoke without preamble, in a fashion that fit a seasoned cop.

Arlene nodded, but remained quiet.

"We think it's possible that he made a copy of your key," Kelly explained.

Arlene's gaze snapped to Kelly. "Why would he—" Her words faded to silence under Kelly's eye. No doubt the woman was getting Kelly's silent communication: no one was that blind and stupid to be facing the evidence and still deny its existence.

Jack took the key ring from Herrera and compared the keys to the one he'd put in the lock. He settled on one and gave it a try. It turned easily.

Jack looked at Arlene, then Bert, then Herrera, finally Kelly.

"Mrs. Reid," Kelly began, "I think you know why your husband would have made a copy of the condo key."

The woman let go of her purse, and it dangled freely from her shoulder. "I have no—"

"I think you do." Kelly softened her approach, stepped closer to the woman. "It's not easy to think about someone you love cheating on you, but—"

"No, he wasn't a cheater." There was a spark in her eyes that belied her claim, and Kelly was curious why she was so adamant about protecting her dead husband's reputation. Or was it more because it would hurt hers, and she'd have to live with the whispers of people.

"Men who cheat are good at hiding it from their wives, their loved ones." Kelly spoke like she knew from personal experience, but the truth was she didn't let herself get entangled romantically. Her primary focus had always been on other things—torn between her career and her caring for her ailing grandfather, who had raised her as his own daughter, until he passed away. Then it had become what she could scrape together for a career. "Many wives don't know about their husband's infidelities," she added, trying to soothe Arlene into a confession of suspicion at least.

Arlene gritted her teeth and fixed her gaze across the hall, past Kelly and seemingly on nothing in particular.

Bert put a hand on his daughter's shoulder. "Darling, why don't you just admit to it? Darrell was a snake."

She shrugged off her father's hand and turned to him. "I'm leaving. I'm not just going to stand around here while you"—she fit in a quick glance at Kelly—"tell me that Darrell was cheating on me." She stormed off toward the elevator bank with Bert on her heels.

Herrera turned to one of his officers. "Make sure they get home all right."

The officer nodded and went down the hall to catch up with Bert and Arlene.

"Well, shall we?" Herrera gestured toward the condo door.

Jack took the first step inside. Kelly followed, then Herrera and the remaining officer walked in. They flipped a wall switch, and ceiling fixtures flooded the room with light.

The layout was open concept and bright. Huge windows would let the sun in during the day when the heavy drapes were pulled back. The space was large, but bulky furniture made it feel smaller. It was definitely furnished with the touch of man's influence. No frilly throw pillows, no knickknacks or personal touches, for that matter. No photographs or anything homey about the place. It was rather cool and reminded Kelly of her childhood home. A place she'd only lived until the age of six when her mother had shot her father. Love hadn't grown in the tiny bungalow but rather dark secrets, ones that eventually broke dirt and gave way to poisonous plants that choked out any resemblance to compassion.

Kelly cleared her throat, willing the sensations of her past to creep into remission again.

The condo had been lived in recently. There were dirty dishes in the sink, a few empty wine bottles on the counter, and a couple of wineglasses. She opened the cabinet under the kitchen sink, and there was garbage in the receptacle.

Herrera came back toward them after having journeyed down the hall. "If Mr. Pryce says he hasn't been here, then someone else has been sleeping in the bed."

Kelly walked along the kitchen counter, closer to the wineglasses. "Ja—Agent Harper." She mentally cursed herself for almost slipping into a more informal address.

Jack looked over at her from the living room.

"There's a wineglass here that has a lipstick print," she said. *A soft coral pink.*

"Darrell entertained here. Not his wife, I gather," Herrera said.

"No," Kelly said. "You missed the part before we came up. The clerk said Reid had been here with women, including one last night."

Herrera put his hands on his hips. "She could tie into Reid's murder."

"We're keeping an open mind," Jack said.

"About a serial killer?" Herrera shot back. "You look surprised I know about the other murders."

Jack's eyes narrowed.

"You didn't bother to tell me about them."

Kelly stepped back.

"We're still investigating whether they are connected to this case."

"Uh-huh, but it's looking pretty damning, I suspect, seeing as you left two of your agents back at the station to dig into them more."

The tension between Jack and Herrera was tangible.

"We're taking it seriously," Jack eventually admitted.

Herrera shook his head and looked around the condo. Kelly took it as a prompt to move and walked around the place. She found more evidence that a woman had been there recently. In the bedroom, there was the faint hint of woman's perfume and the subtle smell of sex. The answer to what Darrell did to entertain his female guests was apparently answered. In a way, Kelly found it disappointing that the cliché was proved again. But were the murders about exacting revenge on cheating husbands, or was there more to Reid's and the other men's murders?

"We'll need to get CSIs in here," Jack said. "See if they can gather prints and DNA. Maybe we'll be able to ID the mystery woman."

"I'll get them up here," Herrera said, surprisingly cooperative given Jack's poor performance at being a team player.

There was a knock on the condo door, and a man called out, "Captain Herrera."

They walked back to the entry and found an officer standing there.

"One of the CSIs sent me in to see you," he started. "Said they've narrowed down the trajectory."

They left Pryce's condo with the officer and headed for the elevator. For Kelly, she couldn't get on the ground floor fast enough.

CHAPTER TWENTY-ONE

Paige and I were en route to Wilson Place when we got the call. We met up with Jack and Kelly in front of the building. They were accompanied by two CSIs and Captain Herrera. We walked up mid-conversation.

"As I was saying, it's most likely our shooter struck from the northeast region." A CSI with a handlebar mustache was pointing in the direction to support his words.

"What type of buildings are that way?" Paige blurted out.

Six sets of eyes went to her, including mine. Jack's expression was one of surprise, and he glanced at me for an explanation.

"We tried reaching you," I said. That wasn't a lie; we had called on the way over and got voice mail.

"We found some interesting things in the packet Nadia had compiled." Paige's gaze danced over the CSIs and Captain Herrera, then back to Jack. "In the previous cases, the sniper's nests were in hotels." Paige looked at Handlebar. "Are there any hotels in the vicinity you mentioned?"

Handlebar's eyes pinched in thought. "There are two that would afford the sniper with the right elevation they'd require."

"Which would be…?" I prompted. "And what floor?" Though I had a good feeling I knew the answer I'd get.

"The shot would have had to come from the eighth to tenth floor."

"The eighth," both Paige and I said at the same time.

"The sniper nests in the three cases Nadia found were all on the eighth floor," I elaborated.

"Could be coincidence," Herrera said.

"Possible but not likely," I replied. "There are notable patterns to the killings, and the location of the sniper nests would be no different. In all the cases, too, there was a circle cut out of the window for the barrel of the rifle to go through."

Jack set his gaze on me and nodded. To Handlebar, he said, "Names of the two hotels."

"The Colonial Hotel and the Royal Plaza."

"I'll get officers to help on the eighth floors," Herrera volunteered.

"Sounds good." Jack looked at Paige and me. "You two go to the Colonial Hotel. Kelly and I will hit the Royal Plaza."

"Just thinking, Jack," Kelly interjected. "The room where the sniper set up must show as occupied, probably with a Do Not Disturb sign on the door, or the cleaning crew would have found a window with a hole in it by now, and it would have been called in."

Jack nodded. "Yes, good point. We need to talk to people who would have been there this morning, too, to see if they heard or saw anything."

"And just so you know," I began, "two of the hotel rooms the sniper used were paid for in cash, but the one used in New Mexico was paid for using a stolen credit card. A path that didn't lead investigators anywhere."

"No description from hotel employees on what the person looked like in any of the cases?" Jack regarded me with disbelief.

I shook my head. "Nope, and no surveillance cameras. The one where the stolen card was used, the hotel has an app that allows its guests to manage everything from check-in to check-out. They are given a code that they use to unlock their hotel rooms. That's what our sniper used."

"That's a scary thought," Herrera lamented. "And an absolute nightmare from a law enforcement standpoint."

"Technology advances are sometimes overrated," Jack said and was on the move.

"I'll get the verbal search warrants for the rooms and get it followed up in writing, but at least you can get started." Herrera put his phone to an ear, and the CSIs started packing up their equipment.

"Oh, Jack," Paige called out, and he turned around. "Brandon and I think our sniper might be a woman." She went on to tell them about Sherman waiting on someone who we suspected was the sniper.

"Wow, she set him up. Talk about brazen," Kelly said. "She's not afraid of showing her face to her victims." She looked at Jack. "We really have to find Reid's mistress."

"Mistress?" My ears perked up, and personal guilt socked me in the gut. "We confirmed he had one?"

"Yeah." Jack told Paige and me what had transpired before we arrived. "All right." He clapped his hands. "Let's move."

Jack and Kelly set off.

Just as Page and I started to leave, Handlebar's colleague mumbled, "Glad we could help."

"You should be," I snapped. "You could have just played a role in finding a serial killer."

The CSI's face went white. "I wasn't being sarcastic."

"Yeah, you were. You're sulking because you never got a big, fat thank-you, but if you're looking for one or a pat on the shoulder, you're in the wrong line of work. Go be a barista."

The CSI scowled and went back to work.

I headed toward our SUV, figuring we'd drive to the Colonial. "I can't believe some people," I seethed.

"Really? I thought you went off on—"

"That guy deserved it."

"Ooookay…."

I looked over at her, and her eyes read, *You sure this isn't about something else?*

"Let's just get this shooter," I said.

The Colonial Hotel was located three blocks north, and Paige parked in their underground garage. At the front desk, she gave them our information and purpose for being in their hotel and obtained a parking pass, which we'd flash on the way out.

Paige's phone chimed, and she looked at it. "Text from Herrera. We've got the green light to search the rooms."

The male clerk at the front desk was wiry and had a long neck that went on inches above his collar. "I'll get the manager for you right now."

"His name?" I said stiffly.

"*Her* name is Anita Cannon." The clerk talked slowly; his offense at my assuming gender was obvious. He picked up the handset on his phone and requested that Anita come to the front desk for the FBI.

Paige and I stepped back and let the clerk register a few guests.

"Are you sure you're okay?" she asked me.

"I'm fine. Let's just focus on our jobs."

She scanned my eyes, sighed, and hitched up her chin. "Very well. Why didn't you mention how the rooms were paid for by the sniper before, back at the station?"

"It didn't exactly come up. And you were so fixated on the eighth floor, then we rushed down—"

A woman in a tight, black skirt suit sashayed toward us, holding a tablet in one hand. Her wavy, dark hair fell over her shoulders and bounced with her steps. Her heels clacked on the marble flooring. She stopped in front of us and smiled pleasantly enough, but it was all business.

"You're with the FBI?" she said, tucking the tablet under one of her arms.

"Special Agents Dawson and Fisher," Paige said. "I'm right to assume you're the manager, Anita Cannon?"

"You are."

"We need access to all the south-facing rooms on your eighth floor," I cut in, eager to move forward.

Cannon regarded me with indifference. "I'm sure you can understand that we can't just let you into the rooms without a warrant."

"We have a verbal one from Judge Whittaker, and one in writing is forthcoming. They just take a little more time—and that's something we're short on."

Ms. Powertrip stood there, unmoved.

"There was a shooting three blocks south this morning. A man was killed. You might have heard it on the news?" I paused, seeing if Anita would give any sort of reaction. Not so much as a slow blink.

"Sure." Spoken like a robot.

"We have reason to believe that the shooter might have set up in one of your rooms," I laid out.

Anita's mouth twitched like she wanted to say something but didn't know what, giving the first sign that my words were hitting between her ears.

"Fine, come this—" Anita's gaze went past us toward the doors.

I turned, and two uniformed officers were there, saw us, and headed over.

A whole two officers, Captain Herrera? There has to be—what?—ten plus rooms on the eighth floor.

"How many rooms face south on the eighth?" I asked Anita.

"I don't have that fact at the top of my head, but I wouldn't imagine any more than fifteen."

"Agents," one of the officers said by way of greeting when he reached us.

I didn't respond. Paige said a simple, "Hi."

"Ms. Cannon," I started, "we're especially interested in rooms that are currently rented out and that may have a Do Not Disturb sign on the door."

Anita's gaze drifted to the front desk, her face a mask of hesitancy, but she nodded. "I'll have that information compiled for you. In the meantime, we can hit up every room, but I'm going to accompany you. I'll deal with any guests we might encounter. There's to be no word of a possible shooting taking place from here."

"If we run into any guests, we'll be asking them if they heard or saw anything unusual this morning about six o'clock," I told her. "As well as during the time leading up to that and after."

"I can appreciate you both have a job to do," Anita said, seeming to leave the uniformed officers out of her statement, "but so do I. The guests of this hotel need to know that they are safe when they stay here."

"And I can appreciate that," I countered.

"Good, then let's proceed." Anita *clacked* her way to the elevator bank, the rest of us following.

I knew I had to shake my irritation and release my baggage. I had to pull from Jack's inculcation: emotions had no real place in an investigation. I just wish I was as good as he was at holding them at bay. Then again, maybe if Jack was face-to-face with a trigger like I was when it came to working next to Paige, and on this case in particular, he might not be so cool either.

CHAPTER TWENTY-TWO

Kelly had always relished the rush that came with closing a case, finding a killer, getting justice. Ask anyone in law enforcement, and they'd tell you it was a high like no other. But her time as a homicide detective investigating, for the most part, single murders paled by comparison to hunting a killer who took out more than one person. She supposed the feeling was similar to when she'd had a part in taking a gang leader nicknamed Rock off the streets and hitting him with five murder charges. That had truly been a good day.

She was next to Jack as they scoured the eighth floor of the Royal Plaza. The place smelled of cleaner and chlorine—comfortable and familiar scents for a hotel. It made Kelly want to snuggle under a fluffy duvet, order pay-per-view and room service. *If only.*

Jack ignored the Do Not Disturb sign and knocked on room 819. They'd taken the rooms to the left of the elevator bank, and two officers went to the ones on the right. Jack made it clear to the uniforms they were to take detailed notes if they ran into any guests, and he provided them the basic questions they should ask.

A third officer watched the elevators and was to make sure no one left the floor until they were spoken to.

Jack knocked a second time, and footsteps approached the door. The chain slid across, and the door opened. A man in dress slacks and an unbuttoned shirt with a tie dangling loose around his neck was standing there looking bedraggled and smelling of whiskey. He perked up at the sight of Kelly.

"Well, hellllooo," he said with a smile.

Oh Lord! Too many men live up to the womanizer stereotype.

"My boss and I would like to talk to you for a minute," she said, sensing from Jack it might work to their advantage if she handled this one.

A cocky grin. "Sure." He opened the door wider.

Jack gestured for Kelly to go inside first. For the guy's leering—and practically drooling—Kelly thought him harmless. Even if Jack wasn't around, she could handle this loser herself.

"Have a hard day?" she asked, making light conversation.

"Very *hard*."

She fought not to roll her eyes, but realized she'd opened the opportunity for a lewd innuendo. She pulled out her badge. "We're agents with the FBI. I'm Kelly Marsh, and this is Supervisory Special Agent in Charge Jack Harper."

"No shit." The man clamped a hand on Jack's shoulder. Jack tensed, and the man removed his hand.

Kelly's guess was Jack preferred not to be touched. "How long have you been staying here?" she asked, though she knew the answer. Before they set out on the eighth floor, they got all the guest information from the front desk, in gratitude to a cooperative hotel manager.

"Since last night."

"Nice. Just to get away for the weekend early?" Kelly was looking past him. The bed was disheveled. The comforter bunched to one side, half on the floor. A glass with amber liquid was on the nightstand, and across the room, a near-empty bottle of Jim Beam sat on a table in front of the window. The drapes had been pulled in about two feet on both sides.

"I lost my job." He belched.

"Sorry to hear that."

"Hey, you're a bright spot."

Kelly pasted on a smile. "We just need to take a look around. Okay?"

"Whatever you want, sunshine." He grabbed his glass.

Kelly walked farther into the room, headed toward the window. She looked down and could see that it had a clear line of sight to Wilson Place, and she swept back the drapes. No hole. She shook her head at Jack, and they went to leave.

"You're leaving already? You just got here."

"Don't destroy your liver just because some boss couldn't appreciate you," she said. "You should be thanking them for letting you go. Now you can take your life in a direction it was meant to go."

The man stood straighter, and a grin spread across his lips. "No shit. You some guru or something?"

Or something... "Take care," she said, closing the door behind her and Jack.

"We can mark room 819 off our list," she said.

"No shit." Jack smiled, and she giggled.

CHAPTER TWENTY-THREE

Paige wished Brandon would let go of the chip on his shoulder before she had to knock his block off. He was going through some personal crisis, and it was affecting the way he was approaching the case. He'd attacked that CSI, and then he'd been brash with the hotel manager. The longer Anita Cannon shadowed them, though, she was starting to get under Paige's skin, too.

Anita insisted on accompanying them to every door and was adamant she be the one to greet the guests when they first answered. Being a responsible manager was one thing, but this over-the-shoulder supervision was another. By the time they reached the thirteenth room, which happened to be number 850, Paige had about enough—but it didn't matter. The terms were Anita was to be with them. Due to that, Paige had asked the officers to position themselves at the elevators and not let anyone go down unless they could confirm they'd been spoken to. Anyone arriving on the floor was to be escorted to their rooms, and Anita, Paige, and Brandon were to be notified.

Somewhere between the ground floor and the first door they knocked on, Anita announced she had the list of guest names, their room numbers, and when they'd checked in. They'd knocked on several doors already, only to find them empty and with no holes in the windows.

Anita pointed a long finger toward room 850 and consulted her tablet. "This one has been unoccupied for the last five days."

"Then the last time maid service would have been in there was when?" Brandon asked.

"Five days ago. Actually, six."

"Is it normal to have a room sit unoccupied for so long?" It seemed odd to Paige.

"It can happen. It all depends on what people want and the way the computer assigns the rooms."

Anita took a step down the hall.

"Wait." Paige remained planted in front of 850. They'd had in mind the sniper had rented a room, like in previous cases, but what if that wasn't the case this time? And what if their expertise extended past a rifle to technology? Had they messed with the hotel's system somehow? Paige flicked a finger toward the door for 850. "Let's take a look inside."

Anita stopped walking and spun. "Do you think that's necessary?"

"If I didn't, I wouldn't have said it."

"Fine then." Anita rapped her knuckles on the door and explained herself. "It's protocol before entering any room in the hotel." There was no response, and Anita proceeded to press the keycard to the lock pad, and the light turned green.

Paige pushed down on the handle and went inside. She'd followed a gut feeling coming in here, but she'd learned early on as an FBI agent to exhaust every possible lead.

The curtains were open most of the way, and the lights from the city skyline cast a reflection on the glass and added a subtle glow to the room. She went straight for the window.

The lights were turned on, and when she glanced back, she saw it had been Brandon to flip the switch.

Paige looked outside, and she had a clear line of sight to Wilson Place. She let her gaze go to the left, then right along the length of the window. The curtain on the right was blowing inward just lightly—and for good reason. Her heart hammered upon seeing the hole in the glass. "Brandon," she called him over.

"What is it?" Anita hastily asked.

Brandon joined Paige at the window, and she first pointed out the line of sight and then swept the curtain back to expose the hole.

"What!" Anita spat. "This is…this is…"

"We're going to need to lock down this room." Brandon's directive left Anita no room for negotiation.

"Oh…okay."

"We'll also need to speak to any guests in the neighboring rooms—even from the other side of the hall," Paige clarified. "Any that could have been here at six o'clock this morning."

"Sure. One minute." Anita's hands shook as she selected a name from her contact list and put her phone to an ear.

Paige listened as Anita told the people at the front desk precisely what she needed. Paige turned to Brandon. "Let's call Herrera, get some CSIs in here to process the room."

"On it." He turned his back to her and made the call.

She returned to staring out the window and pondering. *What is our sniper's motive? And what brought them from New Mexico or even farther away? What is it about Darrell Reid specifically that got their attention?*

"Okay, we have guests in two rooms near this one who were checked in this morning and still are. One across the hall and one next door." Anita fidgeted with her tablet. "I don't understand how someone got in here."

Paige could appreciate the manager was probably in shock. It wasn't every day she'd find out a shooter used a room in the hotel as a sniper's nest. But the answer seemed simple: someone got ahold of an all-access keycard. "It could have been a new hire with access to the room. Do you know of anyone that fits that description?"

Anita shook her head. "No. There's a hiring freeze in place right now. Has been for a few months."

A few months ago, their sniper—running with the assumption the same one was behind the three previous shootings—had been in Arkansas.

"Well, someone got ahold of a keycard for this room." Brandon pocketed his phone and entered the conversation. "Could have been lifted off a maid or janitor."

Anita wriggled her red-painted lips and bit down on the bottom one. "I don't see how. They're supposed to keep it on their person, not leave it sitting around on their cart."

A bad feeling spread over Paige like vines taking hold of brick. "Are all your maids and janitors accounted for?"

Anita tucked her tablet under an arm and rubbed her shoulder. "As far as I know."

"But you're not sure?" Paige pushed.

"Let me call Housekeeping." She took her phone out again.

"It doesn't have to be a maid from this floor or assigned to this room," Paige clarified. "Anyone who would have an all-room-access keycard."

"It's Ms. Cannon," Anita said into the phone. "Do you—" She looked at Paige for direction.

"Ask if anyone on shift yesterday didn't show up today or hasn't been heard from."

Anita nodded and went ahead and asked. "Okay…Uh-huh…" Her cheeks paled in increments, and she was white when she ended the call.

"Ms. Cannon," Paige said, "what did they say?"

"Two maids are unaccounted for." Her eyes rose to meet Paige's. "Are you saying that—"

"I'm not saying anything just yet. Who were they?"

"Tracy Hogan and Marsha Doyle. Tracy had a falling out with her supervisor yesterday and walked off the job."

"And Marsha?" Paige pressed gently.

"She was to start today at three. That was—" Anita juggled the tablet and her phone and looked at her wristwatch "—over seven hours ago. Guess it's safe to say she's not coming in."

"Does Marsha Doyle have a history of not showing up?" Paige asked.

Anita sniffled and shook her head. "According to the Housekeeping manager, she's usually here a half hour before shift." She trembled, and Paige would have loved to guide her to someplace to sit, but this room was off limits until it was processed.

"What was Marsha's shift yesterday?" Paige asked Anita.

Anita shook her head.

"Did she clock out?" Paige was trying to establish a timeline for when the maid could have disappeared.

"I…don't know."

"Just breathe, okay?" Paige wanted to offer a reassurance that all was well but knew she couldn't.

"Oh…'kay." The word came out on two deep exhales. Anita fumbled with her phone, and Paige put her hand on the manager's.

"Do you want me to ask Housekeeping?" Paige offered.

Anita shook her head slowly. "I can do it." She placed the call and, less than a minute later, was finished. "Marsha clocked out at eleven last night."

Paige passed a look at Brandon, and he went into the hall and called for the officer there to come into the room.

"We need to have the hotel checked—every room, every closet," Brandon told the officer. "We believe we might be looking for the body of a maid by the name of Marsha Doyle."

"Dear God," Anita exclaimed and slapped a hand over her mouth.

The officer turned to leave, and Paige called out to him. "Can you see Ms. Cannon to somewhere private where she can sit? A nearby vacant room, perhaps?"

"Yes, ma'am."

Paige cringed at the address, but the more she dipped into her forties, she supposed she better get used to being called *ma'am*.

"Ms. Cannon," the officer addressed the hotel manager, "if you'll come with me."

Anita was staring into space and blinking slowly.

"Ms. Cannon," Paige said, breaking the manager's daze.

"Ah, yes. Coming." Anita gave one more look at Paige before leaving the room with the officer.

Brandon came across the room to Paige. "There's nothing in the previous cases that indicate collateral damage."

"Let's not get ahead of ourselves."

"You know as well as I do the maid's probably dead."

She did; she just didn't want to think about it and what that meant.

"Our killer is starting to unravel. Are they getting sloppy?"

And Brandon puts my fear into words…

"Could be, but they still managed to take out one target on a busy street, from three blocks away." She'd try to cling to hope, but she wasn't one to live in denial, either. "Assuming we're right about the maid, our sniper took her out sometime between the end of her shift last night at eleven and six this morning."

"Well before six, so the sniper could set up, but if the maid was taken out, where did that happen?"

Paige hated talking about Marsha Doyle as if she was already deceased, but it seemed more likely they'd turn up a body than find her alive somewhere.

CHAPTER TWENTY-FOUR

Herrera had picked up some extra-large pizzas and brought them into the conference room down at the station, declaring they came from the best pizza joint in the city. Kelly was having a hard time getting more than a slice in. Not that she was blaming that on the pizza, rather some homesickness. Tomorrow night—or tonight technically, as it was pretty much midnight—she'd be missing the first dinner in six years with her friends, Brianna and Jessica, back in Miami.

Herrera was seated at one end of the table, Jack at the other. It could have been construed as a struggle for power, but Kelly thought Jack took that crown hands down. There was no doubt there was still some tension from Jack's failure to communicate with Herrera about the previous murders. And for that, Kelly couldn't blame Herrera for being upset.

Before heading here, they'd requested video from the Colonial Hotel be sent to Nadia. She'd have to wade through the last five days to see who had entered room 850 and when. If they were lucky, they'd get a face.

Brandon and Paige talked to neighboring guests before coming to the station, and no one had heard or seen anything helpful.

"As we briefly explained earlier, we—" Paige glanced at Brandon "—think the sniper arranged to meet Sherman and then used the opportunity to take him out."

"With Sherman's cheating ways, it's possible the sniper is a woman." The thought excited Kelly for some reason she couldn't pin down.

"Right," Paige confirmed.

"I'm still not on board with that yet," Jack said. "Sherman was unemployed at the time of his death. It could have been an interview or something business-related."

Brandon's eyes met Jack's. "We thought of that, too."

"Yet it sounds like all of you are giving real credit to the sniper being a woman."

"It would allow her to get close to her victims without them suspecting," Kelly rushed out, not understanding how Jack could close his mind to the possibility of a female sniper. Really, it made complete sense. Male victims shot through the heart—adulterous men, at that. It smacked of a woman scorned, but it didn't mean the victims had wronged the female sniper directly. They could have just been surrogates for the actual person who'd caused her pain. Question would then be: what had her traveling from New Mexico to Virginia?

"Now, about the room at the Colonial—" Paige swallowed a mouthful of food and dabbed her lips with a napkin "—how did our sniper know the room wouldn't have been rented out?"

"If possible, we need to find out if their computer system was tampered with." Jack dropped his pizza crust on his paper plate. "I can have Nadia get on that. Now, the other rooms the sniper used…You had mentioned they were rented. Do you have anything more on the stolen credit card that was used to pay for the room in Albuquerque?"

"The card belonged to Edna and David Mavis, a couple in their seventies, out of California."

"Did any of these other hotels, where the sniper set up their nest, have video that could have captured the shooter?" Kelly asked.

Brandon met her gaze. "The ones in New Mexico and Arkansas didn't have video. The hotel in Tennessee did, but the video file was corrupt and of no use."

"We need to get on the ground. Talk to the investigating officers, find out more about any possible eyewitness accounts. That goes for all three shootings, but if I were to focus on one, it would be the first," Jack said.

Kelly fiddled with her greasy plate and eyed her half-eaten slice, but she wasn't hungry anymore. "Any update on the maid, Marsha Doyle?"

"Nothing yet," Herrera said. "Officers have been sent to her apartment, and there was no answer. The building manager, who has keys, has gone out of state for a couple days. Guess his mother fell ill, but the officers got ahold of him by phone, and he said he'd come back tomorrow."

Kelly nodded. And she knew there hadn't been any update from CSIs working over room 850 of the hotel, which she found strange. What hotel room had no hits for DNA or fingerprints? The answer was simple: one that had been wiped down. She supposed that shouldn't shock her, really—not when they were looking for a skilled sniper who seemed to take pride in remaining invisible.

"Was there anything else found on Reid's person or of note from the autopsy?" Jack asked Herrera.

Herrera bobbed his head, swallowed his mouthful of food. "There was epithelial under his fingernails and hair taken from his suit. Besides his keys, Reid had his wallet in his pocket and three individually wrapped breath mints. We collected his cell phone, and a preliminary check shows nothing useful—all business correspondence. His wallet contained his ID, as you know, but also credit cards and two recent receipts."

Kelly sat up straighter. "Where do they tie back?"

Herrera brushed his hands together, ridding them of crumbs from the pizza slice he'd polished off, and opened a folder in front of him. A few seconds later, he said, "Spencer's Sports Bar—it's downtown—and a Starbucks."

"When were the charges made?" If they were lucky, they might be able to piece the last moments of Reid's life together before he'd shown up at Wilson Place on Wednesday night. She was surprised they were just hearing about the receipts now.

"Starbucks yesterday afternoon about three and—" Herrera squinted and held the report a few inches from his face "—the bar was at eleven."

Kelly glanced at Jack. If this information excited him, it wasn't evident. She hesitated to voice her thoughts on the matter for fear of being shot down, but she'd regret it if she didn't say anything. "We need to go to Spencer's and see if Reid was there by himself or had company." Maybe their sniper had shown his or her face again. It does seem that the sniper had arranged the meet-up with Sherman.

"I agree," Paige said. "If we're lucky, he was there with his mistress, or the mystery woman from Pryce's condo, if they are different people. The staff at Spencer's might have some names for us so we can track her—or them—down."

"It's definitely a lead worth following," Jack said.

Kelly smiled inside because she'd been the one to suggest going to the bar in the first place, but she refused to let the expression show, thinking it would come out as a goofy grin. Jack must have been more interested in the receipts than he'd let on.

"On the topic of the mistress, how did the CSIs make out at Pryce's condo?" Jack asked, his attention on Herrera.

"They have a bit of a goldmine there. Semen on the bedsheets. You know about the lipstick on the wineglass. That left us some DNA, and there were also prints there. If the woman's in the system, we'll find her."

Jack tapped his shirt pocket that housed his cigarettes. "All right, here's the plan. Kelly and I are going to work the case from here in Arlington."

Brandon and Paige stiffened in unison.

"And I want you two on a plane for New Mexico. Dig around and find out anything you can about Robert Wise's life before he was shot. His interactions, his relationships. Let's see if we can figure out a trigger for our unsub."

"You don't think it has something to do with cheating men?" Kelly rushed out and regretted doing so immediately.

"Nothing is ever the way it seems on the surface." Jack latched eyes with her as he spoke.

She nodded and felt foolish—and angry. She'd been a homicide detective for six years and a cop for four years before that. She knew very well that things weren't always the way they appeared. She was tiring of being corrected at every turn just for speaking her theories aloud. He was hot and cold; one minute acknowledging the validity of something she said, the next reprimanding her. If things didn't change with Jack, she wasn't sure how she could go on being a part of his team.

CHAPTER TWENTY-FIVE

Driving had always calmed the sniper, and so she had driven needlessly, mindlessly for hours—around and around. But that's what happened when there was nothing left to do, and she hated being idle. It was in those moments the darkness crept in and grabbed on with a viselike grip. Any spark of humanity that sometimes ignited was then snuffed out before it could catch flame.

She didn't need to arrive at her last destination until Sunday, and it was barely Friday. There would be plenty of time to drive to her heart's content, but she needed rest, and she needed a drink—something the doctors advised against, but sometimes she preferred booze to medication. Sure, the former amplified the taunting voices and crystalized images, but it also provided a therapeutic meeting ground to face the demons, tucked away in a cloak of impregnability. She already had her drink of choice sitting in a brown bag on the front passenger seat. She was only moments away from tearing it free, like she had done with gifts on Christmas morning as a child. At least there were a few happy memories of the festive season. Like everything, though, good times had a way of disappearing—if they showed up at all.

She pulled into the lot of a motel that advertised hourly rates and had a flashing neon-green vacancy light. A place like this would probably take cash and ask no questions because with the clientele they'd attract, they wouldn't want answers.

The male clerk behind the desk looked like the walking dead, high on something—or a combination of somethings.

"You take cash?" the sniper asked.

"Yep." The clerk continued staring at the phone in his hands like it held the secrets of the universe.

"I need a room for the night."

The clerk mumbled the rate, and she slapped the bills on the counter.

"Here." The clerk swept the money into his palm and handed her a key. "Room 13."

Superstitiously unlucky, and she didn't want to take any chances. "What about room 8? Is it available?"

"Sure." Indifferent, he swapped out the keys, and she left.

The room smelled like an ashtray and looked like one, full of what appeared to be unwanted furniture plucked from a vintage store for ten dollars apiece or less. But she didn't really care; it was just a resting place, nothing more, nothing less. Much like her life had been in reflection.

She shucked the bottle of Jack Daniel's free of the bag and unscrewed the lid. She took a long pull and closed her eyes as she let herself sink out of reality, into the space of unconsciousness, blissfulness, nonjudgment, nonconformity, freedom. All of this was a lot of pressure on the drink, but it was nothing the 80 proof couldn't handle.

The TV was a little tube television, and she half-expected it to be a black-and-white model, even though "Color TVs" was something that had made it on the sign out front of the motel. She turned on the TV and settled in, drinking until everything around her blended and blurred into indistinct shapes. The one TV becoming two and morphing into the dresser it sat on, the picture on the wall flattening and amalgamating with the wall. Yes, this moment was bliss, where regrets and painful memories weren't allowed to exist—and yet they came. At first seeping into awareness and then rushing in like water overtaking the *Titanic*.

She had killed a lot of people in her lifetime; their faces never forgotten, and she had killed again today. Well, yesterday now, according to the clock, which told her it was after midnight, the technical dawning of a new day.

She lifted the bottle back for another swig and wiped her mouth. An onslaught of images struck with a vengeance. The bullet meeting its target. Darrell Reid falling to the ground. Pedestrians running and screaming, seeking cover.

Darrell wouldn't have had time to question what hit him—unless he inquired from God in heaven after death. That was assuming one existed and if humankind met their maker. She found it hard to believe in the existence of a greater being. If one existed, why didn't they step in and stop war, end terrorism…and the list went on.

"Fuck you!" she cried out, and tears fell down her cheeks. Faith, acceptance—these were for the weak.

Her eyes fell heavy and closed. The vision behind her eyelids waving and vibrating, pulsing. She was drifting off into a land where she was truly untouchable, when something banged against the wall behind her.

She sprang to her feet, then nearly swooning, she recovered, her head light from the whiskey and the room spinning around her.

The banging continued, followed by loud grunting. Another writhing pig. Likely with a hooker or some skank.

"Fuck this!" She grabbed her gloves and went for her bag with the handgun and grabbed the weapon. She tucked it into the waistband of her pants and let it sit under her shirt and set off for the neighboring room.

She pounded on the door.

A woman's scream came from inside, the sound of faked ecstasy. Definitely a hooker giving her john what he paid for—a stroke to his ego and his dick.

She smacked the door again, and it swung open.

"What the hell do you want?" The man would top the scales at well over three hundred pounds. He barely squeezed into his white briefs, his tub belly obscuring the waistband, and he had the face of a gnarled dog. His fingers were stubby and fat like the rest of him, but the sniper's eyes shot to the gold band.

"Shut the fuck up and back up!" she barked.

"Why the hell should I—"

She drew the handgun. Not another word was needed. The man walked backward into the room, the sniper moving with him. Once inside, she closed the door with her foot.

The woman screamed again—sounding more genuine than before—but this time, it was out of pure fear. The sniper had no real interest in her, but she couldn't just let her go, either. Not now.

"Both of you, get on the bed, lace your fingers behind your head."

Tears were pouring down the woman's cheeks, and she seemed oblivious to the fact she sat there completely naked.

"You're married," the sniper spat in the direction of the man.

"What's it to you?"

The man sure was cocky for facing the business end of a gun. Perhaps the afterglow of sex had him feeling invincible. His ugly face was glaring at her, his mouth set in a challenging grimace.

The sniper glared right back and pulled the trigger.

The woman started to scream, and the sniper fired again. Finally…silence.

CHAPTER TWENTY-SIX

Paige and I took a commercial flight to Albuquerque and were crammed in economy seats that weren't wide enough to accommodate my shoulders. And don't get me started on the lack of legroom. We should have booked the exit row.

Paige took the window seat, and I sat in the one next to the aisle. Our elbows were pressed together on the armrest. I understood that airlines had to make money, too, but touching her was driving me a little mad, and the smell of her perfume was intoxicating. I had to squeeze it all out. *Think of Becky. Think of your job.*

Paige looked over at me and smiled awkwardly. She was just as uncomfortable as I was, and I found that comforting. The saying "misery loves company" came to mind.

"This is strange, isn't it?" I said, thinking maybe it was best to put a floodlight on the elephant in the room.

"Us working together? Ah, yeah."

My mother would likely say something to the effect that one's character grew during challenging circumstances, not easygoing times. Maybe personal growth was overrated. "I'm certainly no Zach."

"Nope." She grinned and glanced out the window, not that there was anything to see. We'd left the ground in Washington, DC, around two in the morning and were only an hour into our four-and-a-half-hour flight to Albuquerque, New Mexico.

"Well, you're no Jack, either."

She faced me again. "Ha-ha."

"Take that as a compliment," I said with a smile.

"Uh-huh. I'm probably easier on you."

Yes and no…Depends on how you look at it.

She stared into my eyes. "How are you and Becky, by the way?"

"Ah, good. No complaints." The image of Becky flashed in my mind, and I shoved aside the feelings of guilt that came with it. After all, I hadn't done anything to wrong her. I just didn't want to move in together and had asked her to remove her spare toothbrush from my place. "We're taking things a bit slower than we had been."

"Oh." Summed up in one little utterance, not much more than a guttural response: she pegged our relationship as doomed.

"It's a good thing," I assured her, but wasn't sure whether I was trying to convince her or myself.

"If you say so. Slow can just be stagnant."

"Slow can just be slow, too," I snapped.

Paige just kept looking into my eyes. "You guys are good together. Don't mess it up because you fear commitment."

"You're one to talk!" I lashed back. Being accused of the exact thing I was guilty of stung beyond measure, like alcohol poured on an open wound. "You probably slept with me in the first place because I was married and there'd be no pressure for you to commit to our relationship." The words were out in a torrent, and the pain that washed over her face slammed me in the chest. "I'm sor—"

Her eyes glistened in the dim light of the cabin. "I don't want to hear it. Not at all. Let's just keep things professional. We have a job to do; we do it. All this personal stuff—and the history between us—I'm so over it."

I was wise enough not to point out that she'd been the one to bring up "this personal stuff" when she'd asked about Becky. "Works for me," I said coolly and leaned my head against the back of my chair and closed my eyes.

I didn't open them again until Paige was nudging my elbow.

"Wake up."

I peeked through slits and groaned. "What—"

Paige pointed to the aisle, and I followed the direction of her finger.

A flight attendant was staring back at me. "If you could straighten your chair, sir."

It took a few seconds for her words to penetrate; my mind was so groggy, and I didn't remember reclining the seat. I fumbled for the button on the chair and leaned forward to return the back to an upright position. I felt across my waist, and my belt was still on. I wouldn't have taken it off the entire flight.

"Thank you, sir." The attendant smiled, and I wondered how many more times she'd say *sir* before we landed. She left, and I turned to Paige.

"I didn't even hear the announcement that we were descending." My words probably came across as a mumble.

"You probably couldn't hear it over your snoring."

I felt my cheeks heat—and that was a hard feat to accomplish. "Whatcha gonna do." *Play it cool.*

She smirked. I recalled our argument before I'd nodded off, and my stomach soured.

"You get any sleep?" I asked.

"Not really." Her eyes burrowed into mine.

"Oh, my snoring?"

"Maybe, but it's okay. If it wasn't that, it was—" She gave a furtive glance between our seats and pointed a finger behind us. Between the crack, a young boy was smiling at me, mischievousness smeared all over his face.

"And you wonder why I don't want kids," I whispered.

"Never have, but it's not the kids who are the problem so much as the parents."

I couldn't disagree with her there. For some reason, parents these days let their kids get away with so much more than those from my generation. Lazy parenting? Hard to know precisely, given that I had no personal experience in that regard.

The plane started swerving from side to side like it was sliding on ice.

I gripped the arms of my chair and ended up putting my hand right on top of Paige's and squeezing. She pulled back like she'd been scalded by hot water.

"Sorry. I didn't mean to—"

"It's fine."

A mumbled voice came over the speakers, and all I could make out was, "Ladies and gentlemen…turbulence… nothing to worry about."

I took a steady breath. A plane crash or facing Paige on the ground—I wasn't sure which would be worse. At least with the former, it would be over quickly.

CHAPTER TWENTY-SEVEN

Spencer's Sport Bar lived up to its name. LED signs advertised beers and spirits, and pennants were tagged up everywhere. The bar was positioned in the middle of the room with televisions mounted to shelving that housed bottles of alcohol and glasses.

Kelly hung back a bit, letting Jack lead the way. She was feeling more than a little angry with him. It seemed like every time she opened her mouth, he was ready to criticize. But from her experience, part of what solved cases was tossing out hypotheticals and seeing what stuck. It would seem that wasn't welcome on Jack's team—at least not by her.

The bar was bustling for being close to one o'clock Saturday morning, though Kelly remembered in her twenties she and her friends never left home for the clubs until midnight. Not that Kelly was a major fan of clubbing.

Jack squeezed between a few guys at the bar and flagged down the server behind the counter. Kelly was behind Jack, but she could discern that he was holding up his badge. If nothing else, aggravation on the bartender's face gave that away.

The server waved for Jack to follow him, and Kelly stuck close on his heels. They were taken into the kitchen before the server turned around, crossed his arms.

"What can I do for you, Officer?" The twentysomething guy leveled the question as a challenge on Jack, but briefly slid his gaze to Kelly.

"*FBI*," Jack corrected. "Agents Harper and Marsh. We need to speak to the bartender who was working last night at eleven."

"You're looking at him." He clasped his hands in front of himself and shifted his weight to his heels, like he was posing for a gangster portrait.

"And your name?" Jack prompted.

"Cody Banks."

"Well, Cody, did you see this man in here last night?" Jack pulled out his phone and brought up an image of Darrell Reid, held his screen for the server to see.

"I know him, if that's what you're asking. Name's Darrell Reid, some fancy prosecutor, from what I understand. What about him?"

"You know him, okay, but what I had asked was whether you saw him last night. Did you?"

"I might have."

"A yes or no answer will suffice."

"Yes." The word came out resembling a hiss.

"Was he here by himself?" Kelly cut herself into the conversation. Cody looked at her.

"He was with a woman. Good-looking thing, too." Cody's predatory gaze took in her entire body, and she felt the need for a shower.

Kelly swallowed her instant dislike for this guy. *Thing* was never a way to describe a woman. "Do you know her name?"

"Never got it. Nope." Cody peered into Kelly's eyes, licked his lips.

Unbelievable! Kelly squared her shoulders, peacocked her stance. "What did she look like?"

"Brown hair, long, past her shoulders, and she had almond-shaped eyes, rosebud lips."

Rosebud lips? "Okay, body shape," Kelly said. "Tall? Short?"

"Trim and fine." Cody smiled and flashed a bit of his teeth with the expression. He looked like a carnivore about to snack on his prey. Kelly detested that she was being eyed as the quarry.

"Did she come in with Mr. Reid?" Jack asked.

"No. She met him here, and I think they left together. Now, whether they went somewhere after that, I don't know."

If this woman was also their sniper, Kelly almost respected that she could be so deceitful and put herself so close to her target. "Has she been in here before?"

"She has, and it's always with Mr. Reid. The guy's— what?—in his fifties, and she's maybe thirtysomething. He either knows what he's doing, or he pays for her time."

"She strike you as a hooker?" Jack inquired.

"Nah, not really. Maybe a high-end escort, but definitely not a street hooker. She dressed too nice."

Kelly nodded, only half interested. Cody had said, *"It's always with Mr. Reid."* She asked, "How long have the two of them been coming here together?"

"Say about six months, maybe more."

Six months ago, their sniper had been in New Mexico, so if anything, Cody had just described Reid's mistress— not his would-be killer—but they still needed to speak with her. "She didn't by chance pay her own tab? Maybe by credit card?"

"Nah, that lawyer picked up the check. Don't blame him. Women as fine as that don't have to pay for anything."

Kelly clenched her hands, her fingernails digging into her palms.

"You said they left together," Jack said. "What time was that?"

"Say around eleven."

Jack produced a card from his pocket and handed it to Cody. "You suddenly remember her name, call me. Got it?"

Cody tucked the card into a back pocket. "Sure."

Jack was the first to turn his back on this doofus, but Kelly happily followed his lead.

Outside, she inhaled the fresh night—early morning—air. Who cared that it was riddled with car exhaust and other pollutants? It still worked to clear her mind of Cody and his objectification of women. It was sad to think men like that were still around in the twenty-first century, though she'd dated one a year ago. He was Mr. Charmer until his veneer wore off, which didn't take too long. He was probably why she had a sensitivity to sleazeballs.

Jack stepped up next to her and nudged his head toward the bar. "It was a long shot coming here."

Is he trying to make me feel better or worse?

"Sometimes long shots pay off." The words spilled from her lips, and she pinched her eyes shut. "I'm sorry, Jack. I didn't mean to—"

"Hey, nothing to be sorry for." He started toward the SUV, and she followed. "It only made sense for us to come here."

His comment rendered her silent for a few seconds. "I didn't mean to be disrespectful." Of course, the minute she said the words, she regretted them. Why did she continue to apologize? If anything, he owed her an apology. He'd been disrespectful to her from the start of this case. She felt her temper ripple through her, and she tried to tamp it down with logic. Jack was the boss and, as such, could treat her however he was inclined. He was still a grand improvement over her sergeant in the Miami PD. If she didn't get her emotions under control and watch her mouth, she'd be sent packing and back to him, tail between her legs, and that's the last thing she wanted.

Once in the SUV, she did up her seat belt. "We really do need to find Reid's mistress," she said, keeping all emotion out of her statement. "She's not our sniper, given what Cody said about them coming here for six months together, but the mistress might have seen someone who stood out to her."

"Don't disagree, and we'll find her, but it's likely not to be tonight."

She glanced at the clock on the vehicle's dash. *1:40 AM.* "That's a good bet."

"Pretty much. Let's catch some sleep, reconvene at the station about eight."

"Sounds good," she said—and it did—but she wasn't sure the Sandman would visit her. She'd left everything behind for this job, and she was sure as hell going to make it work. If only the investigation would cooperate with her efforts.

CHAPTER TWENTY-EIGHT

When Paige's eyes fluttered open that morning, her first thought was that she was in New Mexico. The second hit much harder: the memory of Brandon's hand squeezing hers and the damn chemistry that crackled when they'd touched. It was hard for her to imagine as she'd never let herself fall so hard before Brandon, so why now, and why did it have to be him?

"Paige!" Brandon shouted from the passenger seat, jolting her, and causing her to torque the wheel. An oncoming car blared its horn. She swerved back into their lane.

"Are you trying to kill us?"

"Uh, sorry."

"Yeah, I'd say. You want me to drive, just say the word."

"No, I'll be fine."

"Says you. Your mind's run off somewhere."

"I'm fine," she articulated clearly through clenched teeth. To hell with opening up to him about her feelings. She'd tried to make nice on the plane ride, and that had backfired. Yes, professional was how she'd keep things between her and Brandon going forward. She really had to let go of the notion that happily-ever-after existed. *What a schmuck!*

"Tired?" he asked.

She applied more pressure to the gas. They were on the way to speak with Wise's widow, and the sooner they got there, the better. "Like you wouldn't believe. You?"

"You bet. I usually prefer a little more than a few hours' sleep."

Their flight had landed in Albuquerque at sixty thirty local time that morning, and they had picked up an SUV at the local FBI office. When they called Jack to confirm their arrival in New Mexico, he had filled them in about his and Kelly's visit to Spencer's Sport Bar. After that, they'd checked into a hotel and grabbed a few hours' sleep before hitting the road about ten. It was now almost half-past. It felt like they'd packed a day's worth of activity in already.

"In one hundred meters, your destination will be on the right."

Paige canceled the route on the GPS and stopped in front of a modest-size, beige stucco bungalow with a clay-tile roof, packed close to neighboring houses. The front lot was wood chips and stone with a rather sad-looking tree growing in the middle.

"You have reached our destination." Paige mocked what the GPS would have said if it were still on. She got out, led the way to the front door, and knocked.

Footsteps came toward the door, and it opened to reveal a beautiful woman all of maybe five-foot-four with a blond bob. "Yes?"

Paige held up her badge; so did Brandon.

"We're agents with the FBI." Paige introduced them, then asked, "Are you Sonia Wise?"

"Uh-huh."

"We'd like to ask you a few questions—"

"About Robert, let me guess," she cut in and crossed her arms. "That man best be happy he's six feet under, or I'd put him there myself."

Small yet powerful. And feisty!

Paige stepped back. "Can we come inside for a minute or two?"

"Why not? Nothing better to do than talk about that good-for-nothing son of a bitch." Obvious sarcasm—every word—but she swung the door wide open.

Paige gestured for Brandon to go in first.

"I talked with the police. Many times. I don't know what more I can tell you." Sonia reached around them and latched the door. "Certainly can't give you anything new. But honestly, I don't even care if his killer is caught."

"You do—" Paige choked on her own saliva. "Ahem, you don't—"

"Nope, don't care. You catch 'im, I'd like to thank 'im, actually."

Brandon glanced at Paige, back at Sonia. "Do you have someplace we could sit and talk?"

"Yeah, this way." She took them to a living room where she dropped onto a couch and gestured for Brandon and Paige to sit in matching chairs. They took her up on the offer.

"We're sorry for your loss," Paige offered, expecting the condolence to be poorly received.

"Nah, don't be. I'm happier now."

Yep, just as I thought... "Did you and your husband have a rocky marriage?"

Sonia scoffed laughter. "That's putting it mildly. You probably know that we were in marriage counseling?"

Paige nodded. It was the pent-up hostility they hadn't been aware of.

"It wasn't working," Sonia stamped out. "Well, obviously."

Paige glanced at Brandon briefly, then turned her focus back on Sonia. "*Obviously?* I think Agent Fisher and I might be missing something."

"You must be. That man was a cheating bastard 'til the day he died."

Sherman's widow in Tennessee—the shooting from a month ago—had received photographs of her husband with another woman. Had Sonia come into possession of her own? "How do you know he'd cheated on you?"

Sonia sat back in the couch, and her feet dangled a few inches above the floor. "I'd find lipstick on his collar, and his shirts would smell like perfume—not mine."

Paige deflated. It was too much to hope she'd received compromising photos that might advance the case.

Sonia went on. "I'd asked him about it, and he'd always come up with a story to explain it away." She rolled her eyes dramatically. "To even think I ever thought that he wanted to make the marriage work…"

Brandon broke into her thoughts. "Was marriage counseling his idea?"

"Sure was. He even swore to me—said he would on a stack of Bibles—that he wanted to make things right between us."

"As you said, it didn't do any good?" Brandon asked.

"I thought it was helping at first." Color touched Sonia's cheeks. "But apparently it wasn't. I got pictures… You know of him in…" She flailed her hands around. "In situations… with other women."

Paige sat up straighter. Sonia had pictures. "Nothing was said about this in the investigation files."

"I received them a bit after everyone lost interest. Besides, it's embarrassing enough to have your husband cheat on you, but to advertise it all over? No thanks. I'd look like a complete dope."

Paige understood Sonia's bitterness now. It had been seeing her husband in action and the hit to her pride. "You said you got them after everyone lost interest. When was that?"

"Ah, say a few weeks after his death."

"And how did you come into possession of them?" Brandon asked.

"They were in my mailbox." Stated rather bluntly and matter-of-factly.

Paige shuffled to the edge of the cushion. They could have a chance at finding out where they were mailed from and, even more importantly, by whom. "Do you still have them? And the envelope they came in?"

Sonia's eyes flickered, and she shifted her gaze briefly to Brandon. "What am I missing?"

"We believe that the same person who killed your husband may have killed three other men," Brandon laid out.

Sonia's face was stoic, then her mouth twitched, and she laughed.

"Sonia?" Paige wasn't sure what to make of her reaction.

Sonia waved at the air. "Just like Robert. It's not even funny, actually, but look at me." Tears were streaming down her cheeks from laughter.

Watching Sonia's display was unsettling. "What's like Robert?"

"He always loved the spotlight."

Paige would hardly call being the target of a serial killer the spotlight anyone would want.

"And he had a golden touch," Sonia added, sniffling and starting to calm down.

Wise's so-called "golden touch" had some lackluster magic. Murdered and he'd worked as a plumber when he was alive—and he was married to this "treat" of a woman in front of them.

"Ah, I know what you're thinking. *Some golden touch— am I right?*"

Pretty much, yep.

Sonia went on. "Well, we might not have been rolling in dough, but he'd get things handed to him all the time. Rob first met Cecil—that's the owner of Star Plumbing where he'd worked—when he pulled over to help him and his wife at the side of the road. We'd just moved into the area. We came from Walker, California. Anyway, he was still looking for work. I had a little part-time gig at a dentist's office. Manned the desk, answered the phones, scheduled appointments. Real mind-numbing stuff." Sonia pointed a finger-gun to her ear and pulled the trigger. "Anyway, Robert gets to talking with Cecil and his wife, and he mentions that he's looking for work. Cecil took an instant liking to Robert, asked him if he knew anything about plumbing. Robert knew *nada*. Made no difference to Cecil in the end. He took Robert under his wing, taught him everything he knew, helped him get licensed—all while paying him a decent salary."

Sonia had given them everything and a song and dance, but Paige still failed to understand the full scope of "golden touch" as applying to her husband. But how to phrase her confusion… "That's wonderful, but I guess I'm missing how your husband could have had a golden touch when it comes to him being the target of a serial killer."

"You're not going to tell me that the way he went out didn't already draw media attention—and now the FBI thinks there was a serial killer behind his death. The press will have a field day. He'll be famous." She shook her head, frowning, and anger was setting into her eyes. "Just like him to get the limelight without working for it. It just came to him."

If being murdered is how one attains fame, count me out!

"Do you still have those photos?" Paige realized Sonia had never answered that.

"I do." Sonia made no move to get up and looked at Brandon. "The other men you mentioned…Were they all married and cheating scumbags like my Robert?"

Brandon visibly swallowed roughly.

Paige stepped in. "We believe it's possible, yes."

Sonia slapped her knee. "Well, isn't that something. Whoever's pulling the trigger, bravo! Eliminating one more cheating—"

"Murder is against the law, Mrs. Wise," Brandon said firmly.

"You know what? Just call me Sonia. I'm going to revert back to my maiden name. Should've gotten the process started already."

"It doesn't matter who the victim is or what they did or supposedly did," Brandon put out with venom. "Killing people is illegal. In some states, worthy of the death penalty."

Paige faced Brandon and widened her eyes, silently asking that he cool it.

"Yeah, ah, I'll get you those pictures and that envelope. Then I think it's time you be going." Sonia left the room.

Paige turned on Brandon. "What the hell are—"

He turned to face her, his stark expression said it all: *just leave it alone.* But to hell with that. If Brandon wanted to keep things professional between them, then it was about time he realized she was the senior agent and he the subordinate. She was just about to point this out to him when Sonia returned and put the envelope in Paige's face.

"Now, if you'd leave."

Paige took the envelope and frowned upon noticing there wasn't a postmark, just a simple label with Sonia's name printed on it from a computer. It would have just been dropped off and placed it in her mailbox. "Thank you."

"Uh-huh." Sonia crossed her arms, and Paige and Brandon saw themselves out.

Paige was the first to hit the front door, and her angry steps took her to the SUV in a few strides. She waited until she pulled out onto the street. "I don't know what the hell is going on with you—"

"It's none of your—"

"Right, I get that. Our relationship is professional, and trust me, I'm completely fine with that," she snapped. "But as professionals, you're the junior agent in this car. You can't talk to people the way you did in there. It's completely unprofessional and unacceptable."

Brandon didn't say a word and kept facing out the passenger window.

"Did you hear me?" she barked.

"I heard you."

"Good. Then let's get on with it." She might have put her foot down on the gas a little heavier than intended.

CHAPTER TWENTY-NINE

Kelly was able to get some sleep, but only because she'd been able to connect with her friend Brianna before tucking in. Brianna was a defense attorney who kept hours like a vampire and got by on five hours' or less of slumber each night. Kelly had caught Brianna drinking a scotch at By the Drink, a play on the saying "by the book"—something lawyer types seemed to appreciate.

Brianna didn't even need to ask how Kelly was; her astute nature aided her in life more than just in the courtroom. All it took was for Kelly to say, "Hi, how are you?" and Brianna had known something was up with her friend. Kelly went on to share how Jack was treating her, and how ridiculous and small she felt at times as a result.

"He's just applying pressure, seeing if you have what it takes to stick it out."

"I'm starting to wonder if I do."

"Now who's being ridiculous? You don't know the meaning of giving up."

Brianna would know that to be true. She'd seen Kelly's struggle over the years as she tried to come to terms with the fact her mother didn't want to be found.

"But you could have been a lawyer," Brianna said in a singsong voice, as if practicing law was all rose petals.

Kelly had seriously considered that career path—briefly. After all, if her mother had had a better lawyer, she wouldn't have served twenty-five years for a murder she'd made in self-defense. Then maybe everything would be different. But Kelly had decided to be more proactive in her line of work and chose a profession that made it possible to ensure charges were only levied against the guilty.

"I just don't know if I'm cut out for—"

"You are."

Two words, and they might as well have been jackhammered into concrete the way her friend had said them.

"Just give the job time. You've wanted to be FBI for how many years?"

"Oh, let's not dwell on that." She was thirty-three now, but some days, she felt much older. Her twenties felt lightyears behind her.

Brianna laughed her terrific laugh that made a person feel like they'd dipped into a cool spring on a warm day.

"Thanks."

"Anytime, love." With that, Brianna hung up, leaving Kelly feeling better, if not a bit conflicted. Maybe she'd just raised the idea of becoming an FBI agent to impractical standards.

But that pessimism belonged to hours ago, before she got some shut-eye and put in some hours at Arlington PD with Jack. She even managed to keep that enthusiasm when Jack returned from having a smoke break and walked back into the conference room with his phone in his hand and a scowl on his face. Her stomach sank.

"What is it? Paige and Bran—"

"They're fine. Got a call from Bert Pryce, though. We've got to head over to the Reids' place immediately."

She jumped from her chair, then glanced at the coffee left in her mug and briefly wished it was in a to-go cup. "What's happened?"

"Arlene Reid received a package on her doorstep," Jack said as they hurried through the station hallways for the parking lot.

Kelly thought about the previous cases and drew a conclusion. "Did she receive pictures of her husband with another woman?"

He regarded her like she was clairvoyant. "That's right, and from the description of the woman in the photo, it could be the woman from Spencer's Sports Bar."

Bert Pryce answered the door for Kelly and Jack.

"She's not coping with this very well." Bert led them toward the study where they'd last talked yesterday.

There was no sign of other family members milling about, and the driveway had been empty.

"Are you any closer to figuring out who killed Darrell? Not that I care personally, but…"

Sobs could be heard from behind the door to the den.

Bert knocked.

"Ah…come in." There was a series of sniffles, and when Bert opened the door, Arlene was dabbing her eyes with an embroidered handkerchief, similar to the one from yesterday.

On the coffee table in front of her was a manila envelope and a spread of photographs.

"I can't even bring myself to look at them, but at the same time, I can't look away. I just can't believe Darrell would do such a thing. Someone must have doctored these. He was a powerful man. He had enemies."

Was Arlene really that obtuse to believe Darrell had been "husband of the year"? She had been with them at Wilson Place yesterday, when the clerk mentioned Darrell going there with a woman. Still, Kelly said, "We will have the authenticity of the photos examined." She gestured toward them. "Do you mind?"

"Go ahead." Arlene sighed.

Kelly gloved up, and she shuffled through them slowly, studying each one and holding them so Jack could see them, too. There was a total of three. One had been taken from the outside looking in at presumably Pryce's condo and showed a couple having sex against the window. Reid's face was easy enough to make out. Not too smart for a prosecutor to be so blatant; anyone could have seen him. The angle of the shot would indicate it was taken from somewhere higher than the tenth floor; it could have been taken from a higher level in the Colonial Hotel.

Another photo showed Reid and the woman outside a brick building, again it could be Wilson Place. They were sharing a passionate kiss and an intimate embrace. The third showed Reid and the woman nuzzled into a booth at a bar. The glass shelves and layout were familiar. Kelly pointed the photo out to Jack and would tell him back in the car, but this picture had been taken at Spencer's Sports Bar, without a doubt in her mind.

Kelly slipped the photos into a plastic evidence bag when she finished, along with the envelope they'd been delivered in. She noted that the envelope was absent any markings from the postal service and had only a simple printed label that read ARLENE REID.

Arlene leaned into the arm of the couch and angled her body toward Kelly. "Do you think they were forged?"

Kelly could appreciate Arlene wanting to know, but at the same time, her refusal to entertain the evidence before her was either pathetic and naive on her part or a good act. "It's not my realm of expertise," was all Kelly said. But if she were to go by her gut, she'd say the photos were legit.

"Mrs. Reid, your father said these photos were at your door when you woke up," Jack started. "Had anyone knocked?"

Arlene gripped at the hem of her sweater and shook her head. "I used to get the paper off the stoop in the morning for Darrell, but forgot today with everything that happened. And Dad just found it when he was going to step out for some groceries." Her voice cracked, and she pinched her nose, sniffled, dropped her hand.

"And the envelope with the pictures was where exactly?" Jack inquired.

"Underneath the paper."

"When does the paper normally get delivered?" Kelly was hoping to get some sort of a timeline as to when the mysterious messenger had been there. Though she imagined it would have been after the paper delivery.

"It was usually there when I'd check at seven. That's all I really know."

"It's okay," Kelly assured her, but it wasn't, from her standpoint.

"We're going to need to know where you were yesterday morning, Mrs. Reid," Jack said coolly.

"I was here. I'm sure I told you that."

"And you really had no idea that your husband was cheating on you?" Skepticism was deeply embedded in his tone.

"No, and I still don't think he was."

"Even with the evidence before you." Jack gestured toward the bagged envelope and incriminating photographs.

"Who's to say the pictures are even legit?" Arlene glanced hopefully at Kelly, but Kelly wasn't about to come to the woman's defense.

Kelly suspected Jack's tolerance for this woman's naivety had reached its threshold. It could be possible that Arlene was working with the sniper. But if the three previous murders were connected to her husband's, had she been involved with them, too? It would seem unlikely.

"Why do you resist acknowledging even the possibility that your husband was unfaithful?" Jack pressured.

Arlene wet her lips. "The thought…it's…it's humiliating."

Is that the real reason she refuses to acknowledge her husband's affair?

Jack matched his gaze with Arlene's. "You'd want to stop that embarrassment."

Arlene glanced at her father with the desperateness of a drowning person eyeing a life raft. Kelly followed her gaze and realized that Bert hadn't said a word since they came into the room.

"Did you hire someone to kill your husband, Mrs. Reid?" Jack put the question out there with the subtly of a jackhammer.

Arlene blanched, and Bert grimaced.

"How dare you accuse my daughter of such an outrageous thing? We've been nothing but forthcoming, and you—"

Arlene started to sob. Kelly and Jack waited her out for a few minutes.

"Arlene," Kelly eventually said, approaching the woman with kindness.

Arlene blinked slowly. Her eyes had become marbles of pain. She kneaded the handkerchief in her hands. "Fine, yes, I knew about my husband's affairs. I just didn't want you to know."

"Because it would give you motive," Jack concluded.

Arlene didn't give any impression Jack's comment had affected her, and she instead put her attention on her father, who wouldn't meet her gaze and busily picked at the edge of the chair's arm. "Darrell and I have had our share of problems for years now. He was always so busy with his work, and I admired him for that—but it also got very lonely. I don't have to work outside the home. Heck, I don't even need to work *around* the home. I have everything, yet nothing." She dabbed the handkerchief to her nose. "I was so lonely."

Yet, just yesterday, she had told them that Darrell always had time for her. It was hard to believe anything she said.

Arlene carried on. "I had my own lovers. Darrell had his. Please, Daddy, I know how you must feel about this. Such a disappointment I must be."

As Arlene spoke, Bert's eyes filled with tears. By the time she'd finished, they were narrowed and full of indignation. "You have betrayed the sanctity of marriage." He got up, walked to a bar cart in the corner of the room, and poured himself two fingers' worth of an amber liquid from a crystal decanter into a rocks glass.

"If we look at your financial records, are we going to find proof you hired someone to take him out?" Jack asked.

"No." Arlene gulped air, and her chest heaved. "I never killed him or had him killed; I swear to you."

"The truth has a way of coming out."

Arlene clenched her jaw. "Good. Then you'll know I'm innocent!"

"It's time for you to leave." Bert kicked back the rest of his drink and slammed the glass on the cart.

As Kelly and Jack saw themselves out, they could hear Arlene's pleas for her father to forgive her.

In the SUV, Kelly turned to Jack. "You really think she hired someone to kill her husband?"

"It seems to me you suggested a hired gun from the start."

Jack's retort soured in her gut. He was right, but her thinking had shifted. Besides, it would seem Reid's case was connected to three others in which a hired hit couldn't be proven. Then it dawned on her. "You don't really think she paid someone to kill her husband, do you?"

"Nope."

"You just wanted to elicit a reaction you could trust."

Jack nodded. "And I wanted to get a feel for Bert Pryce."

"Oh."

"There's no love spared between father- and son-in-law. That was obvious from our first meeting with Pryce."

"Sure. Are we going to check into his background?"

"Absolutely." Jack lit up a cigarette and drove them off.

Kelly glanced back at the stately Reid house. From the outside, it would appear the people living there had their lives put together, but Kelly'd had a closer look and knew better. But had one of them really commissioned the murder of Darrell Reid, husband, father, and son-in-law?

CHAPTER THIRTY

I'd thought I was miserable before Paige pulled rank. Now, I was downright crabby. We were waiting in a conference room—Paige seated at a table, me looking out a window—at the Albuquerque police station to speak with Sergeant Bell. He'd been the lead investigator on the Wise case. I was hopeful that having a third party around would serve as a buffer for all the unsettled energy. We'd already organized the forwarding of the compromising photos collected from Sonia Wise through the proper channels to Nadia in Quantico. We kept snapshots of the less racy ones on our phones, in case we needed to show the woman's face around.

"Agents." A man's voice cut through the room, and I turned toward the door.

The man was in his fifties and gave off the vibe of someone you wouldn't want to challenge, much like Jack. His life experience had hardened his appearance and was etched in his eyes and in the lines on his face. He wore a button-up shirt, tie, and slacks.

"Sergeant Bell, I presume?" I walked over to him and held out a hand. "I'm FBI Special Agent Brandon Fisher."

"Nice to meet you." Bell took my hand and looked past me to Paige, who introduced herself and shot me a glare for not doing so for her. The sergeant closed the door, then shook her hand. "I understand you're here about the Wise case," he said, tugging on the waist of his pants and taking a seat next to Paige.

"We are," Paige confirmed. "Our analyst has gathered as much information on the case as she could via the database, but sometimes, there are things it can't tell us."

"Everything should be in the file." He pointed to the closed folder in front of Paige, referring to the investigation records as a whole.

Paige left the folder untouched. "I'm more interested in your feelings about the case. For example, what was your impression of the widow? How did she seem to you in the aftermath of her husband's death?"

"Well, I wish I could say I was one of those people who remembered everything, but the shooting was six months ago. I've worked a lot of cases since then."

"Probably some not quite as memorable," I said.

Bell grimaced and said nothing.

For some reason, Bell was on the defense. I dropped into a chair across from him. "We're not here to step on any toes or find fault with how the investigation was handled. We've found ourselves in a situation. You might have heard there was a shooting in Arlington, Virginia, yesterday morning." I paused to give Bell a chance to respond, but he simply kept staring at me. I went on. "A prosecutor was killed. Male. The only victim. Just like in the case of Robert Wise six months ago, here in Albuquerque."

Bell adjusted his tie. "Let me see if I'm understanding what you're saying without actually coming out and saying it. You think the person who killed Wise also killed your prosecutor."

"And two other men in the last three months," Paige interjected.

"An active serial killer?"

"That's the way we're leaning, with a possibility that person may also be a hired gun." I prepared for backlash. Many law enforcement types considered the conclusion of a "serial killer" just hype.

"Nothing about the Wise shooting indicated that. Why blow it up and make it something it isn't? It wasn't anything more than an isolated incident."

"We agree that taken on its own, Wise's shooting didn't indicate an active threat," I assured him. "But now we have three other murders. Trust me when I say we're not here to point blame or accuse the Albuquerque PD—" best to widen the scope and keep it less personal "—for any of the subsequent shootings."

Bell's shoulders slumped. He might have been defensive before; now it seemed he fought with his conscience.

"No one could have seen the other murders coming," I said. "And even if you had, finding the shooter would have been a huge challenge."

"Try *impossible*, because I did all I could," Bell shot back.

"I don't doubt it." This guy had a more volatile temper than I did.

Bell's jaw clenched, and his gaze met mine briefly before he looked off into the distance. "She was upset...Wise's widow. I'm mean, rightfully. She and her husband were working to set their marriage right. Turning it around."

Suddenly, his memory is back!

"Was she open with you about her husband's affairs?" Paige asked.

"I believe you'll find that in the file," Bell said brashly. "But she never cried, which I found strange. They'd been married for twenty-two years. You'd think she'd be able to shed a tear for her dearly departed."

Except he was a cheating son of a bitch, and so am I! My internal judgment came so quickly, so harshly, it stole my breath.

"We paid Mrs. Wise a visit this morning before coming here," Paige admitted, earning Bell's steely gaze.

"I would have appreciated a heads-up."

"We don't have to clear anything past you, Sergeant," Paige said. "As we told you, we believe the same person who killed Wise has killed at least three others. Each time there's a sniping, there's only one victim. All of them are married, all of them with marital problems."

"The husbands were disloyal," I stamped out.

"You're telling me that some person's out there knocking off adulterous men? They'd have their work cut out for them," Bell scoffed, looking at me. His expression was one of man-to-man, as if cheating should be accepted as something guys just did—or was I grasping to feel excused for my actions?

"We don't know the killer's motivation yet, though what you stated is possible," Paige said.

"In at least three cases, the widows received photographs of their husbands in compromising situations with other women," I offered, earning Bell's gaze. Jack had reached us before our meeting here and told us about the photos sent to Arlene Reid.

"Mrs. Wise didn't receive such pictures." He started with confidence, but it melted away the longer he peered into my eyes. "She did?"

I nodded. "But after the interest in solving the case had died down."

"She wasn't really motivated after receiving the pictures, either," Paige contributed. "Doesn't even care if her husband's killer is found. Went so far as to say if we caught his killer, she'd thank them."

"Wow. Okay, here's the thing, though. You brought up the possibility of a hit man, which I couldn't find evidence to support, but answer this: why would a hit man send the type of pictures you described? They'd send pictures of the dead body to prove they finished the job."

I faced Paige; it was starting to sink in that we were after a serial killer acting on his or her own agenda. "Can you excuse us?" I said to Bell and motioned for Paige to follow me to the hall. "Bell's right, and it was under our nose. A hired gun wouldn't have any reason to send compromising photos of the husbands."

"Unless it wasn't the wives who hired the hit, and whoever did wanted to ease their grief by letting them know the type of men their husbands were."

I stared at her blankly. "That's the exact opposite of what you thought yesterday when you said the wives may have been sent the photos to hurt them."

"I know." She sighed. "Okay, so let's say our killer is acting on their own initiative. Then what does the sniper stand to gain from sending the pictures? And why snipe the targets?" Paige paced, circled back.

"We figure the sniper is probably military, someone given the proper training with a rifle," I said. "He or she is using this method to kill, so it makes sense to say sniping is something they're comfortable with doing."

"Maybe they're a sharpshooter, someone who ranked high in their qualifications. But where do we even begin in tracking them down?"

"Well, it's almost like our killer is locked into the mindset of a sniper. They could be someone who served in an active war zone and had to kill people."

"Sure. I'm still missing how we narrow that down," Paige said.

"They—" I stopped short for a second. "I just realized we haven't decided whether our sniper is a man or a woman. I thought we were going with a woman."

"I don't know. Not attaching to either, just remaining objective. Anyway, focus…there's less time between the murders. Maybe they're battling with their own mind?"

"Yeah. Why not? And assuming the sniper saw an active war zone, they could be diagnosed with PTSD," I said. "Still hard to narrow down, I'm sure. There have to be hundreds or thousands who might meet that criteria."

Paige frowned, and I was with her. I hated that the very people who protected our freedoms so often returned damaged, everything they had before, gone—including their health.

"Except I'd say she probably left the service in the last year or even closer to the time she killed Robert Wise. If she does have posttraumatic stress disorder and was discharged earlier than that, I think we'd be looking at more victims," I said.

Paige shrugged. "Maybe we just don't know about them."

I nodded at the solemn thought.

"I think we should let Jack and Kelly know what we're thinking," she said.

"Including what Bell pointed out?"

"Yeah, but I say we leave him out of it."

I smiled.

"And our thoughts on the killer's mental state, possible health," she added.

"I agree." I pulled out my phone, feeling like we were finally making headway with this case.

CHAPTER THIRTY-ONE

Arlington, Virginia
Friday, October 25th, 1:15 PM Local Time

Kelly glanced over at Jack behind the wheel of the SUV. They'd just left the Reids' house and were driving down the street. She assumed they were headed back to Quantico to log the photos into evidence, but she wasn't positive what their next step would be after that. She was about to ask Jack when his phone rang. He answered, and the caller's voice came over the car's speakers.

"Captain Herrera here. Forensics got a hit on fingerprints lifted from a wineglass in Pryce's condo. We now know who our mystery woman is. Sending a picture now."

The message icon showed on the vehicle's display. Jack pulled to the curb, brought up the image on his phone, and held it for Kelly to see.

She'd seen that picture before—in the photos with Darrell Reid. "She's a familiar face."

"You think so, too?" Herrera sounded surprised, which piqued Kelly's curiosity.

The captain wouldn't have seen the compromising pictures yet and might not even know about them. "Where did you see her before?"

"I was going to ask the same of you."

"Arlene Reid received some photographs of her husband with this woman," Jack said. "Your turn."

There was a smoldering silence on the other end.

"Captain?" Jack prompted.

A few more seconds passed before Herrera spoke. It was evident the captain wasn't too impressed with Jack's failure to communicate again. "Remember I mentioned a woman with chest pains yesterday, the one taken to the hospital? Well, that's her."

"They'd probably just left Pryce's condo," Jack reasoned.

Kelly wondered why she hadn't come forward about knowing and being with Reid. Surely, she had to have heard he'd been the one killed unless— "She okay? Did something serious happen to her?" *A heart attack*, Kelly was screaming in her mind, remembering the horror when her grandfather had his.

"No, she was checked at the hospital and released within an hour."

"Did she mention Reid in her statement to your officers?" Jack asked.

"Like I said, there wasn't much conversation."

Jack looked over at Kelly, and if there was one face that said *unimpressed*, she was seeing it: brow furrowed, eyes darkened, mouth set in a scowl.

"What's her name?" Jack prompted.

"Jane Powell, thirty-five," Herrera said. "Police brought her in for solicitation a couple years ago."

"What was Powell's sentence?" Kelly asked.

"Nothing. The prosecution—a.k.a. Darrell Reid—was assigned the case and had the charges dropped. Good for us, her prints weren't removed from the system." Herrera took a pause, then added, "You might also care to know that Powell is a self-made millionaire. She started up some jewelry line called Pixie Jewels six months after the charges were dropped. The company's worth three million today."

"Quite the change in luck," Kelly said, suspicious of whether Powell's success was at all related to Darrell Reid and what—if anything—that could mean.

"I'd say. I'll shoot her info over now. You might want to pay her a visit."

"No question there," Jack replied drily. "Any updates on the missing maid?"

"As you know, we were waiting for the building manager to return. He just got back, so I have officers headed there now, and I plan to meet up with them. I'll keep you posted on what we find." There seemed to be an enclosed request that Jack start doing the same for the captain.

"Thanks." Jack ended the call and selected *Nadia* from the favorites list. She answered on the second ring, and he got right into the reason he called. "We need you to dig a bit into a woman by the name of Jane Powell. She was Reid's mistress. See if she has any connection to the previous victims."

"You got it, Jack."

"Thanks." He clicked off and looked over at Kelly. "We just want to cover all—" Then his phone rang, and caller ID showed it was Brandon.

"Whatcha got?" Jack answered.

"We really think we're looking for a serial killer acting of her own accord," Paige said, and went on to explain how they'd concluded this because of the compromising photos sent to the widows and not proof of death. "Wise's widow received pictures, too. Making three out of four, including Arlene Reid. Now, we figured our sniper has a military background, but Brandon and I think she might have been discharged, say, in the last year."

"I see we're going with a female sniper now?" Jack said.

"Not yet decided," Paige said.

"You said discharged—for what?" Jack turned up the speaker volume.

"Mental instabilities, PTSD, that type of thing." Paige's voice came through loud and clear.

"Oh." Kelly's skin on the back of her neck tightened, and the hairs rose on her arms. "If we're looking at someone with health issues, what about veteran hospitals? There have to be some in the vicinities of the crime scenes."

The line fell silent.

"Did we lose you?" Jack asked.

"No," Paige replied. "Hope you don't mind, Jack, but we went ahead and spoke to Nadia. We're seeing if she can narrow down snipers discharged in the last year with mental and emotional issues. We also asked about VA hospitals."

Kelly felt her heart sink. Every time she thought she'd made a great suggestion, it either went bust or someone else beat her to it.

"Anyway," Paige went on, "Nadia informed us that there's a VA hospital right here in Albuquerque, super close to our current location."

"We can just talk to the person in charge, see if we can get anywhere or if they'd have any names," Brandon added.

"Let's have Nadia do her thing first," Jack said firmly. "We'll make sure to have her check to see if there are any VA hospitals within close proximity of the other shooting sites. It's possible the sniper was treated at different locations. It might help in whittling things down to a name. Unless she's on that already?"

The ensuing silence would have given him the affirmative answer.

"With all these calls to Nadia, did you have time to track down Wise's mistress?"

"Not yet, but Brandon and I were thinking we'd visit the hotel room where the sniper had set up their nest. We could get a feel for the place ourselves and, if we're lucky, turn up a clue that might help us ID the sniper."

"Probably six months too late, but keep me posted."

"We've got an ID on Reid's mistress," Kelly shared.

"We're headed over to see her now." Jack ended the call.

"I knew it, Jack," she squeezed out, though her throat felt stitched together.

"Knew what?" Displeasure seeped into his voice, and she hated that it was directed at her.

She squared her shoulders, trying to find courage to stand up to Jack.

"Knew what, Agent?"

"Fine, I guess there's no time like the present." It was a phrase her grandfather had said often. "I stopped suspecting we were looking at a hired gun a bit ago."

"Why not voice your opinion before now?"

She clenched her hands, digging fingernails into palms. She had never held back saying her thoughts out loud until she'd joined Jack's team. Hypothesizing and talking out theories were often how cases got solved: ideas sparked, epiphanies realized, and *boom*. It also worked the other way, knocking down rubbish and clearing the way to revelations. Really, how much longer could she just keep quiet, mind her tongue, bide herself?

Her chest pinched; her heart rate sped up. "Every time I suggest something, you knock me down. It's met with 'there's not enough to go on' or 'it's too early to jump to a conclusion.' But sometimes you just need to talk out loud, see what sticks." Jack's scowl deepened as she spoke, but she was already in too far. "I say this respectfully, but I'm used to speaking my mind, my thoughts, suspicions, even my feelings—I know emotions are taboo to you. But it seems the rest of your team can say what they're thinking, and you don't jump down their throats." Her shoulders were heaving as she watched Jack and waited for a response. He was no longer scowling. He was just watching her, his eyes scanning hers. She wished he would say something, anything. Scratch that, not *anything*, not that he wanted her to pack her bags and head back to the Miami PD. Maybe she could rescue herself, backpedal. "Jack, my grandfather greatly respected you. I do, too." Her admission came as a shock to her, considering. There was a subtle flicker in his eyes—one she couldn't read. "I didn't mean to upset—"

"Is that all?"

"Yes." She gulped. Tears burned her eyes, thinking of losing this job. Maybe she'd spoken too bluntly, but it was freeing to get out how she was feeling. At the same time, had she been too open, too aggressive?

"Now, tell me why you *don't* think it was a hired gun, Agent Marsh."

"The evidence in front of us, including no proof that money exchanged hands."

"We just might not have found that trail yet. It doesn't mean one doesn't exist."

"The fact the murders are so spread out."

"The hit man is paid well and has the means to travel."

She took a deep breath, steadying herself. "The missing maid. And, yeah, she could just be missing, but if she isn't…" Kelly would leave *alive* unsaid. "She doesn't fit the previous victimology, which could mean the sniper's emotions are involved, and that could create a whole other mess." Not that she had to tell him.

"The maid could have just run off, all of this a coincidence."

She knew Jack was playing devil's advocate, but it was trying her patience. "But the maid could be dead." *There, it was out!* "And if she is, hired guns don't typically kill people for free," she added confidently.

Jack smirked.

Anger curdled in her stomach. "Am I missing something?"

"I was wondering how long it would take." He pulled out a cigarette.

"How long would what take?"

"For you to stand your ground." He lit up his cigarette and exhaled out the window. "A good agent knows when they have something, Marsh. They don't let anyone, not even their superior, talk them out of it."

My boss is a psychopath!

"All this—the way you've been indifferent with me, even rude—was a *lesson*?"

"It was." He took another drag.

Kelly wasn't sure if Jack's confession made her more angry or relieved.

"Now that we have that out of the way, is there anything else you want to tell me?" He was grinning, lopsided, with the right side of his mouth higher than the left.

"No, I think that's all for now." She narrowed her eyes at him, but if he weren't her boss, she would have punched him in the face.

CHAPTER THIRTY-TWO

You really think you're looking at a serial killer who served this country?"

Paige could feel the cynicism in every word of Sergeant Bell's question. She and Brandon had gone back into the conference room and shared an overview of their working theory that the shooter was most likely former military.

"In answer to your question," Brandon started, "we do. The person we're looking for used to be one of the good guys."

Probably still considers themselves to be, Paige thought.

"What happens to some people," Bell groaned.

"Can't disagree with you there," Paige admitted. "We'd like to take a look at the place were Wise was shot and the hotel room where the sniper built their nest."

"What's stopping you? It doesn't seem you need my permission."

Paige chose to ignore the underlying hostility toward their presence by making a peace offering. "We don't need it; you're right, but it might be beneficial for you to come along."

"How so?"

"You know the management at the hotel, for one, and it might make access to the room easier."

Bell crossed his arms.

Paige was also thinking that revisiting the scene might jog something loose from Bell's memory, but the sergeant would probably take such a comment as an accusation that his notetaking was shoddy. "You could be a big help," she added. Flattery worked on pretty much everyone.

"I've got a lot on my plate, Agent, but…" Bell let his words dangle and met her gaze.

"*But* you will?" Paige smiled pleasantly at him.

He dipped his head. "I will."

They left the room and headed to the Enchantment Hotel, where the sniper had set up for the shot that killed Robert Wise. Paige drove herself and Brandon in the SUV. Bell was going to meet them there.

Brandon looked over at her from the passenger seat. "Do you think visiting the hotel will help us find Wise's mistress? Jack's wanting us to find her."

"As I'm well aware."

"Then why not try the pub where he was shot first? They might recognize her."

"We'll get there."

"Well, you're the senior agent, so I should trust you know what you're doing."

"What the hell is going on with you?" she snapped. Maybe raising her voice at him would clear the air—even if it didn't fit the mold of "professional."

His expression was hardened. "You ever feel guilty about us?"

"Why would I—"

"Because I was married, Paige. I was married," he repeated lower.

So…what? He's having a pang of conscience all these years later? "I know that."

"Then, did you ever feel guilty?"

"You might not want to know the answer to that."

"I asked."

She took a deep breath, peered into his eyes, and told a white lie. "Never."

He pinched his eyes shut, and she looked back to the road. A few seconds later, he said, "I did."

His admission might as well have been a spear jabbed into her heart. She didn't think it was possible to regret a good thing, so he mustn't have considered their being together a good thing. At what point had she lost perspective and romanticized their relationship into something it never was? "Maybe it's time you forgave yourself."

"I thought I had," was all he said. Four words that spliced her open.

She blinked back the hurt—mad at herself that she even felt anything—and focused on driving. Not long later, she was parking outside the Enchantment Hotel. Bell was ahead of them and waiting.

Bell held the door for them, but then took off toward the front counter. "I'll go talk to the manager." He was greeted with a smile that turned into a frown when he flashed his badge. The clerk put a phone to his ear.

A few moments later, Bell was headed back to Paige and Brandon.

"The manager's on his way to speak with—" Bell stopped talking, his gaze going behind Paige, and she followed it and saw a man in a suit walking toward them.

"Sergeant Bell," the man said, his eyes traveling over Paige and Brandon.

"These are FBI Agents Paige Dawson and Brandon Fisher."

"I'm Gabriel Rodriquez, the manager of the Enchantment Hotel." He looked Paige over, barely glanced at Brandon. To Bell, he said, "How can I help you today?"

"They would like to see room 892."

"Ah, the infamous room 892. It's usually always rented out, but today you're in luck." Gabriel gestured for them to follow him to the elevator bank. He pushed the Up button, and when they all loaded on, he selected the eighth floor.

The eighth floor... What was it about their sniper and that number? A question they'd considered before, but no less important to answer. The thing with human beings was we were all creatures of habit, programmable. So what had made the number eight personal to the sniper?

Gabriel took them to room 892 and unlocked the door. He pushed it open and said, "Ladies first." He offered Paige a pleasant smile, which she returned.

"Thank you," she replied.

"Don't mention it, and if you need me—for anything at all—I'll be in the hall."

"Appreciate it." She peered deeply into his eyes, knowing exactly what his offer of *anything* included, and wished she could take him up on it.

Keep it in your pants, Dawson! she scolded herself as she walked to the window on the other side of the room and looked out. Bell came up on her left, Brandon on her right.

Bell pointed a few blocks over. "See that green sign with the gold lettering? That's the Lucky Pub."

Though not so lucky for Wise...

Paige nodded and turned to the sergeant. "Can you run us through how the room looked when you came in the day of the shooting?"

Bell rubbed the top of his head, over the little hair he had left. "It looked pretty untouched—except for the hole in the window."

"Had the bed been slept in?" Paige asked.

Bell shook his head. "No, but that makes sense, given the circumstances. Less chance of leaving any trace."

Speaking of trace... "The room was paid for by a stolen credit card. Can you fill us in a bit more on that?"

"Again, that information should be in the file, but the overview? The card belonged to a couple, last name Mavis, from California. They're in their seventies with grown children. And before you ask, we investigated them thoroughly, but didn't get anywhere closer to the sniper."

California. Wise's widow had mentioned they'd moved up from Walker, California. Was that anywhere near the Mavises, and even if so, was it relevant to the investigation?

"Where do the Mavises live exactly?" If the city name was in the file, she didn't recall seeing it.

"I can't remember exactly where off the top, but if you have something in mind, know this: the physical card was never shown."

"The check-in app?" Brandon said.

"That's right. The app makes it so no contact is necessary between guests and hotel staff."

Paige found it an absurd system when she'd first heard about it, and in the case of a stolen credit card, it was a liability to the hotel. "Seems to me the hotel is taking on a lot of risk. They'd be on the line for a fraudulent charge claim from the credit card company."

"Sure—and they probably account for potential losses." Spoken without any emotion.

Not his monkeys, not his circus, Paige supposed. "Okay, so who had access to the Mavises' credit card information? Their kids?"

"Not according to the children or the couple. But, apparently, Mrs. Mavis liked to shop online periodically. She could have just given her information to the wrong place."

The thought of cyber theft wasn't working for Paige. The use of the Mavises' card was more personal—more connected. Otherwise, why not the use of more stolen cards? "When did the Mavises realize their card had been stolen?"

"Only after local cops went to their door."

"And that was…"

"The day after the shooting."

Bell didn't need to explain that the budget for Albuquerque wouldn't accommodate him and his officers to travel to California, nor would they have jurisdiction, anyhow. But given that aspects of the case crossed state lines, Bell should have involved the FBI sooner. "When you found out the credit card came from California, why didn't you call in the FBI?"

"As I mentioned, we believed it was a matter of the information being stolen, not the physical card. Besides, the murder happened here. That, and there was nothing to connect the victim to the Mavises. The case presented itself as a one-off shooting. One victim, one target. The threat was over."

Sadly, it wasn't. Paige sighed.

Bell's face hardened. "If I'd have my crystal ball then—"

"We can't see the future," Paige said firmly. "You did your best with what you had. All anyone can expect." She let her comment sit for a few seconds before continuing, her thoughts not wandering far from the stolen credit card. The Wises came up from California—there had to be some sort of connection between that and the credit card information coming from the state. Otherwise, it just seemed too coincidental, and Paige had learned a long time ago not to believe in coincidences. "Did you subpoena the transaction history on the Mavises' credit card?"

Bell crossed his arms and snuffed out air. "I've been at this job for a while now, Agent."

"That's a yes?" There was nothing in the file Nadia had forwarded that mentioned anything about the transaction history on the card.

"Of course I did."

"And where did that lead?"

"I was tasked with finding the sniper, not investigating credit card fraud."

"But that credit card was a connection to your sniper," she stamped out. "Surely it was a lead worth pursuing."

"Sure. But you hit a wall, you turn back."

Usually, you work your way along the wall until you find an opening. "Did you even try to figure out at what point the card was stolen?"

"Previous charges—before this hotel room—were validated by the Mavises as belonging to them. You also must open your mind to the possibility that the information was stolen over the phone, conned out of them. Sadly, it happens to the elderly all the time. Some person calls, claiming to be with the IRS, tells them they're going to be arrested if they don't pay their past-due taxes right away. The elderly believe them. They come from a time when they could trust people. They provide their credit card information and *boom*."

Such a sad reflection—but accurate portrayal—on the current state of the world: you couldn't trust anyone. "What you're saying, though, is the job of digging into the stolen card was passed to another department."

"You got it. My chief wanted the sniper found, not for me and my officers to become bogged down pursuing an angle that wasn't giving us anything to go on."

Not that the redirection of resources had done much good. Bell and his officers hadn't gotten any closer to finding the sniper. "Well, thank you for joining us here, Sergeant Bell." She offered a pleasant smile. "Agent Fisher and I are going to go over to the Lucky Pub—"

"And see if you get lucky," Bell cut in. "Listen, I'm not too thrilled you're here, I'll be honest. It means I missed something. But good luck."

He left the room, and Paige turned to Brandon, not that there was anything to say. If Bell had given more attention to the Mavises' credit card and following that trail, maybe there wouldn't have been three other victims.

CHAPTER THIRTY-THREE

Kelly couldn't say she was a fan of Jack's teaching tactics—they were a tad psychotic—but they were effective. She'd never forget the lesson to always speak her mind and stand up for herself—not that it did her mother any good. People liked to preach "speak your mind," but unless you were saying what pleased them, they didn't really want to hear it.

Jack knocked on Jane Powell's door, the banging cutting through Kelly's thoughts.

A tall brunette answered the door, and she was unmistakably the one captured in the photographs with Reid. Her lips were painted in a shade of pink coral similar to what had been on the wineglass in Pryce's condo. She wore chunky jewelry around her neck and bangles on her wrists, likely her own designs; a skirt that came mid-thigh; and a blouse with its top three buttons undone.

Kelly pulled her badge. "Jane Powell?" Jack had told her in the car to take the lead on this one.

"I am, and you are?" The woman pursed her lips and let her gaze trail over Kelly to Jack.

"Special Agent Marsh, and this is Supervisory Special Agent in Charge Harper. We have some questions we'd like to ask you."

"About the shooting?" Jane asked, soft-spoken.

"That's right. Do you have someplace we could sit?"

Jane backed up and held the door for them. "This way." She turned and sauntered down a hallway. They were shown to a sitting room that was sparsely furnished, but the pieces chosen made a bold statement of elegance and money. Of course, one could afford extravagant purchases when their company was worth three million dollars.

Each of them dropped into a chair, the seating arranged in a rough circle to encourage conversation.

Kelly leaned slightly forward. "Ms. Powell—"

"Please, call me Jane." She crossed her legs and didn't move to tug down on her skirt that had ridden up and exposed more leg than Kelly or Jack needed to see.

But Kelly studied the woman's eyes. She'd had chest pains, no doubt brought on from the shooting, but Jane wasn't giving any signs that she knew it had been Darrell who'd been killed. *Does she know?* And her energy was calm, as if the FBI visited her every day, as if nothing could faze her.

Kelly shifted her position and clasped her hands. "We understand you were at Wilson Place yesterday morning around the time of the shooting?"

"Yes. And taken to the hospital." Still no trace of emotion.

"This might not be easy to hear," Kelly started, "but Darrell Reid was killed in the shooting."

Jane didn't blink. "I'm aware of that."

Maybe Jane was living in denial. "We have reason to believe you and Darrell were close." The compromising photos were branded on her brain cells.

"Is that a crime?"

"Not at all, but you don't seem too shaken by his death."

"It's not that I'm an unfeeling robot, but our acquaintance was nothing more than sex."

"But that's been going on for a while?" Kelly recalled that the server at Spencer's Sports Bar had seen them come in together for the last six months. Surely even the most casual of "acquaintances" would be missed after that amount of time.

"Yeah, I guess we have."

Kelly wasn't sure why—or how—Jane was being so blasé about Darrell's death. "He helped you get off from solicitation charges a couple years ago." She was hoping to elicit some emotion.

"I 'got off' because I wasn't guilty. Ya know Darrell was the only one who believed in me, but I still didn't fall for him at the time. He was in his fifties. I'm thirty-five."

"Something obviously changed your opinion of him."

"We bumped into each other—then we started *falling* into each other. The fact he was married was perfect; I'm not looking for anything long-term. Deep and meaningful relationships are overrated."

"Is that why you don't seem too shaken up by the news of his murder?" Kelly asked.

Jane narrowed her eyes. "People die, and I know that sounds callous, but I try not to get too attached, ya know, to anyone, anything."

Yet she was shaken enough to have chest pains. Kelly was starting to think the chest pains had more to do with her own brush with death than grief that she'd lost a lover. As for not getting attached, Kelly could relate. It didn't bring anything good. It hadn't for her, anyway. No matter how much love she held in her heart for her mother and brother, it hadn't brought them back into her life.

"I can understand where you're coming from," Kelly said, and noticed that Jack looked over at her. "Do you know if Mr. Reid was seeing other women besides yourself?"

"I don't know for sure, but it wouldn't surprise me. We weren't exclusive."

Kelly nodded, thinking of the calls Reid's aide had received from mystery women. "When did you last see Mr. Reid?"

"We hooked up Wednesday night, and I left his father-in-law's condo Thursday morning, close to six."

"The time Mr. Reid was shot." Kelly delivered rather bluntly. Jane gave no reaction. "You must have come out not far ahead of him," she added.

Jane's shoulders sagged. "Yeah, I was pretty lucky."

"Did you and Mr. Reid go out Wednesday night or stay in?" Kelly was anxious to hear Jane's answer.

"We went to Spencer's Sports Bar for a few drinks then to his father-in-law's condo."

"That picture I showed you a moment ago was taken at Spencer's." Kelly realized now that she hadn't pointed that out to Jack.

Jane licked her lips and sat up. "By whom?"

"That, we don't know, and we were hoping you might be able to tell us."

"I don't see how I'd know." She started fidgeting with her necklace again, then her eyes widened. "There was this one chick that kept staring at Darrell on Wednesday when we were there. I could have decked her for being so obvious. But what really ticked me off was the way Darrell was eyeballing her. And I was sitting right there with him."

They'd pegged their sniper as brazen, as someone who arranged a meet with Sherman and took him out. They knew from the picture that their sniper had been at Spencer's at the same time as Reid and Powell, but Kelly would have thought she'd keep a low profile. "She was staring at him?"

"Oh, yeah, hard to miss."

"And he was looking back at her?" *Did Reid know his killer?*

"He was, but he told me it didn't mean what I thought it did." Jane rolled her eyes. "Men can be such liars. Goes back to my motto not to get attached."

"Did he say why he was looking at her?" Jack interjected.

Jane turned to him. "He tried to tell me she reminded him of someone he knew." Her gaze back on Kelly. "Can you believe that?"

"Someone from his past?" Kelly reasoned.

"What he tried to tell me. Men."

"Did he tell you her name?"

"No," Jane dragged out.

"What did she look like?"

"Plain. Pretty, but plain. She wasn't wearing any jewelry."

"Age?" Kelly asked.

"About my age."

"So, in her thirties?" Kelly flipped back just to verify.

"That's right."

"Hair color? Eye color?" Jack inquired.

"Blond, but it wasn't her natural color. She had dark roots. I didn't get a look at her eyes. The bar's dimly lit, and she was a few tables away from us. I don't remember her eyes, except for they were on Darrell most of the night."

Kelly's heart was pounding. The debate over the gender of their shooter was put to rest as far as she was concerned. "And what was she wearing?"

"A really nice gray, crepe sweater with a plunging neckline and fitted blue jeans."

"Did she approach Darrell?" Kelly inquired. "Interact with him?"

"I would have liked to have seen her try that. I probably would have hit her then."

Kelly noted the irony that jealousy culled out feelings for Darrell, but his death hadn't. "How was her hair styled? How long?" If they were armed with a solid description, she and Jack could revisit Spencer's Sports Bar and talk to the manager again, see if he had anything to offer.

"She had her hair scooped back into a clip, but left some curly strands loose, and they spilled down the side of her cheeks."

"What about her build?" Kelly asked.

"She was trim. Say about your height."

Five-nine. "Was she alone?"

"Yeah, and she must have left before Darrell and me. I didn't see her on the way out, anyway, but she must not have left long before because her untouched glass of wine was still on the table."

"All right." Jack got to his feet. "You think of anything else, call me." He handed Jane his card.

"Thank you for your help, Ms. Powell," Kelly offered. "You've been very helpful."

"Wait." Jane stepped up next to Kelly and put a hand on her elbow. "Did she kill Darrell?"

"It's far too soon to know," Kelly found herself saying and realized she'd been indoctrinated by Jack.

Jane saw the two of them out, and in the hall, Jack's phone rang. He didn't take the call on speaker and hung up less than a minute later. "That was Nadia. She can't find any connection between Powell and our victims."

Can't say I'm surprised, Kelly thought. She was about to respond when Jack's phone rang again. Whatever message his caller was delivering wasn't good. Jack hung up as they loaded onto the elevator.

He looked over at her and said, "That was Herrera. They found the maid."

CHAPTER THIRTY-FOUR

The Lucky Pub, Albuquerque, New Mexico
Friday, October 25th, Noon Local Time

I found it quite ingenious to name a bar the Lucky Pub. It held out such promise to its patrons, but it had failed Wise six months ago. Before that, it was possible that Wise had met up with women there on numerous occasions. We knew from the file that Wise had frequented the pub, but that fact hadn't gotten Bell anywhere closer to finding the shooter. Bell might have wished us good luck, but I don't think he believed we'd have any. If for that reason alone, I'd love to prove him wrong.

It was around noon when we entered the Lucky Pub, and there was a lunch crowd.

"We'll get a table, grab something to eat, and then tend to business," Paige suggested.

I nodded, agreeing with her strategy. A full stomach aided focus, and we needed as much of that as possible. The added benefit to being a customer first was we'd set ourselves on the server's and management's good side. It would be harder to turn us away if we'd just paid for a meal.

A hostess saw us to a booth in a far corner, and I took the spot that had my back to the kitchen door and me facing the dining room. Most of the tables near us were occupied, but the people's conversations couldn't be heard due to the music coming over the speakers. This table would be a good place to talk about the case without fear of being overheard.

"Here you go. Your waitress will be here soon." The hostess handed us laminated menus with drinks and appetizers on one side and entrees on the back—all of which read as comfort fare. Maybe an empty stomach would be better than scarfing down a piece of cottage pie or a serving of macaroni and cheese. It was bad enough that I ate pizza at midnight last night and hadn't hit a gym since leaving home yesterday morning.

A smiling waitress came to our table. Her name tag read PENELOPE. "Can I get either of you started with a drink?" She slapped down coasters in front of us.

"I'll have a water," I said.

"Bottle or tap?"

"Tap's fine."

Penelope nodded and looked at Paige.

"I'll have an iced tea."

"Sweetened or unsweetened?"

"Unsweetened, please."

"I'll be right back with that and to take your meal orders."

Paige read the menu and toyed with the edge of the brown newsprint that was spread over a plastic tablecloth.

The place was a dive with an outdated and unclean feeling. Surfaces were coated in a thin layer of grime that was tacky to the touch. I looked up, and the grates in the ceiling vent had fur.

Yuck. What had ever attracted Wise to this place?

I flipped my menu, and there was something sticky on the backside. *Sticky backside...yummy thought.*

I snatched a napkin from the holder on the table and tried to wipe off whatever it was, but the paper stuck to the menu.

Paige's head was still in hers, studying it with such scrutiny she could have been cramming for a test.

Glancing back at mine, I saw Cobb salad, figured it was probably one of the healthiest choices here, and dropped the menu.

Penelope returned with our drinks, poured into glasses that had been etched by many trips through a dishwasher. "Ready to order?" She held a pen poised over a notepad and looked at me.

"I'll have the Cobb salad."

"Dressing?"

"Balsamic?" It came out sounding like a question, but I didn't eat Cobb salad much and wasn't sure what to pair with it. Balsamic was my favorite dressing, and I didn't think I could go wrong with it.

"Consider it done. And you?" Penelope addressed Paige, but my partner kept her eyes on the menu while biting her bottom lip.

"Paige," I prompted.

"Um, a-yeah, I'll have the same but with traditional Cobb dressing."

"Coming up." Penelope collected the menus and left.

Paige took a sugar packet out of a small bowl that was on the table and tore it open. She dumped the sugar into her iced tea.

"I thought you wanted it unsweetened?" I smiled and raised my brows.

"I do, but I like it with just one sugar pack." Paige looked around us, then met my eyes. "This is quite a dive."

"Was just thinking the same thing."

Silence settled between us with the comfort of a scratchy wool blanket.

Paige's phone rang, and she answered quickly. "Just a minute," she told her caller. To me, she said, "It's Nadia. I'll have to step outside to hear her." She set off for the front doors.

I watched after her, hating that I still harbored feelings for her, about our past. Shouldn't the fact our affair was long over make it easier to release and move forward? It was just this case messing with my head, had to be.

I drained back most of my water, and Penelope came around and topped it up. She left to tend to her other tables, and my gaze settled on a couple in their forties. They were leaned across their table, talking to each other as if they harbored a secret. They held hands under the table, and the way the woman kept laughing and tossing her hair back told me they were lovers. He was wearing a wedding band, and she wasn't.

I turned away, the guilt working to set down roots. Ridiculous. I had nothing to feel guilty about. Besides, as far as I knew, Deb had never found out about Paige and me—but did that make what I had done okay? Maybe if I came clean with my ex and apologized, I'd feel better in some way, but what did I really hope to accomplish? Telling her would only hurt her unnecessarily. No, these feelings were something I had to deal with on my own. I looked down at my water and wished for something much stronger.

"Nadia doesn't have anything for us on the VA-hospital front." Paige slipped back into the booth across from me.

"Well, we both knew that was a reach." The way her face fell, I'd say she'd held out hope for a far more optimistic outcome than I had.

Paige continued. "She said the number of military personnel discharged from service suffering from PTSD is at an all-time high. No way for her to narrow that down with what we have—which isn't much. I think we need to let go of the VA hospitals and focus on the Mavises."

"The people whose credit card information was stolen?"

"Yeah. I had Nadia do a quick check, and the Mavises are from Bridgeport, California and Wise's widow said that they were from Walker, California. Turns out both towns are in Mono County and within half an hour of each other."

"Okay, but we don't even know if California ties into our sniper. What you've mentioned could be nothing more than a coincidence. Bell said that the credit card itself wasn't stolen, so our sniper never had to set foot in California."

"But the Wises were from there," Paige stressed. "And I'm pretty sure our sniper was."

"Why? Because of some credit card information that could have been stolen from online or over the phone? And tell me this, why would the sniper use a card that might lead us to her?"

Paige took a sip of her iced tea. "Well, it didn't lead Bell to her."

"Burn."

She smiled. "Seriously, there are a couple of reasons the unsub would leave a trail. The sniper could get a rush from the chase, or they are trying to tell us something."

"But what?" My mind was trying to piece together a motive here but was falling short. Maybe we needed more background on the Mavises and Wise before anything coherent would stitch together. "Did you find out anything more about the transaction history on the Mavises' card?" I'd cave a little to please Paige. She seemed excited about the California lead.

"Uh-huh." She leaned across the table. "I found out from Nadia the last charge before the fraud came to light was made at the Sunset Diner, and apparently the Mavises frequented the place. I think our sniper gained access to the Mavises' credit card there."

Maybe I'd given her too much rope, because now it felt like she was reaching. "So the sniper worked there?"

Paige sat back and hitched her shoulders. "It's possible."

"If she held a job, then she'd have to be mentally stable. She might not have PTSD."

"Or she has lucid moments, when she's perfectly fine. There may be times when she's getting treatment and times when she's not."

I bobbed my head side to side.

"Anyway, before I forget to tell you, Jack called. I let him and Kelly know about my suspicions that this might link back to California, and he told me that Marsha Doyle's body was found in her apartment."

"I wish I could say that surprises me. How was she killed?"

Penelope shadowed the table, and stood there, motionless, holding our two salads and staring at me with her mouth slightly agape.

I plastered on a smile. "We're talking about this show we binge on Netflix."

Penelope set our food down in front of us and walked away without saying a word.

"Oops," I said to Paige.

Paige was smiling and lifted up her fork. "Let's hurry and eat up. We have work to do."

"I'm good with that." I hated it when meals dragged on. As I ate, I thought about the killer we hunted. They might love the chase, but so did I. Even better was the catch.

CHAPTER THIRTY-FIVE

The victim was shot in the head with a handgun, execution style," Herrera said, standing with Kelly and Jack over Marsha Doyle's body, which was supine on the floor not too far inside her front door. Blood smears showed the body had been dragged farther into the apartment so the shooter could close it inside.

"She answered her door and got a bullet to the head for her troubles," Kelly lamented, though she'd seen far worse crime scenes than this one.

CSIs were busy working over Marsha's apartment and around her body. The medical examiner hadn't arrived yet but had been called.

"It would also seem that the shooter knew Marsha by sight," Kelly reasoned. "There's no indication of hesitation, just cold calculation. The sniper knew that Marsha had what they needed, and they didn't hesitate to act and take it."

"I'd have to agree with that," Herrera said. "So far, we haven't found her keycard or her work ID. I have officers canvassing the building to see if anyone was seen hanging around. We don't have a narrower window for time of death, but we know that she got off work at eleven Wednesday night, and the sniper was at the Colonial Hotel at six Thursday morning. The officers are working with that time frame."

Kelly turned to Jack. "Our unsub is very organized and acting faster. They're becoming more comfortable with killing as they go along and are even willing to take out others to accomplish their end goal. There might be other victims we're not yet aware of, too." The latter was a disheartening thought, but if she was against a hired gun before, she truly was now. There was also the knowledge they had after talking to Jane Powell. Reid had known the woman—the sniper—staring at him. She turned to Jack. "Definitely not the work of a hired gun, and that woman Powell told us about…Reid knew about her, but how and from when and where? How far back do their paths intersect?"

"What woman?" Herrera asked.

Kelly filled the captain in on the mystery woman at Spencer's. "Powell said the woman kept staring at Reid. I think she's the one who snapped the photos of them together." Kelly's heart picked up some speed, and she met Jack's gaze. "Even more than that, I think this woman is our killer."

"A female sniper?"

"Why not," Kelly fired back. "Women can do anything men can do."

Herrera held up his hands. "Not the way I meant it."

Kelly didn't care how he meant it; she took it as she heard it. "Jack, we've discussed how the sniper could be personally motivated, and now she shows her face to her victim within hours of taking him out?"

"Ballsy," Herrera chimed in.

Kelly disregarded Herrera's male-macho terminology. "It was her way of letting Reid know he was going to pay for what he did, whatever that was."

"Hmm." Jack patted his shirt pocket where he kept his cigarettes.

"You don't agree?" Kelly asked.

Jack met her eyes. "I never said that. We definitely need to figure out how the sniper and the victims are connected. We figure our sniper has a military background, but none of the victims did."

"There has to be something they hold in common," Kelly reasoned.

"All the men were cheaters," Herrera said.

"I think there's more to it." Kelly's mind went to the photos sent to the widows. "I think the reason our sniper has targeted these men is personal, but that's not enough. She wants the widows to know the type of men their husbands were, too. So, what's the grander message in that? We also need to figure out why a woman in her thirties—as Powell described the woman at the bar—is killing men in their fifties." Her thoughts went dark. "Sexual abuse when she was younger?"

Jack shook his head. "It's more likely she'd take them out another way…in another spot on their bodies."

The way both men stiffened and shifted their posture told Kelly just the thought of being struck in "another spot" made them uncomfortable.

"But if she was abused as a child, then how would Reid recognize her?" Herrera asked. "You said Powell told you he did."

"Right. So, if it is sexual abuse, she could have been a teenager. Looks don't change so drastically that she'd be unrecognizable as an adult."

"Okay, here's a question," Herrera started. "How did a younger woman come to be in the company of four men twenty years or so older than she was?"

"School? No, only one of them was a teacher." Kelly snapped her fingers. "What about through her mother? She could have been single, had the four victims as boyfriends at different times?"

"Wow, then she really knew how to pick 'em," Herrera stated drily. "Though not unheard of for the cycle to repeat itself."

"The chances that all four men abused her…" Jack raised a skeptical brow.

Maybe I took my theorizing too far.

"Nadia conducted quick backgrounds on the victims, their places of birth—all different states—and dates of birth, but did she dig any deeper? And now that we're thinking that the state of California could somehow tie into the investigation, can we place all the men there at some time?"

"Call Nadia and have her dig deeper."

Kelly took out her phone and stepped into the hall. Nadia answered on the second ring, and Kelly asked her to take a hard look at the victims' pasts for ties to California.

"Wanna hold the line?"

"I do."

Keys were clicked on Nadia's end, and it felt like forever before Nadia's voice came back on the line. "I didn't notice this before, but we weren't focused on California."

"What is it?"

"All of them had addresses in towns that were within a short drive of Bridgeport. Do you think that could mean something?"

"Can you put them there at the same time?"

"Yeah."

Tingles ran down Kelly's arms. "Then, yeah, I'd say it could mean something. When were they all living in the area?" Maybe their shooter had been there during the same time period.

Nadia provided the year range.

Kelly's shoulders sagged. "That would make them all teenagers and young adults in their early twenties. College age. Any of them go to the same school?"

"No, I would have noticed that before now."

So, how had they all come into contact—or had they? Maybe they only had to cross paths with the sniper. If they were in their teens and twenties, though, their sniper wouldn't even have been born yet. *What the hell?* "What ages were the men when they left the state?"

"Well, the three of them moved farther away from Bridgeport, to the north of the state—not close to each other—and at different ages. But they all left California in their thirties. Reid at thirty-three, Miller and Sherman thirty-five, and Wise thirty-seven."

That would put their suspected sniper in her teens, but there didn't seem to be any geographical meeting point to facilitate an assault. "Okay, thanks, Nadia."

"Why do I get the feeling I didn't help?"

"No, you did." Kelly hung up, headed back into Marsha's apartment, and joined Jack. "Can we talk a minute?"

They stepped into the hallway, where she updated him on her conversation with Nadia.

"Okay." Jack's eyes shadowed. "It seems this all stems from something that happened in California."

"I'd say that emotions are certainly at play, too. A hired gun wouldn't leave any type of trail."

"I'll give you that."

"We figure she entered the military, specifically the Marines, given the type of gun used in the shootings. We're running a little tight on leads, but what if she happened to enlist and be trained in the state of California."

"Are there any bases in the vicinity of Bridgeport?"

Kelly brought out her phone and did a quick Google search. "There are thirty-two in the entire state..." She scrolled down and stopped when she got to the Marine Corps Mountain Warfare Training Center in Pickel Meadows. "Ah, Jack...there's a training center right in Pickel Meadows. It's only twenty-four minutes from Bridgeport." She looked up from her phone when Jack didn't say anything. "That's where the Mavises are from—the couple whose credit card was stolen. This can't be a coincidence."

"I'm aware. Tell me more about the training center," he said.

She scanned the article and gave Jack the highlights. "It was originally started to prep soldiers for the Korean War. Most of the troops trained there now are sent to help with peacekeeping efforts in Afghanistan." She slowly pried her gaze from her phone's screen.

Jack rubbed his jaw and walked a few steps. She'd never imagined Jack as a pacer, yet here he was.

"Jack?" she prompted.

He held up his index finger, stopping walking, turned to face her, then pulled out his phone. "Nadia, I need you to find out the names of any females sent to the military training base in Pickel Meadows, California, who were trained as snipers. Narrow the window between thirteen and twenty-two years ago."

Kelly did the quick math in her head. The mystery woman was estimated in her thirties. Accounting for an age range of thirty to thirty-nine, less seventeen—the earliest age anyone can join the Marines—that would put her enlistment between the years Jack had noted.

"Call me back the minute you get anything." Jack pocketed his phone and returned to Marsha's apartment without another word to Kelly.

She found that strange, but she also noticed the way his voice sounded like steel and the glazed-over look to his eyes when he'd made the request of Nadia. It was probably because he felt he was in some way turning on his own by pointing the finger at someone who had served. Kelly knew from her grandfather that the military was a brotherhood, and everyone had the other's back. Whether Jack would admit it or not, Kelly suspected he was struggling with his sense of loyalty—but at the same time, she had no doubts that he'd take down a killer no matter their past service record.

CHAPTER THIRTY-SIX

The sniper's back was stiff, and her hips cracked when she put her legs over the side of the bed and sat up. The mattress in this hovel of a motel was hard as shit. It made her think of earlier days when sacrifices were not only demanded, but expected and par for the course. "Hardships build character," her mother would sometimes say, but life had been one large hardship. One huge mistake, really. Some days she didn't feel she had the right to exist. But maybe there was a reason for everything, and she was tasked to see that atonement was made for the wrongs committed. It was necessary to justify her actions to keep from teetering over the edge of sanity into the pit of insanity. She did the same when deployed. Told herself the ends justified the means, but it didn't make the memories or the images less potent. It didn't ease the burden she carried within herself, the heavy weight knowing that her actions had caused death. One thing she noticed everywhere she went was that people the world over were striving, striving, striving. Searching as if they'd lost something to be found, even if they'd never possessed it in the first place. But she *had* lost something. Correction: something had been taken away, and every day of her life had been about claiming back that which should have remained hers.

She massaged her temple, the whiskey from last night drilling into her skull. Light was filtering in around the ratty curtains, and she squinted at the alarm clock on the nightstand. It was just after two.

Her eyes drifted to the floor, to the bags that held her guns, and a wave of nausea had her gripping her stomach. She'd killed again. The next day was always worse than the moment, than the immediate aftermath. At that point, she was numb and unfeeling. With the dawn of a new day, overwhelming remorse often set in with the subtlety of a jackhammer. But she had to believe she had a reason for doing what she did. She, too, sought to find that which she'd lost—even if it meant taking the lives of evil men to reset the scales of justice.

She grabbed her water glass from the nightstand and took a sip as flashbacks to an earlier time took hold. Mother sitting in the window on a summer's day, her eyes vacant as she looked out onto the street where the sniper played hopscotch with some neighbor kids. The sniper would wave and smile, but her mother never reacted. It was like Mother wasn't looking at her, but rather *through* her. As if Mother was tangled in the webs of her past, apprehended by living nightmares that haunted her while she was awake.

She tried talking to her mother in these moments, but she wasn't sure if her words were sinking in. All Mother would do was nod, and the room felt empty, hollow, solemn, like the walls begged for reverent silence.

She balled her hands into fists but released them, relaxing her hands in her lap. She took another sip of water and set the glass back on the table. Today was a new day, and it was time to get started, though finding motivation to go on was hard. Here she was safe, tucked away and secluded from the world, isolated.

Someone knocked heavily on the door, and her instinct was to retreat. Maybe if she stayed quiet, her visitor would go away.

Then she clued in; it was after two in the afternoon. She should have checked out hours ago.

She started gathering her things. "I'm leaving," she called out.

"It's the police," were the words that returned.

Fear lassoed her, and her chest remained expanded with her last breath. *How did they find me?* She'd been careful, taken necessary precautions.

"Please come to the door. We have questions for you."

Questions?

"One minute." She stuffed her bags into the dresser drawers and went to the door. She stood there, taking a few deep breaths. *Everything will be fine,* she chanted in her mind, and cracked the door. The midday sun blinded her, and the brightness drilled her headache farther into her skull. She pinched her eyes, looking at her callers through slits. There were two of them—a man and woman—both in uniform and staring back at her.

Neither of them said a word, and she felt every millisecond pass. She leaned against the doorframe, doing her best to appear relaxed and casual. "You said you had questions for me?"

"We understand you rented this room last night?" The male officer voiced it like a question and held on to a notepad, his pen pointing toward her.

"That's right." *God, my head hurts!* "What's this about?"

"We just need to know if you heard anything unusual," the female said, a note of impatience inflected in her tone.

"Ah, no." The sniper tried to widen her eyes, but the sunlight was blinding and offensive. "Why would I have—"

"There was a double homicide in the room next to yours."

Only then did she become aware of the flashing squad cars in the lot. Doors on a vehicle marked "Coroner" slammed shut, and a metal gurney clinked and rattled as it was pushed toward the room next door.

There was something skittering on the edge of her mind, but just outside of her grasp. And why the hell hadn't she taken in her surroundings immediately upon opening the door? The damn whiskey had made her stupid—that's why.

"Did you hear me?" The mark of irritation wrinkled the female officer's brow, and she wondered if the woman was always this on edge. "There was a double homicide in the room next to yours," she repeated.

There was something there on the edge of her mind, but it felt just out of grasp. She could bring snapshots to mind of driving to the Reids' house again, early this morning, still drunk, and determined to return to the motel for sleep.

"Did you hear me, ma'am?" the female officer prompted.

"Yes, a double homi—" Then the memories flooded in.

The tissue-paper thin walls.

The grunting.

The banging headboard.

The wedding band.

The hooker.

Her legs buckled slightly as the memories assaulted her. A man and a woman. Shot point-blank. She'd technically killed three people in the past twenty-four hours. She hoped the cops hadn't noticed her composure slip and laid her other hand over her chest to feign shock. "A double homicide?" She got out the full question this time.

"We appreciate this may come as a shock," the female cop said. "But if you could tell us if you heard or saw anything suspicious, it would be a great help."

"No, I'm sorry, I didn't…" The whiskey churned topsy-turvy in her otherwise empty stomach. The blanket of nausea spread over her cheeks, and her mouth salivated. "I'm sorry… I…I drank a lot last night and pretty much passed right out."

Both cops regarded her with trademark suspicion. Lips in a thin line, heads cocked, eyes full of judgment.

"We'll still need your name and a number where we can reach you," the lady cop said with an air of superiority.

"Ah, well…I…" Her eyes went to two people who were talking and standing next to a forensics vehicle.

"Name and number?" the male officer prompted, holding his pen braced over a page.

She brought her focus back on the cops and gave them a name. "That's all I've got for you. Down on my luck right now. Cell phone company shut off my service, and I just got kicked out of my apartment."

"Yeah, sure, okay, I get that. Here—" the male officer handed her a card "—if you think of anything, call me."

She took that as her dismissal and started her retreat inside her room. On the way, she heard the lady cop mumble to her partner, "Why the fuck do people lie straight to our faces?"

Her comment sparked a raging wildfire, and the sniper balled her fists at her sides. If she'd told the lady cop the truth, she probably couldn't handle it.

I killed them and felt nothing!

Likely the woman would stare at her in a daze, only breaking the spell by shouting at her to put her hands up and turn around. She'd be cuffed and off to prison. What a stupid question. *Why do people lie?* To cover their asses!

She clenched her stomach; she could barely handle it herself. And to think of the rotting corpses in the next room…she could have just messed everything up. But one thing was clear: she had to get the hell out of there, and it was probably time to ditch her car.

CHAPTER THIRTY-SEVEN

Paige pushed her plate aside, finished with the Cobb salad. She looked across at Brandon, who had finished a while before her. For a split second, she wanted to broach the personal, but she was smarter than to actually do so. She'd seen this side of him before—the moody edge, the hair-trigger, redheaded temper—and she wasn't eager to provoke him. Instead, she stuck to business and filled him in on what else Jack had told her when he called about the murdered maid. "There was a woman watching Reid and his mistress the night before his murder. Apparently, she was someone from his past."

"There's a glimmer of a break in the case."

"Yeah. We very well could be looking at a woman sniper," she concluded.

The waitress cleared their plates and returned a few minutes later with their check. Paige glanced at the total and put her expense credit card in the sleeve, then identified herself and Brandon as FBI.

"We need to speak with the manager," she said.

Penelope frowned. "Robert Wise? Right? That's who you want to talk about."

"That's right. How did you know?"

"Well, given what happened to him…and you're the FBI," she stated soberly.

Paige nodded; the waitress's deduction made sense. "Did you know him?"

"No, but I know what happened to him. I'll go get the boss man." She snatched the check holder off the table and left.

Not long later, a heavy man, wearing a half apron, was at their table. "I've told the cops everything I know."

"We're not the cops," Paige retorted. "We're federal agents."

"As Penelope told me, but you're really all the same."

Paige chose to ignore that and went on with introductions. "I'm Special Agent Dawson, and this is Special Agent Fisher."

"There's nothing more I can tell you about Mr. Wise that I haven't already said." He wiped his hands on the apron.

"We told you our names. Yours would be…?"

"Drew Hart."

"Well, Mr. Hart, do you recognize this person?" Paige picked up her phone and brought up one of the photographs sent to Wise's widow, angling the screen so Drew could see it. This particular shot captured the woman's face rather clearly, as she had her head tilted to the side, Wise's face in her neck.

His gaze flicked up to Paige's. "You're showing me porn?"

"It's not porn. Tell me, do you recognize her?"

He looked again. "Not sure."

"But you think you've seen her before?" Paige pushed.

"Looks like a customer who came in here with Rob, but I haven't seen her since he died."

"Since he was murdered, you mean," Paige said to stress the importance of this conversation. "We're trying to find out who killed him, and this woman was…close to him."

"Looks like." Drew raised his brows at Brandon.

"Do you know her name?" Brandon asked.

"Sure. It's Josefina Alvarez."

Paige looked at Drew with disbelief and drew his eye.

"You said that Josefina would come in with Mr. Wise?" Paige said.

"That's right." Drew put his hands on his sides, the mannerism emphasizing his potbelly.

"But she hasn't been in since his death..." Paige could imagine returning to where her lover had been killed wouldn't be at the top of Josefina's to-do list. "Did you happen to notice anyone else hanging around, another woman, perhaps, who might have been watching Mr. Wise and Ms. Alvarez?"

His face paled. "There was a woman. She came in a few times."

A pattern may be starting to emerge, but had the mystery woman from Spencer's shown up to watch Reid and Powell more than once? It would make sense that she'd stalked all her victims to know when and where to strike.

Drew continued. "I try to notice new faces. Like I saw yours when you came in. Anyway, customer service is too underrated, as far as I'm concerned, so I like to know as much as I can about my customers."

It was probably why Wise liked coming here. It was Cheers of New Mexico.

"What was memorable about her?" Brandon asked.

"She was always watching Mr. Wise, and she was here the night before he was shot."

The skin on the back of Paige's neck tightened. "Did you mention her to the police?"

"I did, but they didn't seem to care."

Given the fact there wasn't any mention of a mystery woman in Bell's notes, Paige would agree that the sergeant hadn't cared. "Did you get this woman's name?" Paige was hopeful—but doubtful.

"My waitress might have."

Paige perked up.

"Now, whether she'd remember it is another thing. But when I train my servers, I stress that they get customers' names. People like being called by their names."

Penelope must have missed that part of the training as she hadn't asked hers and Brandon's. "Could we speak with the server who would have tended to this woman?" she asked. "You wouldn't happen to be able to find out who—"

"It would be Barbie. She takes care of the patio. Mr. Wise always sat out there, and that woman I mentioned did the last time she came here. Believe it was table ten. Tell Barbie that, and it might help jog her memory." Drew went on his way.

Paige leaned across the table, talking in hushed tones. "Our killer was here, Brandon, just like she was at Spencer's back in Arlington."

"She's wanting the men to know their day of judgment has arrived."

"I think you're right about that."

"Hi-ya." A twentysomething blonde stood at the edge of the table. She wore her hair in a high ponytail and was smiling. "Drew said you wanted to talk to me about a customer."

"We do." Paige introduced herself and Brandon. "And your name is?"

"Barbie Pendleton."

"Ms. Pendle—"

"Oh, Barbie is fine." She smiled wider, flashing a mouth of white teeth.

"*Barbie*," Paige said, hating herself for saying the name, "you served a woman who was sitting at table ten on the patio, around six months ago, and she was apparently interested in Mr. Wise." Paige provided her with a date.

Her face darkened, and she laid a hand over her heart. "Was that the night the poor man was shot?"

"The night before," Paige set her straight. "Is there anything you can tell us about her? What she looked like?"

"She was pretty." Her brow concentrated in thought. "A blonde with green eyes, if I remember right."

The mystery woman from Spencer's had been a blonde, too. "You're sure?"

Barbie's eyes narrowed. "Why are you interested in her?"

"We can't say," Paige said. "Open investigation."

Barbie slid her bottom lip through her teeth and nodded.

"Did you happen to get her name?" Hopefully, Barbie's training had stuck more than Penelope's had.

"Oh my. If she did, I can't remember now, but I would have asked— Oh, her name should be on the receipt. But ya know, she was here more than just once."

"Mr. Hart told us that. A few times?" Brandon asked, stealing Barbie's gaze.

"That's right." She brushed a cheek against a shoulder. "I thought maybe she was an ex of Mr. Wise."

"Why?"

"She seemed obsessed with him. She'd watch him from a distance, and then that night—the one you're asking about—she called ahead and booked table ten. It's in plain view of where Mr. Wise normally sat."

Brandon put his elbows on the table. "When did you see her last?"

"That night...the night before..." Barbie didn't need to finish.

"Maybe if you could get us that receipt now?" Paige prompted.

"Sure, I'll see what I can do." She walked away with the swagger of a runway model, with the long legs and lean body to match, but the stereotype that the beautiful were somehow less intelligent was busted when it came to this Barbie. She was sharp and had an incredible memory.

"The sniper knew Wise's routine, where to strike and when," Brandon said thoughtfully. "We need to talk to Wise's mistress, this Josefina Alvarez."

"Agree."

Barbie paraded back to the table, her ponytail swaying wildly behind her, and she was smiling. "I have a name for you. Estella."

Paige reminded herself it was too soon to get excited. Now, if her name could be verified, possibly by credit card... "How did she settle up?"

"Cash."

So much for tracking her down by credit card. Then again, it could have been another stolen number.

"That doesn't help?" Barbie winced and looked from Paige to Brandon.

"Actually, you've been a big help. Thank you," Paige said, though disappointed they didn't have a payment trail to follow.

"What about video surveillance? Is there any on the patio or even inside?" Brandon asked.

"I can go ask Drew. I know we have cameras, but I don't know if recorded footage from six months ago is still kicking around. Let me go check." She bounced off again.

"Thanks," Brandon called after her, then said to Paige, "We need to update Jack on what we've found here."

"For sure."

A few minutes passed before Barbie returned.

"Drew said we have video. Want to follow me?"

"Absolutely," Paige replied, and she and Brandon quickly rose to follow Barbie through the kitchen doors.

CHAPTER THIRTY-EIGHT

Kelly continued to stare at Marsha's lifeless body like she had been for a couple hours now. It didn't matter how long she looked, she felt nothing emotionally, only a drive to find justice. She also had more questions than answers. The medical examiner had shown up and was being tight-lipped, and Nadia hadn't called back with any new information. Jack's impatience was tangible. He'd even been out for a couple of cigarettes, and his face was all sharp angles and concentration.

"The victim was definitely killed by a gunshot to the head," the medical examiner said, "and considering the amount of stippling, it's likely the gun was fired less than eighteen inches from the victim."

So just as Kelly had thought: Doyle had opened the door and ate a bullet. But did their killer know that Doyle would be on the other side, or was she willing to kill whoever answered, knowing that the all-access hotel keycard was inside the apartment? It hadn't turned up yet, so it seemed easy to conclude that the sniper had taken it to gain access to room 850.

"No one heard a gunshot," Kelly reiterated, chewing on what canvassing officers had been finding thus far. The killer must have used a suppressor, and that means they planned ahead. But, even so, this murder has impulsive elements. Our sniper was brazen enough to shoot from the hall where anyone could have seen her. Would she have killed someone if they came up on her by happenstance?"

"Scary thought." Herrera puffed out a deep breath.

"But all good deductions." With Jack's praise, she found herself standing just a bit taller. Jack added, "In the least, she's feeling a sense of power, and it wouldn't seem she's worried about getting caught."

"Maybe she wants to be stopped?" Herrera asked. "That's what happens with some of these sickos, isn't it?"

Jack frowned at the word *sickos*. "I don't know if she wants to be stopped, but it's almost as if she's indifferent to the idea."

"So…what? She's going with the flow, so to speak?" Kelly asked.

"Yes and no. I'd say she's following a plan," Jack concluded.

Kelly gave consideration to Jack's words, but how many victims did this killer's plan include? Were more people being added to the list all the time, or would there be a natural end to the killing? After all, if the sniper was taking out people in revenge for a past wrongdoing, there could only be a limited number on her hit list. But if she had become addicted to killing along the way, that was another story, and the murders might not stop on their own. "I don't know if she really wants to be caught, though she does leave little strings to pull. She still strikes me as methodical, locked into military mode. She sees her kills as a mission she's taken on. She planned out the execution of her four male victims and was precise in carrying it out. Shooting Marsha Doyle wasn't a whim, either. She tracked her to her apartment for a purpose: the keycard. There's never been any unintended casualties otherwise, as far as we know."

"If she does view those she kills as accomplishing a mission, it could explain the cold calculation. That would remove emotion from the equation." Jack locked gazes with Kelly and didn't need to remind her they'd recently thought the opposite way.

"A mission could make sense. Killing Doyle just became necessary. After all, she literally held the key. I wonder if there were other people taken out because the sniper saw their deaths as necessary, too." Kelly butted her head toward

Marsha's dead body. "Hopefully, the evidence the sniper left behind will give us another string to pull."

The medical examiner looked up from his crouched position next to the body. "We'll have the bullet extracted and analyzed, run through the system."

"Have it rushed," Jack told him.

"Was planning on it."

"It might connect to other murders we aren't yet aware of." Kelly could only get a tad excited about any of this. Even if the gun used to shoot Marsha Doyle had been used in other murders, it only got them so far; it didn't hand them the shooter.

Jack's phone rang, and he answered and headed for the hall. He signaled for Kelly to follow him, and when he disconnected, he informed her it had been Paige and shared her message.

"Estella," Kelly repeated the name he told her. "And they have video?" This could be a break they needed.

"The likelihood of her real name being Estella is slim," Jack said.

"I agree, but I'd say the name might mean something to her."

Jack remained quiet.

Kelly added, "Emotion, no emotion, I don't think our shooter does anything without thinking things through. Maybe she is sending a message with the name or—"

Jack's phone jingled. "Harper here...Yes, okay. What about the name Estella? Any of those show up for you?" He reentered Marsha's apartment with Kelly hot on his heels and went into the kitchen where he put Nadia on speaker. Herrera joined them there.

"The Marines really don't like parting with information," Nadia said. "That's what's taken me so long, but there were five women who were trained at the facility in Pickel Meadows during the time range you gave me and who were also taught to snipe. You said Estella? Do we think that's our sniper's name?"

"The name came up for Paige and Brandon," Jack cut in. "They'll be calling you about it."

"Well, I don't recall any Estellas."

"Any of those five women see an active war zone?" Jack asked. "Suffer PTSD?"

"All of them, Jack. Figured I'd narrow it down based on our previous thinking about mental instability and being trained in sniping."

"Were any of the five women treated in any VA hospitals in or around the cities where the victims were shot?" Kelly asked.

"Not that I can see. The sniper was either not medicating or receiving treatment elsewhere."

"She might not even realize she has a problem," Kelly said. "If she's operating from the standpoint of a mission, then she might just think she's doing what's required of her."

"Send us the list of names you got there," Jack directed. "But I want you to dig into the background of these women. See if the name Estella pops up anywhere."

"You got it, Jack."

He ended the call, and Kelly's phone pinged a text notification, followed afterward by Jack receiving one. She looked at hers, and it was the list of names.

Jack stuffed his phone into a pocket and addressed Herrera. "Keep us posted on what transpires here."

"I can do that."

Jack led the way out of the apartment, and Kelly trailed, not sure where they were headed now.

"Jack?" she called out.

He slowed for her to catch up.

"Where are we going?"

"We're going back to the sniper's nest."

"Because…" She didn't like questioning Jack, but she wasn't sure why they'd be going there.

"Sometimes there are things you miss the first time."

CHAPTER THIRTY-NINE

Paige and I just got situated in Lucky Pub's office in front of a monitor when our phones chimed with message notifications. It was an email from Nadia with a list of five women—any of whom could be our sniper. I scanned the list quickly, but there was no one named Estella. *That would have been too easy.*

"You ready to view it?" Hart asked.

"I am." I glanced at Paige, whose nose was still in her phone. "Paige?"

She pulled her gaze from her screen. "Please, go ahead."

Hart hit Play, and the stilled video on screen came to life. Hart had spent money on his video surveillance system— not HD quality by any means, but not the grainy black-and-white shit we were often given to work with.

The camera was positioned at the end of the patio, so we were given a good overview of the entire area. Barbie was taking orders from a table of four and laughing with her customers.

"Where's Mr. Wise?" I asked.

"Right there." Hart pointed out the backs of a man and woman sitting next to each other. "Now, the woman you're curious about…Watch this table." Hart circled a finger on the monitor, and seconds later, a hostess showed a woman to a table. It was farther away from the camera, but she was facing us.

"Freeze that there," Paige requested, and Hart complied.

The woman was someone you'd least expect to kill four men. She was trim and pretty with blond hair, and she carried herself with grace. But the fact a woman of the same description had shown up the night before Reid's murder, too, was more than coincidence to me. We were getting our first good look at our sniper. I glanced at Paige and nudged my head.

"Can you do a print screen of that image and send it to me?" Paige went on to give Hart her email address.

Hart clicked away, and seconds later, Paige's nose was back in her phone. "I'm just going to forward this to someone real quick." She tapped wildly at the screen, composing a message to Nadia with the photo attached. "Thanks," she said to Hart, and he hit Play again.

On screen, "Estella" watched Wise intently, only to look away every now and then. Wise shifted—as if he were uncomfortable—and took his arm down from Alvarez's shoulder. So what was it about "Estella" that made him anxious? Did they share a past like Reid and the mystery woman—presumably "Estella"—had?

The video went on to show "Estella" placing an order with Barbie and then the waitress setting off to take care of it. "Estella" immediately resumed staring at Wise, even as she unwrapped her cutlery from a paper napkin. Wise continued squirming and sipped on his drink, taking a few in rapid succession.

Barbie returned with something and placed it on the table. It appeared that "Estella" thanked her, still not taking her eyes off Wise. When Barbie left, "Estella" picked up what had been dropped off: a steak knife. She held the hilt in the palm of her right hand and put the tip to the pad of her left index finger.

"She's threatening him, right there," I said, and Paige nodded. Hart remained silent.

Josefina Alverez pecked Wise on the cheek and excused herself.

A bathroom break?

When Wise's mistress was out of sight, he walked over to "Estella" and sat across from her.

They did know each other!

"Estella" was saying something. I wish we had sound, but a lip-reading expert might be able to figure out her words. Her face didn't show any emotion. If anything, she appeared calm as she continued to toy with the knife. Wise, on the other hand, was visibly agitated when he left the table in less than a minute to return to his own. Alvarez reentered the camera range not long after that.

"Can you rewind, zoom in, and play it slowly?" I asked Hart.

He paused the video and looked at me like I was crazy. "I'm doing good playing and pausing. Rewinding, sure, but there's no way I can play it slowly. And don't ask me to zoom in, either. I'm the least tech-savvy person out there."

Again, where was Zach? He had a way with technology. But I'm sure if we got the video to Nadia, she could handle it. "We'll have our analyst do that for us."

"It's just not going to be me."

"Just send the segment of video to Agent Dawson—from the moment Mr. Wise is seated until he, his mistress, and that woman leave the pub." I figured since he already had her email, it would make it easy for him.

"I can send the day's footage. Again, I'm not a wizard. No video editor or splicer here."

"That works," I said. "For now, if you can, let's rewind to when Mr. Wise goes to her table and watch it again."

Hart narrowed his eyes at my dig, but he did as I'd asked without comment. Lips were moving far too fast for me to make out what was being said, but I'd wager the conversation was terse. Given Wise's brisk movements, her few words were all that was necessary to get her point across.

This time, we let the video play out until Wise and Alvarez left, followed shortly by "Estella."

"Well, that's all folks," Hart said. "I'll get you the file."

Paige and I waited until she had the video, then thanked Hart for his help and left.

Back in the SUV, I started first. "I'd really like to know what she said to Wise."

"That makes two of us." She was tapping away on her phone. "I'm forwarding the video to Nadia."

"Have her find someone who can figure out what Estella"—I put finger quotes on the name—"said to Wise."

"Already on that." A few more taps, and Paige looked over at me. "We're getting close, I feel it."

"Yeah, we both saw the way she wielded that knife. I'd say we have our sniper's face."

"There's something bugging me about what we just saw."

I turned to face her more squarely. "And that was…"

"Yes, I agree that she seemed to threaten Wise with the knife play, but how does he go from acting intimidated… You saw how he was squirming in his chair?"

I nodded.

Paige continued. "How does he go from that to being brave enough, as it were, to join her at her table? And when he goes back to his table for the rest of his meal with Josefina, he seems to be more relaxed than before?"

"Good actor? False bravado? Though he was visibly agitated for a bit. And did he say anything to her? We couldn't see his face."

"If he did, she gave no visual tells. But for Wise to be uncomfortable one second, aggravated, possibly cocky the next, he underestimated her."

"Isn't that an understatement." I thought back to "Estella's" steadfast appearance—confident, chin high, and calm. So calm. "Whatever happened to that woman made her a cold-blooded killer." Shivers tore through me. The killers who didn't feel emotion were the hardest for me to comprehend—and the hardest to predict.

CHAPTER FORTY

Kelly and Jack took a few detours on the way to the Colonial Hotel. Paige had called to tell them how she and Brandon had made out with the video from the Lucky Pub and armed them with a photo of "Estella." She and Jack stopped by Powell's, and the mistress positively identified "Estella" as the woman from Spencer's the night before Reid's murder.

After meeting with Powell, they dropped in at Spencer's to see if they could get anywhere with identifying the mystery woman, but they met a wall. She'd paid cash, which was not surprising to Kelly. Something else that didn't come as a surprise was when Brandon told them "Estella" had been devoid of all emotion on the video, even when confronted by Wise at her table. Kelly could feel it in her gut: "Estella" was their sniper. The hard part still remained: finding out her real identity and tracking her down.

As Kelly stepped into room 850 of the Colonial, she noticed immediately that the sniper's hole had been covered with a piece of cardboard taped in place.

Jack was next to her, staring out the window, but he kept turning and looking over the room. "Paige said in all the previous cases, the sniper set up their nest on the eighth floor."

Just like here, Kelly thought, but she wasn't sure if he was talking to her or himself and chose to let his comment pass without a reply.

"Does the killer's motive have something to do with the military?" he asked, then stared blankly at her.

"Jack?" She was certain she didn't have to say it, but the victims were never enlisted—which he'd know.

He waved a hand. "I'm just talking out loud."

She nodded, though he didn't strike her as the talking-it-out type, just as he hadn't seemed like a person who paced. "Serving in the military definitely changes you," she said, and he turned to face her. She'd seen shifts in her grandfather's behavior though he did his best to hide it. "It's gotta be rough witnessing things…" She empathized with those who had seen an active war zone. They'd have seen people killed, maybe even before their own eyes. They could have even been the ones doing the killing. War would seem merciless and unjustifiable, even to those most dedicated to patriotic duty. Surely there'd be moments of reflection when the basic and bitter truth sank in: people were killing people because their governments told them to.

Something coursed across Jack's face—pain, hurt, grief, all three?—and he looked out the window again. "It can get to you if you let it."

Kelly watched his profile. Maybe his military past was responsible for his detached approach to life, his dislike for feelings, emotions. Her grandfather had given her a snapshot of Jack's past—an ex-wife and a son he was rather distant from. Life could have been more kind. "Thank you, Jack."

"For what?" He kept his gaze out the window.

"For your service, for all that you sacrificed."

"When you're in the military, you follow orders, you carry out your missions without question, without emotion."

She replayed Jack's comment in her head. It was similar to a thought she'd had a moment ago about people killing because their governments told them to.

Her eyes widened, and she touched Jack's arm. "Do you think our killer might be acting on orders?"

He peered into her eyes and didn't say a word for what felt like forever. "It's possible, but it's just as possible she's ordering herself. I agree that she's acting with order and logic. And every nest is set up on the eighth floor," he repeated again.

"You really think there's something in that?"

"It wouldn't be the first time a number actually meant something to a killer."

As was the case with the investigation that Jack and his team had helped her with in Miami. That killer had an attachment to the number three. "Okay, so why the number eight? We're thinking she was a Marine. Maybe a battalion or regiment number?" she tossed out the first thing that came to her.

Jack met her eyes. "Could very well be." He proceeded to pull out his phone, and Kelly could see he was looking at the list of names Nadia had sent over. "She didn't include their assignments." He called Nadia on speaker, holding his phone between them. Nadia answered on the second ring. "Nadia, did any of the women from your list serve with a regiment or battalion with the number eight?"

"Hang tight…" Keys clicked, and after a few minutes, she said, "There is one."

Kelly's heart fluttered. "Which one?"

"Lance Corporal Michelle Evans, currently thirty-five," Nadia said slowly. "She served with the third battalion, in the eighth regiment. She was dispatched eleven months ago." There was the sound of more clicking keys.

"Rather vague. Dig into that, but in the meantime, send us everything you have on her so far," Jack directed.

"Wait," Kelly called out, "Does this Evans lady have any Estella in her background?" Jack was watching her, seeking an explanation. "To provide that name to the server at the Lucky Pub, it tells me it means something to her." It might not, but Kelly would rather see clues where they didn't exist than miss any that did.

"Oh—" Nadia seemed to drift away from them as if something else had garnered her attention.

"Nadia?"

"We've got our sniper. You know I was getting the surveillance video from the Colonial Hotel. Well, I've looked at it and enhanced a closeup of someone going into room 850. I'd say she's a positive match for the woman on the Lucky Pub video. But now I have Michelle Evans' photo in front of me. Oh, yeah, we have her."

"Find out everything you can on her immediately," Jack said. "We'll have a conference call with the entire team in one hour from now."

"I'm on it, Jack." Nadia beat Jack to hanging up—and it left Kelly hanging. Who was Estella, and how did she tie in with this Michelle Evans?

CHAPTER FORTY-ONE

The sniper wasn't born a killer; she was made into one. In place of pleasure and satisfaction was shame and regret—but there was also a sense of pride and accomplishment. The seeing through of a mission and getting the job done. She'd be lying to say she didn't love the sense of power and control that came with pulling the trigger. She'd been trained, and she did her job—or she tried. But that fat man and the woman hadn't been a part of the mission. In the field, they'd have been civilian casualties except for she'd killed them intentionally—heat of the moment or not. She'd gone to that door prepared to take life.

She was seated on a bench at a train station, her hands tucked under her legs in an effort to still them. But they continued to quiver like fish frying in oil.

She watched people walk past and assessed each one, sizing them up as if they were targets and she was in the field. She glanced down at the bag she'd tugged close to her side. It held the handgun, but she had to do what she had to do. Her next step would also be off-mission, but maybe it was time to start thinking of herself. She bounced her legs and chewed on a fingernail.

People started looking at her—or at least it felt that way. Their eyes full of condemnation and judgment, ready to turn on her, turn her in, like they knew what she had done. All the people she had killed.

A lone tear spilled down her cheek, and she swiped it away. Her whiskey-induced headache had eased up and given way to her conscience. If only she could get more drugs, but she couldn't risk refilling her prescription.

The FBI could already be onto her, and she needed to avoid arrest for at least two more days to see her entire operation all the way through and reap the full reward. That being the ultimate feeling of approval, acceptance, and praise—all of which sang to her soul, filling her with bliss. The thought of being locked in a cage before she received closure sent tremors tearing through her. Even if a cage was where she belonged.

A toddler walked by, holding his mother's hand, mere feet in front of the sniper, but instead of facing ahead, he was staring at her. His innocent eyes probed hers. His widened a fraction as if he'd discovered her secret and saw the horrors living inside her soul. It took a mere child to see what most adults could not. But adults were too tainted by life's experiences; their perceptions affected and out of focus. And she knew that she, too, was susceptible—and hated that weakness of being human.

She reached for the bag; her hand finally calm. She also became aware of the bag she had strapped to her back that held her sniper rifle. The backpack was just big enough to hold the disassembled gun, helping her move about less conspicuously. It was most unlikely a cop would stop her and ask for her permit to carry.

She might have had her moments of weakness, times when she left clues, consciously or not. A cry for help? Or stupidity? Even she didn't know. But she wasn't stupid enough to draw undue attention. She'd heard the stories of infamous serial killers taken down by happenstance and idiocy, not even related to the murders and atrocities they had committed. The Southern California Strangler, Randy Kraft, came to mind. He was pulled over for drinking and driving with a dead man in his passenger seat, putting an end to his killing spree. She'd heard of others who were brought down because of a broken taillight, an unpaid parking ticket, driving a stolen car, and other such stupid moves. And maybe for her, it wasn't so much getting caught but being *stopped.* Then what would she do? Mission terminated, what would come next for her? That thought was actually more terrifying than prison. She'd either been told what to do or planned out her own life for the past fifteen years, maybe even before the Marines.

The station was emptying out, people having boarded their trains or departing. The path to the lockers was unobscured. The shiny marble floor mocked her, daring her to take a step across it. Challenge accepted.

She stood and grabbed her shoulder bag. The lockers were about thirty feet away. She'd do what she'd came to do and leave.

A loud, ear-piercing smack rang out across the lobby. She dove to the ground and slipped her hand into her bag, but yanked it out quickly as if she'd been bitten by a snake. She'd almost had her fingers wrapped around the handgun. *That was close, but what the hell was that noise?*

She studied her surroundings and spotted a janitor down the hallway righting a metal-handled mop. It must have hit the floor; the marble had amplified the *thwack* like a loudspeaker.

She got back on her feet. She was safe, but her heart was pounding.

Again, she glanced at the lockers. The thirty-some-foot span felt more menacing than before. She returned to the bench, her entire body trembling. She'd almost messed up like other stupid serial killers and drawn her handgun. At least last night she'd been careful; she'd gloved up.

Thoughts started to pour in on her—not fears over leaving trace at last night's murder scene, but the kills themselves.

She pulled out the empty drug bottle from her inside jacket pocket and shook it. Ridiculous, really. Pills couldn't magically manifest overnight. But, God, they'd take the edge off, afford her some peace of mind, let her breathe. If only. But she had none, no prescribed Band-Aid to seal her insanity. She jammed the bottle back into her pocket, her mind retreating to the past, to Afghanistan, to her nightmarish memories no one should have.

CHAPTER FORTY-TWO

Michelle Evans didn't sound like a name that would belong to a killer, but rather someone Paige would be friends with. But the fact that killers functioned like chameleons in society was why they'd always exist. People would often say of even the most heinous murderers before arrests were made that "they were so quiet" or "they wouldn't hurt a fly."

Paige and Brandon were set up in a meeting room at the local FBI field office with their laptop at the ready for a video conference with Jack and Kelly. The system rang, and Brandon moved his chair closer to her, bumping her shoulder with his. She rolled away to put some distance between them.

Paige clicked the button to answer. "Hey, guys."

"Hi," Kelly replied, and Jack just dipped his head. They were still waiting on Nadia to join them.

"Have you gotten anywhere further with the identity of Wise's mistress?" Jack asked.

"Her name's Josefina Alvarez," Paige said. "No one's seen her at the pub since Wise's murder. She's probably staying away because of the bad memories, but we'll pay her a visit." Paige didn't want to think Josefina was dead.

"Do that."

"She was next on our list," she said. They would probably be at Josefina's door now if Jack hadn't called the meeting.

There was another ring, and Nadia joined the conference. She looked ragged; her hair that was normally smooth and straight was a little frizzy. She was also wearing red-framed glasses instead of contact lenses. She held a file folder in both hands and smacked its edge against her desk, then opened it.

"Oh, it's not looking good for Michelle Evans," Nadia said, playing up the drama.

"Just tell us what you have," Jack said coolly.

"Michelle Evans is the daughter of Estella Evans."

Kelly was grinning. "I knew it."

"You knew the sniper's mother was named Estella?" Brandon tossed out.

"No." Kelly angled her head. "Just that the name had personal meaning to her. Doesn't get much more personal than the woman who brought you into the world." As she spoke, Kelly's voice darkened. Paige didn't know her past but imagined there were complications between her and her mother.

"Even so, what made her provide her mother's name to the waitress at the Lucky Pub?" Paige said, thinking. "Her mother must have been on her mind."

"There'd be good reason for that," Nadia replied. "Estella died eight months ago. Doctors diagnosed Michelle with PTSD about three months before that and sent her home."

"How did the mother die?" Jack inquired.

Nadia looked straight at the camera and said somberly, "She had early-onset Alzheimer's."

Jack's mother had lost the battle with the mind-altering disease last year, and it was probably why Nadia had put Estella's illness so delicately.

Nadia went on. "Estella had suffered for about a year after being diagnosed and was in a home where she was cared for. It just so happened around the time Michelle was discharged, her mother's mind had taken a swift turn for the worse, too."

Paige ran through the timeline of the murders in her head and came to a conclusion. "Her mother's death could have been Michelle's trigger. Wise was killed only two months after."

"Still, why those particular men?" Brandon asked.

Paige looked at him. "There must have also been a connection with the mother."

"Possible abuse, as we've theorized before?" Kelly suggested. "What about Michelle's father, Nadia? Who is he, and was he in the picture when she was growing up?"

"I'm going to guess no. Frank Evans enlisted in the Marines twenty-nine years ago."

"Michelle would have been six," Kelly said, sorrow tinging her voice. "Tender age."

"Is he still alive? Serving?" Brandon asked.

"He's alive, but he left the Marines five years ago with an honorable discharge. He's currently fifty-six and working as an engineer with a company in Baltimore, Maryland, where he lives now."

Fifty-six, Paige considered that. Was it a coincidence that all the men who were shot were ages fifty-five and fifty-six— her father's age range? Paige was also curious if Frank Evans had reentered his daughter's life, possibly at the funeral service. Maybe his appearance had been the trigger more than the mother's death. "Is there any indication that Frank Evans was a part of Estella's life in more recent years? Did he pay for his wife's care?"

"Nope," Nadia said. "There's no indication Frank even kept in touch with his wife and child. No money was sent for them, and when I called the home where Estella was up until her death, they told me she paid for her own care. She had quite a nest egg that was left to her by her wealthy parents when they died. That was when Estella was twenty-one."

"They were wealthy?" Paige asked. "What did they do?"

"Honestly, I didn't have time to dig into that."

"Regardless, end of day, Frank Evans went off to serve his country and truly abandoned his family." Paige was disgusted.

"It happens," Jack snapped, and Paige could have smacked herself. Jack might see himself guilty of that same thing. She'd apologize, but that would only antagonize him.

Paige took a deep breath and exhaled through her mouth. "Michelle was raised by her mother, had a father who didn't have anything to do with her, the mother gets sick, and still no sign of the father. Or so it would seem," Paige summarized. "How does all this tie into the four victims? We know that Michelle was acquainted with Wise and Reid in the past. But how?" Paige didn't even know where she was going with her comments, but speaking thoughts out loud often helped. *In the past...* If only they could find out what Michelle had said to Wise when he'd joined her. "Nadia, did you get the video I sent over from the Lucky Pub?"

"I did and forwarded it along to a colleague who is an expert at lip-reading. We're at the mercy of his schedule."

"Tell him it's part of a murder investigation," Jack said.

"I have, Jack, and I'll let you know once I hear from him." Nadia paused, and a smile played on the edges of her mouth. "I can also connect Michelle with the Sunset Diner."

"She did work there," Paige blurted out.

"She did," Nadia affirmed.

Paige nudged Brandon in the arm.

"I called the diner and spoke with the owner. Michelle waitressed there about eight months ago for about a month. She told the owner she needed to pay off her mother's health bill and for the funeral."

"You said that Estella had money, so...what am I missing?" Paige asked.

"Nothing. Something's not adding up. And when Estella died, she left a sizable amount to Michelle."

"A sizeable amount being...?" Jack prompted.

"A few hundred thousand."

No one said anything for a few beats; Jack was the first to speak.

"I think we need to get on the ground..." Jack kept talking, but Paige didn't want to hear him. She had a bad feeling. "Go to Bridgeport, California." He was looking at the camera, and she swore right at her. "Paige?"

"Yes?" Her chest tightened.

"Did you hear me? I want you and Brandon to get on a flight to California."

Coolness blanketed her. The last time Paige was there, she was arrested for murder. It was only because Jack, Brandon, and Zach literally flew to her rescue and cleared her name that she was released. "I hear you," she forced out.

Paige could feel Brandon staring at her profile and wished he'd stop. *Focus on the case*, she told herself. "Nadia, you said Michelle was a waitress for only a month. Why did she leave?"

"Why, I don't know, but apparently she just didn't show up for her shift."

"Huh." Paige was running through all that Nadia had just told them. "So she took a job under false pretenses, ran off about a month before the first murder. It seems conclusive now that she stole the Mavises' credit card information, but what drew Michelle to the Sunset Diner in the first place? And had she planned to steal from the Mavises, or was it just a matter of convenience?"

"She's leaving breadcrumbs," Kelly said, "between the credit card, the Sunset Diner, and giving the name Estella to the Lucky Pub, she wants us to look at Bridgeport. I'd say her trigger happened there. Her reason for wanting the four men dead happened there. Like Jack and I were discussing, she's adhering to a mission, even if it's one that she's given herself, and I think she's being intentional about what she leaves behind."

Jack looked from Kelly to the screen. "Do you have an address on Michelle Evans?"

"I do. Last known is a one-bedroom apartment in Bridgeport, California. I contacted the building manager, and he said the place is paid up until the end of the year, but he hasn't seen Michelle in months. She has a Toyota Corolla, and it's in the apartment's lot. I've tried tracking her phone, but no luck. I also looked her up online, but her social media hasn't been active since not long after she was enlisted."

"Which was when?" Paige asked. She didn't remember Nadia saying.

"Fifteen years ago. She was twenty. I have her bank accounts and credit cards being monitored. She touches her money, and we'll know about it."

"What about any registered weapons?" Brandon asked, and Paige tilted her head. He shrugged. "Hey, you never know."

"None," Nadia said.

"Not the easiest to get a sniper rifle off the street, but not impossible," Paige concluded. "A handgun's easier."

"Both are easy enough if you have greenbacks to throw around." Brandon smirked.

"We need to find out all we can on this Michelle Evans, what triggered her," Jack stated with authority. "If it did involve her mother's death, what about it? How does that make targets of the four men she killed? Paige, you and Brandon need to visit the diner, talk to the owner, and go to Michelle's last known address and get inside. Nadia, get local uniforms there to watch the place for any sign of Michelle, and we'll need the father's address in Baltimore. Kelly and I will pay him a visit."

"I'll send it to you right away, Jack," Nadia said.

"And Michelle's last known to Paige and Brandon."

"Of course."

"Paige, before you board a plane for California, visit Wise's mistress and see if she can offer anything to the investigation."

Paige nodded, and with that, they all had their marching orders. Nadia was the first to sign off, followed by Jack and Kelly, then Paige and Brandon.

Paige turned the laptop off but held her finger over the power button. *Why California, of all the places in the world?*

"Not looking forward to a trip back to the Golden State?" On the surface, Brandon's words could have been taken as jest, but his face was somber.

She slowly shook her head. She could easily conjure up the feeling of being held in that jail cell, treated like a murderer. She wrapped her arms around herself.

"Guess I can't say I blame you." Brandon reached in front of her and shut the lid on the computer. "Come on, we've got to get another flight booked *and* fit in a visit to Wise's mistress."

"Yeah."

"Hey, at least you have me to travel with." He flashed her a cheesy grin, and she rolled her eyes.

CHAPTER FORTY-THREE

Instead of just one thing causing tension, there were two. My guilt and Paige trying to suppress bad memories from her last visit to California. Hopefully, the fact it was a large state, and she'd had her problems in Valencia, a few hundred miles south of Bridgeport, would help her release the past. I was out of luck with that until I decided to forgive myself— apparently easier said than done. But regardless of feelings and personal drama, Paige and I would be boarding a flight at ten minutes after seven, in just over three hours, so we had to make our visit to Josefina Alverez a quick one.

Paige rapped her knuckles against Alvarez's apartment door a second time. "Ms. Alvarez, it's the FBI. Please open the door."

"One minute," a woman said, followed shortly by the sound of bare feet padding across the floorboards toward them. The door swung open, and a thirtysomething Alverez stood there, tying the strap on a thigh-length silk robe. What little modesty she showed still didn't cover up her long, tanned legs and ample cleavage.

Not that I noticed. I was always the professional. I cleared my throat and held up my badge. "We're Agents Fisher and Dawson with the FBI. You're Josefina Alvarez?" Not so much a question, as I recognized her from the compromising photos.

"I am." She was soft-spoken, but the devil danced in her eyes.

"I hope now's a good time, but we have a few questions for you about Robert Wise. Can we come in?" I adhered to the more-bees-with-honey approach, unlike Jack, who would have presented such a question as a request. Alvarez wasn't moving, though, so maybe a little more force was necessary. "It's important that we talk with you," I stressed, hoping to sound closed to negotiation.

She took a half-step back when a man came up behind her, wearing a T-shirt and a pair of boxers, and put an arm around her waist. He eyed me with instant dislike.

"Who are these people?" he asked Alvarez.

"The FBI," she said, turning to face him and putting them cheek to cheek. "They're here about Robert."

The man took a dominating position behind Alvarez and put his hands on her shoulders. "This isn't a good time right now."

"Actually, this is the perfect time," I countered. "We have a plane to catch and need to ask Josefina a few questions before we leave."

"Maybe when you get back, then." The man was smug.

"We won't be back," I said firmly.

Alvarez put a hand over the man's. "It's okay, Garrett." She moved back, and Garrett moved with her. "Come in," she told us.

Paige and I entered the apartment, and Alvarez and her boy toy just stood there and made no offer of a place to sit.

"We shouldn't be long, but it still might be more comfortable for you if we were seated," Paige said as if reading my mind.

Alvarez and Garrett moved as a unit toward a sofa, where they sat snugly beside each other. Paige and I dropped into chairs across from the sofa.

"We understand that you and Robert were lovers," Paige said.

"We were."

"We're sorry for your loss."

"Thank you." Alvarez blinked slowly.

"You and Robert were close?" Paige put it as a question as her gaze drifted over Boy Toy. I hated that I even felt a twinge of jealousy. I was in great shape, too, and worked out every chance I got—which hadn't been often lately. Ate healthy. I sucked in my flat gut even more and sat up straighter, squaring my shoulders.

"Guess you could say that," Alvarez admitted. "I cared about him, but Rob and I were rather casual. He was married and just having fun. So was I…having fun, anyway." She gave a smoldering look at Boy Toy, who put his finger to her lips and eyed her like he was going to take her right then and there.

Okay!

I glanced at Paige, but she wasn't looking at me.

"So you never developed any real feelings for him, despite it being 'for fun'?" Paige's gaze danced briefly to me, and I flushed with a rush of new guilt, feeling like I'd used her. That's what my sleeping with Paige had been to me: fun. *But* I had been married. The affair had been exciting and risqué, off-limits, like forbidden fruit.

"No, I did," Alvarez admitted.

Spikes of self-flagellation exploded in my chest.

"But I knew we weren't going anywhere," Alvarez said. "He wasn't going to leave his wife, and they were in counseling."

"Have you ever returned to the Lucky Pub since he was shot?" Paige asked.

"No interest." A shiver visibly tore through her, and Garrett wrapped an arm around her.

"We understand that you had dinner with Robert at the Lucky Pub the night before he was murdered," Paige said.

"That's right. We were there most nights, actually. He was obsessed with the patio and insisted we sit out there whenever the weather was nice enough."

"Did you notice anything or anyone unusual the night before the shooting?" I asked, not wanting to come out and show her Michelle Evans's picture.

"There was a woman who kept staring at Robert. She was driving me nuts the way she was looking at him."

"And how was that?" Paige asked. "Like she was interested in him?"

"I wouldn't say so. More like she had something against him. I asked him about her."

My curiosity piqued. "What did he say?"

"He didn't want to talk about her. And I let it go at the restaurant because I didn't want to make a scene."

"But after you left," Paige pressed, "did you pick up the conversation?"

"Oh, yeah. I was furious, but he still refused to talk about her. He wouldn't even tell me her name, but he knew it. I knew he did. I told him I wasn't having sex with him until he told me about her. He bid me a 'good night.' Can you believe it?" Alvarez consulted her companion, who shook his head and swept a strand of her black hair behind an ear and kissed her cheek.

Whatever had transpired between Evans and Wise was still volatile—and raw after many years. What the heck had happened? "Did you mention this woman to investigating officers?"

"I never did. Do you really think some chick killed Robert? 'Cause I don't. I think he messed with that girl somehow for sure, but I don't think she killed him. That's why I never brought her up to the police."

I leaned forward, clasped my hands between my knees. "Messed with her how?"

Alvarez bit on a bottom lip and shrugged, and the robe slid down the curve of her shoulder a few inches. "It would only be a guess, but I'd say he slept with her."

"Broke her heart?" Paige inquired.

"I wouldn't know, but she was pissed about something."

I thought back to Evans's emotionless expressions on the video. Something didn't jibe here. I was pretty certain Alvarez was talking about Evans like we were, but we should make sure before we continued. "What did this woman look like?"

"She had blond hair, pretty," Alvarez spoke slowly, like she wasn't sure why all this mattered.

There was one more way of verifying we were all talking about Michelle. "At the pub, the night before Robert's murder, where was she seated?"

"At a table, facing us."

It was clear we were talking about the same person, except for the face I remembered from the video, the one that had been devoid of emotion. "What made you think she was mad?"

"Well, I could tell Robert was mad. It was just oozing from him. He was normally cool under pressure, slow to anger, but this woman had him livid. His face was all scrunched up, and he said something to her."

"When was this?" I glanced at a clock on the wall, only to realize things were getting interesting and we had a plane to catch—soon.

"I'd stepped out to use the restroom. Really it was because I needed a break from this woman's constant staring. I came back and saw Robert sitting at her table. He didn't know I saw him. I hung back."

I'd have to look at the video again, but I don't remember seeing Alvarez standing back and watching Wise and Evans. It was possible that she was just out of the camera's range.

"Did you know she had the audacity to follow us back here?"

"She came to your apartment and spoke with you or Robert?" Paige asked.

Alvarez shook her head. "No, but I found a note under my door the next morning. I know she put it there."

"How do you know she left the note?" I was interested in proof, not suspicion.

A flicker of irritation crossed her eyes. "The note told me that Rob was a dangerous man. The handwriting was certainly a woman's. We're typically neater."

What a generalization! She's never seen my mother's handwriting. "Can we see the note?"

"I threw it out. It scared me at the time. Some wacko stares at us all through dinner and then gives me a note like that. It had to be her, who else?"

"Okay, thank you for your time," Paige said and led the way out of the apartment.

In the SUV, Paige turned it on and commented, "So Josefina calls Michelle a wacko, admits she was scared of her but doesn't report her after Rob was murdered? Some people are crazy."

"Uh-huh." My thoughts kept steamrolling me with guilt. *It was for fun.*

"Three widows receive compromising photos of their husbands," Paige began. "Now Wise's mistress says she received a note, essentially warning her away from Robert. It's almost as if part of Michelle's mission is to expose these men to all the women in their lives."

"All right, so we have the Marines, a diner, the Mavises, four male victims, two mistresses—"

"And a partridge in a pear tree." Paige chuckled.

"Yeah, I have no idea how it all fits together yet."

"Good, because neither do I, and as the senior agent among us, I should figure it out before you do."

I fell silent, thinking that was her way of apologizing for pulling the seniority card the other day. But if anyone owed anyone an apology... "Paige—"

"Brandon—"

"You go first," I told her.

Her face went serious. "I did feel guilty. Still do sometimes. Not for falling in love with you, not for sleeping with you, but for hurting Deb—that's if she ever found out. But only a little. You weren't happy, Brandon, not with her. If you were, you never would have..." She didn't need to finish, and I nodded.

"We'd been drifting apart," I admitted, grabbing the morsel of justification she'd extended.

"And like it had been for Josefina and Robert, what we had when you were in the academy was casual."

"It didn't feel that way sometimes."

"No, it didn't." She locked her gaze with mine. "But all that's behind us now. You and Deb, well, you're divorced, and you're happy with Becky. I'm happy for both of you." She smiled one of those sorrowful smiles you gave people when your heart was breaking.

"I'm sorry, Paige."

"For—"

"Please, let me get this out." *Before I find an excuse not to.* "I'm sorry for hurting you, for putting you through everything I have." I loved Becky, but in another life, if things were entirely different, I could see myself with Paige; I loved her, too.

She sniffled and batted a hand of dismissal. "We were adults. We both knew what we were doing."

"Yeah."

"Besides, the past is harmless if we just leave it there. It's not like we can go back and do things differently anyway." She attempted a smile, but her eyes darkened. I sensed she was revisiting the lesson she'd learned her last time in California. She'd gone to hunt down one of the men responsible for raping her friend when she was on spring break in college— but it had snowballed into a legal nightmare when he'd turned up dead and Paige looked good for his murder. But even that trip to the past had a silver lining: we'd uncovered a serial killer and brought him to justice.

No more was said as Paige put the SUV into drive and took us to the airport. My heart hurt for the women in my life—past and present. But the past wasn't something I could change, just as Paige had cleverly pointed out. My only hope was that over time I might forgive myself. I also had the lesson to make smarter choices moving forward and utilize a little thing called self-control. I just hoped I had some.

CHAPTER FORTY-FOUR

Kelly looked out the windshield at the colored lights whizzing by as Jack sped down the interstate toward Baltimore, her mind miles away and years in the past. Her six-year-old self had watched her mother shoot her father as if from a distance, through someone else's eyes. Even all this time later, the image never crystalized beyond a flat, cardboard-like representation of the event. Shrinks told her she needed to allow herself to the feel the moment and immerse herself in it, but she'd never been successful. That didn't mean the horror she'd witnessed hadn't affected her. Really, how could it not when six was such a tender age, a time when impressions were made and memories formed. Kelly couldn't help but empathize with Michelle. She'd experienced trauma of her own; her father had left her as a young girl. Feelings of abandonment were left to churn in his absence and to curdle like spilt milk over time.

"She didn't show any emotion. Cool, calm, devoid of emotion…" Kelly ruminated out loud what Paige and Brandon had told them about the Michelle Evans they'd seen on the pub's surveillance video.

Jack took an exit for Baltimore and didn't say anything.

Kelly started thinking about Paige's call that updated them on her and Brandon's visit to Josefina Alverez. "If our sniper is the one who left the note for Wise's mistress—which it would seem she had—she viewed Wise as a dangerous man. But she didn't show any signs of being afraid of him. It's not lining up."

"She views herself in a position of control and power—and she is the one holding the gun." He glanced over at her, a smirk playing on his lips, and Kelly smiled.

"Suppose you're right about that." She hoped that Frank Evans, Michelle's father, would be able to shed some light on her past, but he also hadn't seen his daughter since she was six—that they knew of. It was even more of a stretch to think he'd have any clues to offer as to her current whereabouts. But he might be able to tell them more about the Mavises and the Sunset Diner than they already knew, which was very little.

It was about thirty minutes of city driving, after getting off the highway, to reach Frank Evans's address. Jack pulled into the lot of a rundown apartment building. The sight of the crumbling brick and broken asphalt hurt Kelly's heart.

"This is where a Marine vet with an honorable discharge ends up? Something's wrong with the system. Some 'thanks for your service.'"

"The men and women who sign up to serve this country don't do it for the money." Jack got out of the SUV, and she felt like a child who'd had her hand slapped. Her cheeks flushed warm, and she unbuckled her seatbelt and joined him outside.

"Sorry, Jack, that's not what I was saying." She walked around the front of the vehicle.

"No harm done."

"I was just saying that vets should be compensated for their trouble." Her defensive words spilled out, and she instantly felt like a fool. How could compensation even begin to smooth over what active service men and women had seen and done?

"I'm not going to argue with you." Jack led the way into the apartment building.

There was an overhang above the front door, and Kelly looked up to study it, almost fearing it would fall on top of them. She shuffled into the main lobby as quickly as possible.

Jack pressed the button for Frank Evans's apartment, and they waited.

"I realize that many of them go in without a trade and come out with one, but I still feel there could be more our country could do for them." For some reason, Kelly couldn't let the matter go. Maybe it was because the man she loved the most in this world had served his country and should have received far more acknowledgment for his efforts.

Jack rang Frank's apartment a second time.

"Who's it?" A man's slurred voice came over the intercom.

"Mr. Frank Evans?" Jack asked.

"Who's is it?"

Who's is it? The guy sounded shit-faced drunk.

"It's the FBI. We need to talk to you."

There was thundering silence for a span of time, and just when Kelly wondered if he'd passed out or was making a run for it for some reason, there was the buzzing of the door unlocking. They made their way to Frank's apartment, but the door was closed, and there was no response to Jack's first knock. He knocked again.

There was a thump against on the back of the door, and Kelly imagined Frank was looking at them through the peephole. "Go away."

Oh, this is going to be fun.

"Mr. Evans, open the door," Jack said in a no-nonsense manner.

The door cracked open the amount the chain would allow, and Frank squeezed his face through the opening.

Jack put his badge a few inches from his nose.

"Geez." Frank crossed his eyes and pulled back. The door was shut, the chain slid, and the door opened wide. He stood there cradling a beer bottle in his right hand. "I don't know why the Feds wanna talk to—" He burped and wiped his mouth with the back of his hand.

Kelly wanted to fan the air. If smell had color, they'd all have been shrouded in a green haze.

"Can we come in?" Jack didn't wait for an answer and started inside the place.

"Surrreee, come on in." Frank bobbed his eyebrows at Kelly, and she gave him a cordial smile, taking shallows breaths but still getting inundated by the odor of whiskey. *Beer, whiskey...what else has he been drinking?*

A Cat 4 hurricane would have left less of a mess than what was before them. The living area of the apartment were all visible from the entry and littered with trash. Take-out boxes tossed here and there. Every sitting surface but where Frank must have had his butt parked was covered. The tabletops were packed with empty bottles, with barely enough room to set down a fresh drink. Maybe that's why Frank traveled with one.

As she continued to scan the room, she found a rocks glass—the whiskey and source of the reeky belch—nestled between remote controls and a pizza box. The apartment smelled like a man's gym locker—nauseating body odor.

"*Takes* a seat where you'd like." Frank gestured around and rocked on his feet.

"Steady there," she said.

"Nah, I'm fine." Frank batted a hand in the air but made his way to a pocket of space on the couch.

How did a former Marine end up in this hovel, with such a horrible addiction? Her mind raised the question, though the answer could be textbook: it was to drown out the memories of what couldn't be unseen. Her grandfather had taken to drink for a brief time, but thankfully, he had her, *and* he was willing to help himself. That was the key. You can only help those who want to help themselves.

Jack laced his hands in front of himself. "We're hoping you can answer some questions we have about your daughter Michelle."

Frank frowned. Gone was the rather harmless drunk as a storm moved across his eyes. "I don't have a daughter." He punched back some beer.

"The birth record says otherwise," Jack countered.

Frank downed the rest of the beer and set the bottle on the table with some force.

"We need to find Michelle Evans." Jack didn't give any impression the man's strong reaction even fazed him. "Do you know where she might be?"

"Do I—" Frank smirked then laughed. "Why would I? I haven't seen her in the better part of thirty years."

Kelly could see that he was trying to hide the regrets and pain that had dug trenches in his soul behind amusement. Maybe if she pointed out the good he'd accomplished, it would help matters. "It's understandable that you would have fallen out of touch with Michelle." She paused to give him a warm smile. "We understand that you served with the Marines. Thank you for your service." She'd offered the sentiment for strategy, but she also meant every word.

Frank closed his mouth, as if he'd been prepared to say something smart, and dipped his head. Typical, she thought, as her grandfather had been the same way—viewing service as his patriotic duty.

Frank's face softened, and he seemed to sober. "It was the hardest thing I had to do…leaving Michelle."

"I can imagine it would have been." Kelly waited a few seconds. "You said you haven't reconnected with Michelle, but what about with your wife, Estella?" Kelly asked gingerly, not really wanting to tear scabs from old wounds. But it had to be done.

"Wow. I haven't heard that name in a long time. Not that I've ever forgotten her."

"I can feel that you loved her." Kelly was speaking from her heart. Who knew what drove some people away from their loved ones? If only life was black and white and not so complicated.

"I did. Very much." His eyes filled with tears, and he patted the arm of the chair. "I heard she died eight months ago."

Kelly wanted to ask how he'd heard that but didn't want to shut him down. Besides, it would be understandable if he'd kept some sort of tabs on the woman he'd loved—but if that was the case, had he also kept them on Michelle? And if he had, why be so adamant he hadn't seen her in about thirty years?

The room fell silent for a few minutes, Kelly and Jack letting Frank sit in reflection.

Frank sniffled and eyed Jack. "Why is the FBI looking for Michelle?"

"She's a person of interest," he provided the textbook response.

"Don't give me some blanket response. Why is she of interest? And don't tell me you can't say."

"Your daughter became a Marine, like you," Jack said, throwing a curveball and causing Frank to narrow his eyes.

"I might have heard that," he said.

So he did keep tabs on Michelle. "She was trained as a sniper, and from what we understand, she was a very good one."

If Frank was making any connection between the recent sniping in Arlington and their presence, it wasn't showing on the man's face or in his body language. His forehead was bunched up like he was confused and had a headache.

"What are you trying to tell me? I'm not in the mood for games."

"You might have heard about a recent shooting that took place in Arlington," Jack said.

"Sure, I— Oh. You don't think that...?" Frank's eyes widened.

"Michelle Evans is of interest to the FBI." Jack squared his shoulders as if erecting a wall of defense for the Bureau.

Frank's gaze flicked to Jack. "You do think that she— Whoa. I'm not going to sit here and tell you she wouldn't do something like, uh, kill people. I didn't know her past the age of six. But I'd like to think that she wouldn't. Did she serve time in an active war zone?" He looked to Kelly for the answer, and she nodded. "Well, that can change a person." He pinched his eyes shut.

"It does." Jack's hand traced over his shirt pocket that housed his cigarettes, and then he let his arm fall to his side.

"You served?"

"I did." Jack's admission carried on a measured exhale.

Frank remained quiet, watching Jack, as if hoping for an elaboration. But Jack was a man of few words, and he liked to portray himself as impenetrable. Kelly was aware it was the sensitive souls who burrowed inward to protect themselves from the outside world. *The sensitive souls.* She felt more understanding for Jack and his stance on controlling one's emotions. It wasn't because he didn't feel them; it was because he felt them strongly. Maybe it was time to touch a bit more on Frank's.

"Mr. Evans, it's admirable that you served your country, as I said before," she began, "but I don't think you left your family completely behind. You've kept tabs on them through the years, by the sound of it."

"Still hardly makes me husband or father of the year."

"Many in military service leave their families to carry out their patriotic duty, but they keep in contact with their loved ones." Kelly wasn't making any accusations but building to a delicate question. "Why did you fall out of touch with your family?" If Frank could answer that, they might be able to figure out more about Michelle's mindset.

Frank clenched his jaw. "It's time for you to leave." He jumped up from the couch and thrust a pointed finger toward the door.

"Please, we haven't even had a chance to ask—"

"I don't care."

She was going to say they hadn't asked about the Mavises and the Sunset Diner. *Guess we'll have to do that on a future visit.* She took a few steps toward the door. "Thank you for your time—"

"Enough platitudes. Out!" he barked.

Kelly was shaking when she hit the hall with Jack. "All I did was ask why he left his family."

"I'd say you touched a raw nerve." Jack pulled out his pack of cigarettes as they walked down the hall and outside.

She stopped clear of the overhang and faced Jack. "Raw nerve for sure. He's living with a lot of regrets, but I also think he's hiding something. He says he heard about Estella's death and Michelle joining the Marines. I think he kept an eye on them. For how long, who knows? He loved Estella—even admitted as much. It's just the way he…" Her thoughts went to Frank's strong reaction to her asking why he'd cut off his family.

"Agent," Jack prompted.

She stood a little taller at hearing her title. "Okay, here's what I'm thinking. It's almost like he felt forced to leave or maybe even…was pushed away? He can't even decide from one minute to the next if Michelle is his daughter or not."

"Could just be that he doesn't feel worthy of her."

She gulped back memories she wanted to hold on to of an idyllic childhood—the one she'd only known through the pages of fairy tales. "When Mom left us—Grandpa, me, my brother—after she was released from prison, Grandpa told us she didn't feel worthy of us anymore. I don't know if he believed that or if it's something he said to help us all feel better. But it didn't help. To think that Mom felt unworthy made me feel responsible. Had I said or done something that made her feel that way? Was it something I didn't do or say?" This was her first time admitting this out loud, and tears were close to falling. "But I've come to believe Mom made the choice to leave—one I had nothing to do with." *Am I lying to myself?* She sighed. "If Frank Evans made the choice to leave his family on his own, shouldn't he be able to move forward and accept his decision?"

"If only life worked that way." Jack slipped a cigarette out of the pack. "Some choices can haunt you forever and have long repercussions."

Did that mean Mom may be out there regretting hers? Kelly shook the thought aside, not wanting to dwell on it for any length of time. Hope could be cruel.

Jack lit his cigarette and took a puff. "Regrets are born when the consequences of our decisions aren't what we'd planned for, kiddo."

Kiddo? The nickname warmed her, and she tried to ignore the surge of emotion whelming into her chest.

"Yeah, you're right." She took a few calming breaths and tried to call on logic, but it had left her stranded on an island of insecurity and doubt. She looked up at the moon and wondered where on God's green earth her mother was, and wherever that might be, was she looking up at the sky right now and asking the same thing about her daughter?

CHAPTER FORTY-FIVE

Bridgeport, California
Saturday, October 26th, 8:35 AM, Local Time

The sunshine that had been streaming in around the curtains in Paige's hotel room had her waking up in a good mood—until it sank in that she was back in California, and Brandon's apology from yesterday bubbled up from her subconscious. It was endearing that he felt for what he'd put her through—and irritating, as the consideration he'd shown her only made her like him more. But the healthy thing to do was tamp down any personal feelings and focus on the case. And that was getting easier with every sip of coffee she took from a jumbo to-go cup she'd gotten from a local restaurant. It also helped that in Bridgeport she could almost forget she was in California. Royal palms didn't line the road, and the town was small with a population of six hundred.

It was eight thirty by the time she and Brandon were getting out of the SUV, which they'd rented at Mammoth Yosemite Airport, in the lot at Michelle's apartment building. The sun was already beating down, and sweat was gathering at the back of Paige's neck. She hated the feeling.

Brandon had gulped back the rest of his coffee before exiting the rental vehicle, like he didn't want to leave a drop, and she knew the feeling. But that's what happened when you hopped on a red-eye and still had to drive an hour from the airport to your destination. Paige wondered if he'd had a hard time nodding off like she had.

She spotted a deputy's car from the Mono County Sheriff's Office immediately and headed over. He put his window down and greeted them with a hearty "Good day."

"We're FBI Agents Paige Dawson and Brandon Fisher."

"Deputy Mitchell." He squinted and looked at Brandon.

"Any sign of Michelle since you've been watching the place?" Paige asked.

"Nope. Nothing." Mitchell pinched the bridge of his nose and looked more exhausted than she felt. Stakeouts were boring as hell.

"You the FBI?" A rotund man in his fifties was making his way toward them from across the gravel lot.

"We are," Paige said.

"Well, I'm glad I was right about that. Could have been embarrassing otherwise. You know that saying about when you assume…"

Paige glanced at Brandon and raised her eyebrows. *You make an ass out of you and me.*

He held out his hand. "Anyway, I'm Dan Player, the manager here. I saw you from my window." Dan pointed up to a second-story balcony. "I was just having a coffee and waiting for you. Hey, would you like one?"

"No, we've just finished one—" Paige tossed out a brief smile "—but thank you. I'm Special Agent Dawson, and this is Special Agent Fisher."

"Let's go see the place, shall we?" He turned and waved a hand over his shoulder for them to follow.

"We shall," she whispered to Brandon, and before walking off, she whispered her thanks to Mitchell.

"I told your analyst… Nadia, isn't it?" Dan paused, working the key in the apartment door, and looked over a shoulder.

"That's right," Paige said.

"I told her, which you probably know, but I haven't seen Michelle in months. Strange, too, as she paid up for a full year. Only a month left on the lease now."

So, Michelle had moved in at about the same time she was discharged from the Marines.

Dan finished with the lock, twisted the handle, and opened the door for them.

Paige took in the space. It was one main room with the kitchen to the back and two doors off to the right—a bathroom and a bedroom. The place felt empty with only a couch, an end table, a small study desk, and a chair. There were no bookshelves, no TV, no computer, and no personal effects in the main area, though Michelle may have had those things in the bedroom. First impression made it hard to believe that Michelle had ever spent any real time here. It was a rather dark apartment with only one window in the living area behind the desk.

"What can you tell us about Michelle?" Brandon asked.

"Huh. Guess it depends on what you'd want to know." Dan angled his head and fidgeted with the key that was still in his hand.

"Anything and everything," Paige replied. "What is she like?"

"She's quiet and sticks mainly to herself."

Isolation wouldn't help a person who needed to sort out emotional issues. "You never saw any friends come over?" Paige asked.

"I saw a man come by a couple of times."

"When was this?" Paige asked.

"Probably about two to three months after she moved in. Like I said, though, it was just a couple of times. It doesn't mean he wasn't here more, but if he was, I didn't see him."

Paige nodded thoughtfully. That would be around the time of Estella's death. If they could find out who that man was, it might get them closer to finding Michelle. "Can you tell us anything about him? What he looked like? His name?"

"Nah, sorry. I didn't meet him, only saw him."

"What did he look like?" Brandon repeated the other half of her inquiry.

"Um, nice-looking guy, above-average, but he was in his fifties. Thought he was a little old for her, but who am I to judge? To each their own."

Paige felt tingles down her arms. All the victims were in their fifties. Had this man done something that triggered the killing? "Did you happen to catch what kind of vehicle he drove?"

"No." Dan stopped fiddling with the key and looked briefly down at his hands. He slowly lifted his gaze to meet Paige's eyes. "Is Michelle all right?"

"As far as we know." Paige felt comfortable in saying that; Michelle was far from all right. She'd killed four men and one woman—that they knew of.

He let out a deep breath. "Oh, that's a relief to hear. But wait— Why is the FBI interested in her, then?"

"All I can tell you is Michelle Evans is a person of interest to the FBI."

"*Ohhh.* You're trying to find her, so you think she's done something."

"I'm not at liberty to say, Mr. Player," Paige said.

"Very well. I guess things are what they are." Dan handed the key to Paige. "You hold on to this for as long as you need. I'm in apartment 101 if you need me."

"Thank you."

Dan left and closed the door behind him.

"A man in his fifties?" Brandon raised his eyebrows. "Interesting."

"I thought the same, but until we figure out who…" Paige let her words trail off. "Let's spread out and see what we can find."

"I'll take the bedroom." Brandon set off in that direction, and she went to the study desk.

She proceeded to glove up and open the top drawer. Pens, highlighters, markers, sticky notes. Nothing personal.

The next drawer offered much of the same, but Paige found a folded map. She opened it on the desk. It was a map of the United States, but a red marker outlined a path along I-40/I-81/I-66 and starred the cities of Albuquerque, Little Rock, Knoxville, Arlington, and Baltimore.

"Brandon, get out here."

He rushed over to her.

"Look what I've found." She gestured wildly to the map. "Michelle planned out her route. She knew where Wise, Miller, Sherman, and Reid were."

"Seems like solid proof of that." Brandon dragged his finger along the red line.

"I'd say." Paige fixed her gaze on Baltimore, Maryland, and pressed her fingertip next to the asterisk there. "Michelle's father lives in Baltimore." She slowly turned to look at Brandon. "Is she going to target him next?"

Brandon had his phone out and to his ear quickly, filling in Jack and Kelly. He hung up a moment later. "Good news is Jack and Kelly are already back in Baltimore. They were going to pay Frank Evans another visit today. Guess he was drunk when they showed up to talk last night."

"Hopefully, they can figure out why Michelle might want to target her father."

"Assuming she does, but I know how it looks with the map."

"Ah, yeah. Considering men were shot in all the other cities, which leads to another question. How did Michelle know where to find the men?"

"It's called the internet."

"Very funny, smart-ass."

Brandon shrugged. "Hey, just saying."

"Not everyone's online these days. Remember, Nadia said Michelle wasn't active on social media."

"Doesn't mean she can't use a search engine."

"Fine, I'll give you that."

Paige tugged on the drawer, intent on pulling it out and spilling the rest of the contents on the desk to examine them there, but she met with resistance. "Something's…" She slid her hand along the inside of the drawer, trying to figure out what was interfering with the drawer opening—and felt something stuck to the top and bunching in the track. She hunched down, her head almost upside down trying to see what was there, and made out the corner of a piece of paper that had been taped there. She gently worked it free and held it in the light coming through the window.

It was a photo of five young men, in their late teens, early twenties. Four of the faces, though decades younger, were unmistakable. There were standing in front of a teal-painted building.

Brandon leaned in, his shoulder pressing against hers. "Is that—"

"Yep, all four of our victims. I'll be damned. All of them knew each other."

"Who's this guy?" Brandon pointed a finger toward the fifth man.

"I don't…" Paige took a closer look. There was something familiar about the bridge of his nose and the distance between his eyes. "Bring up Frank Evans's license photo."

Brandon did so and held his phone's screen toward her.

"Number five is Frank Evans," she said with certainty. "Michelle's father not only knew the men she killed, but by the looks of this photo, Frank was good friends with them."

"The possibility was mentioned that Michelle might have been assaulted by the victims. What if it had been Frank who'd brought them into Michelle's life?"

"Sure, but what the hell happened?" Paige wasn't sure she really wanted the answer.

CHAPTER FORTY-SIX

Kelly stood next to Jack as he banged on Frank's door—a little loud for any time of day. But given how heavily Frank had been into the drink last night, he might still be passed out. So far, it was like rousing the dead. They'd buzzed his apartment, but there'd been no response, and Jack had gotten them into the building by way of calling another tenant.

Like rousing the dead. Her thought repeated, and she feared Paige and Brandon might have been right about Frank Evans being target number five. What if Michelle had already gotten to him?

Kelly raised her hand to knock, and the door swung open.

Frank was massaging his forehead. "You again? What do you want? I told you I don't know anything." He was peering at them with half-mast eyes.

Kelly's impression last night had been that Frank was an alcoholic who sought regular comfort in a bottle, but for him to be feeling the effects of overindulgence this much, it wasn't a habit for him. The state of his place would indicate he'd probably been drinking for a few days or so, though. What had caused him to turn to the bottle? Did it have something to do with one of his old buddies recently turning up dead? But he had acted like the shooting in Arlington was no big deal—or was that what he wanted them to believe?

"Here, we brought you this." Kelly extended a take-out cup of coffee, which had been her idea, and Jack had agreed to it. If they were going to get Frank to talk, they had to come as allies.

Frank took the coffee. "Thanks," he mumbled.

"It's just black. Figured if you like cream and sugar, you'd have that here," Kelly said.

"Black is fine." He slurped from the small hole in the lid and stepped back to let them into the apartment.

The place still looked like a hurricane had run through—not that Frank would have been in the mood to clean after they'd left last night.

Frank went into the living area and gathered the take-out containers from the sofa and stacked them onto the coffee table. "What is it you'd like to talk about today? Come on, sit." He pointed to the recently cleared cushions, and Kelly and Jack sat down.

Frank grabbed a dining chair from around a small table and plopped down on it. He let out an involuntary groan as he did so. "Paying the piper today," he said. "Sure, ain't like drinking back in my younger years. Everything hurts this morning."

"Did you know the man who was shot in Arlington, Virginia, a couple days ago?" Jack asked, obviously unmoved by Frank's complaints about his self-inflicted joint problems.

Frank slurped his coffee. "I heard it was some prosecutor."

"We're pretty sure you can do better than that," Jack said firmly.

Frank took another gulp of coffee and ripped into a coughing fit. He tapped fingers against his throat, then held one up for them to wait. Eventually, he said, "I'm an engineer. He was a prosecutor. Where would our paths have crossed?"

Kelly shifted on the lumpy sofa cushion and kept her eye on Frank. They'd come here thinking he might be his daughter's next target, but that didn't explain why he was acting so strangely and hiding his association with Darrell Reid.

"Does Bridgeport, California, sound familiar?" Jack asked.

"Sure, I lived there for a bit, but—"

"It's better for you and us if you just tell us the truth," Kelly jumped in, playing good cop.

Frank met her gaze. "Fine, I might have known Darrell at one time in my life, but that's ancient history."

"What about Robert Wise?"

Frank turned his attention to Jack. "Yeah, I know him. What about him?"

"He was shot. Albuquerque, New Mexico, six months ago."

Frank wiped his forehead that glistened with sweat. "I had no idea."

"You have television and internet, I assume," Jack said.

"Sure, but—"

"What about Gregory Miller. Do you know him?" Jack had Frank under rapid fire.

So much for presenting ourselves as allies.

Frank closed his eyes for a few seconds. "Used to."

"He was shot in Arkansas three months ago." Jack leaned forward. "And Dennis Sherman? Know him?"

"Yes. Again." Frank set his coffee cup on the floor. "If you think I killed any of these men, think again. I can provide you with alibis. Call my work, and they'll tell you I haven't taken any vacation time in the last year. Not even any sick days."

"Kelly pulled out her phone and brought up the photo that Paige had found. She held her screen for Frank to see. How do you know these men?"

He glared at her. "If you knew I knew them, then why did you…" He shook his head and took a deep breath. "We met in an after-school program."

"What kind of program?" Kelly asked.

"It was really more like summer school. None of us were doing that great in our classes, so our parents had us taking courses during the summer to boost our grades."

Colleges and universities would show on their backgrounds, but it's not likely extra course credits would. That's why Nadia hadn't been able to link the men. Kelly also thought of the variety of occupations among the five men. "None of you ended up in the same field. What did you study in the summer?"

"Math. None of us were really great with the subject."

"That must have changed." She remembered clearly that Robert Wise became a plumber; Gregory Miller a teacher; Dennis Sherman an electrician; Darrell Reid a prosecutor; and Frank Evans an engineer. "Did you stay in touch over the years?"

Frank shook his head. "Ancient history. I got married, went off to serve. They moved on." He grabbed the coffee cup, pressed his scowl to the lid, and took a long sip.

"Did the five of you have a falling out?"

"You could say that." A pulse started tapping in his cheek. Something bad had happened. *Something that led to four men's murders?*

"Tell us what it was," Jack demanded.

Frank clenched his jaw and shook his head. "No, I have a right to my privacy, Agent. And I hardly believe whatever us kids squabbled about has anything to do with why they are dead."

Squabbled? Frank was failing at downplaying the significance of what had happened. "Your friends were murdered," Kelly said, earning Frank's gaze. "And you were hardly kids. You were in—what?—your early twenties in this picture?"

Frank rolled his shoulders. "I don't even remember when it was taken or where," he snuffed out, cavalier, but his body language was betraying him. The subject of his former friends had struck a nerve. "Where did you get that photo?"

"It was found in an apartment Michelle kept in Bridgeport," Kelly delivered, and Frank went white and bristled.

"You—you were in her apartment? Why?"

Kelly noted that he didn't ask how Michelle had come into possession of the photo. "As we told you last night, Mr. Evans, your daughter is of interest to the FBI."

"And as I told you, she's not my daughter."

Kelly cocked her head. That was his original stance last night, but then he'd gone on to talk about her as if she was, so which was it? And why the confusion? "You might want to start talking to us, Mr. Evans, because we believe your daughter plans on killing you next."

"She what?" Frank spat. "She wants to…kill me?"

Kelly felt Jack watching her, but she wasn't going to look at him. Maybe she'd gone too far laying out how it was, but they had to shake Frank into talking, and there was only so long they could dance around 'she's of interest to the FBI.'

Frank looked from her to Jack.

"Do you know why your daughter would want you dead?" he asked.

Frank hugged his cup with both hands, and his body shook. His eyes were full of tears; his face a mask of panic. "I might."

CHAPTER FORTY-SEVEN

It was going on midmorning by the time Paige and I arrived at the Sunset Diner. Before leaving Michelle's apartment, we told Deputy Mitchell we needed the place processed to see if they could find anything Paige and I might have overlooked. He was going to call for help with that and have officers take a thorough look at Michelle's car that we'd found parked around the back of the building. Without dedicated crime scene investigators, officers stepped up to collect evidence and process crime scenes.

Sunset Diner's exterior was teal-painted brick and had faded over the years, but I'd bet this was where the photo of our victims and Michelle's father had been photographed. "Paige, can I see that picture you found again?"

"Sure." She brought it up on her phone, as the original was bagged and tagged and with local law enforcement.

I compared the image to what was before us. "I'd say that it was taken right here." I touched the corner of a brick that had a chunk missing out of its corner and matched identically to the picture.

"Good eye. Maybe that has something to do with why Michelle was drawn to get a job here."

"Let's go see if we can find out."

Paige walked to the door of the restaurant, but I cut in front and grabbed the door for her. Chimes rang overhead.

"Thanks," she said as she walked in, "but I could have gotten it for myself."

"Good day." A plump waitress in her sixties, wearing a full apron over a teal uniform to match the exterior brick, came over to us. "Welcome to the Sunset Diner."

Paige smiled at her, and I looked around the restaurant. It was having an identity crisis, with a jukebox in a corner and black-and-white floor tiles paired with heavily varnished blond-pine tables and spindle-back chairs. Fifties-era diner meets country restaurant. Regardless, there wasn't a customer in sight.

"We'd like to speak with Earl Gilbert," Paige said and added, "if he's in."

"Oh, he's in or the doors would be shut." The woman gestured to a cut-out in the wall that opened to the kitchen. "He's just cleaning the grill, getting ready for the lunch crowd."

I couldn't see anyone back there, but I could hear clanging and scrubbing.

"Maybe I can help ya? I'm his wife, Harriett."

Typical hospitality as expected in a small town without the usual curiosity and suspicion.

"That you might." Paige gestured toward a table as if seeking permission to take a seat and, at the same time, inviting Harriett to join us.

We all sat, careful not to upset the table that was set up with paper placemats and paper-wrapped cutlery.

"We're FBI Special Agents Paige Dawson and Brandon Fisher," Paige said.

Harriett dropped into the chair with a *humph*. "FBI?" Her mouth fell in a straight line. "What brings the FBI to my door?"

"Our analyst back at Quantico spoke with your husband about a former employee of yours, Michelle Evans, and we'd like to ask some questions about her."

"Earl!" Harriett bellowed.

"What in blazing—" A man's face appeared in the cut-out, then disappeared. He burst through the kitchen door and hustled toward us. He eyeballed Paige and me. "Who are you?"

"They're the FBI, Earl. They said they spoke to you. Why didn't you tell me anything about that?" Harriett set a glare on her husband, but he seemed unfazed.

"Earl," Harriett prompted him. "Start talkin'."

"Listen, woman, I don't have to tell you everything."

"You better start."

Earl's turn to glare at his wife.

"Mr. and Mrs. Gilbert, we'd just like to know what you could tell us about Michelle Evans," I said.

The couple looked at me for a long moment, then Earl said, "I told that lady on the phone all I really know about her. She worked here about eight months ago and only stuck around for a month. I was sad to see her go, too. She was a hard worker."

"Why did she leave?" I went to lean my elbows on the table and remembered the place settings, so I threw an arm over the back of my chair instead.

"Don't really know, truth be told. She just didn't show, and we've not been able to reach her since."

"Would you sit down, Earl? You're hanging over us like a bat," Harriett complained.

"I'm just fine standing, Harriett."

It was amazing the two of them survived one day to the next and hadn't taken each other out yet. That must have been love. But what was bugging me was they probably knew exactly why Michelle had left and weren't saying. Either way, it would have been about a month after her mother's death, but neither Gilbert brought it up. "Did she just take off or…"

"Well, we heard her momma died," Harriett said.

Earl nodded.

They probably hadn't just heard; they likely had attended the funeral. Another thing with small towns was everyone knew everyone—and everybody's business. Harriett made it sound like she and Earl didn't know Michelle and her family, but Estella had grown up in Bridgeport and stayed here all her life. They were holding back on us.

"Do you know why Michelle came to you for a job?" I asked.

"I suppose it was for the same reason as everyone else; she needed money," Harriett said.

"We were thinking more that it might have something to do with her family's past, a connection here."

Harriett traced the placemat in front of her with her fingertip. "I don't know all of it. Earl and I just picked up the diner about ten years ago."

Michelle would have been in the Marines, but Estella would have been around. And ten years was plenty of time to get welcomed in by the residents of a small town and privy to the gossip. "Did Michelle ask you any questions about the diner or her parents?"

Harriett stopped moving her finger and looked at her husband. "I know she was curious about the diner's history."

"What about it?" I asked.

"Oh, just mostly about the customers. Do the same ones always come around, that sort of thing." Harriett looked across the room, and again I had a feeling she wasn't telling us everything, but I wasn't sure why she'd be withholding.

I was curious if Michelle had asked about Wise, Miller, Sherman, and Reid. She might have even shown the Gilberts the picture we'd found.

"Speaking of the diner's history," Paige said, pulling out her phone. "Do either of you recognize these men?"

They say great minds think alike.

Earl leaned down, his cheek close to his wife's, and they studied the photograph of the five men taken outside the diner.

"I don't. What about you, Harriett?" Earl straightened up to a full standing position again.

Harriett didn't respond to her husband and kept her eyes on the screen.

"As my wife told ya, we just picked up the diner ten years ago, so maybe this was from before our time?"

I nodded and kept my eye on Harriett. "We believe it was taken about thirty-three to thirty-five years ago."

"Yep, before us," Earl said.

Neither Paige nor I said anything. Harriett was fussing with her apron beneath the table. Just because they'd taken possession of the diner ten years ago didn't mean they weren't around town before then.

"How long have you lived in Bridgeport, Mrs. Gilbert?" It was time to apply a little pressure.

Harriett slowly raised her gaze to meet mine. "All my life, and for Earl, most of his. His family moved in when he was ten."

Huh, so they do know more than they're saying. "You'd be privy to a lot of what went on in this town, even without owning the diner."

Neither Gilbert said a word.

"Did either of you know Michelle before she came to work here?" Paige asked.

"Only as a girl. She went off to join the Marines when she was twenty. I know she wanted to before then, but Estella wouldn't allow it. She was devastated when the girl left."

"So you knew Estella? What about Michelle's father?"

"Oh, yeah, I knew both of them. And that man…" Harriett pursed her lips and looked up to the ceiling. "He left his young family to fend for themselves. Little Michelle was only six."

Earl sat beside his wife, and they made eye contact, an unspoken conversation passing between them.

I leaned forward. "Is there something else?"

They both shook their heads. Just like residents of a small town to protect their own from outsiders. If we wanted to get any sort of inkling as to Michelle's possible whereabouts now, we'd have to approach it the right way. We wouldn't get anywhere saying that Michelle was a threat. "We believe that Michelle's unwell and that she needs help." Not entirely a lie.

"Is she sick?" Earl asked.

"Don't tell me she has early-onset Alzheimer's," Harriett said. "What Estella suffered through, no one should."

"Michelle is unwell, but we can't comment further than that," Paige offered. "But the sooner we find her, the better."

"I haven't seen her in town in months," Harriett said sorrowfully.

"Mrs. Gilbert, you commented on Michelle's father leaving town when she was a young girl," Paige started, "but have you seen him since he enlisted?"

Harriett looked away and crossed her arms. "I haven't, no."

"Okay." Paige nodded. "Would you happen to know why Michelle's father left his young family?"

Again husband and wife met each other's eyes and held a private, silent conversation.

"Should we tell them, Earl?" Harriett said, barely above a whisper.

Earl's mouth set in a frown. "It was just rumor."

I sat up straighter. "What was rumor?" The thing with rumors was they usually contained a nugget of truth.

Harriett flicked her gaze from her husband to me. "It wasn't no rumor. It was the truth."

"Mrs. Gilbert, it might help us," Paige said gently.

Harriett's left hand started to shake, and she cradled it in her right. "When Estella was in college, she was raped. Dang sad, too, because she was in love with Frank. He married her, though, not long after."

Paige clenched her teeth. "And...Michelle, she—"

"Yes," Harriett said. "She could be the possible result of the rape."

I leaned back in my chair. Frank might not even be Michelle's biological father. Had Michelle found out about the rape, and did it have anything to do with her killing spree?

"What my wife hasn't said..." Earl paused, and his mouth twitched like he didn't want to put what he had to say next into words. "The rumor was that Estella hadn't just been raped by one man, but by four."

Four men? Was it Wise, Miller, Sherman, and Reid? I felt the blood drain from my face.

Harriett sniffled, and tears were beading in her eyes. I glanced at Paige, and she was pale and barely holding herself together. The man she'd set out to talk to in California was one of four who'd raped her friend.

The chime over the door sounded, and a man wearing blue jeans and a sweat-stained T-shirt came into the diner.

"Hey, Earl, Harriett," he said as a greeting.

"George," Earl replied.

"Just sit wherever you'd like, and we'll be with ya in a second," Harriett added, her voice rather quaky.

George sat at a table in the back corner. He must have sensed our conversation was more of a confidential nature.

"Before we go," I said, "can you take another look at the photo Paige showed you?"

Paige brought it up for them again. "Are any of the men who raped Estella in that photograph?"

"Allegedly," Earl said firmly. "Who *allegedly* raped her. My wife and I don't want to be gettin' anyone in trouble."

"Is that a yes or a no?" I pressured.

"Earl's right." Harriett reached for her husband's hand. "We can't say. We weren't there."

"But you lied when you said you didn't recognize them," I confronted them.

Harriett's face became a hardened mask. "We're not going to be bullied into talking."

Earl stood again, positioning himself behind his wife. "It's time for you to leave."

"Is there a problem there, Earl?" George asked.

Earl held up a hand to stay the local wannabe hero. "We're fine. Be right with you."

George grimaced at Paige and me.

Paige made the first move to leave the diner, and I followed her lead.

"Not exactly warm and fuzzy at the Sunset Diner," Paige said, pulling out her sunglasses.

"Especially when we started talking about the rape. And we didn't even have a chance to ask them about the Mavises."

"Maybe Jack and Kelly will have luck on that front with Frank Evans."

"Maybe." I was starting to think the credit card theft was just a presented opportunity for Michelle.

Paige's eyes went dark and glazed over like her mind was on something else, and I had a feeling I knew what. "You all right?"

"Yeah, I'll be fine."

We loaded into the SUV, and I snapped my seat belt into place. "Guess we could have just gotten our motive, though."

"Quite possibly. Her mother was raped, and she was the product of that assault," Paige summarized, "but how does that trigger Michelle now after all these years? I think we can both agree that it was likely the four victims who'd raped the mother?"

"I'd say that seems likely."

"Still, why now?"

Paige's question had me stumped for a few seconds as I sorted through the facts we knew. Michelle had joined the Marines, maybe in search of her father. Had Estella told her daughter, and she ran away to deal with it, to get answers from Frank? Estella had died eight months ago, her mind a mess from the merciless disease. *Eight months ago.* That was two months before the first murder. Had the rape come out as a deathbed confessional, or had the ugly truth been festering inside of Michelle for years?

Paige looked away and shook her head. Her voice was carried on a fine breath. "I can't even imagine being Michelle and finding out I was the result of rape, and assuming she didn't know until she left the Marines... That had to cut even more. Before that, she would have thought her biggest heartbreak had been her father leaving."

"Then she'd be faced with not even knowing if the man she'd grieved from childhood was, in fact, her father."

"Yeah, it's sickening. She'd feel so unwanted, like she didn't belong."

"Maybe like she shouldn't even exist."

"I think we definitely found our trigger," she said with conviction.

Silence fell between us for a few seconds.

"A couple things, though." Paige spoke slowly and deliberately. "It looks like Frank Evans is Michelle's next target. But why?"

"Could be that Michelle didn't know which men had raped her mother?" I hitched my shoulders. "Or maybe she still held him responsible for it happening, for some reason."

"Okay," Paige said but didn't sound satisfied by my response. "And here's something niggling at me. Reid and Wise recognized Michelle. How? Michelle would have just been a young girl, or a baby, last they knew. Did they keep tabs on her, and if so, why?"

"Huh, I have another idea." I took out my phone and called Nadia. "Can you fire me over a photo of Estella Evans?"

Seconds later, Paige and I were looking at the spitting image of Michelle Evans.

CHAPTER FORTY-EIGHT

Kelly couldn't imagine being wanted dead by her own flesh and blood. She wondered if her dad had known that one day his raised fists would cost him his life at his wife's hand. But she couldn't dwell on that. Whenever she gave her father a personality, feelings, she'd start down a dark, twisty rabbit hole she didn't to visit. But Frank Evans seemed to be handling the possibility better than most people might.

Frank had finished his coffee, and the empty cup sat at his feet. He'd just told them that Estella had been raped when they'd been engaged. "At the time, I had no idea about the rape or that Michelle could have been one of theirs. We eloped within a month of her pregnancy, which I came to find out later—much later—was because she wanted to get married before she got a baby bump. I was just flattered she wanted to get married right away. Estella never told me why she'd been in such a rush until after we'd been married for six years. She started putting on weight and eating anything she could get her hands on, until one day, she just broke down. She told me she was eating to fill a hole and then came out about the rape." Frank screwed up his face in disgust and rage.

Kelly'd seen victims of sexual assault struggle with self-worth for decades, even after going on to find love, getting married, and having children. So many didn't realize rape was a violation that lasted a lifetime. "And that's when you left?" The question was off Kelly's lips before she could think them through; her heart was thumping, and her stomach tossing. When Estella needed Frank the most, he'd bolted—and he had the nerve to tell them he loved Estella last night! But then, how could a person deal with the fact they'd lived a lie for six years?

"Yeah," he replied sourly. "I'm douche of the year."

"You told us you met the four men at summer school. Tell us a bit more," Jack requested.

"Um…" Frank hitched his shoulders. "We hit it off as quick friends and started hanging out after class and on weekends. I introduced them to Estella, and everything seemed fine. They liked her, and she liked them." He bit his bottom lip. "Everything was great—at least I thought it was. It makes it easier when the girl you love likes your friends, and they her." He was staring into space and wringing his hands. "Guess they liked her too much. Every one of them took a turn." He balled his fists.

Kelly glanced at Jack to see if he'd noticed, and he glimpsed at her. He'd caught it.

"Some friends, eh," Frank added. "All four of them even had the nerve to stand up for me at my wedding. Fucking sons of bitches."

Kelly couldn't imagine what it would have been like for Estella if these men, a.k.a. friends of her husband, were always hanging around. "It must have been hard on you, too," she empathized.

"That's why I left. She'd betrayed me by not telling me, and I looked—and felt—like a damn fool. And I couldn't stand looking at her anymore. Estella or Michelle—truth be told. But it was mostly me who I hated, who I wanted to punish. If it hadn't been for me, Estella never would have had to go through what she had. And Michelle, well, every time I looked at her, I wondered who the father was. One day I'd see Rob in her; another day Darrell; and around it would go with all four of them."

"Did you ever confront any of your so-called friends?" Jack asked.

"Nope." A pulse tapped in Frank's cheeks. "Another reason I enlisted. If I ever saw any of their faces again, I'd have killed them."

Kelly was finding it hard to believe he just ran away like a scared dog with its tail tucked between its legs, and Jack must have, too, given the question he'd just asked.

"That would have taken a lot of self-control," she said, shivers dancing across the back of her neck, over her shoulders, and down her arms. Something was starting to feel way off here. Was his current anger evidence of pent-up emotions, or indicative that Frank had taken action himself? Then there was another possibility that flittered through Kelly's mind as quick as a flash of lightning. "Mr. Evans, you're aware that we found a photo of you with these men when you were all younger in Michelle's apartment."

"Yeah, you showed it to me."

"Do you know where she would have gotten the photo?"

"Maybe Estella? She's the one who took the picture. That's all I can think, anyway." Frank wiped his sweaty forehead with the palm of his left hand again.

"Really? She held on to a photo of her husband, who left her, and the four men who raped her?" Kelly didn't bother to mask her skepticism. She wanted a reaction.

"She must have…I mean, I don't know where else Michelle would have gotten it from."

Kelly wasn't buying his words, and a theory was starting to form in her mind. "You think that Michelle found out that her mother was raped—and possibly by these men? Estella showed her the picture even?"

"It's possible," Frank said.

"Then, maybe she…" Kelly rolled her hand.

Frank's eyes widened. "She killed them for what they did to her mother."

Kelly's approach had worked: father had turned on the daughter in a flash. But she wanted to know one more thing before she asked Jack to join her in the hall. "Mr. Evans, do you know a couple named Edna and David Mavis? They're from Bridgeport, California, where you grew up."

Frank's brow crinkled. "The name sounds familiar. Ah, yeah, Rachelle Mavis. She was Edna and David's daughter and a good friend of Estella's. They'd known each other since they were little."

Kelly tried to contain her excitement at finally having a connection between the stolen card and Michelle. Just like Michelle had done with dropping the name Estella at the Lucky Pub, she was leaving a breadcrumb back to California—back to the scene of the real crime in her mind—by swiping the Mavises' credit card information. She looked at Jack and said, "Can we talk in the hall for a minute?"

Jack led the way out, and they walked to the end of the corridor, well out of earshot from Frank's apartment, but still within view if he tried to leave.

"I think Frank's involved—and maybe even working with Michelle," she put out. "You saw how quickly he turned on Michelle in there. Yesterday, he was defending her. I apply a little pressure, hook him, and he's all about her guilt. He knows exactly how Michelle came into possession of that photo, because he gave it to her. I feel it. There's no way Estella would hold on to that photo. Frank took advantage of Michelle's vulnerability, of her fragile state of being. I think he moved in around the time of Estella's death. Michelle would be at her lowest point, having just lost her mother, having experienced an active war zone, suffering from PTSD. She'd be wanting a place to belong in the world—even more so if she'd just found out how she'd come into the world. That's assuming Estella told her, but it could have just as well been Frank. I think he commissioned his own daughter to carry out the murders. Though he says he hasn't seen her in years."

"People say a lot of things." Jack tapped his shirt pocket.

"Sadly true. We've got to have Nadia do a full background on this guy. I really don't think he's Michelle's next target; I think that he's her conspirator. Both would have motive. You heard him—if he saw their faces again, he'd kill them."

Jack pulled out his phone. "We've got to let Frank think we're on his side for now, assuming we haven't already made him think otherwise."

"Sorry, Jack, if I was a little straightforward in there."

"It's fine. What's done is done, and he might not even have picked up on your implications. But let's see what we can do to salvage the situation." He called Nadia, and Kelly listened as Jack asked her to subpoena Frank's phone records and financials. "The guy says he hasn't taken any vacation or sick leave in the last year, but that doesn't mean he couldn't have hopped on a plane on his days off. See if you can find any record of travel, too," Jack told Nadia. "Also pull up information on Rachelle Mavis. She's the daughter of the couple whose card was stolen. I'll hold the line." Jack, ever so softly, tapped the carpet with his foot while he listened to Nadia. "Okay. And one more thing. Quickly check to see if Frank has any weapons registered to him."

Kelly felt herself go cold at thoughts of how quickly this could go sideways.

A few moments later, Jack hung up, but he didn't put his phone away. "He doesn't show any registered weapons, but when we go back in there, we still approach with caution. Talk to him like a friend, like we still fear for his life, got it?"

She nodded, but adrenaline was pumping through her and making her quaky.

"But we're going to call in for backup first."

"Makes complete sense."

Jack made another call to the local police department. He let them know where they were, the potential situation, and that their subject could be armed and dangerous.

"We hold off going back in until they get here," Jack added. "Should be about fifteen minutes."

"What did Nadia say about Rachelle Mavis?"

"She died a couple years ago."

"Oh." She could have provided some insight into Estella and Michelle.

"I'm going to update Paige and Brandon on our suspicions about Frank and let them know about Rachelle." He made the call and told them, then said, "Okay, go back and see if you can get anywhere with that. Keep us posted, and we'll do likewise. Bye." Jack pocketed his phone.

"What is it, Jack?"

"They said that the building manager where Michelle has her apartment remembered seeing a man with Michelle there once or twice. He described him as being in his fifties. I have them going back to see if the manager recognizes any of the men in the photo."

CHAPTER FORTY-NINE

Bridgeport, California
Saturday, October 26th, 10:40 AM Local Time

Jack's call had Paige and me sitting in stunned silence for a few minutes. "A conspiracy between father and daughter," I said. "Never saw that coming."

"Me neither."

"But how does that coincide with the asterisk on Michelle's map?"

Paige looked over at me in the passenger seat. "Could just be where she plans on ending up."

"She marked the victim's locations with asterisks." I wasn't so sure that Frank Evans was in the clear—just yet.

"Could represent destinations to her," Paige reasoned.

"Still. Arlington to Baltimore isn't that far. An hour and a half?" I latched eyes with Paige. "If they're working together, Frank could be hiding Michelle." I called Jack on speaker and pointed out the possibility.

Before the call ended, Jack told us, "Smart thinking."

Paige pulled out of the diner's parking lot, headed in the direction of Michelle's apartment building, and about ten minutes later, we were standing in the hall outside apartment 101.

"Agents." Dan Player smiled at us when he opened his door. "I thought you were finished here. I got Michelle's key back. Do you need it again?"

Paige shook her head. "We have a follow-up question for you."

"Certainly." Player stepped back into his apartment.

We entered and stayed just inside the door.

"You told us that a man came here with Michelle." I pulled up a photo spread on my phone of Wise, Miller, Sherman, Reid, and Evans. "Do any of these men look familiar to you?"

"Just a second." Player padded to a nearby living area and grabbed a pair of readers off a coffee table, put them on. "All right." He took my phone and studied the screen. "Yeah, him." Player pointed at Frank Evans. "He's definitely who was here with Michelle."

I glanced at Paige. *So much for not seeing his daughter in years!*

"You both look surprised," Player said.

Yes and no… "We are a bit," I admitted. "When was it you saw him again?"

"Say, around the time of her mother's funeral."

"Thank you, Mr. Player," Paige said.

"That all now? Or do you think you'll need back in her place?"

"We'll keep you posted," she said.

Paige and I smiled at him and saw ourselves out.

In the parking lot, we talked in the privacy of the SUV.

"Frank Evans lied. He was probably at the funeral, which means the Gilberts probably lied to us, too. But now we have someone who places him with Michelle around the time we figure she was triggered," Paige said.

"So he comes back to conscript her, as it were, to kill the four men who'd raped Estella."

"Could be. Maybe he just wanted to see Michelle and make amends, but it became something else?"

"Sounds like a conspiracy to commit murder times four."

"You could say times five, including the maid," Paige corrected.

"And if he knew about the funeral, he could have also been keeping tabs on his four ol' buddies all this time."

"And fed that information to Michelle so she'd know where to find them. I was wondering how she knew where they all were."

"Did Frank openly discuss the murders with Michelle, or did she take the mission on herself? Did he give her the photo of the men so she knew who they were? For her to see with her own eyes how they'd all been buddy-buddy to her father's face and had committed such a horrible evil behind his back?"

"Well, the visual would have amped up hatred in Michelle."

"Uh-huh," I agreed. "I really think Frank sent his daughter on a killing mission. Otherwise, why cover up the fact he was here and that he saw Michelle? He told Jack and Kelly he hadn't seen her in years."

"He didn't want us to know he was here, that's for sure."

A blond, twentysomething woman was running across the parking lot toward us and waving.

Paige lowered her window.

"Are you the FBI?" she asked, panting.

"We are. Agents Dawson and Fisher."

Paige and I got out of the vehicle.

"You're looking for Michelle Evans?" The woman squinted in the late morning sun.

"We are," Paige said. "What's your name?"

"Karen Ross." She attempted a smile, but the expression didn't give full birth.

"Do you know Michelle and where she might be?" I leaned against the SUV but quickly righted myself. The sun had heated the black paint to boiling.

"We were friends."

"*Were*?" I asked.

"When she left, she told me she might not be coming back."

Paige lifted her sunglasses onto her forehead. "Do you know where she went?"

"She didn't tell me."

"Tell us what you do know about Michelle," Paige encouraged.

"Just that she was a nice woman, if not a little strange, but who isn't around here?" A nervous little chortle. "Should I be worried about her now that the FBI is looking for her?"

"We believe she might have gotten herself mixed up in something, but we're doing what we can to find her," I said, my mind stuck on the part about Michelle not having plans to return. *What is her endgame?* "Her car's here, so did she leave with someone?" I asked.

"She took a taxi. I don't know to where."

I nodded.

"Poor Michelle was never the same after her mom died," Karen volunteered.

"She took it hard?" Paige asked conversationally.

"Sure did. She didn't want to talk as much. We used to have coffee in the back. There's a small green space with some picnic tables next to the lot. Anyway, she kept telling me she wasn't feeling well. I don't think her time in Afghanistan helped her either."

"War zones rarely do." I probably said that a little drier than intended. "Did she ever say anything to you about her father?"

"She was very tight-lipped about him, but he showed up here, ya know, and to her momma's funeral." Karen kicked the toe of her shoe into the gravel of the parking lot.

It never got less disgusting to think that Frank had taken advantage of Michelle at her most vulnerable moment—whether he'd originally planned to do the killings himself or not.

"How did Michelle handle his return?" Paige asked.

"She was an utter mess. Like I said, she didn't want to talk about him much. If it had been me, and my daddy had shown up all these years later, I'd have slammed the door in his face."

I nodded. We already had Player's testimony that he'd seen Frank Evans—and more than once. It was evident that Michelle hadn't sent her old man packing.

"Michelle was a gentle soul. She told me that she owed it to her father to forgive him," Karen said, as if pulling from my mind. "She said people do things they don't mean to sometimes."

For this extension of forgiveness, father and daughter had to have found a common ground, and that was looking to be the murder of four men who'd wronged the woman they'd both loved.

"Did you believe her when she told you that?" I asked.

Karen met my eyes and took a deep breath. "I think so. She seemed sincere."

"Thank you for speaking with us." Paige handed Karen her card. We got Karen's information, too. "If you think of anything else, call me."

"I will."

Paige and I returned to the SUV and headed out. I didn't even know where we were going, and I wasn't sure Paige did, either.

"Michelle forgave her father," Paige began. "It hardly sounds like she plans to kill him."

"I agree. Maybe the asterisks are more to mark destinations, after all. But why not take the map with her then?"

"She has a reason, but you know what else all this means?" Paige blinked slowly. "Both father and daughter were working as a team. We've got to share what we've found out with Jack about Frank being here."

We were quiet for a moment, working through the tangled mess.

"Frank Evans obviously lied," I said, slicing into the silence between us. "He told Jack he hadn't seen his daughter in nearly thirty years, but somehow he got down here for Estella's funeral—which was another lie, because he said he didn't go to it."

"And by the sounds of it, he was in Bridgeport for a bit," Paige added. "Yeah, we've got to update Jack. The sooner, the better."

CHAPTER FIFTY

As Kelly and Jack headed back to Frank's apartment, she took a deep breath, preparing herself to play nice *and* to be on the offensive—especially after Paige and Brandon's call. Not to mention that Frank had already shown them his moods were temperamental and fluctuated rather easily. And if he was hiding Michelle, things could turn ugly fast.

Jack knocked on Frank's door, and Frank called out from inside, "Go away."

"We have news about Michelle," Jack shouted back.

A bald-faced lie, but it might sway him to—

The door swung open, and Frank was standing there with a shot of whiskey in his hand. He kicked it back. "What about her?"

Jack brushed past him, and so did Kelly. At least for the moment, it didn't seem that Frank was any sort of threat to them—to his liver, possibly. They'd certainly touched a nerve to drive him to drink again. Guilty consciences were often loud, and booze could drown out the voices.

Frank slammed his door shut and stood there, back to the wall. "What happened to Michelle?"

"Let's sit down, Mr. Evans." Jack spoke with calm authority, and Frank did as he was asked, resuming his place on the dining chair again. Jack and Kelly sat back on the couch.

"What is it?" Frank's hand was shaking as he met Kelly's eyes. "She killed them, didn't she?"

"When was it you said you last saw her?" Kelly asked, disregarding his question.

"I told you. The day I left, almost thirty years ago." Frank averted his gaze.

"That's right." Kelly said it apologetically, as if she'd had a lapse in memory. "And Estella? Did you attend her funeral?"

Frank clenched his jaw. "I told you I didn't."

"We both know that's not true," she countered. The plan before had been to return as allies, not adversaries, but that was before they knew he'd lied to them, before it would seem all had been forgiven between daughter and father as they found common purpose.

Frank paled. "I'm telling you the truth."

"You're still sticking with that?" she volleyed back. "Who are you protecting?"

Jack got off the couch and started for the hall in the apartment that would lead to a bedroom or two and the bathroom.

Frank sprung from his chair. "Hey, wait, where do you think you're—"

"Just using the washroom, if that's all right." Jack studied him, and Frank backed down.

"You could have just asked."

The guy's more than a little twitchy.

Frank returned to his chair and regarded Kelly. "I didn't tell you about going to the funeral because I didn't think you'd understand. I left Estella, broke her heart. We were childhood sweethearts, got married before we even finished college. And I turned my back on her—and none of it was her fault." Frank's eyes welled up with tears, but Kelly wasn't sure she was buying his act.

Jack returned and shook his head subtly for Kelly's benefit; Frank didn't notice. But it told her that Jack hadn't found Michelle in the apartment. It didn't mean Frank wasn't keeping her somewhere else, though.

Frank glanced at Jack but resumed talking to Kelly. "I had no right to be there, but when I saw Shelly… She looked just like her mother. I was hurled into the past, only this time, I swear to God, it hurt even more."

Kelly noted how Michelle had become "Shelly," indicating a closeness he seemed so intent on hiding. "Did Michelle recognize you?"

"No. I mean, why would she?"

"Was that when you showed her that picture of you and your old buddies outside the Sunset Diner?"

"Yeah," he mumbled.

Kelly had thought before it would be odd for Estella to hold on to a picture that showed the faces of her rapists, but it was just as strange for Frank to keep it—unless he'd harbored it for ill intent. "Did you give her the photo to keep?" Kelly treaded delicately.

"I did, but I made a copy of it for myself," he said, adding the latter part seemingly as an afterthought.

Strange… But if Kelly confronted him on why he'd held on to it—or asked to see it—he'd certainly become defensive and stop talking to them.

"Did you tell Michelle what they did to her mother?" Jack asked.

"I didn't have to. She knew."

Kelly leaned forward. "Estella told her?"

"She told me that in Estella's last days, she'd babble, almost incoherently, and it slipped out that she might not be mine. Between that and other things she'd said, Shelly figured it out."

"She figured out the men in the photo you showed her were the men who raped her mother?" Kelly would side in favor of Estella coming out and telling Michelle, rather than her just "figuring it out."

"You say you held on to the picture of them," Jack started. "Did you keep tabs on them? It seems they were never far from your mind."

Frank licked his lips and grimaced.

"Did you know where these men were living?" Jack raised his voice with this question, and it was almost a bellow in the small apartment.

Frank crossed his arms. "I'd like a lawyer before I say anymore."

"Fine by me." Jack stood to his feet. "You'll be coming with us."

Kelly guided Frank from the chair and put him in cuffs. As she did so, she could only imagine the sadness her grandfather would have felt with her bringing in a former Marine. But good service only took a bad man so far.

CHAPTER FIFTY-ONE

Paige and I went back to the inn we were staying at in Bridgeport and were on a conference call with Jack and Kelly. We had considered going to visiting the Mavises to see if they could shed more light on the Evans family, but Jack had us proceeding otherwise—and for good reason. Nadia had come through with some findings on Frank Evans, and it would appear that he was lying about a lot of things.

"His phone records show that he received a call from a pay phone in Bridgeport two weeks after the mother's funeral. The conversation lasted fifteen minutes," Nadia said.

"Michelle called him, but for what?" I asked, knowing, unless we were suddenly mind readers, we'd have to get Frank to tell us.

"Really, it's just an assumption that Michelle was the one to make the call," Kelly pointed out.

I shook my head, not that she could see. We were doing this meeting via telephone. The Wi-Fi in the hotel was spotty at best. The closest FBI field office was in San Francisco, the better part of a five-hour drive away. "I think it's a good assumption. And to talk on a pay phone tells me the conversation was probably something Michelle didn't want traced."

"Like they were conspiring to commit murder," Kelly finished.

"Exactly like that."

"Well, the guy's lawyered up, so I'd say he has something to hide," Jack updated us.

Nadia continued. "I was able to confirm that Frank Evans did fly out to California at the time of his wife's funeral."

"He lied about taking time off from his job, too," Paige said.

"Seems like."

Jack and Kelly would have had their hands full with Frank and not had time to speak with Frank's employer to confirm what he'd originally told them.

"Now, I've got more for you," Nadia said. "Several calls were made to Frank Evans along the stretch of I-40/I-81/I-66. Each phone call got shorter and shorter. And all the calls were made using pay phones. There were also calls from the cities where the shootings took place, and they were placed two days afterward."

"It's like Michelle was reporting in, telling her father that the murders had been done." As I said the words, a chill ran down my spine. "What slime, using his daughter to do the killing."

"But Frank's not even sure Michelle is his daughter," Kelly said. "And, really, she could be any one of the men's who raped her mother."

"Maybe that made it easier for Frank to use Michelle the way he has?" Paige tossed out.

"He's certainly not father of the year, or human being of the year, for that matter," Kelly seethed.

"Not that it helps, but there's no question that Frank Evans is aiding his daughter." Nadia's voice cut into the room. "There was another charge from the same airline Frank took to fly to California, and when I followed that up, I was told that it was for a flight to Albuquerque for one passenger—"

"Let me guess, Michelle Evans," I interrupted.

"Yes, Brandon." Nadia didn't sound happy that I'd cut her off. "It had her landing there seven months ago. From there, there's another charge that was made at Auto Rentals in Albuquerque. I called and found out that a Honda Accord was rented, and it was just returned to a depot in Arlington, Virginia, yesterday."

"Wow, she kept the same car all this time. That's ballsy," I commented.

"No, I think it's more breadcrumbs," Kelly said.

"Breadcrumbs?"

"Uh-huh. I've thought it before, but I almost think Michelle wants to be caught."

Kelly's theory sat out there.

"If that's the case, I want to grant her wish," I said. "Arlington, you said... But the map Paige and I found indicates her last destination is Baltimore, Maryland. Why ditch the car?"

"She is done with the killing." Kelly sounded confident.

"We need to figure out how she's getting from Arlington to Baltimore and how she's paying for it," Jack stated.

"It has to be cash," Nadia began. "As I said, nothing new is popping up on credit cards—Frank's or Michelle's."

"Where's the breadcrumb now?" I mumbled.

"I said 'breadcrumb,' not homing beacon," Kelly retorted.

"Nadia," Paige started, "you said calls were made to Frank two days after the murders. Did any come after Reid's?"

"No," Nadia confirmed.

"Maybe she's planning to update her father in person that the job was taken care of," I reasoned. "But then what? Father and daughter reunited run off into the sunset, a twist on Bonnie and Clyde?"

"Except for other pieces in this investigation don't fully fit," Kelly cut in. "The breadcrumbs she keeps leaving behind."

I got the distinct impression she was using the word just to bug me now.

"Why show her face at all? Why the note to Wise's mistress— Oh, we haven't heard back from Jane Powell, Jack, as to whether she got any note about Reid being a dangerous man."

"I'll call her again after we're finished here," he said.

Kelly went on. "And why the photos to the widows, warnings to the mistresses—assuming that was a pattern, too—and why give her mother's name to the waitress at the Lucky Pub? Why leave the map and photo at her apartment?"

I hated to admit it, but it did feel like Michelle was leaving us a trail to follow. "She's trying to find belonging," I said. "And approval from Frank—who may not be her father. Possibly killing to impress him. He is the only father figure she's ever known. And then he shows up in her life, in one of her darkest moments, just after she lost her mother. Biological father or not, she'd cling to him."

"Michelle may see killing the men as a way to move forward, to get back with her father, to heal," Paige picked up. "The little clues she's leaving may indicate she wants to do what's right, but she's also driven by revenge at some level or she wouldn't keep pulling the trigger."

"I disagree." This came from Kelly, and the rest of us fell silent.

"About what?" Jack eventually prompted her.

"I think revenge is Frank Evans's motive. It might have fueled Michelle to start, but I think she was more driven by getting her father's approval. Think about it. She joined the Marines to probably find him. Maybe even that was an act of seeking his approval, following in his footsteps. For Michelle, I think it was more about a mission, or at least that's how she reasoned and justified her actions in her mind. She was at war—only this time, it was on the four men who raped her mother—and the commander-in-chief was Frank."

I gave consideration to everything that Kelly had just said, and it could explain everything. "Frank Evans used his daughter to get revenge," I reiterated.

"Frank doesn't even view Michelle as his daughter half the time," Kelly pointed out. "As far as he's concerned, she could be one of the rapist's. Remember he even told us he couldn't stand to look at her face, Jack? Part of why he'd left?"

"Ouch," Nadia interjected. I'd almost forgotten she was still on the line. "Guys, there's a couple other things I need to tell you. First, I heard back from the lip-reading expert, and he was able to read Michelle's lips in the Lucky Pub video. She told Wise, 'You know what you did.'"

"Sounds like an enclosed threat," I said.

"I'd say so," Paige shot back. "We both saw that video and his strong reaction."

"The second thing," Nadia began. "I also looked into the computer system at the Colonial and worked with their tech. It would seem the system was hacked so room 850 would remain empty."

"So Michelle has tech skills," I concluded.

"I'm not sure about her, but Frank Evans does. I followed my gut and contacted Frank's old commanding officer in the Marines, and he told me that Frank could have come out and found a job in computers or engineering."

"We've got Frank in custody," Kelly rushed out with urgency. "There has to be something we can do with that."

With her plea, an idea struck me. "Jack?"

"I haven't gone anywhere."

Always the wise ass.

"The evidence points to father and daughter working together," I began. "What if we have Frank arrange a meet with Michelle? He's got to have a way of reaching her. And he's obviously all about protecting his own hide."

"Hmm."

I was tempted to say his name again to jolt an actual response consisting of real words, but I resisted the urge.

"That could work," Jack finally said. "But we have to make sure precautions are taken." He was talking slower than normal, evidently deep in thought. He must have been seriously considering what I'd proposed. "I don't think he presents any physical threat to Michelle," he then muttered under his breath.

"Well, we'll all be there. We could even name the place." This was our best chance of getting our hands on Michelle. "If Frank hesitates to hand her in, we dangle a deal in front of him. Just a feeling here, but I am pretty sure he'll jump on it." It made me sick to think how far this former Marine had fallen from grace. He'd let the horrific acts of other people break him. But sadly, he wasn't the first and wouldn't be the last.

"I say we do this," Jack declared. "Paige and Brandon, get on the first plane back here. Kelly and I are going to question Frank as soon as his lawyer gets here. Depending on how things go, we might proceed with setting up a meet. We've got to flush Michelle out somehow, and that might be the easiest way to do it."

With that, Jack hung up, and all of us were severed from the conference call.

I sat there, relishing in the fact that Jack could be running with my idea. It always felt good when the big dog respected you.

CHAPTER FIFTY-TWO

Kelly couldn't let go of the fact Frank had denied Michelle as his daughter half of the time. He showed emotion regarding her when he felt it helped his case. He didn't love Michelle, that much felt apparent. He probably came to hate her as much as the men who'd raped Estella, viewing her as tainted. The best way to get Frank's cooperation in bringing in Michelle was by making it seem as if he was the good guy—the hero—aiding the FBI in bringing in a killer. But first, they had to show him they had him cornered and create desperation.

She and Jack were at the Baltimore police station, and Frank was in an interview room. While they were all here, local field agents were searching Frank's apartment for anything that smacked of a murderous conspiracy.

Jack led the way into the interview room. Frank was seated at a table next to his lawyer, a man by the name of Joe Crawford, who carried all his weight in his gut.

Jack and Kelly sat across from them.

"Our conversation will be recorded, Mr. Evans," Jack said. "Do you have any objections to that?"

Frank waved a hand of dismissal.

"All right, then. For the record, Mr. Evans, when did you last see your daughter?"

A pulse tapped in Frank's cheek. "I last saw Michelle at her apartment."

"And that was after your wife's funeral?"

Frank looked at his lawyer, who nodded.

Frank answered, "Yes."

"And where was the funeral?" Jack leaned back in his chair.

"Bridgeport, California."

"You grew up there, didn't you?"

"I did." Frank pulled on the collar of his T-shirt as if it were suffocating him.

"Before the funeral, how long had you been away?"

"The better part of thirty years."

"Uh-huh." Jack opened a file folder and slowly tapped his index finger. "When you showed up, was your daughter there?"

"Yes. You know all this."

"It's just for the record. When you left all those years ago, Michelle Evans was just six years old, is that correct?"

"You know that," Frank hissed, and the lawyer put a hand on Frank's forearm to calm him.

"Did your daughter recognize you?"

"No."

Hearing this admission again, Kelly got tingles up her spine. He'd really manipulated the entire situation. He probably told Michelle about the rape—not the mother—and got her to empathize with him and to understand why he'd abandoned her and her mother.

Jack went on. "Did you introduce yourself to your daughter?"

Frank consulted his lawyer, who spoke up. "Relevance, Agent?"

Jack leveled a glare on the man. "The relevance is that we believe your client conspired with Michelle Evans in the murder of five people—unless he can prove otherwise."

"I believe it's on the prosecution to prove guilt, Agent," the lawyer said.

"I'm innocent," Frank claimed. "Michelle killed five people?"

Frank certainly went from being defensive to cooperative in a flash when he thought it served his purpose.

"Someone did," Jack said stiffly.

"Well, it wasn't me."

"You and your daughter stay in contact after the funeral?" Jack carried on casually.

Frank stared at Jack, briefly let his gaze drift to Kelly. "Why don't you tell me?"

"We noticed that you received a phone call from Bridgeport a couple weeks after Estella's funeral. Was that Michelle?"

"No idea. Probably a telemarketer."

"From a pay phone?"

Frank grimaced.

"The call also lasted fifteen minutes. Care to try again?" Jack asked.

"Fine, it was Michelle." Frank shifted in his chair. "All this was her idea, okay? I didn't say anything because…because, well, she's my daughter."

Oh, she's his daughter again…whenever it benefits him.

"She said she wanted to kill the men who did this to her mom," Frank said. "And she wanted us to be a family again. That's why when you said you thought she was going to kill me, I couldn't believe it."

Time to turn this interview around. "Only thing is you weren't looking for a family anymore, were you?" Kelly jumped in.

Frank met her gaze.

"You just wanted revenge on the men who raped your wife," Kelly said.

He slouched, crossed his arms like a petulant child.

"You got your daughter to carry it out with the promise it would bring you together, give you both a purpose."

Frank rolled his eyes dramatically.

Jack retook the stage. "We have proof that you aided your daughter in murdering those men."

"I highly doubt that," Frank scoffed.

The lawyer bristled. "What have you got, Agent?"

Jack pulled out the receipt from the car rental made in Albuquerque, New Mexico. "That's a receipt for a Honda Accord rented out using your client's credit card."

"Impossible. I've never—"

Joe held up a hand to silence his client.

"The rental company confirms that you were called—and your phone records prove it—about the charge. You authorized it."

The twitch was back in Frank's cheek.

"Before that, you booked a flight for Michelle Evans to Albuquerque. Your credit card confirms this."

Frank said nothing.

"Your phone records also show that you received a call two days after every murder," Kelly pitched in.

Frank turned to his lawyer. "Joe, do something about this."

"There's nothing I can do at this point, Mr. Evans," the lawyer said calmly.

"Unbelievable."

"You're looking at a lot of years in prison," Kelly said. "Five murders—"

"Five murders. You keep saying five." He looked from Kelly to Jack.

He pulled a crime scene photo of Marsha Doyle from the file and tossed it across the table. It came to rest in front of Frank.

"I have no idea who that woman is," Frank snarled.

"She was a maid at the Colonial Hotel where Michelle set up her sniper nest to take out Darrell Reid," Kelly said.

"What does any of this have to do with me?"

Kelly would love to cuff him upside the head, but she held back her temper. "You sent your daughter on a mission. She's a trained Marine, and she'd do whatever was necessary to carry it out. You used her training against her, her vulnerability, and manipulated her emotions."

"I want a deal," he snapped.

And we have him where we want him.

Jack leaned across the table. "You're not denying the allegations against you?"

Frank slammed a flattened hand on the table. "Those shits raped the only woman I've ever loved. One of them made her pregnant with…with that…" His lips were furled, and his nostrils flaring.

With *that*? *Ouch.* Kelly hurt for Michelle. Frank didn't care about her; he only saw her as a weapon to fulfill his purpose.

"Tell us where Michelle is," Jack demanded.

"I have no idea. She was supposed to call me after taking out Darrell. I haven't heard from her."

Joe dropped his head into his hands and sighed.

Jack calmly put his arms on the table and leaned forward. "You're confessing to conspiracy to murder four men and one woman?"

Frank didn't say anything but was huffing.

"Do you have a way of reaching her?" Kelly asked.

"No." He shook his head. "She calls from pay phones."

Joe turned to Frank. "I suggest that you keep quiet."

"There has to be some way you can reach her. If not, you're going down all by yourself for five murders." Jack pointed at Marsha's photo.

"But I never pulled the trigger," he seethed.

"Conspiracy to commit murder carries the same penalty whether you carry out the act yourself or not," Kelly stressed.

"Which you'd have to prove."

"You as good as admitted it, but as we speak, there are techs working over your apartment, your computer," Jack said. "If there's something there, they'll find it. You admitted a day didn't go by that you never thought of Estella. I'd bet the same was true about the men who raped your wife, 'the only woman you ever loved.'"

There was a pregnant pause.

"What do you want from me?" Frank raked his fingers through his hair and gripped his skull like a man gone mad.

Jack sat back, crossed his arms. "We want you to flush out your daughter."

Kelly angled her head. "What's it gonna be? Life in prison—no deals—going down for five murders, or are you going to help us bring Michelle to justice?"

Frank looked at his lawyer.

"He'll cooperate," Joe said.

"We're going to need you to call her," Jack stated.

Frank clenched his jaw again. "Won't need to—and it's probably best that I don't so she doesn't catch on. She might be off her rocker, but she's smart. We planned to meet tomorrow night at ten thirty."

"Where?"

"The Regency. It's a bar here in Baltimore where people respect your privacy, if you know what I mean."

Translation: It's a place frequented by criminals.

"You're going to keep your appointment, Mr. Evans, and we're going to be there in your ear." With that, Jack got up and left the room. Kelly followed.

"We've got to keep a close eye on this. I don't want anything going sideways. We'll need agents in place to play the roles of bartenders, waitresses, customers. We don't need to scare her off. The four of us—you and I, and Paige and Brandon, will pose as customers. I want us close if we need to make a move."

Kelly could tell by her boss's face he'd seen enough of these operations go sideways, and he didn't want one on his watch. She also picked up on the fact that, while mention of a deal was dangled, none were made—and that pleased her. She hated affording leniencies to criminals, especially killers.

CHAPTER FIFTY-THREE

Baltimore, Maryland
Sunday, October 27th, 10:30 AM Local Time

By the time Paige and I landed in Baltimore and booked into a hotel, I could have slept for a week, not that I had the luxury. We'd gotten about three hours of slumber, though, which was better than some nights on an active case. But it was the jet lag from all the different time zones we'd hit in the last couple days that was making it worse. It was almost half past eight when Paige and I entered the conference room at the Baltimore PD, where we'd be meeting up with Jack and Kelly.

I beelined straight for a take-out cup of coffee that was on the table and pulled back the tab. Steam oozed out, carrying with it a robust aroma. I took a sip and savored every second of it before I had to swallow. I'd just finished a coffee, but I'd take it intravenous today.

"You like that?" a man's voice said, startling me a bit, and I turned around. He held out his hand. "I'm Officer McCauley."

"Brandon Fisher," I said, taking his hand. "And this is Paige Dawson."

He shook her hand and said, "The coffee's from Sophie's Beans. They make the best coffee in the city, if you ask me." He tagged on a smile. He was far too cheery for first thing in the morning—even if it wasn't technically *first* thing, though it was for me, since I'd just crawled out of bed, the sheets not even warm.

"Thanks for bringing it in." Paige grabbed a coffee for herself.

"No problem."

Jack and Kelly were already seated and drinking their own java.

"I'll leave you to it." Officer McCauley closed the door, and Paige and I joined Jack and Kelly at the table.

"Nadia's forwarded some findings from the Marsha Doyle murder," Jack started. "She was shot at point-blank range with a 9mm bullet. As requested of Captain Herrera with the Arlington PD, the forensics are being handled through the FBI's lab in Quantico. The ballistics were rushed and showed they were fired from a Glock G19 handgun."

"Common," I said.

"And easy to get off the street," Kelly added.

Oh, it's so good to be working side by side with Miss Show-off again, I thought sarcastically. Actually, she wasn't that bad. Some people were just put on the planet to test our patience and maybe expand us as human beings…maybe.

"We have no way of knowing where the gun came from," Jack said. "But more of note—and we just found out—is that the handgun was used in two murders a couple of days ago in a Baltimore motel."

I almost swallowed my coffee the wrong way. "Do we know of any connection to our sniper?"

Jack shook his head. "But it appears that either Michelle or Frank was behind the deaths. Now, Forensics found a bullet casing in Marsha Doyle's apartment that had rolled under a table next to the door. Prints on it came back a match to Frank."

I sat back, surprised. "He loaded the gun used to shoot Doyle."

"I think it's possible he pulled the trigger," Jack said grimly. "A tenant told one of Herrera's canvassing officers that they saw a man outside the building a couple of times, usually in the evening, about the time Doyle would be returning from work."

"Did they provide a description?" Paige asked.

"They did, and it lines up with Frank's build and coloring. I'm having Herrera send officers back with a photo spread to see if they can positively ID Frank Evans."

"Frank Evans killed Marsha Doyle," I said. "Possibly the two in the motel."

"So it would seem."

I glanced at Kelly, back to Jack, thankful that the two of them were fine. They'd approached Frank as an innocent initially, as the next potential target. Little had they known going in.

Jack continued. "The weapon itself hasn't been recovered. No sign of the Glock in Frank's apartment. It's possible Michelle has it in her possession, but it's also just as possible that the weapon was discarded. Regardless, we all take precautions with Michelle tonight. We'd be fools to think she won't be armed. There haven't been other leads from a forensic standpoint, but Kelly and I got in touch with Jane Powell, Reid's mistress. She said she never received a note about Reid."

"Either that was something Michelle did with Wise's mistress and no one else or the other notes were lost," I said.

"Without tracking all the other mistresses, we have no way to know if it was a pattern typical for Michelle or not, but I'm not worried about that at this time. We just need to get her into custody." Jack flipped to another report. "A search of Frank's apartment did turn up something. Nothing definitive to support a conspiracy between him and Michelle, but browser history on his computer indicates he cyberstalked Wise, Miller, Sherman, and Reid over the years. He even had sites bookmarked."

"One cocky son of a bitch," I said and earned a glare from Jack for my language. "Sorry." I gave it a few seconds and said, "Okay, so we probably have a witness to put him outside Doyle's building, and his fingerprint was on the casing from the bullet used to kill her. We have him connected to one murder anyhow."

"Yeah, the one he denied knowing anything about," Kelly said. "The man's sick himself, if you didn't guess that already. The last thirty years of his life have been about Estella's rape. That's a long time to plot revenge."

"Some things stick with you," Paige said somberly, and I had the feeling her mind was back on California and further back to the rape of her friend.

"You think he was planning this for that long?" I asked, skeptical.

"There's a lot of history on his computer to indicate that's possible," Jack said.

"Is there any other forensic evidence to hang Frank?" Paige asked.

Jack shook his head. "That's all on that front, but we heard from the sheriff's office in Bridgeport, California. Deputies collected an empty envelope that came from Ancestry Labs in Michelle's car. They specialize in DNA testing. I have Nadia following up there to see if she can get any details."

I'd try not to get my hopes up too high. "Speaking of Frank, he's in holding?"

"Yes, and we need to come up with a plan of attack for tonight." Jack filled us in on the meet tonight at the Regency. "I've already alerted the FBI director, and he's authorized agents to come to assist from Quantico. They're going to pose as customers and workers at the bar."

"Makes sense," I said.

If Jack was the type to roll his eyes, he would have right then; I could feel it.

"We're going to get a script for Frank to stick to. Any deviation, and we move in, and the entire thing is put to an end." Jack's body stiffened. "Any deviation. Got it?" He looked over his team, and we all nodded.

CHAPTER FIFTY-FOUR

The Regency, Baltimore, Maryland
Sunday, October 27th, 10:30 PM Local Time

By the time ten thirty came around, we'd been through so much preparation, it almost felt like it should be later than it was. Then again, that might be the jet lag talking. Either way, time was up.

Paige and I were seated at a table to the left of Frank's, under the guise of a date, and Jack and Kelly were on the other side. Other agents were positioned throughout the Regency.

An agent from Quantico was tending bar, and two others were posing as servers. Out front, undercover agents were keeping civilians from entering the bar as discreetly as possible.

At ten thirty-five, the front door opened, and Michelle Evans walked in. I found myself holding my breath. She was right there, and I just wanted to move in, but Jack wanted to see if we could get a confession from her through Frank. The more evidence, the better, when it came to getting convictions.

Michelle wandered through the restaurant, and I was careful to watch but not appear as if I was. She was just as I'd expected from pictures I'd seen of her: pretty, trim, blonde, but there was certainly something off about how slowly she was walking and how she was diligently checking out her surroundings. Something she'd probably learned from being a Marine. Her gaze swept over everyone, but I had no doubt she was cataloging us all, trying to assess us.

But if I did say so myself, we were all looking the parts we were playing. Paige's hair was backcombed and frizzy, and she was wearing jeans and a matching jacket. Her gray T-shirt had a hole in it with some band's name scrawled across the front, tour dates on the back. I was done up much the same, but I had a knock-off leather coat, which I had hanging on the back of my chair. Both of us had pints of beer in front of us, along with two empties. We hadn't been drinking on the job, of course, but it was made to look like we had enjoyed some beer already and that the staff was slow to clear the tables, which would fit with the feel of the place. It could definitely benefit from a thorough cleaning. My Dr. Martens stuck to the tile floor. Even the tabletops were tacky—that took me right back to the Lucky Pub.

Michelle spotted Frank and sat across from him. She didn't take off the thigh-length trench coat she wore, but she undid it. She didn't say a word.

"Michelle, you made it," Frank said. We could hear him through earpieces, as we had the music playing at a loud volume that was regular for the joint and he was recording the conversation, which we could hear live. "You did it? The prosecutor, that was you, Shelly?"

"Yes." Michelle was smiling; it traveled in her single-word response.

Frank held out a hand for Michelle's, and slowly she raised hers and extended it across the table. "I'm so proud of you," he said.

"Thank you." Michelle was quiet, shy, tentative like a little girl talking to her father.

"You took care of all of it. You cleared your mother's name."

Michelle stiffened and withdrew her arm. "Mother never needed her name cleared." Heat coated her tone, and it made the skin tighten on the back of my neck. I glanced quickly at Jack, starting to get a bad feeling.

Frank didn't seem fazed. "What did you do with the rifle?"

"Just what you told me to do. It's at the bottom of the Patapsco River."

"And the leftover ammunition?"

"With it." Michelle shifted her position, slowly, and her demeanor was calm.

"You did a good thing, Shelly, killing those men."

"I'm not so sure."

"You did. Now we can be a family again, Shelly. A family," Frank cooed, using her pet name so much that it made me cringe.

Michelle flashed a brief, insincere smile that disappeared faster than it formed. She shuffled her feet in slow, precise movements and looked my direction. I laughed and took a sip of beer as if Paige and I were having an engaging conversation, but my mind was on the fact something was off about her.

Images of the interstate map found in Michelle's apartment flashed in my mind. The asterisks noted at each stop she intended to make along the way. The ones marking her targets. We had thought at one point that Frank was a target, but we'd become distracted by the fact he was an accomplice. Her friend Karen told us Michelle had forgiven her father, but what if she hadn't? We'd pegged Michelle for the patsy, but maybe she wasn't as naive as we thought.

"We need to abort now," I said for the benefit of the comm, trying not to jump up and put an end to it myself.

"We let it play out a bit longer," came Jack's reply.

"What do you mean you're not sure, Shelly?" Frank said. "I love—"

Michelle reached inside her coat, and I bolted to my feet.

I was too slow. She'd pulled a gun and squeezed the trigger.

Blood was draining from Frank's forehead as his head hit the table.

She put the gun on the table in front of her and laughed when she saw us and raised her hands in the air. "Thank you. Thank you," she repeated with a wide smile.

I glanced at Paige. *Guess there's a first for everything.*

Paige collected the gun—not a Glock G19—but a Sig Sauer P938, an easy acquisition off the street.

Jack cuffed Michelle and started to read her the Miranda rights. "You have the right to—"

"He used me!" she snarled and spit on Frank's lifeless body. "He turned his back on my mother. On me. That man doesn't know love. I shouldn't even exist."

Jack hauled her to her feet and finished off the Miranda rights.

Michelle then said, "Prison will be a better place for me. At least my mother will know peace now. She was an angel on earth, and now she watches over me." She blew a kiss toward the ceiling, then started to sob, her body racking fiercely under the pressure of years of emotional turmoil finally giving birth.

CHAPTER FIFTY-FIVE

Jack would probably be in meetings with the director of the FBI for the foreseeable future. While the director had given his approval for the operation, its traumatic ending necessitated some explanation. I wasn't sure what was going to happen to Jack, and I was feeling the weight of that burden on my shoulders. After all, I had been the one to suggest a meet between Frank and Michelle. My mind kept going around and around, trying to untangle it all. Even looking back, given what I'd known then, I probably would have suggested it all over again—that is, without knowing the outcome. We should have just moved on her when she walked in the door, but we'd blindly wanted to go for the confession, for the solid proof. If only we'd known just how much she wanted for this all to end, to see her mission through. It pained me to admit how right on the mark Kelly had been about her leaving breadcrumbs for us to follow. But things were always clearer looking backward. The calls between Frank and Michelle had become shorter and shorter. There was already a wedge growing between them. We'd failed to discern the meaning.

Jack had assigned me with the task of interviewing Michelle Evans, and I had yet to meet such an interesting—and conflicted—person. I'd sat down with her after we brought her in from the Regency to the Baltimore police station. Michelle was sitting in the interview room, shoulders and chin high when I entered.

. . .

"Frank Evans was the devil." Michelle speaks with such clarity and definitiveness.

"He was also your father." Ancestry Labs had confirmed such to Nadia. Michelle had sent a sample of her hair and Frank's for comparison.

"That's just DNA." She traces a finger in a circle on the table. "I'll only be my mother's daughter."

I let a few seconds pass in silence, then proceed to remove crime scene photos of Wise, Miller, Sherman, Reid, Marsha Doyle, and the two victims from the Baltimore motel. I set out each one slowly and facing her.

Michelle's gaze goes to each one as I lay it down, and she touches the corners for every one but Doyle's. She stops all movement, sitting there still and pale, like she'd been struck.

"Ms. Evans—"

"Please call me Ms. Foster, my mother's maiden name."

"Who killed her?" I gesture to Doyle's photo, and Michelle pushes it toward me.

"The devil killed her." She sniffles and refuses eye contact.

She'd led us to the location of the Glock G19 that had been used to murder Doyle and the M40 that she'd used for sniping. She claimed both had been bought off the street months ago.

I lift the picture of Doyle. "Did you and your father work together to kill the maid?"

"No!" she screams.

"What about them?" I point to the motel victims.

"Check the handgun for prints! You won't find mine on it."

I straighten, slowly. Herrera's officers who went back to Marsha Doyle's building found a witness who was able to positively ID Frank Evans as hanging around the building. I tend to believe that he pulled the trigger on Doyle. I'm not sure where I stand on the motel victims yet. Neither Frank or Michelle can be placed at the motel, but management wasn't exactly being cooperative with us or the police.

I put a photo of Frank on the table.

Michelle snatches it and crumples it into a ball. "I hate that man." Tears fall down her cheeks, but otherwise, she doesn't look to be crying. "He put me up to all of this. He put it into my head that they needed to pay for what they did to my mother. My mother was nothing but good and sweet and kind." She throws the photo, and it just misses the side of my head. "She believed in forgiveness. Frank was evil, a coward. He left us to fend for ourselves. Mom was devastated. I…I…"

"You what?" I say kindly.

"I grew up, joined the Marines, and tried to find him."

"You wanted to know why he'd left."

"I did." A sickly-sweet admission carries on a honeycomb voice. "I sought—no, hungered for—his approval."

"Did you ask him why he left when you saw him at your mother's funeral?"

Michelle bites on her bottom lip and nods.

"And what did he tell you, Ms. Foster?"

Her eyes glisten at the name, and a brief smile lifts the corners of her mouth. "He told me it was the fault of these men." She spits on the photos of her victims. "He said their actions set all the heartbreak into motion for our family, and it was time to hurt them."

"But you sent hurtful photos to some of their widows," I say. "Why hurt them?"

"I sent them to all of the women." She meets my gaze.

So, some must not have mentioned them or received them for one reason or another.

"You had to know the pictures would hurt the women." I still wish for an answer as to why she'd sent them.

"I thought that by knowing what kind of men their husbands were, I might ease their grief."

I nod, stuffing down any remnants of my personal guilt into a dark, dark place inside of me.

She looks down at the photos of all the victims again, and I see both sorrow and satisfaction sweep across her face when her gaze touches the four who raped her mother. "It's over now," she says and closes her eyes.

. . .

"Brandon?" Kelly's bark pulled me out of my recollection. From the way she was staring at me with her brows arched, she must have been trying to get my attention for a while.

"Yeah?"

"You okay over there?" She was sitting at her desk, what used to be Zach's desk, near mine.

"I'm good." If I said *fine,* she'd jump all over that and try to profile me. "Guess I don't need to ask how your first case was." The best way to shift the attention from oneself was to quickly direct it elsewhere.

"Not really." She took a deep breath. "I keep thinking I should have known this was going to happen."

I wasn't about to admit the same thing. Call it a matter of pride. "Sometimes things go sideways."

She met my eyes, and I realized how ridiculous that was to say.

"Do you think Jack's going to be all right?" she asked.

"I sure hope so."

Paige walked toward us, holding a coffee. "How was that for your first case with the BAU?"

Kelly looked from Paige to me. "We were just talking about that."

"I bet it was nothing like working with the Miami PD," Paige said.

"Not even close. I was just telling Brandon that I wished there was some way we could have known she was going to shoot him and stopped it. If we had, Frank would be still alive, and Jack wouldn't be fighting on our behalf with the director."

"You don't need to worry about Jack." Paige took a sip of her coffee. "You *never* have to worry about Jack."

I wished I had her confidence, but I really didn't want to question it. Let me go on thinking everything would be fine, that we crossed all the T's, dotted all the I's. I noticed the worry shadowing Kelly's face and felt like I had to bolster the new girl. "You're right, Paige."

"Of course I am. I'm always right." She smiled, but I could see a fracture in the expression—only because I knew her so well.

It had been a rough case, and it had caused a lot of self-reflection. Something I personally wasn't a fan of, but sometimes it couldn't be helped. We rarely grasped how our actions had far-reaching consequences—so many, we could never see coming. Like those men who'd raped Estella wouldn't have seen their act avenged decades later. They probably never even considered the emotional destruction they'd wreaked upon Estella and a young family she'd come to lose—might not have even cared. Or the suffering of a young girl hungry to belong and coming to feel she didn't even have the right to exist. Or the pain of a man that tore him from his family and made him plot murder.

Sometimes I thought a crystal ball would be nice, especially when the feelings of guilt and regret resurfaced, but maybe not seeing the future was a good thing. If we knew what was coming next, there'd be times we'd swerve, and by doing so, maybe we'd become stagnant, living in fear. We'd certainly avoid the journey, and while it might be safer—more comfortable even—there'd be no fun or growth in that.

Catch the next book in the
Brandon Fisher FBI series!

Sign up at the weblink listed below
to be notified when new Brandon Fisher titles are available
for pre-order:

CarolynArnold.net/BFupdates

By joining this newsletter, you will also receive exclusive
first looks at the following:

Updates pertaining to upcoming releases in the series, such
as cover reveals, book descriptions, and firm release dates

Sneak peeks of teasers and special content

Behind-the-Tape™ insights that give you an inside look at
Carolyn's research and creative process

There is no getting around it: reviews are important and so is word of mouth.

With all the books on the market today, readers need to know what's worth their time and what's not. This is where you come into play.

If you enjoyed *Past Deeds*, please help others find it by posting a brief, honest review on the retailer site where you purchased this book and recommend it to family and friends.

Also, Carolyn loves to hear from her readers, and you can reach her at Carolyn@CarolynArnold.net.

Upon receipt of your e-mail, you will be added to her newsletter mailing unless you express your desire otherwise.

Keep on reading for a sample of *One More Kill*, book 9 in the Brandon Fisher FBI series.

CHAPTER ONE

The moon was brilliant in the night sky, giving him all the light he needed to see his prey. They entered the woods, and he was right on their tail. What a rush! The thrill of the hunt had adrenaline pumping through his veins. It had been far too long since he'd felt this level of euphoria.

He stepped into the woods and listened. The snapping of twigs and the crunching of rocks underfoot. And they thought they'd be safe in the woods. Foolish—and a grave mistake. The Leopard smiled to himself.

He was skilled at the art of listening, of homing in on his targets. He sniffed the air and caught the scent of the woman's perfume. She'd certainly come through this way, and if his instinct was right, she was nearby. He smiled and lifted his archery bow, took a few steadying breaths, and pivoted, searching for his target.

"Come out, come out wherever you are," he prattled off in a singsong voice that he hoped sent chills through her very being.

The sound of deep breathing, the bristling of movement— then he saw her. About ten yards ahead. Easy-peasy shot. He pulled back on the bow and let the arrow fly. It catapulted through the air and found its target.

She screamed, and he grinned again, taking such extreme pleasure in her pain and frustration. There would be no one to hear her screams out here! And, oh, how loud people could be! They were certainly louder than animals in the face of their mortality, and more visceral. He loved toying with them the way a cat bats around a mouse in its claws.

Prey One went down in a heap, and he caught up to her, towering above her.

She was still wailing and clutching at the back of her thigh where his arrowhead had pierced into her meaty flesh and rendered her immobile. From the look of the blood pooling on the dirt, he'd struck an artery. He smiled down at her, and her face, a panicked mask, contorted into an expression of absolute horror, and her yells became mute.

"Show your fear," he told her and briefly shut his eyes. "Let me feel your terror." He ripped the arrow from her leg, and she howled into the night.

But there was another noise interfering.

Prey Two—the man. No doubt he had plans of grandeur and that of playing hero.

How lovely, the Leopard thought. "Your white knight is coming, my lady, but he will die just like you."

She let out an ear-piercing, strangled cry that resonated through him, filling him with absolute bliss.

Prey Two emerged from behind a thicket of evergreens. He stood in a bath of moonlight that made its way through a small clearing in the forest, presenting a confident stance, but the Leopard could smell fear. A distinct odor—unpleasant, repulsive. A stench that he needed to put to an end. But first, he had something else to attend to. He needed to make sure the woman wasn't going to risk moving, not that she'd get far if she tried.

The Leopard crouched next to her and removed his Bowie from its sleeve. He held it up for her to see and picked up on the small nuance of her widened eyes reflected in the blade. She tried to back away from him but was unsuccessful.

Her horrified protests became louder—the most pleasant sound to his ears, but there was even better yet to come.

He lunged forward, quickly slicing across her torso, from one side of her belly button to the other. Her intestines spilled from her, and her cries were near deafening.

Much better... A soothing lullaby to my ears...

Prey Two reacted, screaming and coming at the Leopard. Did he not realize that it was far too late to do anything remotely effective?

The Leopard resumed full height and lifted his archery bow. Depending on the male prey, they either ran at this point or challenged him. He so hoped for the latter, as it made it far more fun when they actually thought they could beat him.

"Get away from her!" the man barked.

He was like a tiny chihuahua taking on a bullmastiff. How admirable, yet foolish. The Leopard reloaded the arrow that he'd used on the woman, slipped it into the bow, and released.

It was like the man wasn't even going to try to escape his pending fate—until the last second, when he turned and started to run. The arrow hit him in the back of the leg, and he yelled out, dropping to the ground. The Leopard smiled.

Perfect. He wanted him alive to have fun with next.

He returned to the woman. It was time to get to work before she died from blood loss. The next step was much more entertaining with the prey still conscious, but he'd be fighting against the clock.

He bent down next to her and slapped her face until her eyes popped open. What many people didn't know was they could live with their entrails hanging outside of their body, sometimes for quite a while. The body was miracle and hell—depending on perspective. Her body trembled beneath his touch, but she didn't try to move. She wouldn't be able to anyway.

The man was crying about ten yards away where he'd dropped, sputtering nonsensical, incoherent words, but he was no threat.

The Leopard ignored him—for now. He'd get to him soon enough. He traded his Bowie for another blade, this one smaller, super sharp, allowing him straighter, more precise lines. Finally, it was time to finish what he'd started before he'd been so rudely interrupted. He held her head still, which wasn't hard as she was beginning to slip away into unconsciousness.

He came at her left eye first, and she screamed in terror. *Fantastic!* He proceeded to stab the tip of the blade into her eye socket and began cutting with care and precision. She was bucking now, just slightly, her body more or less twitching like it was having an epileptic seizure. Sadly, it wouldn't be long now, and his fun with her would be over…

He flicked away the flesh of the eyelid. He held the eye he'd extracted for her to see with her remaining eye, but there was no light there, and her chest had stopped moving. He became livid. No! She was to be conscious and alert for both removals! He did, after all, live, breathe, and prey on his victims' fear and helplessness at his hands—at proving himself the superior hunter.

He put the removed eye into one of two small jars that he had in a pocket of his camouflage jacket. Then he extracted the second eye and put it with the first. Both bobbed in the preservative fluid, and he put the jar back in his vest.

Next, he extracted two large, yellow cat's-eye marbles from another pocket. Prey One was almost complete.

He set the marbles in her now-empty eye sockets and admired his work.

Beautiful, but the fun with her is over!

Still, not all was lost. He had reason to be thrilled. There was one more prey to toy with.

He stood and turned to where the man had fallen, but there was no sign of him. Excitement whirled through his veins.

The hunt continues…

CHAPTER TWO

Four days later
FBI Office, Quantico, Virginia
Thursday, 12:50 PM Local Time

The vultures were circling… That could be said of a couple of things, but it immediately applied to the discovery of two murder victims found in the woods of rural Arkansas.

Currently, I, FBI Special Agent Brandon Fisher, was in a briefing room at Quantico with the rest of my team members with the Behavioral Analysis Unit. That included Paige Dawson, Kelly Marsh, and the latest addition, a man named Tony Manning. He was technically our boss—for now. I liked to believe that Supervisory Special Agent Jack Harper would be back soon. Mid-forties, Tony seemed more concerned with carving out his reputation as a badass than actually being effective, though in all fairness, we hadn't hit the field yet. I had a feeling that was about to change.

Also in the room was Nadia Webber, our team's assigned analyst. She was handling the latest briefing, an investigation that promised to finally free us from our cubicles. We'd been keeping them warm ever since our case last month went belly-up—also the reason Jack wasn't around. The director and other higher-ups of the Bureau, who might also be considered circling vultures, had decided it was a good time to dredge Jack's past for any hint of wrongdoing they could hold against him.

We were all seated at a round conference table, while Nadia stood next to a large flat-screen mounted on the wall with a tablet in her hands.

On the screen were images of two victims—one male, one female. Both were sprawled in a wooded patch, but the screen was split vertically up the middle. From what we'd already been told, they were found in the same area of the woods, though not next to each other. As for their bodies, the massacre was similar. Blood was pooled out on the ground in front of them, along with…

Bile rose in the back of my throat, and I swallowed roughly, as I concluded that I was looking at their intestines.

Nadia continued to bring us up to speed. "The victims, identified as Mark and Stephanie Duran, were forty-eight and forty-seven respectively. They were found Monday morning by a local farmer in a patch of woods on their property. They lived in the house on the land but didn't work the fields. They leased that out."

"One of the leasing farmers made the discovery. Name of Keith Owen," Manning inserted out of some sense of self-importance, I figured. Nadia was managing just fine.

"They were both shot with arrows in the back of the upper leg," Nadia added.

Arrows? That was different. Our team hunted the most sadistic serial killers under the sun, but this was a first—at least for me. But I clued into something else this may tell us about our unsub—or unknown subject. "I'm guessing these wounds were not the cause of death." The mess on the ground could lead me to that conclusion, but my mind was starting to formulate something else. I just needed a little more to go on.

Nadia shook her head. "They didn't help, but cause of death was exsanguination." She swept her finger on the screen of her tablet. On the TV screen there was now a satellite image of the property on the left side, and on the right, a shot from ground level. There was a farmhouse on the land, surrounded by fields, which were skirted by woods. "The Durans were believed to have been chased through their property into the woods where they were then each shot with an arrow," Nadia said.

The picture in my mind was taking on more shape and distinction. The woods were a fair distance from the farmhouse, but the entire property appeared remote and isolated. The killer would be able to do whatever he or she wanted with no one to hear their victims' screams. It made me wonder why an arrow and not a gun. But one thing was clear. "Our killer is a hunter," I said. "After the thrill. Chases the victims, shoots them with an arrow, guts them…" As I spoke, I looked around the room and latched my gaze with Kelly's.

She flicked a finger toward the screen and said, "Go back to the crime scene photos, Nadia." She might be new to the team, but she was probably one of the least squeamish. It made me wonder about the cases she'd worked previously when she was with the Miami PD's homicide division.

The crime scene returned to the monitor.

"They *were* hunted," Kelly reiterated exactly what I had said as if she were surprised that she was in agreement with me. But that was what the two of us did—disagreed first, joined forces later. She continued. "They were shot with an arrow simply to immobilize them. He—because often thrill killers, specifically those who are hunters, are male—wanted them to be alive and conscious while he worked through his MO."

It was certainly a sick method of operation judging from the display in front of us, and her driving home the sad fact the victims were probably alive for all of this suffering had a dark, suffocating cloud descending over the room.

"Were the arrows recovered? Can they tell us anything helpful?" I asked.

"They haven't been found. It's believed that the killer removed them and took them with him," Nadia said.

"To use again," Kelly muttered.

"Arrows, even if they were left behind, wouldn't give forensics much to work with, not like that of a bullet," Paige said. "And bows and arrows are not a registered weapon."

"True enough," Manning piped in. "But if we did find out what brand was used, that might help lead us to the killer's identity." He shrugged when all eyes went to him. "I also know a little about archery. I used to go north with my dad and uncle when I was young. Anyway, continue, Nadia."

"All we know about the arrows is they had a lot of pressure behind them and penetrated deeply enough to chip bone," Nadia said. "It's believed that he is using either a crossbow or a compound bow."

"Both are rather accurate if handled by an experienced archer." Manning cut in again to show how smart he was. "Both those bows are used in hunting, though the compound bow is more traditional. Of course, not as much as the longbow. Think Robin Hood. With that one, however, it's all driven by manpower and packs less punch. With a compound bow, it utilizes a pulley system that assumes some of the weight on the drawback. The shooter would still get the feel of a longbow without needing as much strength, and the arrow would pack more wallop. Didn't mean to interrupt, Nadia."

Sure you did...

Nadia changed the image on the screen, and I'd expected it would be a more graphic display of the Durans' guts, but it was something else that was equally as disturbing. Their eyes and eyelids were gone, and in their place were large, yellow cat's-eye marbles.

Paige groaned, and I glanced over at her—implying concern, but it simply masked my desire to avoid the screen for a second or two. But if someone like Paige who had been FBI for years could react like that, I had a right. I'd only been a Fed for four years. Kelly, as expected, didn't really show much of a visceral reaction, except for maybe some sadness for the plight of the victims.

I sometimes wondered about Kelly's mind. I was aware she'd witnessed her mother shoot her father at the age of six. Regardless of whether the man was abusive, and the murder was technically self-defense, that had to affect a young psyche. Not to mention her mother ended up being charged with manslaughter and going to prison for fifteen years.

"They were alive when he took their eyes." Nadia put a hand over her stomach. "The type of knife is yet to be determined. But as you can see the cuts were made rather cleanly. It's believed that something sharp and non-serrated was used, most likely a scalpel."

"And to slice their abdomen?" Kelly asked.

"Likely something larger, a type of hunting knife."

"He takes their eyes as trophies." Paige's voice was low, and she kept her gaze on the screen as she spoke.

"That fits with a hunter," I said. "He probably wants to relive the kill and be reminded of it." The marbles in the Durans' eye sockets had my mind going to a mounted stag and brought something else to my attention. "He's also proud of what he's done."

The door to the briefing room opened, and Jack poked his head in. He made eye contact with Manning and said, "In the hall." In usual Jack fashion, it was more directive than question or request.

Manning stiffened and made a show of looking around the room at us. "We're in the middle of a briefing, Harper. Can't it wait?"

"In the hall," Jack said again, then retreated.

Manning sighed and got up, rebuttoning his suit jacket as he did so. Just before leaving the room and shutting the door, he said, "Prepare yourselves for wheels up."

Wheels up, meaning we'd be boarding a government jet for Arkansas as soon as possible. It also meant we might be about to find out how useful Manning was in the field. But there was a part of me that stirred at Jack's appearance, and I hoped my feeling was right. My confidence in Manning wasn't founded, and it was already shaken. For him to tell us to "prepare," he was off the mark. As field agents, we were always prepared, and though we'd been riding desks for about a month, we all had a go bag at the ready.

"Wonder what that's about?" Kelly bobbed her head toward the door, saying what we were all thinking.

"We'll probably find out soon enough." Me, the voice of reason, whenever it suited to irritate Kelly. Our relationship had started off as one of animosity, both longing for Jack's approval, but we'd moved beyond that—mostly—and settled into a sort of sibling relationship. Hence the "disagree, then agree" shtick we had going.

Kelly glared at me briefly and smirked. "Just always have to be the smart-ass."

"Don't mind him. He's good at it." Paige shot me a narrow-eyed glance and snickered. I wasn't amused.

"Let's just focus on…" I nudged my head toward the screen.

Nadia dropped into a chair. She wasn't saying anything, but her roving eyes were telling.

"You know what's going on," I guessed.

"Don't worry about me. Worry about the monster behind that." Nadia pointed at the gruesome crime scene on display.

I turned back to the images, allowing them to really sink in, as gross as they were, and balanced it with what I'd learned about this case already. I was quite confident of one thing. "Whoever's behind this, it wasn't their first time out. Not given the organization I'm already seeing, the forethought. He's murdered before."

The door opened, and Jack came in. There was no sign of Manning.

Jack regarded me, his face dark shadows and hard lines. "You'd be right, Brandon. I believe the man behind the Arkansas murders has finally come out of hiding."

CHAPTER THREE

Jack Harper was tired of jumping through hoops and answering to barking superiors who all had their own way of doing things. They couldn't agree on protocol if it bit them in the ass, and with the rules changing all the time, no one had a chance of deciphering them. Still, he'd messed up; he'd take that burden on his shoulders. Someone had died. Someone who didn't need to. Someone who would still be alive if he'd only figured out another plan to ensnare the serial killer that he and his team had hunted last month. But the past was the past, and Jack was well aware at fifty-four, there was no going back—no do-overs. Yet here he was again, haunted by his past. He was just grateful the FBI director had agreed to reinstate him for this investigation. Then again, it would have been stupid of him not to.

Jack and his team were on an FBI jet headed to Arkansas. They'd land in Fayetteville, meet up with those from the local FBI field office, and then make the half-hour drive to Huntsville. They had four and a half hours until touch-down, providing them ample opportunity to become more familiar with the person they were hunting.

"He calls himself the Leopard," Jack said. "Male, as you may have already concluded. He's been dormant for fifteen years. Before that, we believe the same man was responsible for the murders of six people—all couples, all Caucasian—in the past twenty-five years. The same killing method was used for all of them. And then there's the killer's signature."

"Caucasian," Kelly said, not touching on the "signature" bit. "So the killer probably is as well."

Jack nodded. "As we all know here, a serial killer rarely crosses ethnic lines, though there are always exceptions. In this case, you're correct, Agent Marsh. He is a white male, estimated to currently be in his mid-to-late forties."

"'The Leopard'? Why that name?" Paige asked.

"Leopards are quite the hunters. They ambush or stalk their prey and hunt alone." Jack's face twisted with shadows. "They are solitary animals, opportunistic, and hard to find."

"That's on the mark for this killer by the sounds of it already." Paige sighed.

Jack nodded, deciding to loop back around to the killer's final touch. "Then there's the cat's-eye marbles. His signature. The victims' eyes are removed, and we can only assume he takes these with him as his trophies. In the past, we theorized that the killer might have wanted to be the last thing his victims ever saw, and that's why he removed their eyes. We also figure he chose a golden yellow, and not green or some other color, to more closely resemble a leopard."

"But fifteen years is a long time to be dormant," Brandon tossed out. "Maybe he's killed victims we're not aware of."

Jack met Brandon's gaze. "There's no way." *Or is there, and I missed finding them?* What Brandon and the others didn't know was Jack had stayed vigilant for any signs of this killer's MO, and nothing had popped in the system. Anywhere.

"Even out of state?" Brandon added, as if reading his mind.

"Anywhere." Jack heard the bite to his tone, and it had his team looking at him, but he wasn't apologetic for it. He'd been doing this job for almost as long as Brandon had been alive.

"All right, then," Paige said gingerly. "It only leaves the possibility that something had prevented our unsub from killing. Those who kill for pleasure don't typically stop unless they're forced to do so."

Jack nodded at Paige, glad to have her on his team. The two of them went way back. "That's correct, but this guy also has a pattern. For the three sets of murders that we're aware of besides this latest one, five years had passed between each one."

"So, couple one twenty-five years ago," Paige began. "Couple two twenty years ago. Couple three, as already touched on, fifteen years ago. Now the Durans. So what prevented him from killing? Incarceration or illness perhaps?"

"Could be anything. It's far too soon to know."

"Five years in between kills, though, seems very specific," Kelly started. "Did you ever figure out why that was the case, Jack?"

"Not really. Obviously he can control his urges to kill."

"He could have chosen to lie low." Brandon shrugged when they all looked at him, and added, "It would make it easier for him to evade capture."

Jack nodded. "This case was the first one I picked up as FBI—twenty-five years ago. And, as I touched on a moment ago, this killer is a chameleon. He gets off by first immersing himself into his victims' lives, blending into small communities. He stayed in each location for five years before killing his victims."

"Now that's commitment," Kelly said.

"And dedication. As you know, that was not the case with the Durans, so we'll need to figure out why he changed that aspect of his MO. All of you have a recap of the previous case files in the folders in front of you." He gestured to them. "You'll get the gist of the investigation's progress which, sad to say, hasn't been much. In the past cases, though, the unsub leased farm property. Each one had a farmhouse, a barn, fields, and woods. He integrated himself into the community and became one of them."

"That would have been more of a...high." Brandon had shuddered as the plane buffeted with some turbulence.

"Absolutely," Jack agreed. "He was a killer, but no one would have had a clue. In fact, he became everyone's friend in the small towns he chose. He got involved with the communities. Built up trust. You have photos taken by the townspeople of the unsub—but don't get excited. He disguises his true appearance."

"He thinks of everything," Brandon mumbled.

Jack was ready to get ahead of the curve. "Yes, so we can't discount him. He knows exactly what he's doing. He's organized, methodical, intelligent. It's believed that childhood trauma may have led to him doing what he does."

"How did he get the victims to his place?" Paige asked.

"The unsub would invite his would-be prey over for dinner. They'd go without hesitation because, as I said, he was a friend."

"Huh," Paige said. "Wonder how he worked things with the Durans."

"We'll certainly need to do some digging. He still could have inserted himself into the community. History, at least, tells us he was good at stalking his victims and becoming a part of their worlds. There's no doubt he utilized some of these gifts this time around too. His method of disposal was different with the Durans than the past cases as well. The Durans were left in the woods to bleed out, but with the previous six victims, he dragged them back to the barn where he hung them from the rafters. By the time anyone noticed the victims were missing, the Leopard was long gone."

"You said he rented the properties in the past," Brandon said. "Were you able to narrow in on him with financial records?"

"Nope." Jack had this gnawing in his gut. There were times this case had him feeling like a failure and questioning his abilities as an investigator. "Nothing much to find. He did open bank accounts but did so under assumed names. He also used these aliases to rent the properties. Each name was different and led nowhere, just like the money. For each account, only a single cash deposit was made to open it, from which he paid for rent and living expenses."

"Cash deposit, so no tracking there. Unless he was captured on bank video," Kelly said.

"And he was, but it still didn't get us anywhere. As I mentioned a minute ago, he changes his appearance. He had money at his disposal, but where that source is, we have yet to find out."

"I can't believe he stayed at the various rental properties for five years," Brandon said.

Paige shook her head. "He has to be a psychopath to blend in and become everyone's friend."

Brandon angled his head, studied Jack's eyes. "Did you ever get close to him?"

The answer to that question pained him more than almost anything—*almost*. "Not really. He never leaves anything behind that we can use forensically to track him, no prints or DNA." Jack's mind fed him a haunting recollection from the first scene twenty-five years ago.

"There's something you need to see." An FBI crime scene investigator comes over to him.

Jack's been staring at the bodies dangling from the beams since he stepped into the barn at least an hour before. He's counting the passing seconds until they are down on the ground and afforded some human dignity. A medical examiner and his assistant, along with some investigators, are working on that now.

"Jack," the CSI prompts.

"Ah, yeah." He turns, and the CSI is holding two small evidence bags.

He extends one to Jack. Inside is a handwritten note that reads, "I'll never stop." It is signed, "The Leopard."

Jack feels rage curdle up within him, but he turns to the other bag and points. "What's that?" he asks the CSI.

"The other part of the message. Though I'm not quite sure what to make of it." The CSI hands this bag to him.

If it's possible to feel something from an object, Jack is sensing something just holding the items through the plastic. It is hard to pin down what exactly, but he lands on darkness and pure evil. Still, he doesn't give it back to the investigator.

Yellow cat's-eye marbles.

"I'll never stop." Jack feels himself go cold and rushes toward where the bodies are being taken down.

The female is already freed, and her remains are on a black tarp. Jack gets in closer, despite grumblings from the ME, whom he waves off. Jack has a suspicion… When the victims had been hanging, something was off with their faces, though it was hard to figure out what with how far up they'd been, but their cheeks were stained with blood.

He holds up the bag with the cat's-eye marbles and crouches down next to the woman. His image is reflected back at him in the marbles that are in her eye sockets. He looks over his shoulder at the CSI, who had trailed him to get his evidence back. "It was part of the message, all right."

"I'll never stop…"

"Jack?" Paige prompted him.

"I'll never stop," he repeated. "Those are the words the killer wrote in a note that he left at the crime scene twenty-five years ago. His first couple. He even left an extra set of marbles to show his intent. Brandon's right. Maybe I just haven't been looking in the right place. Maybe this guy wants us to think he's been dormant all this time, but he hasn't been." Jack fell silent, guilt rolling over him.

"His circumstances could have changed," Paige offered.

"Actually, Jack, if he had killed in the last fifteen years—sticking to his MO and signature, anyway—I'm sure you would have seen something in the ViCap database," Brandon said.

ViCap—the Violent Criminal Apprehension Program—was a national, searchable database used by the FBI to house statistical data from serial violent crimes.

Jack considered and sighed. "Obviously, we're missing something, but he could have altered his MO more than we know."

"So we look at different aspects of it, let each methodology stand on its own," Kelly suggested. "Maybe he hasn't targeted couples during the last fifteen years or cut out eyes… The list of possible variation goes on."

"I'll have Nadia run some searches, plucking for the various elements." He hated that he hadn't thought of that himself—particularly the couples' bit. It just seemed like such a critical part of the unsub's MO, Jack found it hard to imagine that he'd let that go.

"I'm sure it's in here"—Paige patted the folder in front of her—"but what else stands out about victimology, besides the fact the victims were all Caucasian and targeted as couples? You mentioned they were from small towns?"

"Yes. Also something to keep in mind… He seems to choose people who are about the same age as he is, so the age of the victims would change as time goes on. Oh, and another thing. With the previous cases, the victims had secrets they'd held from the rest of the world. Could go as far as saying some of them had led double lives."

"Such as adultery and domestic abuse?" Kelly asked.

Jack regarded her, well aware of her past and understanding why she'd gone there. "Yes to both. As you read the past files, you'll find this out. One was in hock with gambling debt, another was a highly functioning alcoholic, and so on. Best all of you can do right now is get familiar with what's in those folders. This guy's always been one step ahead, and it's time for us to get ahead of him."

Jack's eyes landed on Brandon, who held his gaze, then nodded and turned his attention to the folder in front of him. Kelly already had her nose in a report. When he shifted to Paige, he noted she was watching him. She'd always been able to see through him, whether he liked it or not. She'd probably witnessed his desperation to close this case, possibly more.

But he was no longer in the mood for talking. He was in the mood for a cigarette, in part thanks to this killer who had him starting the filthy habit in the first place. But he had hours to go before he could light up and take a few deep hits of nicotine.

Jack pulled out his phone and called Nadia. He'd have her check country-wide for the different aspects of the killer's MO, including single murders, see if anything popped. As he made the request, it returned to his ears as a shot in the dark, but he couldn't just surrender. If he stood any chance of actually bringing the big cat down this time, he had to try every possible angle he could conjure up.

ONE MORE KILL

Book 9 in the Brandon Fisher FBI series

He told her to run. And she did. As fast as her legs would take her, but it wasn't fast enough…

The **bodies of a husband and wife are found in a patch of woods in small-town, rural Arkansas** by a neighboring farmer. They were shot with an arrow, gutted, and left to bleed out. The killer also removed their eyes and replaced them with large cat's-eye marbles. **The murder method and signature are too bizarre to point toward an isolated incident, and FBI Special Agent Brandon Fisher recognizes this right away. His boss with the Behavioral Analysis Unit, Supervisory Special Agent Jack Harper, confirms that he's crossed paths with this killer several years ago, and he has a voracious appetite for blood. In fact, Jack's seen his work firsthand—six times, three couples, in three states.**

Brandon, Jack, and the rest of the team head to Arkansas for one purpose: **to bring down the ruthless and elusive serial killer who calls himself "the Leopard."** Versatile and adaptive, this madman hunts his prey like a wild, hungry cat—tracking them, then striking with swift viciousness. But just as the FBI think they might finally be getting closer to the Leopard's true identity, he adapts his method and starts killing people faster than ever before.

Racing to catch up, and struggling to get one step ahead, **the FBI comes to uncover buried family secrets that aid the** investigation—while at the same time, flipping it on its head. **Suddenly, the hunters are now the hunted. And while this case has haunted Jack since he joined the Bureau, things are about get more personal and dangerous than he ever would have imagined. If he and his team aren't careful, one of them—or someone they love—may become the Leopard's next victim.**

CAROLYN ARNOLD is an international bestselling and award-winning author, as well as a speaker, teacher, and inspirational mentor. She has several continuing fiction series and has many published books. Her genre diversity offers her readers everything from cozy to hard-boiled mysteries, and thrillers to action adventures. Her crime fiction series have been praised by those in law enforcement as being accurate and entertaining. This led to her adopting the trademark: POLICE PROCEDURALS RESPECTED BY LAW ENFORCEMENT™.

Carolyn was born in a small town and enjoys spending time outdoors, but she also loves the lights of a big city. Grounded by her roots and lifted by her dreams, her overactive imagination insists that she tell her stories. Her intention is to touch the hearts of millions with her books, to entertain, inspire, and empower.

She currently lives near London, Ontario, Canada with her husband and two beagles.

CONNECT ONLINE
CarolynArnold.net
Facebook.com/AuthorCarolynArnold
Twitter.com/Carolyn_Arnold

And don't forget to sign up for her newsletter for up-to-date information on release and special offers at CarolynArnold.net/Newsletters.

CPSIA information can be obtained
at www.ICGtesting.com
Printed in the USA
LVHW102158121022
730605LV00023B/486